Praise for #1 *New York Times* bestselling author Linda Lael Miller

"Linda Lael Miller creates vibrant characters and stories I defy you to forget."
—#1 *New York Times* bestselling author
Debbie Macomber

"Miller is one of the finest American writers in the genre."
—*RT Book Reviews*

"[Linda Lael] Miller tugs at the heartstrings as few authors can."
—*Publishers Weekly*

Praise for *New York Times* bestselling author Brenda Jackson

"[Brenda] Jackson has the sexiest cowboy to ever ride the range."
—*RT Book Reviews* on *A Wife for Westmoreland*
(4½ stars)

"[Brenda] Jackson is a master at writing."
—*Publishers Weekly*

The daughter of a town marshal, **Linda Lael Miller** is the author of more than one hundred historical and contemporary novels. Now living in Spokane, Washington, the "First Lady of the West" hit a career high when all three of her 2011 Creed Cowboy books debuted at #1 on the *New York Times* list. In 2007, the Romance Writers of America presented her their Lifetime Achievement Award. She personally funds her Linda Lael Miller Scholarships for Women. Visit her at www.lindalaelmiller.com.

Brenda Jackson is a *New York Times* bestselling author of more than one hundred romance titles. Brenda lives in Jacksonville, Florida, and divides her time between family, writing and traveling. Email Brenda at authorbrendajackson@gmail.com or visit her on her website at www.brendajackson.net.

#1 *New York Times* Bestselling Author

LINDA
LAEL MILLER

PART OF THE
BARGAIN

HARLEQUIN® BESTSELLING AUTHOR COLLECTION

ISBN-13: 978-0-373-53784-6

Part of the Bargain

Copyright © 2017 by Harlequin Books S.A.

The publisher acknowledges the copyright holders of the individual works as follows:

Part of the Bargain
Copyright © 1985 by Linda Lael Miller

A Wife for a Westmoreland
Copyright © 2011 by Brenda Streater Jackson

Recycling programs for this product may not exist in your area.

Printed in U.S.A.

www.Harlequin.com

CONTENTS

PART OF THE BARGAIN

Linda Lael Miller

In loving and grateful memory of Laura Mast.

Chapter 1

The landing gear made an unsettling *ka-thump* sound as it snapped back into place under the small private airplane. Libby Kincaid swallowed her misgivings and tried not to look at the stony, impassive face of the pilot. If he didn't say anything, she wouldn't have to say anything either, and they might get through the short flight to the Circle Bar B ranch without engaging in one of their world-class shouting matches.

It was a pity, Libby thought, that at the ages of thirty-one and thirty-three, respectively, she and Jess still could not communicate on an adult level.

Pondering this, Libby looked down at the ground below and was dizzied by its passing as they swept over the small airport at Kalispell, Montana, and banked eastward, toward the Flathead River. Trees so green that they had a blue cast carpeted the majestic mountains rimming the valley.

Womanhood being what it is, Libby couldn't resist watching Jess Barlowe surreptitiously out of the corner of her eye. He was like a lean, powerful mountain lion waiting to pounce, even though he kept his attention strictly on the controls and the thin air traffic sharing the big Montana sky that spring morning. His eyes were hidden behind a pair of mirrored sunglasses, but Libby knew that they would be dark with the animosity that had marked their relationship for years.

She looked away again, trying to concentrate on the river, which coursed beneath them like a dusty-jade ribbon woven into the fabric of a giant tapestry. Behind those mirrored glasses, Libby knew Jess's eyes were the exact same shade of green as that untamed waterway below.

"So," he said suddenly, gruffly, "New York wasn't all the two-hour TV movies make it out to be."

Libby sighed, closed her eyes in a bid for patience and then opened them again. She wasn't going to miss one bit of that fabulous view—not when her heart had been hungering for it for several bittersweet years.

Besides, Jess had been to New York dozens of times on corporation business. Who did he think he was fooling?

"New York was all right," she said, in the most inflamatory tone she could manage. *Except that Jonathan died,* chided a tiny, ruthless voice in her mind. *Except for that nasty divorce from Aaron.* "Nothing to write home about," she added aloud, realizing her blunder too late.

"So your dad noticed," drawled Jess in an undertone that would have been savage if it hadn't been so carefully modulated. "Every day, when the mail came, he fell on it like it was manna from heaven. He never stopped hoping—I'll give him that."

"Dad knows I hate to write letters," she retorted defensively. But Jess had made his mark, all the same—Libby felt real pain, picturing her father flipping eagerly through the mail and trying to hide his disappointment when there was nothing from his only daughter.

"Funny—that's not what Stace tells me."

Libby bridled at this remark, but she kept her composure. Jess was trying to trap her into making some foolish statement about his older brother, no doubt, one that he could twist out of shape and hold over her head. She raised her chin and choked back the indignant diatribe aching in her throat.

The mirrored sunglasses glinted in the sun as Jess turned to look at her. His powerful shoulders were taut beneath the blue cotton fabric of his workshirt, and his jawline was formidably hard.

"Leave Cathy and Stace alone, Libby," he warned with blunt savagery. "They've had a lot of problems lately, and if you do anything to make the situation worse, I'll see that you regret it. Do I make myself clear?"

Libby would have done almost anything to escape his scrutiny just then, short of thrusting open the door of that small four-passenger Cessna and jumping out, but her choices were undeniably limited. Trembling just a little, she turned away and fixed her attention on the ground again.

Dear heaven, did Jess really think that she would interfere in Cathy's marriage—or any other, for that matter? Cathy was her *cousin*—they'd been raised like sisters!

With a sigh, Libby faced the fact that there was every chance that Jess and a lot of other people would believe she had been involved with Stacey Barlowe. There had, after all, been that exchange of correspondence, and Stace had even visited her a few times, in the thick of her traumatic divorce, though in actuality he had been in the city on business.

"Libby?" prodded Jess sharply, when the silence grew too long to suit him.

"I'm not planning to vamp your brother!" she snapped. "Could we just drop this, please?"

To her relief and surprise, Jess turned his concentration on piloting the plane. His suntanned jaw worked with suppressed annoyance, but he didn't speak again.

The timbered land below began to give way to occasional patches of prairie—cattle country. Soon they would be landing on the small airstrip serving the prosperous 150,000-acre Circle Bar B, owned by Jess's father and overseen, for the most part, by Libby's.

Libby had grown up on the Circle Bar B, just as Jess had, and her mother, like his, was buried there. Even though she couldn't call the ranch home in the legal sense of the word, it was *still* home to her, and she had every right to go there—especially now, when she needed its beauty and peace and practical routines so desperately.

The airplane began to descend, jolting Libby out of her reflective state. Beside her, Jess guided the craft skillfully toward the paved landing strip stretched out before them.

The landing gear came down with a sharp snap, and

Libby drew in her breath in preparation. The wheels of the plane screeched and grabbed as they made contact with the asphalt, and then the Cessna was rolling smoothly along the ground.

When it came to a full stop, Libby wrenched at her seat belt, anxious to put as much distance as possible between herself and Jess Barlowe. But his hand closed over her left wrist in a steel-hard grasp. "Remember, Lib—these people aren't the sophisticated if-it-feels-good-do-it types you're used to. No games."

Games. *Games?* Hot color surged into Libby's face and pounded there in rhythm with the furious beat of her heart. "Let go of me, you bastard!" she breathed.

If anything, Jess's grip tightened. "I'll be watching you," he warned, and then he flung Libby's wrist from his hand and turned away to push open the door on his side and leap nimbly to the ground.

Libby was still tugging impotently at the handle on her own door when her father strode over, climbed deftly onto the wing and opened it for her. She felt such a surge of love and relief at the sight of him that she cried out softly and flung herself into his arms, nearly sending both of them tumbling to the hard ground.

Ken Kincaid hadn't changed in the years since Libby had seen him last—he was still the same handsome, rangy cowboy that she remembered so well, though his hair, while as thick as ever, was iron-gray now, and the limp he'd acquired in a long-ago rodeo accident was more pronounced.

Once they were clear of the plane, he held his daughter at arm's length, laughed gruffly, and then pulled her close again. Over his shoulder she saw Jess drag her suitcases and portable drawing board out of the Cessna's luggage compartment and fling them unceremoniously into the back of a mud-speckled truck.

Nothing if not perceptive, Ken Kincaid turned slightly, assessed Senator Cleave Barlowe's second son, and grinned. There was mischief in his bright blue eyes when he faced Libby again. "Rough trip?"

Libby's throat tightened unaccountably, and she wished she could explain *how* rough. She was still stung by Jess's insulting opinion of her morality, but how could she tell her father that? "You know that it's always rough going where Jess and I are concerned," she said.

Her father's brows lifted speculatively as Jess got behind the wheel of the truck and sped away without so much as a curt nod or a halfhearted so-long. "You two'd better watch out," he mused. "If you ever stop butting heads, you might find out you like each other."

"Now, that," replied Libby with dispatch, "is a horrid thought if I've ever heard one. Tell me, Dad—how have you been?"

He draped one wiry arm over her shoulders and guided her in the direction of a late-model pickup truck. The door on the driver's side was emblazoned with the words CIRCLE BAR B RANCH, and Yosemite Sam glared from both the mud flaps shielding the rear tires. "Never mind how I've been, dumplin'. How've *you* been?"

Libby felt some of the tension drain from her as her father opened the door on the passenger side of the truck and helped her inside. She longed to shed her expensive tailored linen suit for jeans and a T-shirt, and— oh, heaven—her sneakers would be a welcome change from the high heels she was wearing. "I'll be okay," she said in tones that were a bit too energetically cheerful.

Ken climbed behind the wheel and tossed one searching, worried look in his daughter's direction. "Cathy's waiting over at the house, to help you settle in and all that. I was hoping we could talk...."

Libby reached out and patted her father's work-worn hand, resting now on the gearshift knob. "We can talk tonight. Anyway, we've got lots of time."

Ken started the truck's powerful engine, but his wise blue eyes had not strayed from his daughter's face. "You'll stay here awhile, then?" he asked hopefully.

Libby nodded, but she suddenly found that she had to look away. "As long as you'll let me, Dad."

The truck was moving now, jolting and rattling over the rough ranch roads with a pleasantly familiar vigor. "I expected you before this," he said. "Lib..."

She turned an imploring look on him. "Later, Dad—okay? Could we please talk about the heavy stuff later?"

Ken swept off his old cowboy hat and ran a practiced arm across his forehead. "Later it is, dumplin'." Graciously he changed the subject. "Been reading your comic strip in the funny papers, and it seems like every kid in town's wearing one of those T-shirts you designed."

Libby smiled; her career as a syndicated cartoonist was certainly safe conversational ground. And it had all started right here, on this ranch, when she'd sent away the coupon printed on a matchbook and begun taking art lessons by mail. After that, she'd won a scholarship to a prestigious college, graduated, and made her mark, not in portraits or commercial design, as some of her friends had, but in cartooning. Her character, Liberated Lizzie, a cave-girl with modern ideas, had created something of a sensation and was now featured not only in the Sunday newspapers but also on T-shirts, greeting cards, coffee mugs and calendars. There was a deal pending with a poster company, and Libby's bank balance was fat with the advance payment for a projected book.

She would have to work hard to fulfill her obligations—there was the weekly cartoon strip to do, of course, and the panels for the book had to be sketched in. She hoped that between these tasks and the endless allure of the Circle Bar B, she might be able to turn her thoughts from Jonathan and the mess she'd made of her personal life.

"Career-wise, I'm doing fine," Libby said aloud, as much to herself as to her father. "I don't suppose I could use the sunporch for a studio?"

Ken laughed. "Cathy's been working for a month to get it ready, and I had some of the boys put in a skylight. All you've got to do is set up your gear."

Impulsively Libby leaned over and kissed her father's beard-stubbled cheek. "I love you!"

"Good," he retorted. "A husband you can dump—a daddy you're pretty well stuck with."

The word "husband" jarred Libby a little, bringing an unwelcome image of Aaron into her mind as it did, and she didn't speak again until the house came into sight.

Originally the main ranch house, the structure set aside for the general foreman was an enormous, drafty place with plenty of Victorian scrollwork, gabled windows and porches. It overlooked a sizable spring-fed pond and boasted its own sheltering copse of evergreens and cottonwood trees.

The truck lurched a little as Ken brought it to a stop in the gravel driveway, and through the windshield

Libby could see glimmering patches of the silver-blue sparkle that was the pond. She longed to hurry there now, kick off her shoes on the grassy bank and ruin her stockings wading in the cold, clear water.

But her father was getting out of the truck, and Cathy Barlowe, Libby's cousin and cherished friend, was dashing down the driveway, her pretty face alight with greeting.

Libby laughed and stood waiting beside the pickup truck, her arms out wide.

After an energetic hug had been exchanged, Cathy drew back in Libby's arms and lifted a graceful hand to sign the words: "I've missed you so much!"

"And I've missed you," Libby signed back, though she spoke the words aloud, too.

Cathy's green eyes sparkled. "You haven't forgotten how to sign!" she enthused, bringing both hands into play now. She had been deaf since childhood, but she communicated so skillfully that Libby often forgot that they weren't conversing verbally. "Have you been practicing?"

She had. Signing had been a game for her and Jonathan to play during the long, difficult hours she'd spent at his hospital bedside. Libby nodded and tears of love and pride gathered in her dark blue eyes as she surveyed her cousin—physically, she and Cathy bore no resemblance to each other at all.

Cathy was petite, her eyes wide, mischievous emeralds, her hair a glistening profusion of copper and chestnut and gold that reached almost to her waist. Libby was of medium height, and her silver-blond hair fell just short of her shoulders.

"I'll be back later," Ken said quietly, signing the

words as he spoke so that Cathy could understand, too. "You two have plenty to say to each other, it looks like."

Cathy nodded and smiled, but there was something sad trembling behind the joy in her green eyes, something that made Libby want to scurry back to the truck and beg to be driven back to the airstrip. From there she could fly to Kalispell and catch a connecting flight to Denver and then New York....

Good Lord—surely Jess hadn't been so heartless as to share his ridiculous suspicions with Cathy!

The interior of the house was cool and airy, and Libby followed along behind Cathy, her thoughts and feelings in an incomprehensible tangle. She was glad to be home, no doubt about it. She'd yearned for the quiet sanity of this place almost from the moment of leaving it.

On the other hand, she wasn't certain that she'd been wise to come back. Jess obviously intended to make her feel less than welcome, and although she had certainly never been intimately involved with Stacey Barlowe, Cathy's husband, sometimes her feelings toward him weren't all that clearly defined.

Unlike his younger brother, Stace was a warm, outgoing person, and through the shattering events of the past year and a half, he had been a tender and steadfast friend. Adrift in waters of confusion and grief, Libby had told Stacey things that she had never breathed to another living soul, and it was true that, as Jess had so bitterly pointed out, she had written to the man when she couldn't bring herself to contact her own father.

But she wasn't in love with Stace, Libby told herself firmly. She had always looked up to him, that was all— like an older brother. Maybe she'd become a little too dependent on him in the bargain, but that didn't mean she cared for him in a romantic way, did it?

She sighed, and Cathy turned to look at her pensively, almost as though she had heard the sound. That was impossible, of course, but Cathy was as perceptive as anyone Libby had ever known, and she often *felt* sounds.

"Glad to be home?" the deaf woman inquired, gesturing gently.

Libby didn't miss the tremor in her cousin's hands, but she forced a weary smile to her face and nodded in answer to the question.

Suddenly Cathy's eyes were sparkling again, and she caught Libby's hand in her own and tugged her through an archway and into the glassed-in sunporch that overlooked the pond.

Libby drew in a swift, delighted breath. There was indeed a skylight in the roof—a big one. A drawing table had been set up in the best light the room offered, along with a lamp for night work, and there were flowering plants hanging from the exposed beams in the ceiling. The old wicker furniture that had been stored in the attic for as long as Libby could remember had been painted a dazzling white and bedecked with gay floral-print cushions. Small rugs in complementary shades of pink and green had been scattered about randomly, and there was even a shelving unit built into the wall behind the art table.

"Wow!" cried Libby, overwhelmed, her arms spread out wide in a gesture of wonder. "Cathy, you missed your calling! You should have been an interior decorator."

Though Libby hadn't signed the words, her cousin

had read them from her lips. Cathy's green eyes shifted quickly from Libby's face, and she lowered her head. "Instead of what?" she motioned sadly. "Instead of Stacey's wife?"

Libby felt as though she'd been slapped, but she recovered quickly enough to catch one hand under Cathy's chin and force her head up. "Exactly what do you mean by that?" she demanded, and she was never certain afterward whether she had signed the words, shouted them, or simply thought them.

Cathy shrugged in a miserable attempt at nonchalance, and one tear slid down her cheek. "He went to see you in New York," she challenged, her hands moving quickly now, almost angrily. "You wrote to him."

"Cathy, it wasn't what you think—"

"Wasn't it?"

Libby was furious and wounded, and she stomped one foot in frustration. "Of course it wasn't! Do you really think I would do a thing like that? Do you think Stacey would? He *loves* you!" *And so does Jess,* she lamented in silence, without knowing why that should matter.

Stubbornly Cathy averted her eyes again and shoved her hands into the pockets of her lightweight cotton jacket—a sure signal that as far as she was concerned, the conversation was over.

In desperation, Libby reached out and caught her cousin's shoulders in her hands, only to be swiftly rebuffed by an eloquent shrug. She watched, stricken to silence, as Cathy turned and hurried out of the sunporch-turned-studio and into the kitchen beyond. Just a moment later the back door slammed with a finality that made Libby ache through and through.

She ducked her head and bit her lower lip to keep the tears back. That, too, was something she had learned during Jonathan's final confinement in a children's hospital.

Just then, Jess Barlowe filled the studio doorway. Libby was aware of him in all her strained senses.

He set down her suitcases and drawing board with an unsympathetic thump. "I see you're spreading joy and good cheer as usual," he drawled in acid tones. "What, pray tell, was *that* all about?"

Libby was infuriated, and she glared at him, her hands resting on her trim rounded hips. "As if you didn't know, you heartless bastard! How could you be so mean…so thoughtless…"

The fiery green eyes raked Libby's travel-rumpled form with scorn. Ignoring her aborted question, he offered one of his own. "Did you think your affair with my brother was a secret, princess?"

Libby was fairly choking on her rage and her pain. "What affair, dammit?" she shouted. "We didn't *have* an affair!"

"That isn't what Stacey says," replied Jess with impervious savagery.

Libby felt the high color that had been pounding in her face seep away. *"What?"*

"Stace is wildly in love with you, to hear him tell it. You need him and he needs you, and to hell with minor stumbling blocks like his wife!"

Libby's knees weakened and she groped blindly for the stool at her art table and then sank onto it. "My God…"

Jess's jawline was tight with brutal annoyance.

"Spare me the theatrics, princess—I know why you came back here. Dammit, *don't you have a soul?*"

Libby's throat worked painfully, but her mind simply refused to form words for her to utter.

Jess crossed the room like a mountain panther, terrifying in his grace and prowess, and caught both her wrists in a furious, inescapable grasp. With his other hand he captured Libby's chin.

"Listen to me, you predatory little witch, and listen well," he hissed, his jade eyes hard, his flesh pale beneath his deep rancher's tan. "Cathy is good and decent and she loves my brother, though I can't for the life of me think why she condescends to do so. And I'll be *damned* if I'll stand by and watch you and Stacey turn her inside out! Do you understand me?"

Tears of helpless fury and outraged honor burned like fire in Libby's eyes, but she could neither speak nor move. She could only stare into the frightening face looming only inches from her own. It was a devil's face.

When Jess's tightening grasp on her chin made it clear that he would have an answer of some sort, no matter what, Libby managed a small, frantic nod.

Apparently satisfied, Jess released her with such suddenness that she nearly lost her balance and slipped off the stool.

Then he whirled away from her, his broad back taut, one powerful hand running through his obsidian hair in a typical gesture of frustration. "Damn you for ever coming back here," he said in a voice no less vicious for its softness.

"No problem," Libby said with great effort. "I'll leave."

Jess turned toward her again, this time with an ominous leisure, and his eyes scalded Libby's face, the hollow of her throat, the firm roundness of her high breasts. "It's too late," he said.

Still dazed, Libby sank back against the edge of the drawing table, sighed and covered her eyes with one hand. "Okay," she began with hard-won, shaky reason, "why is that?"

Jess had stalked to the windows; his back was a barrier between them again, and he was looking out at the pond. Libby longed to sprout claws and tear him to quivering shreds.

"Stacey has the bit in his teeth," he said at length, his voice low, speculative. "Wherever you went, he'd follow."

Since Libby didn't believe that Stacey had declared himself to be in love with her, she didn't believe that there was any danger of his following her away from the Circle Bar B, either. "You're crazy," she said.

Jess faced her quickly, some scathing retort brewing in his eyes, but whatever he had meant to say was lost as Ken strode into the room and demanded, "What the hell's going on in here? I just found Cathy running up the road in tears!"

"Ask your daughter!" Jess bit out. "Thanks to her, Cathy has just gotten *started* shedding tears!"

Libby could bear no more; she was like a wild creature goaded to madness, and she flung herself bodily at Jess Barlowe, just as she had in her childhood, fists flying. She would have attacked him gladly if her father hadn't caught hold of her around the waist and forcibly restrained her.

Jess raked her with one last contemptuous look and moved calmly in the direction of the door. "You ought to tame that little spitfire, Ken," he commented in passing. "One of these days she's going to hurt somebody."

Libby trembled in her father's hold, stung by his double meaning, and gave one senseless shriek of fury. This brought a mocking chuckle from a disappearing Jess and caused Ken to turn her firmly to face him.

"Good Lord, Libby, what's the *matter* with you?"

Libby drew a deep, steadying breath and tried to quiet the raging ten-year-old within her, the child that Jess had always been able to infuriate. "I hate Jess Barlow," she said flatly. "I hate him."

"Why?" Ken broke in, and he didn't look angry anymore. Just honestly puzzled.

"If you knew what he's been saying about me—"

"If it's the same as what Stacey's been mouthing off about, I reckon I do."

Libby stepped back, stunned. "What?"

Ken Kincaid sighed, and suddenly all his fifty-two years showed clearly in his face. "Stacey and Cathy have been having trouble the last year or so. Now he's telling everybody who'll listen that it's over between him and Cathy and he wants you."

"I don't believe it! I—"

"I wanted to warn you, Lib, but you'd been through so much, between losing the boy and then falling out with your husband after that. I thought you needed to be home, but I knew you wouldn't come near the place if you had any idea what was going on."

Libby's chin trembled, and she searched her father's honest, weathered face anxiously. "I... I haven't been fooling around with C-Cathy's husband, Dad."

He smiled gently. "I know that, Lib—knew it all

along. Just never mind Jess and all the rest of them—if you don't run away, this thing'll blow over."

Libby swallowed, thinking of Cathy and the pain she had to be feeling. The betrayal. "I can't stay here if Cathy is going to be hurt."

Ken touched her cheek with a work-worn finger. "Cathy doesn't really believe the rumors, Libby—think about it. Why would she work so hard to fix a studio up for you if she did? Why would she be waiting here to see you again?"

"But she was crying just now, Dad! And she as much as accused me of carrying on with her husband!"

"She's been hurt by what's been said, and Stacey's been acting like a spoiled kid. Honey, Cathy's just testing the waters, trying to find out where you stand. You can't leave her now, because except for Stace, there's nobody she needs more."

Despite the fact that all her instincts warned her to put the Circle Bar B behind her as soon as humanly possible, Libby saw the sense in her father's words. As incredible as it seemed, Cathy would need her—if for nothing else than to lay those wretched rumors to rest once and for all.

"These things Stacey's been saying—surely he didn't unload them on Cathy?"

Ken sighed. "I don't think he'd be that low, Libby. But you know how it is with Cathy, how she always knows the score."

Libby shook her head distractedly. "Somebody told her, Dad—and I think I know who it was."

There was disbelief in Ken's discerning blue eyes, and in his voice, too. "*Jess?* Now, wait a minute…"

Jess.

Libby couldn't remember a time when she had gotten along well with him, but she'd been sure that he cared deeply for Cathy. Hadn't he been the one to insist that Stace and Libby learn signing, as he had, so that everyone could talk to the frightened, confused little girl who couldn't hear? Hadn't he gifted Cathy with cherished bullfrogs and clumsily made valentines and even taken her to the high-school prom?

How could Jess, of all people, be the one to hurt Cathy, when he knew as well as anyone how badly she'd been hurt by her handicap and the rejection of her own parents? How?

Libby had no answer for any of these questions. She knew only that she had separate scores to settle with both the Barlowe brothers.

And settle them she would.

Chapter 2

Libby sat at the end of the rickety swimming dock, bare feet dangling, shoulders slumped, her gaze fixed on the shimmering waters of the pond. The lines of her long, slender legs were accentuated, rather than disguised, by the old blue jeans she wore. A white eyelet suntop sheltered shapely breasts and a trim stomach and left the rest of her upper body bare.

Jess Barlowe studied her in silence, feeling things that were at wide variance with his personal opinion of the woman. He was certain that he hated Libby, but something inside him wanted, nonetheless, to touch her, to comfort her, to know the scent and texture of her skin.

A reluctant grin tilted one corner of his mouth. One tug at the top of that white eyelet and...

Jess caught his skittering thoughts, marshaled them back into stern order. As innocent and vulnerable as

Libby Kincaid looked at the moment, she was a viper, willing to betray her own cousin to get what she wanted.

Jess imagined Libby naked, her glorious breasts free and welcoming. But the man in his mental scenario was not himself—it was Stacey. The thought lay sour in Jess's mind.

"Did you come to apologize, by any chance?"

The question so startled Jess that he flinched; he had not noticed that Libby had turned around and seen him, so caught up had he been in the vision of her giving herself to his brother.

He scowled, as much to recover his wits as to oppose her. It was and always had been his nature to oppose Libby Kincaid, the way electricity opposes water, and it annoyed him that, for all his travels and his education, he didn't know why.

"Why would I want to do that?" he shot back, more ruffled by her presence than he ever would have admitted.

"Maybe because you were a complete ass," she replied in tones as sunny as the big sky stretched out above them.

Jess lifted his hands to his hips and stood fast against whatever it was that was pulling him toward her. *I want to make love to you,* he thought, and the truth of that ground in his spirit as well as in his loins.

There was pain in Libby's navy blue eyes, as well as a cautious mischief. "Well?" she prodded.

Jess found that while he could keep himself from going to her, he could not turn away. Maybe her net reached farther than he'd thought. Maybe, like Stacey and that idiot in New York, he was already caught in it.

"I'm not here to apologize," he said coldly.

"Then why?" she asked with chiming sweetness.

He wondered if she knew what that shoulderless blouse of hers was doing to him. Damn. He hadn't been this tongue-tied since the night of his fifteenth birthday, when Ginny Hillerman had announced that she would show him hers if he would show her his.

Libby's eyes were laughing at him. "Jess?"

"Is your dad here?" he threw out in gruff desperation.

One shapely, gossamer eyebrow arched. "You know perfectly well that he isn't. If Dad were home, his pickup truck would be parked in the driveway."

Against his will, Jess grinned. His taut shoulders rose in a shrug. The shadows of cottonwood leaves moved on the old wooden dock, forming a mystical path—a path that led to Libby Kincaid.

She patted the sun-warmed wood beside her. "Come and sit down."

Before Jess could stop himself, he was striding along that small wharf, sinking down to sit beside Libby and dangle his booted feet over the sparkling water. He was never entirely certain what sorcery made him ask what he did.

"What happened to your marriage, Libby?"

The pain he had glimpsed before leapt in her eyes and then faded away again, subdued. "Are you trying to start another fight?"

Jess shook his head. "No," he answered quietly, "I really want to know."

She looked away from him, gnawing at her lower lip with her front teeth. All around them were ranch sounds—birds conferring in the trees, leaves rustling in the wind, the clear pond water lapping at the mossy pilings of the dock. But no sound came from Libby.

On an impulse, Jess touched her mouth with the tip of one index finger. Water and electricity—the analogy came back to him with a numbing jolt.

"Stop that," he barked, to cover his reactions.

Libby ceased chewing at her lip and stared at him with wide eyes. Again he saw the shadow of that nameless, shifting ache inside her. "Stop what?" she wanted to know.

Stop making me want to hold you, he thought. *Stop making me want to tuck your hair back behind your ears and tell you that everything will be all right.* "Stop biting your lip!" he snapped aloud.

"I'm sorry!" Libby snapped back, her eyes shooting indigo sparks.

Jess sighed and again spoke involuntarily. "Why did you leave your husband, Libby?"

The question jarred them both: Libby paled a little and tried to scramble to her feet; Jess caught her elbow in one hand and pulled her down again.

"Was it because of Stacey?"

She was livid. "No!"

"Someone else?"

Tears sprang up in Libby's dark lashes and made then spiky. She wrenched free of his hand but made no move to rise again and run away. "Sure!" she gasped. "'If it feels good, do it'—that's my motto! By God, I *live* by those words!"

"Shut up," Jess said in a gentle voice.

Incredibly, she fell against him, wept into the shoulder of his blue cotton workshirt. And it was not a delicate, calculating sort of weeping—it was a noisy grief.

Jess drew her close and held her, broken on the shoals of what she was feeling even though he did not know its name. "I'm sorry," he said hoarsely.

Libby trembled beneath his arm and wailed like a wounded calf. The sound solidified into a word usually reserved for stubborn horses and income-tax audits.

Jess laughed and, for a reason he would never understand, kissed her forehead. "I love it when you flatter me," he teased.

Miraculously, Libby laughed, too. But when she tilted her head back to look up at him, and he saw the tear streaks on her beautiful, defiant face, something within him, something that had always been disjointed, was wrenched painfully back into place.

He bent his head and touched his lips to hers, gently, in question. She stiffened, but then, at the cautious bidding of his tongue, her lips parted slightly and her body relaxed against his.

Jess pressed Libby backward until she lay prone on the shifting dock, the kiss unbroken. As she responded to that kiss, it seemed that the sparkling water-light of the pond danced around them both in huge, shimmering chips, that they were floating inside some cosmic prism.

His hand went to the full roundness of her left breast. Beneath his palm and the thin layer of white eyelet, he felt the nipple grow taut in that singular invitation to passion.

Through the back of his shirt, Jess was warmed by the heat of the spring sun and the tender weight of Libby's hands. He left her mouth to trail soft kisses over her chin, along the sweet, scented lines of her neck.

All the while, he expected her to stiffen again, to thrust him away with her hands and some indignant—

and no doubt colorful—outburst. Instead, she was pliant and yielding beneath him.

Enthralled, he dared more and drew downward on the uppermost ruffle of her suntop. Still she did not protest.

Libby arched her back and a low, whimpering sound came from her throat as Jess bared her to the soft spring breeze and the fire of his gaze.

Her breasts were heavy golden-white globes, and their pale rose crests stiffened as Jess perused them. When he offered a whisper-soft kiss to one, Libby moaned and the other peak pouted prettily at his choice. He went to it, soothed it to fury with his tongue.

Libby gave a soft, lusty cry, shuddered and caught her hands in his hair, drawing him closer. He needed more of her and positioned his body accordingly, careful not to let his full weight come to bear. Then, for a few dizzying moments, he took suckle at the straining fount of her breast.

Recovering himself partially, Jess pulled her hands from his hair, gripped them at the wrists, pressed them down above her head in gentle restraint.

Her succulent breasts bore his assessment proudly, rising and falling with the meter of her breathing.

Jess forced himself to meet Libby's eyes. "This is me," he reminded her gruffly. "Jess."

"I know," she whispered, making no move to free her imprisoned hands.

Jess lowered his head, tormented one delectable nipple by drawing at it with his lips. "This is real, Libby," he said, circling the morsel with just the tip of his tongue now. "It's important that you realize that."

"I do...oh, God... Jess, *Jess*."

Reluctantly he left the feast to search her face with disbelieving eyes. "Don't you want me to stop?"

A delicate shade of rose sifted over her high cheekbones. Her hands still stretched above her, her eyes closed, she shook her head.

Jess went back to the breasts that so bewitched him, nipped at their peaks with gentle teeth. "Do you…know how many…times I've wanted…to do this?"

The answer was a soft, strangled cry.

He limited himself to one nipple, worked its surrendering peak into a sweet fervor with his lips and his tongue. "So…many…times. My God, Libby…you're so beautiful…."

Her words were as halting as his had been. "What's happening to us? We h-hate each other."

Jess laughed and began kissing his way softly down over her rib cage, her smooth, firm stomach. The snap on her jeans gave way easily—and was echoed by the sound of car doors slamming in the area of the house.

Instantly the spell was broken. Color surged into Libby's face and she bolted upright, nearly thrusting Jess off the end of the dock in her efforts to wrench on the discarded suntop and close the fastening of her jeans.

"Broad daylight…" she muttered distractedly, talking more to herself than to Jess.

"Lib!" yelled a jovial masculine voice, approaching fast. "Libby?"

Stacey. The voice belonged to Stacey.

Sudden fierce anger surged, white-hot, through Jess's aching, bedazzled system. Standing up, not caring that his thwarted passion still strained against his jeans, visible to anyone who might take the trouble to look, he glared down at Libby and rasped, "I guess re-inforcements have arrived."

She gave a primitive, protesting little cry and shot to her feet, her ink-blue eyes flashing with anger and hurt. Before Jess could brace himself, her hands came to his chest like small battering rams and pushed him easily off the end of the dock.

The jolting cold of that spring-fed pond was welcome balm to Jess's passion-heated flesh, if not his pride. When he surfaced and grasped the end of the dock in both hands, he knew there would be no physical evidence that he and Libby had been doing anything other than fighting.

Libby ached with embarrassment as Stacey and Senator Barlowe made their way down over the slight hillside that separated the backyard from the pond.

The older man cast one mischievously baleful look at his younger son, who was lifting himself indignantly onto the dock, and chuckled, "I see things are the same as always," he said.

Libby managed a shaky smile. *Not quite,* she thought, her body remembering the delicious dance Jess's hard frame had choreographed for it. "Hello, Senator," she said, rising on tiptoe to kiss his cheek.

"Welcome home," he replied with gruff affection. Then his wise eyes shifted past her to rest again on Jess. "It's a little cold yet for a swim, isn't it, son?"

Jess's hair hung in dripping ebony strands around his face, and his eyes were jade-green flares, avoiding his father to scald Libby's lips, her throat, her still-pulsing breasts. "We'll finish our...discussion later," he said.

Libby's blood boiled up over her stomach and her breasts to glow in her face. "I wouldn't count on that!"

"I would," Jess replied with a smile that was at once tender and evil. And then, without so much as a word to his father and brother, he walked away.

"What the hell did he mean by that?" barked Stacey, red in the face.

The look Libby gave the boyishly handsome, caramel-eyed man beside her was hardly friendly. "You've got some tall explaining to do, Stacey Barlowe," she said.

The senator, a tall, attractive man with hair as gray as Ken's, cleared his throat in the way of those who have practiced diplomacy long and well. "I believe I'll go up to the house and see if Ken's got any beer on hand," he said. A moment later he was off, following Jess's soggy path.

Libby straightened her shoulders and calmly slapped Stacey across the face. "How dare you?" she raged, her words strangled in her effort to modulate them.

Stacey reddened again, ran one hand through his fashionably cut wheat-colored hair. He turned, as if to follow his father. "I could use a beer myself," he said in distracted, evasive tones.

"Oh, no you don't!" Libby cried, grasping his arm and holding on. The rich leather of his jacket was smooth under her hand. "Don't you *dare* walk away from me, Stacey—not until you explain why you've been lying about me!"

"I haven't been lying!" he protested, his hands on his hips now, his expensively clad body blocking the base of the dock as he faced her.

"You have! You've been telling everyone that I... That we..."

"That we've been doing what you and my brother were doing a few minutes ago?"

If Stacey had shoved Libby into the water, she couldn't have been more shocked. A furious retort rose to the back of her throat but would go no further.

Stacey's tarnished-gold eyes flashed. "Jess was making love to you, wasn't he?"

"What if he was?" managed Libby after a painful struggle with her vocal cords. "It certainly wouldn't be any of your business, would it?"

"Yes, it would. I love you, Libby."

"You love *Cathy!*"

Stacey shook his head. "No. Not anymore."

"Don't say that," Libby pleaded, suddenly deflated. "Oh, Stacey, don't. Don't do this…."

His hands came to her shoulders, fierce and strong. The topaz fever in his eyes made Libby wonder if he was sane. "I love you, Libby Kincaid," he vowed softly but ferociously, "and I mean to have you."

Libby retreated a step, stunned, shaking her head. The reality of this situation was so different from what she had imagined it would be. In her thoughts, Stacey had laughed when she confronted him, ruffled her hair in that familiar brotherly way of old, and said that it was all a mistake. That he loved Cathy, wanted Cathy, and couldn't anyone around here take a joke?

But here he was declaring himself in a way that was unsettlingly serious.

Libby took another step backward. "Stacey, I need to be here, where my dad is. Where things are familiar and comfortable. Please…don't force me to leave."

Stacey smiled. "There is no point in leaving, Lib. If you do, I'll be right behind you."

She shivered. "You've lost your mind!"

But Stacey looked entirely sane as he shook his handsome head and wedged his hands into the pockets of his jacket. "Just my heart," he said. "Corny, isn't it?"

"It's worse than corny. Stacey, you're unbalanced or something. You're fantasizing. There was never anything between us—"

"No?" The word was crooned.

"No! You need help."

His face had all the innocence of an altar boy's. "If I'm insane, darlin', it's something you could cure."

Libby resisted an urge to slap him again. She wanted to race into the house, but he was still barring her way, so that she could not leave the dock without brushing against him. "Stay away from me, Stacey," she said as he advanced toward her. "I mean it—stay away from me!"

"I can't, Libby."

The sincerity in his voice was chilling; for the first time in all the years she'd known Stacey Barlowe, Libby was afraid of him. Discretion kept her from screaming, but just barely.

Stacey paled, as though he'd read her thoughts. "Don't look at me like that, Libby—I wouldn't hurt you under any circumstances. And I'm not crazy."

She lifted her chin. "Let me by, Stacey. I want to go into the house."

He tilted his head back, sighed, met her eyes again. "I've frightened you, and I'm sorry. I didn't mean to do that."

Libby couldn't speak. Despite his rational, settling words, she was sick with the knowledge that he meant to pursue her.

"You must know," he said softly, "how good it could

be for us. You needed me in New York, Libby, and now I need you."

The third voice, from the base of the hillside, was to Libby as a life preserver to a drowning person. "Let her pass, Stacey."

Libby looked up quickly to see Jess, unlikely rescuer that he was. His hair was towel-rumpled and his jeans clung to muscular thighs—thighs that only minutes ago had pressed against her own in a demand as old as time. His manner was calm as he buttoned a shirt, probably borrowed from Ken, over his broad chest.

Stacey shrugged affably and walked past his brother without a word of argument.

Watching him go, Libby went weak with relief. A lump rose in her throat as she forced herself to meet Jess's gaze. "You were right," she muttered miserably. "You were *right*."

Jess was watching her much the way a mountain cat would watch a cornered rabbit. For the briefest moment there was a look of tenderness in the green eyes, but then his expression turned hard and a muscle flexed in his jaw. "I trust the welcome-home party has been scheduled for later—after Cathy has been tucked into her bed, for instance?"

Libby gaped at him, appalled. Had he interceded only to torment her himself?

Jess's eyes were contemptuous as they swept over her. "What's the matter, Lib? Couldn't you bring yourself to tell your married lover that the welcoming had already been taken care of?"

Rage went through Libby's body like an electric current surging into a wire. "You don't seriously think that I would... That I was—"

"You even managed to be alone with him. Tell me, Lib—how did you get rid of my father?"

"G-get rid…" Libby stopped, tears of shock and mortification aching in her throat and burning behind her eyes. She drew a deep, audible breath, trying to assemble herself, to think clearly.

But the whole world seemed to be tilting and swirling like some out-of-control carnival ride. When Libby closed her eyes against the sensation, she swayed dangerously and would probably have fallen if Jess hadn't reached her in a few strides and caught her shoulders in his hands.

"Libby…" he said, and there was anger in the sound, but there was a hollow quality, too—one that Libby couldn't find a name for.

Her knees were trembling. Too much, it was all too much. Jonathan's death, the ugly divorce, the trouble that Stacey had caused with his misplaced affections— all of those things weighed on her, but none were so crushing as the blatant contempt of this man. It was apparent to Libby now that the lovemaking they had almost shared, so new and beautiful to her, had been some sort of cruel joke to Jess.

"How could you?" she choked out. "Oh, Jess, how could you?"

His face was grim, seeming to float in a shimmering mist. Instead of answering, Jess lifted Libby into his arms and carried her up the little hill toward the house.

She didn't remember reaching the back door.

"What the devil happened on that dock today, Jess?" Cleave Barlowe demanded, hands grasping the edge of his desk.

His younger son stood at the mahogany bar, his shoulders stiff, his attention carefully fixed on the glass of straight Scotch he meant to consume. "Why don't you ask Stacey?"

"Goddammit, I'm asking *you!*" barked Cleave. "Ken's mad as hell, and I don't blame him—that girl of his was shattered!"

Girl. The word caught in Jess's beleaguered mind. He remembered the way Libby had responded to him, meeting his passion with her own, welcoming the greed he'd shown at her breasts. Had it not been for the arrival of his father and brother, he would have possessed her completely within minutes. "She's no 'girl,'" he said, still aching to bury himself in the depths of her.

The senator swore roundly. "What did you say to her, Jess?" he pressed, once the spate of unpoliticianly profanity had passed.

Jess lowered his head. He'd meant the things he'd said to Libby, and he couldn't, in all honesty, have taken them back. But he knew some of what she'd been through in New York, her trysts with Stacey notwithstanding, and he was ashamed of the way he'd goaded her. She had come home to heal—the look in her eyes had told him that much—and instead of respecting that, he had made things more difficult for her.

Never one to be thwarted by silence, no matter how eloquent, Senator Barlowe persisted. "Dammit, Jess, I might expect this kind of thing from Stacey, but I thought you had more sense! You were harassing Libby about these blasted rumors your brother has been spreading, weren't you?"

Jess sighed, set aside the drink he had yet to take a sip from, and faced his angry father. "Yes," he said.

"Why?"

Stubbornly, Jess refused to answer. He took an interest in the imposing oak desk where his father sat, the heavy draperies that kept out the sun, the carved ivory of the fireplace.

"All right, mulehead," Cleave muttered furiously, "don't talk! Don't explain! And don't go near Ken Kincaid's daughter again, damn you. That man's the best foreman I've ever had and if he gets riled and quits because of you, Jess, you and I are going to come to time!"

Jess almost smiled, though he didn't quite dare. Not too many years before the phrase "come to time," when used by his father, had presaged a session in the woodshed. He wondered what it meant now that he was thirty-three years old, a member of the Montana State Bar Association, and a full partner in the family corporation. "I care about Cathy," he said evenly. "What was I supposed to do—stand by and watch Libby and Stace grind her up into emotional hamburger?"

Cleave gave a heavy sigh and sank into the richly upholstered swivel chair behind his desk. "I love Cathy, too," he said at length, "but Stacey's behind this whole mess, not Libby. Dammit, that woman has been through hell from what Ken says—she was married to a man who slept in every bed but his own, and she had to watch her nine-year-old stepson die by inches. Now she comes home looking for a little peace, and what does she get? Trouble!"

Jess lowered his head, turned away—ostensibly to take up his glass of Scotch. He'd known about the bad marriage—Ken had cussed the day Aaron Strand was born often enough—but he hadn't heard about the little boy. My God, he hadn't known about the boy.

"Maybe Strand couldn't sleep in his own bed," he said, urged on by some ugliness that had surfaced inside him since Libby's return. "Maybe Stacey was already in it."

"Enough!" boomed the senator in a voice that had made presidents tremble in their shoes. "I like Libby and I'm not going to listen to any more of this, either from you or from your brother! Do I make myself clear?"

"Abundantly clear," replied Jess, realizing that the Scotch was in his hand now and feeling honor-bound to take at least one gulp of the stuff. The taste was reminiscent of scorched rubber, but since the liquor seemed to quiet the raging demons in his mind, he finished the drink and poured another.

He fully intended to get drunk. It was something he hadn't done since high school, but it suddenly seemed appealing. Maybe he would stop hardening every time he thought of Libby, stop craving her.

Too, after the things he'd said to her that afternoon by the pond, he didn't want to remain sober any longer than necessary. "What did you mean," he ventured, after downing his fourth drink, "when you said Libby had to watch her stepson die?"

Papers rustled at the big desk behind him. "Stacey says the child had leukemia."

Jess poured another drink and closed his eyes. *Oh, Libby,* he thought, *I'm sorry. My God, I'm sorry.* "I guess Stacey would know," he said aloud, with bitterness.

There was a short, thunderous silence. Jess expected his father to explode into one of his famous tirades, was genuinely surprised when the man sighed instead. Still, his words dropped on Jess's mind like a bomb.

"The firewater isn't going to change the fact that you love Libby Kincaid, Jess," he said reasonably. "Making her life and your own miserable isn't going to change it, either."

Love Libby Kincaid? Impossible. The strange needs possessing him now were rooted in his libido, not his heart. Once he'd had her—and have her he would, or go crazy—her hold on him would be broken. "I've never loved a woman in my life," he said.

"Fool. You've loved one woman—Libby—since you were seven years old. Exactly seven years old, in fact."

Jess turned, studying his father quizzically. "What the hell are you talking about?"

"Your seventh birthday," recalled Cleave, his eyes far away. "Your mother and I gave you a pony. First time you saw Libby Kincaid, you were out of that saddle and helping her into it."

The memory burst, full-blown, into Jess's mind. A pinto pony. The new foreman arriving. The little girl with dark blue eyes and hair the color of winter moonlight.

He'd spent the whole afternoon squiring Libby around the yard, content to walk while she rode.

"What do you suppose Ken would say if I went over there and asked to see his daughter?" Jess asked.

"I imagine he'd shoot you, after today."

"I imagine he would. But I think I'll risk it."

"You've made enough trouble for one day," argued Cleave, taking obvious note of his son's inebriated state. "Libby needs time, Jess. She needs to be close to Ken. If you're smart, you'll leave her alone until she has a chance to get her emotional bearings again."

Jess didn't want his father to be right, not in this instance, anyway, but he knew that he was. Much as he wanted to go to Libby and try to make things right, the fact was that he was the last person in the world she needed or wanted to see.

"Better?"

Libby smiled at Ken as she came into the kitchen, freshly showered and wrapped in the cozy, familiar chenille robe she'd found in the back of her closet. "Lots better," she answered softly.

Her father was standing at the kitchen stove stirring something in the blackened cast-iron skillet.

Libby scuffled to the table and sat down. It was good to be home, so good. Why hadn't she come sooner? "Whatever you're cooking there smells good," she said.

Ken beamed. In his jeans and his Western shirt, he looked out of place at that stove. He should, Libby decided fancifully, have been crouching at some campfire on the range, stirring beans in a blue enamel pot. "This here's my world-famous red-devil sauce," he grinned, "for which I am known and respected."

Libby laughed, and tears of homecoming filled her eyes. She went to her father and hugged him, needing to be a little girl again, just for a moment.

Chapter 3

Libby nearly choked on her first taste of Ken's taco sauce. "Did you say you were known and respected for this stuff, or known and feared?"

Ken chuckled roguishly at her tear-polished eyes and flaming face. "My calling it 'red devil' should have been a clue, dumplin'."

Libby muttered an exclamation and perversely took another bite from her bulging taco. "From now on," she said, chewing, "I'll do the cooking around this spread."

Her father laughed again and tapped one temple with a calloused index finger, his pale blue eyes twinkling.

"You deliberately tricked me!" cried Libby.

He grinned and shrugged. "Code of the West, sweetheart. Grouse about the chow, and presto—you're the cook!"

"Actually," ventured Libby with cultivated innocence, "this sauce isn't too bad."

"Too late," laughed Ken. "You already broke the code."

Libby lowered her taco to her plate and lifted both hands in a gesture of concession. "All right, all right—but have a little pity on me, will you? I've been living among dudes!"

"That's no excuse."

Libby shrugged and took up her taco again. "I tried. Have you been doing your own cooking and cleaning all this time?"

Ken shook his head and sat back in his chair, his thumbs hooked behind his belt buckle. "Nope. The Barlowes' housekeeper sends her crew down here once in a while."

"What about the food?"

"I eat with the boys most of the time, over at the cook shack." He rose, went to fill two mugs from the coffeepot on the stove. When he turned around again, his face was serious. "Libby, what happened today? What upset you like that?"

Libby averted her eyes. "I don't know," she lied lamely.

"Dammit, you *do* know. You fainted, Libby. When Jess carried you in here, I—"

"I know," Libby broke in gently. "You were scared. I'm sorry."

Carefully, as though he feared he might drop them, Ken set the cups of steaming coffee on the table. "What happened?" he persisted as he sat down in his chair again.

Libby swallowed hard, but the lump that had risen in her throat wouldn't go down. Knowing that this conversation couldn't be avoided forever, she managed to reply, "It's complicated. Basically, it comes down to the fact that Stacey's been telling those lies."

"And?"

"And Jess believes him. He said…he said some things to me and…well, it must have created some kind of emotional overload. I just gave out."

Ken turned his mug idly between his thumb and index finger, causing the liquid to spill over and make a coffee stain on the tablecloth. "Tell me about Jonathan, Libby," he said in a low, gentle voice.

The tears that sprang into Libby's eyes were not related to the tang of her father's red-devil taco sauce. "He died," she choked miserably.

"I know that. You called me the night it happened, remember? I guess what I'm really asking you is why you didn't want me to fly back there and help you sort things out."

Libby lowered her head. Jonathan hadn't been her son, he'd been Aaron's, by a previous marriage. But the loss of the child was a raw void within her, even though months had passed. "I didn't want you to get a firsthand look at my marriage," she admitted with great difficulty—and the shame she couldn't seem to shake.

"Why not, Libby?"

The sound Libby made might have been either a laugh or a sob. "Because it was terrible," she answered.

"From the first?"

She forced herself to meet her father's steady gaze, knew that he had guessed a lot about her marriage from her rare phone calls and even rarer letters. "Almost," she replied sadly.

"Tell me."

Libby didn't want to think about Aaron, let alone talk about him to this man who wouldn't understand so many things. "He had…he had lovers."

Ken didn't seem surprised. Had he guessed that, too? "Go on."

"I can't!"

"Yes, you can. If it's too much for you right now, I won't press you. But the sooner you talk this out, Libby, the better off you're going to be."

She realized that her hands were clenched in her lap and tried to relax them. There was still a white mark on her finger where Aaron's ostentatious wedding ring had been. "He didn't care," she mourned in a soft, distracted whisper. "He honestly didn't care...."

"About you?"

"About Jonathan. Dad, he didn't care about his own son!"

"How so, sweetheart?"

Libby dashed away tears with the back of one hand. "Th-things were bad between Aaron and me b-before we found out that Jonathan was sick. After the doctors told us, it was a lot worse."

"I don't follow you, Libby."

"Dad, Aaron wouldn't have anything to do with Jonathan from the moment we knew he was dying. He wasn't there for any of the tests and he never once came to visit at the hospital. Dad, that little boy cried for his father, and Aaron wouldn't come to him!"

"Did you talk to Aaron?"

Remembered frustration made Libby's cheeks pound with color. "I *pleaded* with him, Dad. All he'd say was, 'I can't handle this.'"

"It would be a hell of a thing to deal with, Lib. Maybe you're being too hard on the man."

"Too hard? *Too hard?* Jonathan was terrified, Dad,

and he was in pain—constant pain. All he asked was that his own father be strong for him!"

"What about the boy's mother? Did she come to the hospital?"

"Ellen died when Jonathan was a baby."

Ken sighed, framing a question he was obviously reluctant to ask. "Did you ever love Aaron Strand, Libby?"

Libby remembered the early infatuation, the excitement that had never deepened into real love and had quickly been quelled by the realities of marriage to a man who was fundamentally self-centered. She tried, but she couldn't even recall her ex-husband's face clearly—all she could see in her mind was a pair of jade-green eyes, dark hair. Jess. "No," she finally said. "I thought I did when I married him, though."

Ken stood up suddenly, took the coffeepot from its back burner on the stove, refilled both their cups. "I don't like asking you this, but—"

"No, Dad," Libby broke in firmly, anticipating the question all too well, "I don't love Stacey!"

"You're sure about that?"

The truth was that Libby *hadn't* been sure, not entirely. But that ill-advised episode with Jess at the end of the swimming dock had brought everything into clear perspective. Just remembering how willingly she had submitted to him made her throb with embarrassment. "I'm sure," she said.

Ken's strong hand came across the table to close over hers. "You're home now," he reminded her, "and things are going to get better, Libby. I promise you that."

Libby sniffled inelegantly. "Know something, cowboy? I love you very much."

"Bet you say that to all your fathers," Ken quipped. "You planning to work on your comic strip tomorrow?"

The change of subject was welcome. "I'm six or eight weeks ahead of schedule on that, so I'm not worried about my deadline. I think I'll go riding, if I can get Cathy to go with me."

"I was looking forward to watching you work. What's your process?"

Libby smiled, feeling sheltered by the love of this strong and steady man facing her. She explained how her cartoons came into being, thinking it was good to talk about work, to think about work.

Disdainful as he had been about her career, it was the one thing Aaron had not been able to spoil for her.

Nobody's fool, Ken drew her out on the subject as much as he could, and she found herself chattering on and on about cartooning and even her secret hope to branch out into portraits one day.

They talked, father and daughter, far into the night.

"You deserve this," Jess Barlowe said to his reflection in the bathroom mirror. A first-class hangover pounded in his head and roiled in his stomach, and his face looked drawn, as though he'd been hibernating like one of the bears that sometimes troubled the range stock.

Grimly he began to shave, and as he wielded his disposable razor, he wondered if Libby was awake yet. Should he stop at Ken's and talk to her before going on to the main house to spend a day with the corporation accountants?

Jess wanted to go to Libby, to tell her that he was sorry for baiting her, to try to get their complex relationship—

if it *was* a relationship—onto some kind of sane ground. However, all his instincts told him that his father had been right the day before: Libby needed time.

His thoughts strayed to Libby's stepson. What would it be like to sit by a hospital bed, day after day, watching a child suffer and not being able to help?

Jess shuddered. It was hard to imagine the horror of something like that. At least Libby had had her husband to share the nightmare.

He frowned as he nicked his chin with the razor, blotted the small wound with tissue paper. If Libby had had her husband during that impossible time, why had she needed Stacey?

Stacey. Now, there was someone he could talk to. Granted, Jess had not been on the best of terms with his older brother of late, but the man had a firsthand knowledge of what was happening inside Libby Kincaid, and that was reason enough to approach him.

Feeling better for having a plan, Jess finished his ablutions and got dressed. Normally he spent his days on the range with Ken and the ranch hands, but today, because of his meeting with the accountants, he forwent his customary blue jeans and cotton workshirt for a tailored three-piece suit. He was still struggling with his tie as he made his way down the broad redwood steps that led from the loftlike second floor of his house to the living room.

Here there was a massive fireplace of white limestone, taking up the whole of one wall. The floors were polished oak and boasted a number of brightly colored Indian rugs. Two easy chairs and a deep sofa faced the hearth, and Jess's cluttered desk looked out over the ranchland and the glacial mountains beyond.

Striding toward the front door, in exasperation he gave up his efforts to get the tie right. He was glad he didn't have Stacey's job; not for him the dull task of overseeing the family's nationwide chain of steakhouse franchises.

He smiled. Stacey liked playing the dude, doing television commercials, traveling all over the country.

And taking Libby Kincaid to bed.

Jess stalked across the front lawn to the carport and climbed behind the wheel of the truck he'd driven since law school. One of these times, he was going to have to get another car—something with a little flash, like Stacey's Ferrari.

Stacey, Stacey. He hadn't even seen his brother yet, and already he was sick of him.

The truck's engine made a grinding sound and then huffed to life. Jess patted the dusty dashboard affectionately and grinned. A car was a car was a car, he reflected as he backed the notorious wreck out of his driveway. The function of a car was to transport people, not impress them.

Five minutes later, Jess's truck chortled to an asthmatic stop beside his brother's ice-blue Ferrari. He looked up at the modernistic two-story house that had been the senator's wedding gift to Stacey and Cathy and wondered if Libby would be impressed by the place.

He scowled as he made his way up the curving white-stone walk. What the hell did he care if Libby was impressed?

Irritated, he jabbed one finger at the special doorbell that would turn on a series of blinking lights inside the house. The system had been his own idea, meant to make life easier for Cathy.

His sister-in-law came to the door and smiled at him somewhat wanly, speaking with her hands. "Good morning."

Jess nodded, smiled. The haunted look in the depths of Cathy's eyes made him angry all over again. "Is Stacey here?" he signed, stepping into the house.

Cathy caught his hand in her own and led him through the cavernous living room and the formal dining room beyond. Stacey was in the kitchen, looking more at home in a three-piece suit than Jess ever had.

"You," Stacey said tonelessly, setting down the English muffin he'd been slathering with honey.

Cathy offered coffee and left the room when it was politely declined. Distractedly Jess reflected on the fact that her life had to be boring as hell, centering on Stacey the way it did.

"I want to talk to you," Jess said, scraping back a chrome-and-plastic chair to sit down at the table.

Stacey arched one eyebrow. "I hope it's quick—I'm leaving for the airport in a few minutes. I've got some business to take care of in Kansas City."

Jess was impatient. "What kind of man is Libby's ex-husband?" he asked.

Stacey took up his coffee. "Why do you want to know?"

"I just do. Do I have to have him checked out, or are you going to tell me?"

"He's a bastard," said Stacey, not quite meeting his brother's eyes.

"Rich?"

"Oh, yes. His family is old-money."

"What does he do?"

"Do?"

"Yeah. Does he work, or does he just stand around being rich?"

"He runs the family advertising agency; I think he has a lot of control over their other financial interests, too."

Jess sensed that Stacey was hedging, wondered why. "Any bad habits?"

Stacey was gazing at the toaster now, in a fixed way, as though he expected something alarming to pop out of it. "The man has his share of vices."

Annoyed now, Jess got up, helped himself to the cup of coffee he had refused earlier, sat down again. "Pulling porcupine quills out of a dog's nose would be easier than getting answers out of you. When you say he has vices, do you mean women?"

Stacey swallowed, looked away. "To put it mildly," he said.

Jess settled back in his chair. "What the hell do you mean by that?"

"I mean that he not only liked to run around with other women, he liked to flaunt the fact. The worse he could make Libby feel about herself, the happier he was."

"Jesus," Jess breathed. "What else?" he pressed, sensing, from Stacey's expression, that there was more.

"He was impotent with Libby."

"Why did she stay? Why in God's name did she stay?" Jess mused distractedly, as much to himself as to his brother.

A cautious but smug light flickered in Stacey's topaz eyes. "She had me," he said evenly. "Besides, Jonathan was sick by that time and she felt she had to stay in the marriage for his sake."

The spacious sun-filled kitchen seemed to buckle and shift around Jess. "Why didn't she tell Ken, at least?"

"What would have been the point in that, Jess? He couldn't have made the boy well again or transformed Aaron Strand into a devoted husband."

The things Libby must have endured—the shame, the loneliness, the humiliation and grief, washed over Jess in a dismal, crushing wave. No wonder she had reached out to Stacey the way she had. No wonder. "Thanks," he said gruffly, standing up to leave.

"Jess?"

He paused in the kitchen doorway, his hands clasping the woodwork, his shoulders aching with tension. "What?"

"Don't worry about Libby. I'll take care of her."

Jess felt a despairing sort of anger course through him. "What about Cathy?" he asked, without turning around. "Who is going to take care of her?"

"You've always—"

Jess whirled suddenly, staring at his brother, almost hating him. "I've always *what?*"

"Cared for her." Stacey shrugged, looking only mildly unsettled. "Protected her..."

"Are you suggesting that I sweep up the pieces after you shatter her?" demanded Jess in a dangerous rasp.

Stacey only shrugged again.

Because he feared that he would do his brother lasting harm if he stayed another moment, Jess stormed out of the house. Cathy, dressed in old jeans, boots and a cotton blouse, was waiting beside the truck. The pallor in her face told Jess that she knew much more about the state of her marriage than he would have hoped.

Her hands trembled a little as she spoke with them. "I'm scared, Jess."

He drew her into his arms, held her. "I know, baby," he said, even though he knew she couldn't hear him or see his lips. "I know."

Libby opened her eyes, yawned and stretched. The smells of sunshine and fresh air swept into her bedroom through the open window, ruffling pink eyelet curtains and reminding her that she was home again. She tossed back the covers on the bed and got up, sleepily making her way into the bathroom and starting the water for a shower.

As she took off her short cotton nightshirt, she looked down at herself and remembered the raging sensations Jess Barlowe had ignited in her the day before. She had been stupid and self-indulgent to let that happen, but after several years of celibacy, she supposed it was natural that her passions had been stirred so easily—especially by a man like Jess.

As Libby showered, she felt renewed. Aaron's flagrant infidelities had been painful for her, and they had seriously damaged her self-esteem in the bargain.

Now, even though she had made a fool of herself by being wanton with a man who could barely tolerate her, many of Libby's doubts about herself as a woman had been eased, if not routed. She was not as useless and undesirable as Aaron had made her feel. She had caused Jess Barlowe to want her, hadn't she?

Big deal, she told the image in her mirror as she brushed her teeth. *How do you know Jess wasn't out to prove that his original opinion of you was on target?*

Deflated by this very real possibility, Libby combed

her hair, applied the customary lip gloss and light touch of mascara and went back to her room to dress. From her suitcases she selected a short-sleeved turquoise pull-over shirt and a pair of trim jeans. Remembering her intention to find Cathy and persuade her to go riding, she ferreted through her closet until she found the worn boots she'd left behind before moving to New York, pulling them on over a pair of thick socks.

Looking down at those disreputable old boots, Libby imagined the scorn they would engender in Aaron's jet-set crowd and laughed. Problems or no problems, Jess or no Jess, it was good to be home.

Not surprisingly, the kitchen was empty. Ken had probably left the house before dawn, but there was coffee on the stove and fruit in the refrigerator, so Libby helped herself to a pear and sat down to eat.

The telephone rang just as she was finishing her second cup of coffee, and Libby answered cheerfully, thinking that the caller would be Ken or the house-keeper at the main house, relaying some message for Cathy.

She was back at the table, the receiver pressed to her ear, before Aaron spoke.

"When are you coming home?"

"Home?" echoed Libby stupidly, off-balance, unable to believe that he'd actually asked such a question. "I *am* home, Aaron."

"Enough," he replied. "You've made your point, exhibited your righteous indignation. Now you've got to get back here because I need you."

Libby wanted to hang up, but it seemed a very long way from her chair to the wall, where the rest of the telephone was. "Aaron, we are divorced," she reminded him calmly, "and I am never coming back."

"You have to," he answered, without missing a beat. "It's crucial."

"Why? What happened to all your...friends?"

Aaron sighed. "You remember Betty, don't you? Miss November? Well, Betty and I had a small disagreement, as it happens, and she went to my family. I am, shall we say, exposed as something less than an ideal spouse.

"In any case, my grandmother believes that a man who cannot run his family—she was in Paris when we divorced, darling—cannot run a company, either. I have six months to bring you back into the fold and start an heir, or the whole shooting match goes to my cousin."

Libby was too stunned to speak or even move; she simply stood in the middle of her father's kitchen, trying to absorb what Aaron was saying.

"That," Aaron went on blithely, "is where you come in, sweetheart. You come back, we smile a lot and make a baby, my grandmother's ruffled feathers are smoothed. It's as simple as that."

Sickness boiled into Libby's throat. "I don't believe this!" she whispered.

"You don't believe what, darling? That I can make a baby? May I point out that I sired Jonathan, of whom you were so cloyingly fond?"

Libby swallowed. "Get Miss November pregnant," she managed to suggest. And then she added distractedly, more to herself than Aaron, "I think I'm going to be sick."

"Don't tell me that I've been beaten to the proverbial draw," Aaron remarked in that brutally smooth, caustic way of his. "Did the steak-house king already do the deed?"

"You are disgusting!"

"Yes, but very practical. If I don't hand my grandmother an heir, whether it's mine or the issue of that softheaded cowboy, I stand to lose millions of dollars."

Libby managed to stand up. A few steps, just a few, and she could hang up the telephone, shut out Aaron's voice and his ugly suggestions. "Do you really think that I would turn any child of mine over to someone like you?"

"There is a child, then," he retorted smoothly.

"No!" Five steps to the wall, six at most.

"Be reasonable, sweetness. We're discussing an empire here. If you don't come back and attend to your wifely duties, I'll have to visit that godforsaken ranch and try to persuade you."

"I am not your wife!" screamed Libby. One step. One step and a reach.

"Dear heart, I don't find the idea any more appealing than you do, but there isn't any other way, is there? My grandmother likes you—sees you as sturdy peasant stock—and she wants the baby to be yours."

At last. The wall was close and Libby slammed the receiver into place. Then, dazed, she stumbled back to her chair and fell into it, lowering her head to her arms. She cried hard, for herself, for Jonathan.

"Libby?"

It was the last voice she would have wanted to hear, except for Aaron's. "Go away, Stacey!" she hissed.

Instead of complying, Stacey laid a gentle hand on

her shoulder. "What happened, Libby?" he asked softly. "Who was that on the phone?"

Fresh horror washed over Libby at the things Aaron had requested, mixed with anger and revulsion. God, how self-centered and insensitive that man was! And what gall he had, suggesting that she return to that disaster of a marriage, like some unquestioning brood mare, to produce a baby on order!

She gave a shuddering cry and motioned Stacey away with a frantic motion of her arm.

He only drew her up out of the chair and turned her so that he could hold her. She hadn't the strength to resist the intimacy and, in her half-hysterical state, he seemed to be the old Stacey, the strong big brother.

Stacey's hand came to the back of her head, tangling in her freshly washed hair, pressing her to his shoulder. "Tell me what happened," he urged, just as he had when Libby was a child with a skinned knee or a bee sting.

From habit, she allowed herself to be comforted. For so long there had been no one to confide in except Stacey, and it seemed natural to lean on him now. "Aaron... Aaron called. He wanted me to have his...his baby!"

Before Stacey could respond to that, the door separating the kitchen from the living room swung open. Instinctively Libby drew back from the man who held her.

Jess towered in the doorway, pale, his gaze scorching Libby's flushed, tear-streaked face. "You know," he began in a voice that was no less terrible for being soft, "I almost believed you. I almost had myself convinced that you were above anything this shabby."

"Wait—you don't understand...."

Jess smiled a slow, vicious smile—a smile that took in his startled brother as well as Libby. "Don't I? Oh, princess, I wish I didn't." The searing jade gaze sliced menacingly to Stacey's face. "And it seems I'm going to be an uncle. Tell me, brother—what does that make Cathy?"

To Libby's horror, Stacey said nothing to refute what was obviously a gross misunderstanding. He simply pulled her back into his arms, and her struggle was virtually imperceptible because of his strength.

"Let me go!" she pleaded, frantic.

Stacey released her, but only grudgingly. "I've got a plane to catch," he said.

Libby was incredulous. "Tell him! Tell Jess that he's wrong," she cried, reaching out for Stacey's arm, trying to detain him.

But Stacey simply pulled free and left by the back door.

There was a long, pulsing silence, during which both Libby and Jess seemed to be frozen. He was the first to thaw.

"I know you were hurt, Libby," he said. "Badly hurt. But that didn't give you the right to do something like this to Cathy."

It infuriated Libby that this man's good opinion was so important to her, but it was, and there was no changing that. "Jess, I didn't do anything to Cathy. Please listen to me."

He folded his strong arms and rested against the door jamb with an ease that Libby knew was totally feigned. "I'm listening," he said, and the words had a flippant note.

Libby ignored fresh anger. "I am not expecting Stacey's baby, and this wasn't a romantic tryst. I don't even know why he came here. I was on the phone with Aaron and he—"

A muscle in Jess's neck corded, relaxed again. "I hope you're not going to tell me that your former husband made you pregnant, Libby. That seems unlikely."

Frustration pounded in Libby's temples and tightened the already constricted muscles in her throat. "I am not pregnant!" she choked out. "And if you are going to eavesdrop, Jess Barlowe, you could at least pay attention! Aaron wanted me to come back to New York and have his baby so that he would have an heir to present to his grandmother!"

"You didn't agree to that?"

"Of course I didn't agree! What kind of monster do you think I am?"

Jess shrugged with a nonchalance that was belied by the leaping green fire in his eyes. "I don't know, princess, but rest assured—I intend to find out."

"I have a better idea!" Libby flared. "Why don't you just leave me the hell alone?"

"In theory that's brilliant," he fired back, "but there is one problem—I want you."

Involuntarily Libby remembered the kisses and caresses exchanged by the pond the day before, relived them. Hot color poured into her face. "Am I supposed to be honored?"

"No," Jess replied flatly, "you're supposed to be kept so busy that you won't have time to screw up Cathy's life any more than you already have."

If Libby could have moved, she would have rushed across that room and slapped Jess Barlowe senseless. Since she couldn't get her muscles to respond to the orders of her mind, she was forced to watch in stricken silence as he gave her a smoldering assessment with his eyes, executed a half salute and left the house.

Chapter 4

When the telephone rang again, immediately after Jess's exit from the kitchen, Libby was almost afraid to answer it. It would be like Aaron to persist, to use pressure to get what he wanted.

On the other hand, the call might be from someone else, and it could be important.

"Hello?" Libby dared, with resolve.

"Ms. Kincaid?" asked a cheerful feminine voice. "This is Marion Bradshaw, and I'm calling for Mrs. Barlowe. She'd like you to meet her at the main house if you can, and she says to dress for riding."

Libby looked down at her jeans and boots and smiled. In one way, at least, she and Cathy were still on the same wavelength. "Please tell her that I'll be there as soon as I can."

There was a brief pause at the other end of the line, followed by, "Mrs. Barlowe wants me to ask if you have a car down there. If not, she'll come and pick you up in a few minutes."

Though there was no car at her disposal, Libby declined the offer. The walk to the main ranch house would give her a chance to think, to prepare herself to face her cousin again.

As Libby started out, striding along the winding tree-lined road, she ached to think that she and Cathy had come to this. Fresh anger at Stacey quickened her step.

For a moment she was mad at Cathy, too. How could she believe such a thing, after all they'd been through together? How?

Firmly Libby brought her ire under control. *You don't get mad at a handicapped person,* she scolded herself.

The sun was already high and hot in the domelike sky, and Libby smiled. It was warm for spring, and wasn't it nice to look up and see clouds and mountaintops instead of tall buildings and smog?

Finally the main house came into view. It was a rambling structure of red brick, and its many windows glistened in the bright sunshine. A porch with marble steps led up to the double doors, and one of them swung open even as Libby reached out to ring the bell.

Mrs. Bradshaw, the housekeeper, stepped out and enfolded Libby in a delighted hug. A slender middle-aged woman with soft brown hair, Marion Bradshaw was as much a part of the Circle Bar B as Senator Barlowe himself. "Welcome home," she said warmly.

Libby smiled and returned the hug. "Thank you, Marion," she replied. "Is Cathy ready to go riding?"

"She's gone ahead to the stables—she'd like you to join her there."

Libby turned to go back down the steps but was stopped by the housekeeper. "Libby?"

She faced Marion, again, feeling wary.

"I don't believe it of you," said Mrs. Bradshaw firmly.

Libby was embarrassed, but there was no point in trying to pretend that she didn't get the woman's meaning. Probably everyone on the ranch was speculating about her supposed involvement with Stacey Barlowe. "Thank you."

"You stay right here on this ranch, Libby Kincaid," Marion Bradshaw rushed on, her own face flushed now. "Don't let Stacey or anybody else run you off."

That morning's unfortunate scene in Ken's kitchen was an indication of how difficult it would be to take the housekeeper's advice. Life on the Circle Bar B could become untenable if both Stacey and Jess didn't back off.

"I'll try," she said softly before stepping down off the porch and making her way around the side of that imposing but gracious house.

Prudently, the stables had been built a good distance away. During the walk, Libby wondered if she shouldn't leave the ranch after all. True, she needed to be there, but Jonathan's death had taught her that sometimes a person had to put her own desires aside for the good of other people.

But would leaving help, in the final analysis? Suppose Stacey did follow her, as he'd threatened to do? What would that do to Cathy?

The stables, like the house, were constructed of red brick. As Libby approached them, she saw Cathy leading two horses out into the sun—a dancing palomino gelding and the considerably less prepossessing pinto mare that had always been Libby's to ride.

Libby hesitated; it had been a long, long time since she'd ridden a horse, and the look in Cathy's eyes was cool. Distant. It was almost as though Libby were a troublesome stranger rather than her cousin and confidante.

As if to break the spell, Cathy lifted one foot to the stirrup of the Palomino's saddle and swung onto its back. Though she gave no sign of greeting, her eyes bade Libby to follow suit.

The elderly pinto was gracious while Libby struggled into the saddle and took the reins in slightly shaky hands. A moment later they were off across the open pastureland behind the stables, Cathy confident in the lead.

Libby jostled and jolted in the now unfamiliar saddle, and she felt a fleeting annoyance with Cathy for setting the brisk pace that she did. Again she berated herself for being angry with someone who couldn't hear.

Cathy rode faster and faster, stopping only when she reached the trees that trimmed the base of a wooded hill. There she turned in the saddle and flung a look back at the disgruntled Libby.

"You're out of practice," she said clearly, though her voice had the slurred meter of those who have not heard another person speak in years.

Libby, red-faced and damp with perspiration, was not surprised that Cathy had spoken aloud. She had learned to talk before the childhood illness that had made her deaf, and when she could be certain that no one else would overhear, she often spoke. It was a secret the two women kept religiously.

"Thanks a lot!" snapped Libby.

Deftly Cathy swung one trim blue-jeaned leg over the neck of her golden gelding and slid to the ground. The fancy bridle jingled musically as the animal bent its great head to graze on the spring grass. "We've got to talk, Libby."

Libby jumped from the pinto's back and the action engendered a piercing ache in the balls of her feet. "You've got that right!" she flared, forgetting for the moment her earlier resolve to respect Cathy's affliction. "Were you trying to get me killed?"

Watching Libby's lips, Cathy grinned. "Killed?" she echoed in her slow, toneless voice. "You're my cousin. That's important, isn't it? That we're cousins, I mean?"

Libby sighed. "Of course it's important."

"It implies a certain loyalty, don't you think?"

Libby braced herself. She'd known this confrontation was coming, of course, but that didn't mean she wanted it or was ready for it. "Yes," she said somewhat lamely.

"Are you having an affair with my husband?"

"No!"

"Do you want to?"

"What the hell kind of person do you think I am, Cathy?" shouted Libby, losing all restraint, flinging her arms out wide and startling the horses, who nickered and danced and tossed their heads.

"I'm trying to find that out," said Cathy in measured and droning words. Not once since the conversation began had her eyes left Libby's mouth.

"You already know," retorted her cousin.

For the first time, Cathy looked ashamed. But there was uncertainty in her expression, too, along with a great deal of pain. "It's no secret that Stacey wants you,

Libby. I've been holding my breath ever since you decided to come back, waiting for him to leave me."

"Whatever problems you and Stacey have, Cathy, I didn't start them."

"What about all his visits to New York?"

Libby's shoulders slumped, and she allowed herself to sink to the fragrant spring-scented ground, where she sat cross-legged, her head down. With her hands she said, "You knew about the divorce, and about Jonathan. Stacey was only trying to help me through—we weren't lovers."

The lush grass moved as Cathy sat down too, facing Libby. There were tears shining in her large green eyes, and her lower lip trembled. Nervously she plied a blade of grass between her fingers.

"I'm sorry about your little boy," she said aloud.

Libby reached out, calmer now, and squeezed Cathy's hands with her own. "Thanks."

A lonely, haunted look rose in Cathy's eyes. "Stacey wanted us to have a baby," she confided.

"Why didn't you?"

Sudden color stained Cathy's lovely cheeks. "I'm deaf!" she cried defensively.

Libby released her cousin's hands to sign, "So what? Lots of deaf people have babies."

"Not me!" Cathy signaled back with spirited despair. "I wouldn't know when it cried!"

Libby spoke slowly, her hands falling back to her lap. "Cathy, there are solutions for that sort of problem. There are trained dogs, electronic devices—"

"Trained dogs!" scoffed Cathy, but there was more anguish in her face than anger. "What kind of woman needs a dog to help her raise her own baby?"

"A deaf woman," Libby answered firmly. "Besides, if you don't want a dog around, you could hire a nurse."

"No!"

Libby was taken aback. "Why not?" she signed after a few moments.

Cathy clearly had no intention of answering. She bolted to her feet and was back in the palomino's saddle before Libby could even rise from the ground.

After that, they rode without communicating at all. Knowing that things were far from settled between herself and her cousin, Libby tried to concentrate on the scenery. A shadow moved across the sun, however, and a feeling of impending disaster unfolded inside her.

Jess glared at the screen of the small computer his father placed so much store in and resisted a caveman urge to strike its side with his fist.

"Here," purred a soft feminine voice, and Monica Summers, the senator's curvaceous assistant, reached down to move the mouse and tap the keyboard in a few strategic places.

Instantly the profit-and-loss statement Jess had been trying to call up was prominently displayed on the screen.

"How did you do that?"

Monica smiled her sultry smile and pulled up a chair to sit down beside Jess. "It's a simple matter of command," she said, and somehow the words sounded wildly suggestive.

Jess's collar seemed to tighten around his throat, but he grinned, appreciating Monica's lithe, inviting body, her profusion of gleaming brown hair, her impudent mouth and soft gray eyes. Her visits to the ranch were usually brief, but the senator's term of office was almost over, and he planned to write a long book—with which Monica was slated to help. Until that project was completed, she would be around a lot.

The fact that the senior senator did not intend to campaign for reelection didn't seem to faze her—it was common knowledge that she had a campaign of her own in mind.

Monica had made it clear, time and time again, that she was available to Jess for more than an occasional dinner date and subsequent sexual skirmish. And before Libby's return, Jess had seriously considered settling down with Monica.

He didn't love her, but she was undeniably beautiful, and the promises she made with her skillfully made-up eyes were not idle ones. In addition to that, they had a lot of ordinary things in common—similar political views, a love of the outdoors, like tastes in music and books.

Now, even with Monica sitting so close to him, her perfume calling up some rather heated memories, Jess Barlowe was patently unmoved.

A shower of anger sifted through him. He *wanted* to be moved, dammit—he wanted everything to be the way it was before Libby's return. Return? It was an invasion! He thought about the little hellion day and night, whether he wanted to or not.

"What's wrong, Jess?" Monica asked softly, perceptively, her hand resting on his shoulder. "It's more than just this computer, isn't it?"

He looked away. The sensible thing to do would be to take Monica by the hand, lead her off somewhere private and make slow, ferocious love to her. Maybe that would exorcise Libby Kincaid from his mind.

He remembered passion-weighted breasts, bared to him on a swimming dock, remembered their nipples blossoming sweetly in his mouth. Libby's breasts.

"Jess?"

He forced himself to look at Monica again. "I'm sorry," he said. "Did you say something?"

Mischief danced in her charcoal eyes. "Yes. I offered you my body."

He laughed.

Instead of laughing herself, Monica gave him a gentle, discerning look. "Mrs. Bradshaw tells me that Libby Kincaid is back," she said. "Could it be that I have some competition?"

Jess cleared his throat and diplomatically fixed his attention on the computer screen. "Show me how you made this monster cough up that profit-and-loss statement," he hedged.

"Jess." The voice was cool, insistent.

He made himself meet Monica's eyes again. "I don't know what I feel for Libby," he confessed. "She makes me mad as hell, but..."

"But," said Monica with rueful amusement, "you want her very badly, don't you?"

There was no denying that, but neither could Jess bring himself to openly admit to the curious needs that had been plaguing him since the moment he'd seen Libby again at the small airport in Kalispell.

Monica's right index finger traced the outline of his jaw, tenderly. Sensuously. "We've never agreed to be faithful to each other, Jess," she said in the silky voice that had once enthralled him. "There aren't any strings tying you to me. But that doesn't mean that I'm going to step back and let Libby Kincaid have a clear field. I want you myself."

Jess was saved from answering by the sudden appearance of his father in the study doorway.

"Oh, Monica—there you are," Cleave Barlowe said warmly. "Ready to start working on that speech now? We have to have it ready before we fly back to Washington, remember."

Gray eyes swept Jess's face in parting. "More than ready," she replied, and then she was out of her chair and walking across the study to join her employer.

Jess gave the computer an unloving look and switched it off, taking perverse pleasure in the way the images on the screen dissolved. "State of the art," he mocked, and then stood up and strode out of the room.

The accountants would be angry, once they returned from their coffee break, but he didn't give a damn. If he didn't do something physical, he was going to go crazy.

Back at the stables, Libby surrendered her horse to a ranch hand with relief. Already the muscles in her thighs were aching dully from the ride; by morning they would be in savage little knots.

Cathy, who probably rode almost every day, looked breezy and refreshed, and from her manner no one would have suspected that she harbored any ill feelings toward Libby. "Let's take a swim," she signed, "and then we can have lunch."

Libby would have preferred to soak in the hot tub, but her pride wouldn't allow her to say so. Unless a limp betrayed her, she wasn't going to let Cathy know how sore a simple horseback ride had left her.

"I don't have a swimming suit," she said, somewhat hopefully.

"That's okay," Cathy replied with swift hands. "It's an indoor pool, remember?"

"I hope you're not suggesting that we swim naked," Libby argued aloud.

Cathy's eyes danced. "Why not?" she signed impishly. "No one would see us."

"Are you kidding?" Libby retorted, waving one arm toward the long, wide driveway. "Look at all these cars! There are *people* in that house!"

"Are you so modest?" queried Cathy, one eyebrow arched.

"Yes!" replied Libby, ignoring the subtle sarcasm.

"Then we'll go back to your house and swim in the pond, like we used to."

Libby recalled the blatant way she'd offered herself to Jess Barlowe in that place and winced inwardly. The peaceful solace of that pond had probably been altered forever, and it was going to be some time before she could go there comfortably again. "It's spring, Cathy, not summer. We'd catch pneumonia! Besides, I think it's going to rain."

Cathy shrugged. "All right, all right. I'll borrow a car and we'll drive over and get your swimming suit, then come back here."

"Fine," Libby agreed with a sigh.

She was to regret the decision almost immediately. When she and Cathy reached the house they had both grown up in, there was a florist's truck parked out front.

On the porch stood an affable young man, a long, narrow box in his hands. "Hi, Libby," he said.

Libby recognized Phil Reynolds, who had been her

classmate in high school. *Go away, Phil,* she thought, even as she smiled and greeted him.

Cathy's attention was riveted on the silver box he carried, and there was a worried expression on her face.

Phil approached, beaming. "I didn't even know you were back until we got this order this morning. Aren't you coming into town at all? We got a new high school...."

Simmonsville, a dried-up little community just beyond the south border of the Circle Bar B, hadn't even entered Libby's thoughts until she'd seen Phil Reynolds. She ignored his question and stared at the box he held out to her as if it might contain something squirmy and vile.

"Wh-who sent these?" she managed, all too conscious of the suspicious way Cathy was looking at her.

"See for yourself," Phil said brightly, and then he got back into his truck and left.

Libby took the card from beneath the red ribbon that bound the box and opened it with trembling fingers. The flowers couldn't be from Stacey, please God, they couldn't!

The card was typewritten. *Don't be stubborn, sweetness,* the message read. *Regards, Aaron.*

For a moment Libby was too relieved to be angry. "Aaron," she repeated. Then she lifted the lid from the box and saw the dozen pink rosebuds inside.

For one crazy moment she was back in Jonathan's hospital room. There had been roses there, too—along with mums and violets and carnations. Aaron and his family had sent costly bouquets and elaborate toys, but not one of them had come to visit.

Libby heard the echo of Jonathan's purposefully cheerful voice. *Daddy must be busy,* he'd said.

With a cry of fury and pain, Libby flung the roses away, and they scattered over the walk in a profusion of long-stemmed delicacy. The silver box lay with them, catching the waning sunlight.

Cathy knelt and began gathering up the discarded flowers, placing them gently back in their carton. Once or twice she glanced up at Libby's livid face in bewilderment, but she asked no questions and made no comments.

Libby turned away and bounded into the house. By the time she had found a swimming suit and come back downstairs again, Cathy was arranging the rosebuds in a cut-glass vase at the kitchen sink.

She met Libby's angry gaze and held up one hand to stay the inevitable outburst. "They're beautiful, Libby," she said in a barely audible voice. "You can't throw away something that's beautiful."

"Watch me!" snapped Libby.

Cathy stepped between her cousin and the lush bouquet. "Libby, at least let me give them to Mrs. Bradshaw," she pleaded aloud. "Please?"

Glumly Libby nodded. She supposed she should be grateful that the roses hadn't been sent by Stacey in a fit of ardor, and they *were* too lovely to waste, even if she herself couldn't bear the sight of them.

Libby remembered the words on Aaron's card as she and Cathy drove back to the main house. *Don't be stubborn.* A tremor of dread flitted up and down her spine.

Aaron hadn't been serious when he'd threatened to come to the ranch and "persuade" her to return to New York with him, had he? She shivered.

Surely even Aaron wouldn't have the gall to do that, she tried to reassure herself. After all, he had never come to the apartment she'd taken after Jonathan's death, never so much as called. Even when the divorce had been granted, he had avoided her by sending his lawyer to court alone.

No. Aaron wouldn't actually come to the Circle Bar B. He might call, he might even send more flowers, just to antagonize her, but he wouldn't come in person. Despite his dismissal of Stacey as a "soft-headed cowboy," he was afraid of him.

Cathy was drawing the car to a stop in front of the main house by the time Libby was able to recover herself. To allay the concern in her cousin's eyes, she carried the vase of pink roses into the kitchen and presented them to Mrs. Bradshaw, who was puzzled but clearly pleased.

Inside the gigantic, elegantly tiled room that housed the swimming pool and the spacious hot tub, Libby eyed the latter with longing. Thus, it was a moment before she realized that the pool was already occupied.

Jess was doing a furious racing crawl from one side of the deep end to the other, his tanned, muscular arms cutting through the blue water with a force that said he was trying to work out some fierce inner conflict. Watching him admiringly from the poolside, her slender legs dangling into the water, was a pretty dark-haired woman with beautiful gray eyes.

The woman greeted Cathy with an easy gesture of her hands, though her eyes were fixed on Libby, seeming to assess her in a thorough, if offhand, fashion.

"I'm Monica Summers," she said, as Jess, apparently oblivious of everything other than the furious course he was following through the water, executed an impressive somersault turn at the poolside and raced back the other way.

Monica Summers. The name was familiar to Libby, and so, vaguely, was the perfect fashion-model face.

Of course. Monica was Senator Barlowe's chief assistant. Libby had never actually met the woman, but she had seen her on television newscasts and Ken had mentioned her in passing, on occasion, over long-distance telephone.

"Hello," Libby said. "I'm—"

The gray eyes sparkled. "I know," Monica broke in smoothly. "You're Libby Kincaid. I enjoy your cartoons very much."

Libby felt about as sophisticated, compared to this woman, as a Girl Scout selling cookies door-to-door. And Monica's subtle emphasis on the word "cartoons" had made her feel defensive.

All the same, Libby thanked her and forced herself not to watch Jess's magnificent body moving through the bright blue water of the pool. It didn't bother her that Jess and Monica had been alone in this strangely sensual setting. It didn't.

Cathy had moved away, anxious for her swim.

"I'm sorry if we interrupted something," Libby said, and hated herself instantly for betraying her interest.

Monica smiled. Clearly she had not been in swimming herself, for her expensive black swimsuit was dry, and so was her long, lush hair. Her makeup, of course, was perfect. "There are always interruptions," she said, and then she turned away to take up her adoring-spectator position again, her gaze following the play of the powerful muscles in Jess's naked back.

My thighs are too fat, mourned Libby, in petulant

despair. She took a seat on a lounge far removed from
Jess and his lovely friend and tried to pretend an interest in Cathy's graceful backstroke.

Was Jess intimate with Monica Summers? It certainly seemed so, and Libby couldn't understand, for
the life of her, why she was so brutally surprised by
the knowledge. After all, Jess was a handsome, healthy
man, well beyond the age of handholding and fantasies-
from-afar. Had she really ever believed that he had just
been existing on this ranch in some sort of suspended
animation?

Cathy roused her from her dismal reflection by flinging a stream of water at her with both hands. Instantly
Libby was drenched and stung to an annoyance out of
all proportion to the offense. Surprising even herself,
she stomped over to the hot tub, flipped the switch that
would make the water bubble and churn, and after hurl-
ing one scorching look at her unrepenting cousin, slid
into the enormous tile-lined tub.

The heat and motion of the water were welcome balm
to Libby's muscles, if not to her spirit. She had no right
to care who Jess Barlowe slept with, no right at all. It
wasn't as though she had ever had any claim on his affections.

Settling herself on a submerged bench, Libby tilted
her head back, closed her eyes, and tried to pretend
that she was alone in that massive room with its slop-
ing glass roof, lush plants and lounges.

The fact that she was sexually attracted to Jess Barlowe was undeniable, but it was just a physical phe-
nomenon, certainly. It would pass.

All she had to do to accelerate the process was allow

herself to remember how very demeaning Aaron's love-making had been. And remember she did.

After Libby had caught her husband with the first of his lovers, she had moved out of his bedroom permanently, remaining in his house only because Jonathan, still at home then, had needed her so much.

Before her brutal awakening, however, she had tried hard to make the rapidly failing marriage work. Even then, bedtime had been a horror.

Libby's skin prickled as she recalled the way Aaron would ignore her for long weeks and then pounce on her with a vicious and alarming sort of determination, tearing her clothes, sometimes bruising her.

In retrospect, Libby realized that Aaron must have been trying to prove something to himself concerning his identity as a man, but at the time she had known only that sex, much touted in books and movies, was something to be feared.

Not once had Libby achieved any sort of satisfaction with Aaron—she had only endured. Now, painfully conscious of the blatantly masculine, near-naked cowboy swimming in the pool nearby, Libby wondered if lovemaking would be different with Jess.

The way that her body had blossomed beneath his seemed adequate proof that it would be different indeed, but there was always the possibility that she would be disappointed in the ultimate act. Probably she had been aroused only because Jess had taken the time to offer her at least a taste of pleasure. Aaron had never done that, never shown any sensitivity at all.

Shutting out all sight and sound, Libby mentally decried her lack of experience. If only she'd been with even one man besides Aaron, she would have had some frame of reference, some inkling of whether or not the soaring releases she'd read about really existed.

The knowledge that so many people thought she had been carrying on a torrid affair with Stacey brought a wry smile to her lips. If only they knew.

"What are you smiling about?"

The voice jolted Libby back to the here and now with a thump. Jess had joined her in the hot tub at some point; indeed, he was standing only inches away.

Startled, Libby stared at him for a moment, then looked wildly around for Cathy and the elegant Ms. Summers.

"They went in to have lunch," Jess informed her, his eyes twinkling. Beads of water sparkled in the dark down that matted his muscular chest, and his hair had been towel-rubbed into an appealing disarray.

"I'll join them," said Libby in a frantic whisper, but the simple mechanics of turning away and climbing out of the hot tub eluded her.

Smelling pleasantly of chlorine, Jess came nearer. "Don't go," he said softly. "Lunch will wait."

Anger at Cathy surged through Libby. Why had she gone off and left her here?

Jess seemed to read the question in her face, and it made him laugh. The sound was soft—sensuously, wholly male. Overhead, spring thunder crashed in a gray sky.

Libby trembled, pressing back against the edge of the hot tub with such force that her shoulder blades ached. "Stay away from me," she breathed.

"Not on your life," he answered, and then he was so near that she could feel the hard length of his thighs against her own. The soft dark hair on his chest tickled her bare shoulders and the suddenly alive flesh above her swimsuit top. "I intend to finish what we started yesterday beside the pond."

Libby gasped as his moist lips came down to taste hers, to tame and finally part them for a tender invasion. Her hands went up, of their own accord, to rest on his hips.

He was naked. The discovery rocked Libby, made her try to twist away from him, but his kiss deepened and subdued her struggles. With his hands, he lifted her legs, draped them around the rock-hard hips she had just explored.

The imposing, heated length of his desire, now pressed intimately against her, was powerful proof that he meant to take her.

Chapter 5

Libby felt as though her body had dissolved, become part of the warm, bubbling water filling the hot tub. When Jess drew back from his soft conquering of her mouth, his hands rose gently to draw down the modest top of her swimsuit, revealing the pulsing fullness of her breasts to his gaze.

It was not in Libby to protest: she was transfixed, caught up in primal responses that had no relation to good sense or even sanity. She let her head fall back, saw through the transparent ceiling that gray clouds had darkened the sky, promising a storm that wouldn't begin to rival the one brewing inside Libby herself.

Jess bent his head, nipped at one exposed, aching nipple with cautious teeth.

Libby drew in a sharp breath as a shaft of searing pleasure went through her, so powerful that she was nearly convulsed by it. A soft moan escaped her, and she tilted her head even further back, so that her breasts were still more vulnerable to the plundering of his mouth.

Inside Libby's swirling mind, a steady voice chanted a litany of logic: she was behaving in a wanton way—Jess didn't really care for her, he was only trying to prove that he could conquer her whenever he desired—this place was not private, and there was a very real danger that someone would walk in at any moment and see what was happening.

Thunder reverberated in the sky, shaking heaven and earth. And none of the arguments Libby's reason was offering had any effect on her rising need to join herself with this impossible, overbearing man feasting so brazenly on her breast.

With an unerring hand, Jess found the crux of her passion, and through the fabric of her swimsuit he stroked it to a wanting Libby had never experienced before. Then, still greedy at the nipple he was attending, he deftly worked aside the bit of cloth separating Libby's womanhood from total exposure.

She gasped as he caught the hidden nubbin between his fingers and began, rhythmically, to soothe it. Or was he tormenting it? Libby didn't know, didn't care.

Jess left her breast to nibble at her earlobe, chuckled hoarsely when the tender invasion of his fingers elicited a throaty cry of welcome.

"Go with it, Libby," he whispered. "Let it carry you high…higher.…"

Libby was already soaring, sightless, mindless, conscious only of the fiery marauding of his fingers and the strange force inside her that was building toward something she had only imagined before. "Oh," she gasped as he worked this new and fierce magic. "Oh, Jess..."

Mercilessly he intensified her pleasure by whispering outrageously erotic promises, by pressing her legs wide of each other with one knee, by caressing her breast with his other hand.

A savage trembling began deep within Libby, causing her breath to quicken to a soft, lusty whine.

"Meet it, Libby," Jess urged. "Rise to meet it."

Suddenly Libby's entire being buckled in some ancient, inescapable response. The thunder in the distant skies covered her final cry of release, and she convulsed again and again, helpless in the throes of her body's savage victory.

When at last the ferocious clenching and unclenching had ceased, Libby's reason gradually returned. Forcing wide eyes to Jess's face, she saw no demand there, no mockery or revulsion. Instead, he was grinning at her, as pleased as if he'd been sated himself.

Wild embarrassment surged through Libby in the wake of her passion. She tried to avert her face, but Jess caught her chin in his hand and made her look at him.

"Don't," he said gruffly. "Don't look that way. It wasn't wrong, Libby."

His ability to read her thoughts so easily was as unsettling as the knowledge that she'd just allowed this man unconscionable liberties in a hot tub. "I suppose you think... I suppose you want..."

Jess withdrew his conquering hand, tugged her swimsuit back into place. "I think you're beautiful," he supplied, "and I want you—that's true. But for now, watching you respond like that was enough."

Libby blushed again. She was still confused by the

power of her release, and she had expected Jess to demand his own satisfaction. She was stunned that he could give such fierce fulfillment and ask nothing for himself.

"You've never been with any man besides your husband, have you, Libby?"

The outrageous bluntness of that question solidified Libby's jellylike muscles, and she reached furiously for one of the towels Mrs. Bradshaw had set nearby on a low shelf. "I've been with a thousand men!" she snapped in a harsh whisper. "Why, one word from any man, and I let him… I let him…"

Jess grinned again. "You've never had a climax before," he observed.

How could he guess a thing like that? It was uncanny. Libby knew that the hot color in her face belied her sharp answer. "Of course I have! I've been married— did you think I was celibate?"

The rapid-fire hysteria of her words only served to amuse Jess, it seemed. "We both know, Libby Kincaid, that you are, for all practical intents and purposes, a virgin. You may have lain beneath that ex-husband of yours and wished to God that he would leave you alone, but until a few minutes ago you had never even guessed what it means to be a woman."

Libby wouldn't have thought it possible to be as murderously angry as she was at that moment. "Why, you arrogant, *insufferable*…"

He caught her hand at the wrist before it could make the intended contact with his face. "You haven't seen anything yet, princess," he vowed with gentle force. "When I take you to bed—and I assure you that I will— I'll prove that everything I've said is true."

While Libby herself was outraged, her traitorous body yearned to lie in his bed, bend to his will. Having reached the edges of passion, it wanted to go beyond, into the molten core. "You egotistical bastard!" Libby hissed, breaking away from him to lift herself out of the hot tub and land on its edge with an inelegant, squishy plop, "You act as if you'd invented sex!"

"As far as you're concerned, little virgin, I did. But have no fear—I intend to deflower you at the first opportunity."

Libby stood up, wrapped her shaky, nerveless form in a towel the size of a bedsheet. "Go to hell!"

Jess rose out of the water, not the least bit self-conscious of his nakedness. The magnitude of his desire for her was all too obvious.

"The next few hours will be just that," he said, reaching for a towel of his own. Naturally, the one he selected barely covered him.

Speechless, Libby imagined the thrust of his manhood, imagined her back arching to receive him, imagined a savage renewal of the passion she had felt only minutes before.

Jess gave her an amused sidelong glance, as though he knew what she was thinking, and intoned, "Don't worry, princess. I'll court you if that's what you want. But I'll have you, too. And thoroughly."

Having made this incredible vow, he calmly walked out of the room, leaving Libby alone with a clamoring flock of strange emotions and unmet needs.

The moment Jess was gone, she stumbled to the nearest lounge chair and sank onto it, her knees too weak to support her. *Well, Kincaid,* she reflected wryly, *now you know. Satisfied?*

Libby winced at the last word. Though she might have wished otherwise, given the identity of the man involved, she was just that.

With carefully maintained dignity, Jess Barlowe strode into the shower room adjoining the pool and wrenched on one spigot. As he stepped under the biting, sleetlike spray, he gritted his teeth.

Gradually his body stopped screaming and the stubborn evidence of his passion faded. With relief, Jess dived out of the shower stall and grabbed a fresh towel.

A hoarse chuckle escaped him as he dried himself with brisk motions. Good God, if he didn't have Libby Kincaid soon, he was going to die of pneumonia. A man could stand only so many plunges into icy ponds, only so many cold showers.

A spare set of clothes—jeans and a white pullover shirt—awaited Jess in a cupboard. He donned them quickly, casting one disdainful look at the three-piece suit he had shed earlier. His circulation restored, to some degree at least, he toweled his hair and then combed it with the splayed fingers of his left hand.

A sweet anguish swept through him as he remembered the magic he had glimpsed in Libby's beautiful face during that moment of full surrender. *My father was right,* Jess thought as he pulled on socks and old, comfortable boots. *I love you, Libby Kincaid. I love you.*

Jess was not surprised to find that Libby wasn't with Cathy and Monica in the kitchen—she had probably made some excuse to get out of joining them for lunch and gone off to gather her thoughts. God knew, she had to be every bit as undone and confused as he was.

Mostly to avoid the sad speculation in Monica's eyes,

Jess glanced toward the kitchen windows. They were already sheeted with rain.

A crash of thunder jolted him out of the strange inertia that had possessed him. He glanced at Cathy, saw an impish light dancing in her eyes.

"You can catch her if you hurry," she signed, cocking her head to one side and grinning at him.

Did she know what had happened in the hot tub? Some of the heat lingering in Jess's loins rose to his face as he bolted out of the room and through the rest of the house.

His truck, an eyesore among the other cars parked in front of the house, patently refused to start. Annoyed, Jess "borrowed" Monica's sleek green Porsche without a moment's hesitation, and his aggravation grew as he left the driveway and pulled out onto the main road.

What the hell did Libby think she was doing, walking in this rain? And why had Cathy let her go?

He found Libby near the mailboxes, slogging despondently along, soaked to the skin.

"Get in!" he barked, furious in his concern.

Libby lifted her chin and kept walking. Her turquoise shirt was plastered to her chest, revealing the outlines of her bra, and her hair hung in dripping tendrils.

"Now!" Jess roared through the window he had rolled down halfway.

She stopped, faced him with indigo fury sparking in her eyes. "Why?" she yelled over the combined roars of the deluge and Monica's car engine. "Is it time to teach me what it means to be a woman?"

"How the hell would I know what it means to be a woman?" he shouted back. "Get in this car!"

Libby told him to do something that was anatomically impossible and then went splashing off down the road again, ignoring the driving rain.

Rasping a swearword, Jess slipped the Porsche out of gear and wrenched the emergency brake into place. Then he shoved open the door and bounded through the downpour to catch up with Libby, grasp her by the shoulders and whirl her around to face him.

"If you don't get your backside into that car *right now*," he bellowed, "I swear to God I'll *throw* you in!"

She assessed the Porsche. "Monica's car?"

Furious, Jess nodded. Christ, it was raining so hard that his clothes were already saturated and she was standing there talking details!

An evil smile curved Libby's lips and she stalked toward the automobile, purposely stepping in every mud puddle along the way. Jess could have sworn that she enjoyed sinking, sopping wet, onto the heretofore spotless suede seat.

"Home, James," she said smugly, folding her arms and grinding her mud-caked boots into the lush carpeting on the floorboard.

Jess had no intention of taking Libby to Ken's place, but he said nothing. Envisioning her lying in some hospital bed, wasted away by a case of rain-induced pneumonia, he ground the car savagely back into gear and gunned the engine.

When they didn't take the road Libby expected, the smug look faded from her face and she stared at Jess with wide, wary eyes. "Wait a minute..."

Jess flung an impudent grin at her and saluted with one hand. "Yes?" he drawled, deliberately baiting her.

"Where are we going?"

"My place," he answered, still angry. "It's the classic situation, isn't it? I'll insist you get out of those wet clothes, then I'll toss you one of my bathrobes and pour brandy for us both. After that, lady, I'll make mad love to you."

Libby paled, though there was a defiant light in her eyes. "On a fur rug in front of your fireplace, no doubt!"

"No doubt," Jess snapped, wondering why he found it impossible to deal with this woman in a sane and reasonable way. It would be so much simpler just to tell her straight out that he loved her, that he needed her. But he couldn't quite bring himself to do that, not just yet, and he was still mad as hell that she would walk in the pouring rain like that.

"Suppose I tell you that I don't want you to 'make mad love' to me, as you so crudely put it? Suppose I tell you that I won't give in to you until the first Tuesday after doomsday, if then, brandy and fur rugs notwithstanding?"

"The way you didn't give in in the hot tub?" he gibed, scowling.

Libby blushed. "That was different!"

"How so?"

"You…you *cornered* me, that's how."

His next words were out of his mouth before he could call them back. "I know about your ex-husband, Libby."

She winced, fixed her attention on the overworked windshield wipers. "What does he have to do with anything?"

Jess shifted to a lower gear as he reached the road leading to his house and turned onto it. "Stacey told me about the women."

The high color drained from Libby's face and she would not look at him. She appeared ready, in fact, to thrust open the door on her side of the car and leap out. "I don't want to talk about this," she said after an interval long enough to bring them to Jess's driveway.

"Why not, Libby?" he asked, and his voice was gentle, if a bit gruff.

One tear rolled over the wet sheen on her defiant rain-polished face, and Libby's chin jutted out in a way that was familiar to him, at once maddening and appealing. "Why do you want to talk about Aaron?" she countered in low, ragged tones. "So you can sit there and feel superior?"

"You know better."

She glared at him, her bruised heart in her eyes, and Jess ached for her. She'd been through so much, and he wished that he could have taken that visible, pounding pain from inside her and borne it himself.

"I don't know better, Jess," she said quietly. "We haven't exactly been kindred spirits, you and I. For all I know, you just want to torture me. To throw all my mistakes in my face and watch me squirm."

Jess's hands tightened on the steering wheel. It took great effort to reach down and shut off the Porsche's engine. "It's cold out here," he said evenly, "and we're both wet to the skin. Let's go inside."

"You won't take me home?" Her voice was small.

He sighed. "Do you want me to?"

Libby considered, lowered her head. "No," she said after a long time.

The inside of Jess's house was spacious and uncluttered. There were skylights in the ceiling and the second floor appeared to be a loft of some sort. Lifting her eyes to the railing above, Libby imagined that his bed was just beyond it and blushed.

Jess seemed to be ignoring her; he was busy with newspaper and kindling at the hearth. She watched the play of the muscles in his back in weary fascination, longing to feel them beneath her hands.

The knowledge that she loved Jess Barlowe, budding in her subconscious mind since her arrival in Montana, suddenly burst into full flower. But was the feeling really new?

If Libby were to be honest with herself—and she tried to be, always—she had to admit that the chances were good that she had loved Jess for a very long time.

He turned, rose from his crouching position, a small fire blazing and crackling behind him. "How do you like my house?" he asked with a half smile.

Between her newly recognized feelings for this man and the way his jade eyes seemed to see through all her reserve to the hurt and confusion hidden beneath, Libby felt very vulnerable. Trusting in an old trick that had always worked in the past, she looked around in search of something to be angry about.

The skylights, the loft, the view of the mountains from the windows beyond his desk—all of it was appealing. Masculine. Quietly romantic.

"Perfect quarters for a wealthy and irresponsible playboy," she threw out in desperation.

Jess stiffened momentarily, but then an easy grin creased his face. "I think that was a shot, but I'm not going to fire back, Libby, so you might as well relax."

Relax? Was the man insane? Half an hour before, he had blithely brought her to climax in a hot tub, for God's sake, and now they were alone, the condition of their clothes necessitating that they risk further intimacies by stripping them off, taking showers. If they couldn't fight, what *were* they going to do?

Before Libby could think of anything to say in reply, Jess gestured toward the broad redwood stairs leading up to the loft. "The bathroom is up there," he said. "Take a shower. You'll find a robe hanging on the inside of the door." With that, he turned away to crouch before the fire again and add wood.

Because she was cold and there seemed to be no other options, Libby climbed the stairs. It wasn't until she reached the loft that her teeth began to chatter.

There she saw Jess's wide unmade bed. It was banked by a line of floor-to-ceiling windows, giving the impression that the room was open to the outdoors, and the wrinkled sheets probably still bore that subtle, clean scent that was Jess's alone....

Libby took herself in hand, wrenched her attention away from the bed. There was a glass-fronted wood-burning stove in one corner of the large room, and a long bookshelf on the other side was crammed with everything from paperback mysteries to volumes on veterinary medicine.

Libby made her way into the adjoining bathroom and kicked off her muddy boots, peeled away her jeans and shirt, her sodden underwear and socks. Goosebumps leapt out all over her body, and they weren't entirely related to the chill.

The bathtub was enormous, and like the bed, it was framed by tall uncurtained windows. Bathing here would be like bathing in the high limbs of a tree, so sweeping was the view of mountains and grassland beyond the glass.

Trembling a little, Libby knelt to turn on the polished brass spigots and fill the deep tub. The water felt good against her chilled flesh, and she was submerged to her chin before she remembered that she had meant to take a quick shower, not a lingering, dreamy bath.

Libby couldn't help drawing a psychological parallel between this tub and the larger one at the main house, where she had made such a fool of herself. Was there some mysterious significance in the fact that she'd chosen the bathtub over the double-wide shower stall on the other side of the room?

Now you're really getting crazy, Kincaid, she said to herself, settling back to soak.

Somewhere in the house, a telephone rang, was swiftly answered.

Libby relaxed in the big tub and tried to still her roiling thoughts and emotions. She would not consider what might happen later. For now, she wanted to be comforted, pampered. Deliciously warm.

She heard the click of boot heels on the stairs, though, and sat bolt upright in the water. A sense of sweet alarm raced through her system. Jess wouldn't come in, actually *come in,* would he?

Of course he would! Why would a bathroom door stop a man who would make such brazen advances in a hot tub?

With frantic eyes Libby sought the towel shelf. It was entirely too far away, and so was the heavy blue-and-white velour robe hanging on the inside of the door. She sank into the bathwater until it tickled her lower lip, squeezed her eyes shut and waited.

"Lib?"

"Wh-what?" she managed. He was just beyond that heavy wooden panel, and Libby found herself hoping...

Hoping what? That Jess would walk in, or that he would stay out? She honestly didn't know.

"That was Ken on the phone," Jess answered, making no effort to open the door. "I told him you were here and that I'd bring you home after the rain lets up."

Libby reddened, there in the privacy of that unique bathroom, imagining the thoughts that were probably going through her father's mind. "Wh-what did he say?"

Jess chuckled, and the sound was low, rich. "Let me put it this way—I don't think he's going to rush over here and defend your virtue."

Libby was at once pleased and disappointed. Wasn't a father *supposed* to protect his daughter from persuasive lechers like Jess Barlowe?

"Oh," she said, her voice sounding foolish and uncertain. "D-do you want me to hurry? S-so you can take a shower, I mean?"

"Take your time," he said offhandedly. "There's another bathroom downstairs—I can shower there."

Having imparted this conversely comforting and disenchanting information, Jess began opening and closing drawers. Seconds later, Libby again heard his footsteps on the stairs.

Despite the fact that she would have preferred to lounge in that wonderful bathtub for the rest of the day, Libby shot out of the water and raced to the towel bar. This was her chance to get dried off and dressed in something before Jess could incite her to further scandalous behavior.

She was wrapped in his blue-and-white bathrobe, the belt securely tied, and cuddled under a knitted afghan by the time Jess joined her in the living room, looking reprehensibly handsome in fresh jeans and a green turtleneck sweater. His hair, like her own, was still damp, and there was a smile in his eyes, probably inspired by the way she was trying to burrow deeper into her corner of the couch.

"There isn't any brandy after all," he said with a helpless gesture of his hands. "Will you settle for chicken soup?"

Libby would have agreed to anything that would get Jess out of that room, even for a few minutes, and he would have to go to the kitchen for soup, wouldn't he? Unable to speak, she nodded.

She tried to concentrate on the leaping flames in the fireplace, but she could hear the soft thump of cupboard doors, the running of tapwater, the singular whir of a microwave oven. The sharp *ting* of the appliance's timer bell made her flinch.

Too soon, Jess returned, carrying two mugs full of steaming soup. He extended one to Libby and, to her eternal gratitude, settled in a chair nearby instead of on the couch beside her.

Outside, the rain came down in torrents, making a musical, pelting sound on the skylights, sliding down the windows in sheets. The fire snapped and threw out sparks, as if to mock the storm that could not reach it.

Jess took a sip of the hot soup and grinned. "This doesn't exactly fit the scenario I outlined in the car," he said, lifting his cup.

"You got everything else right," Libby quipped, referring to the bath she'd taken and the fact that she was wearing his robe. Instantly she realized how badly she'd slipped, but it was too late to call back her words, and the ironic arch of Jess's brow and the smile on his lips indicated that he wasn't going to let the comment pass.

"Everything?" he teased. "There isn't any fur rug, either."

Libby's cheekbones burned. Unable to say anything, she lowered her eyes and watched the tiny noodles colliding in her mug of soup.

"I'm sorry," Jess said softly.

She swallowed hard and met his eyes. He did look contrite, and there was nothing threatening in his manner. Because of that, Libby dared to ask, "Do you really mean to…to make love to me?"

"Only if you want me to," he replied. "You must know that I wouldn't force you, Libby."

She sensed that he meant this and relaxed a little. Sooner or later, she was going to have to accept the fact that all men didn't behave in the callous and hurtful way that Aaron had. "You believe me now—don't you? About Stacey, I mean?"

If that off-the-wall question had surprised or nettled Jess, he gave no indication of it. He simply nodded.

Some crazy bravery, carrying her forward like a reckless tide, made Libby put aside her carefully built reserve and blurt out, "Do you think I'm a fool, Jess?"

Jess gaped at her, the mug of soup forgotten in his hands. "A fool?"

Libby lowered her eyes. "I mean…well…because of Aaron."

"Why should I think anything like that?"

Thunder exploded in the world outside the small cocoonlike one that held only Libby and Jess. "He was… he…"

"He was with other women," supplied Jess quietly. Gently.

Libby nodded, managed to look up.

"And you stayed with him." He was setting down the mug, drawing nearer. Finally he crouched before her on his haunches and took the cup from her hands to set it aside. "You couldn't leave Jonathan, Libby. I understand that. Besides, why should the fact that you stuck with the marriage have any bearing on my attitude toward you?"

"I just thought…"

"What?" prodded Jess when her sentence fell away. "What did you think, Libby?"

Tears clogged her throat. "I thought that I couldn't be very desirable if my o-own husband couldn't… wouldn't…"

Jess gave a ragged sigh. "My God, Libby, you don't think that Aaron was unfaithful because of some lack in you?"

That was exactly what she'd thought, on a subliminal level at least. Another woman, a stronger, more experienced, more alluring woman, might have been able to keep her husband happy, make him want her.

Jess's hands came to Libby's shoulders, gentle and insistent. "Lib, talk to me."

"Just how terrific could I be?" she erupted suddenly, in the anguish that would be hidden no longer. "Just how desirable? My husband needed other women because he couldn't bring himself to make love to me!"

Jess drew her close, held her as the sobs she had restrained at last broke free. "That wasn't your fault, Libby," he breathed, his hand in her hair now, soothing and strong. "Oh, sweetheart, it wasn't your fault."

"Of course it was!" she wailed into the soft green knit of his sweater, the hard strength of the shoulder beneath. "If I'd been better...if I'd known how..."

"Shhh. Baby, don't. Don't do this to yourself."

Once freed, Libby's emotions seemed impossible to check. They ran as deep and wild as any river, swirling in senseless currents and eddies, causing her pride to founder.

Jess caught her trembling hands in his, squeezed them reassuringly. "Listen to me, princess," he said. "These doubts that you're having about yourself are understandable, under the circumstances, but they're not valid. You are desirable." He paused, searched her face with tender, reproving eyes. "I can swear to that."

Libby still felt broken, and she hadn't forgotten the terrible things Aaron had said to her during their marriage—that she was cold and unresponsive, that he hadn't been impotent before he'd married her. Time and time again he had held up Jonathan as proof that he had been virile with his first wife, taken cruel pleasure in pointing out that none of his many girlfriends found him wanting.

Wrenching herself back to the less traumatic present, Libby blurted out, "Make love to me, Jess. Let me prove to myself—"

"No," he said with cold, flat finality. And then he released her hands, stood up and turned away as if in disgust.

Chapter 6

"I thought you wanted me," Libby said in a small, broken voice.

Jess's broad back stiffened, and he did not turn around to face her. "I do."

"Then, why...?"

He went to the fireplace, took up a poker, stoked the blazing logs within to burn faster, hotter. "When I make love to you, Libby, it won't be because either one of us wants to prove anything."

Libby lowered her head, ashamed. As if to scold her, the wind and rain lashed at the windows and the lightning flashed, filling the room with its eerie blue-gold light. She began to cry again, this time softly, wretchedly.

And Jess came to her, lifted her easily into his arms. Without a word, he carried her up the stairs, across the storm-shadowed loft room to the bed. After pulling back the covers with one hand, he lowered her to the sheets. "Rest," he said, tucking the blankets around her.

Libby gaped at him, amazed and stricken. She couldn't help thinking that he wouldn't have tucked Monica Summers into bed this way, kissed *her* forehead as though she were some overwrought child needing a nap.

"I don't want to rest," Libby said, insulted. And her hands moved to pull the covers down.

Jess stopped her by clasping her wrists. A muscle knotted in his jaw, and his jade-green eyes flashed, their light as elemental as that of the electrical storm outside. "Don't Libby. Don't tempt me."

She *had* been tempting him—if he hadn't stopped her when he did, she would have opened the robe, wantonly displayed her breasts. Now, she was mortally embarrassed. What on earth was making her act this way?

"I'm sorry," she whispered. "I don't know what's the matter with me."

Jess sat down on the edge of the bed, his magnificent face etched in shadows, his expression unreadable. "Do we have to go into that again, princess? Nothing is wrong with you."

"But—"

Jess laid one index finger to her lips to silence her. "It would be wrong if we made love now, Libby—don't you see that? Afterward, you'd be telling yourself what a creep I was for taking advantage of you when you were so vulnerable."

His logic was unassailable. To lighten the mood, Libby summoned up a shaky grin. "Some playboy you are. Chicken soup. Patience. Have you no passion?"

He laughed. "More than I know what to do with," he

said, standing up, walking away from the bed. At the top of the stairs he paused. "Am I crazy?"

Libby didn't answer. Smiling, she snuggled down under the covers—she was just a bit tired—and placidly watched the natural light show beyond the windows. Maybe later there would be fireworks of another sort.

Downstairs, Jess resisted a fundamental urge to beat his head against the wall. Libby Kincaid was up there in his bed, for God's sake, warm and lush and wanting him.

He ached to go back up the stairs and finish what they'd begun that morning in the hot tub. He couldn't, of course, because Libby was in no condition, emotionally, for that kind of heavy scene. If he did the wrong thing, said the wrong thing, she could break, and the pieces might not fit together again.

In a fit of neatness, Jess gathered up the cups of cold chicken soup and carried them into the kitchen. There he dumped their contents into the sink, rinsed them, and stacked them neatly in the dishwasher.

The task was done too quickly. What could he do? He didn't like the idea of leaving Libby alone, but he didn't dare go near her again, either. The scent of her, the soft disarray of her hair, the way her breasts seemed to draw at his mouth and the palms of his hands—all those things combined to make his grasp on reason tenuous.

Jess groaned, lifted his eyes to the ceiling and wondered if he was going to have to endure another ice-cold shower. The telephone rang, startling him, and he reached for it quickly. Libby might already be asleep, and he didn't want her to be disturbed.

"Hello?"

"Jess?" Monica's voice was calm, but there was an undercurrent of cold fury. "Did you take my car?"

He sighed, leaning back against the kitchen counter. "Yeah. Sorry. I should have called you before this, but—"

"But you were busy."

Jess flinched. Exactly what could he say to that? "Monica—"

"Never mind, Jess." She sighed the words. "I didn't have any right to say that. And if you helped yourself to my car, you must have had a good reason."

Why the hell did she have to be so reasonable? Why didn't Monica yell at him or something, so that he could get mad in good conscience and stop feeling like such an idiot? "I'm afraid the seats are a little muddy," he said.

"Muddy? Oh, yes—the rain. Was Libby okay?"

Again Jess's gaze lifted to the ceiling. Libby was not okay, thanks to him and Stacey and her charming ex-husband. But then, Monica was just making polite conversation, not asking for an in-depth account of Libby's emotional state. "She was drenched."

"So you brought her there, got her out of her wet clothes, built a fire—"

The anger Jess had wished for was suddenly there. "Monica."

She drew in a sharp breath. "All right, all right—I'm sorry. I take it our dinner date is off?"

"Yeah," Jess answered, turning the phone cord between his fingers. "I guess it is."

Monica was nothing if not persistent—probably that quality accounted for her impressive success in political circles. "Tomorrow night?"

Jess sighed. "I don't know."

There was a short, uncomfortable silence. "We'll talk later," Monica finally said brightly. "Listen, is it okay if I send somebody over there to get my car?"

"I'll bring it to you," Jess said. It was, after stealing it, the least he could do. He'd check first, to make sure that Libby really was sleeping, and with luck, he could be back before she woke up.

"Thanks," sang Monica in parting.

Jess hung up the phone and climbed the stairs, pausing at the edge of the bedroom. He dared go no farther, wanting that rumple-haired little hellion the way he did. "Libby?"

When there was no answer, Jess turned and went back down the stairs again, almost grateful that he had somewhere to go, something to do.

Monica hid her annoyance well as she inspected the muddy splotches on her car's upholstery. Overhead, the incessant rain pummeled the garage roof.

"I'm sorry," Jess said. It seemed that he was always apologizing for one thing or another lately. "My truck wouldn't start, and I was in a hurry...."

Monica allowed a flicker of anger to show in her gray eyes. "Right. When there is a damsel to be rescued, a knight has to grab the first available charger."

Having no answer for that, Jess shrugged. "I'll have your car cleaned," he offered when the silence grew too long, and then he turned to walk back out of the garage and down the driveway to his own car, which refused to start.

He got out and slammed the door. "Damn!" he bellowed, kicking yet another dent into the fender.

"Problems?"

Jess hadn't been aware of Ken until that moment,

hadn't noticed the familiar truck parked nearby. "It would take all day to list them," he replied ruefully.

Ken grinned a typical sideways grin, and his blue eyes twinkled. He seemed oblivious of the rain pouring off the brim of his ancient hat and soaking through his denim jacket and jeans. "I think maybe my daughter might be at the top of the list. Is she all right?"

"She's..." Jess faltered, suddenly feeling like a high-school kid. "She's sleeping."

Ken laughed. "Must have been real hard to say that," he observed, "me being her daddy and all."

"It isn't... I didn't..."

Again Ken laughed. "Maybe you should," he said.

Jess was shocked—so shocked that he was speechless.

"Take my truck if you need it," Ken offered calmly, his hand coming to rest on Jess's shoulder. "I'll get a ride home from somebody here. And, Jess?"

"What?"

"Don't hurt Libby. She's had enough trouble and grief as it is."

"I know that," Jess replied, as the rain plastered his hair to his neck and forehead and made his clothes cling to his flesh in sodden, clammy patches. "I swear I won't hurt her."

"That's good enough for me," replied Libby's father, and then he pried the truck keys out of his pocket and tossed them to Jess.

"Ken..."

The foreman paused, looking back, his eyes wise and patient. How the hell was Jess going to ask this man what he had to ask, for Libby's sake?

"Spit it out, son," Ken urged. "I'm getting wet."

"Clothes—she was… Libby was caught in the rain, and she needs dry clothes."

Ken chuckled and shrugged his shoulders. "Stop at our place and get some of her things then," he said indulgently.

Jess was suddenly as confused by this man as he was by his daughter. What the hell was Ken doing, standing there taking this whole thing so calmly? Didn't it bother him, knowing what might happen when Jess got back to that house?

"See ya," said Ken in parting.

Completely confused, Jess got into Ken's truck and drove away. It wasn't until he'd gotten a set of dry clothes for Libby and reached his own house again that he understood. Ken trusted him.

Jess let his forehead rest on the truck's steering wheel and groaned. He couldn't stand another cold shower, dammit. He just couldn't.

But Ken trusted him. Libby was lying upstairs in his bed, and even if she was, by some miracle, ready to handle what was destined to happen, Jess couldn't make love to her. To do so would be to betray a man who had, in so many ways, been as much a father to him as Cleave Barlowe had.

The problem was that Jess couldn't think of Libby as a sister.

Jess sat glumly at the little table in the kitchen, making patterns in his omelet with a fork. Tiring of that, he flung Libby a beleaguered look and sneezed.

She felt a surge of tenderness. "Aren't you hungry?"

He shook his head. "Libby…"

It took all of her forbearance not to stand up, round

the table, and touch Jess's forehead to see if he had a fever. "What?" she prompted softly.

"I think I should take you home."

Libby was hurt, but she smiled brightly. "Well, it *has* stopped raining," she reasoned.

"And I've got your dad's truck," added Jess.

"Um-hmm. Thanks for stopping and getting my clothes, by the way."

Outside, the wind howled and the night was dark. Jess gave the jeans and loose pink sweater he had picked up for Libby a distracted look and sneezed again. "You're welcome."

"And you, my friend, are sick."

Jess shook his head, went to the counter to pour coffee from the coffeemaker there. "Want some?" he asked, lifting the glass pot.

Libby declined. "Were you taking another shower when I got up?" she ventured cautiously. The peace between them, for all its sweet glow, was still new and fragile.

Libby would have sworn that he winced, and his face was unreadable. "I'm a clean person," he said, averting his eyes.

Libby bit the inside of her lower lip, suddenly possessed by an untimely urge to laugh. Jess had been shivering when he came out of that bathroom and unexpectedly encountered his newly awakened houseguest.

"Right," she said.

Jess sneezed again, violently. Somehow, the sound unchained Libby's amusement and she shrieked with laughter.

"What is so goddamn funny?" Jess demanded, setting his coffee cup down with an irritated thump and scowling.

"N-nothing," cried Libby.

Suddenly Jess was laughing, too. He pulled Libby out of her chair and into his arms, and she deliberately pressed herself close to him, delighting in the evidence of his desire, in the scent and substance and strength of him.

She almost said that she loved him.

"You wanted my body!" she accused instead, teasing.

Jess groaned and tilted his head back, ostensibly to study the ceiling. Libby saw a muscle leap beneath his chin and wanted to kiss it, but she refrained.

"You were taking a cold shower, weren't you, Jess?"

"Yes," he admitted with a martyrly sigh. "Woman, if I die of pneumonia, it will be your fault."

"On the contrary. I've done everything but throw myself at your feet, mister, and you haven't wanted any part of me."

"Wrong." Jess grinned wickedly, touching the tip of her breast with an index finger. "I want this part..." The finger trailed away, following an erotic path. "And this part..."

It took all of Libby's courage to say the words again, after his brisk rejection earlier. "Make love to me, Jess."

"My God, Libby—"

She silenced him by laying two fingers to his lips. Remembering the words he had flung at her in the Cessna the day of her arrival, she said saucily, "If it feels good, do it."

Jess gave her a mock scowl, but his arms were around her now, holding her against him. "You were a very mean little kid," he muttered, "and now you're a mean adult. Do you know what you're doing to me, Kincaid?"

Libby moved her hips slightly, delighting in the contact and the guttural groan the motion brought from Jess. "I have some vague idea, yes."

"Your father trusts me."

"My father!" Libby stared up at him, amazed. "Is that what you've been worried about? What my father will think?"

Jess shrugged, and his eyes moved away from hers. Clearly he was embarrassed. "Yes."

Libby laughed, though she was not amused. "You're not serious!"

His eyes came back to meet hers and the expression in their green depths was nothing if not serious. "Ken is my best friend," he said.

"Shall I call him up and ask for permission? Better yet, I could drive over there and get a note!"

The taunts caused Jess to draw back a little, though their thighs and hips were still touching, still piping primitive messages one to the other. "Very funny!" he snapped, and a muscle bunched in his neck, went smooth again.

Libby was quietly furious. "You're right—it isn't funny. This is my body, Jess—mine. I'm thirty-one years old and I make my own living and I *damned well* don't need my daddy's permission to go to bed with a man!"

The green eyes were twinkling with mischief. "That's a healthy attitude if I've ever heard one," he broke in. "However, before we go up those stairs, there is one more thing I want to know. Are you using me, Libby?"

"Using you?"

"Yes. Do I really mean something to you, or would any man do?"

Libby felt as though she'd just grabbed hold of a high-voltage wire; in a few spinning seconds she was hurled from pain to rage to humiliation.

Jess held her firmly. "I see the question wasn't received in the spirit in which it was intended," he said, his eyes serious now, searching her burning, defiant face. "What I meant to ask was, are we going to be making love, Libby, or just proving that you can go the whole route and respond accordingly?"

Libby met his gaze bravely, though inside she was still shaken and angry. "Why would I go to all this trouble, Jess, if I didn't want you? After all, I could have just stopped someone on the street and said, 'Excuse me, sir, but would you mind making love to me? I'd like to find out if I'm frigid or not.'"

Jess sighed heavily, but his hands were sliding up under the back of Libby's pink sweater, gently kneading the firm flesh there. The only sign that her sarcasm had rankled him was the almost imperceptible leaping of the pulsepoint beneath his right ear.

"I guess I'm having a little trouble understanding your sudden change of heart, Libby. For years you've hated my guts. Now, after confiding that your ex-husband put you through some kind of emotional wringer and left you feeling about as attractive as a sink drain, you want to share my bed."

Libby closed her eyes. The motion of his hands on her back was hypnotic, making it hard for her to breathe, let alone think. When she felt the catch of her bra give way, she shivered.

She should tell him that she loved him, that maybe, despite outward appearances, she'd always loved him, but she didn't dare. This was a man who had thought the worst of her at every turn, who had never missed a chance to get under her skin. Allowing him inside the fortress where her innermost emotions were stored could prove disastrous.

His hands came slowly around from her back to the aching roundness of her breasts, sliding easily, brazenly under the loosened bra.

"Answer me, Libby," he drawled, his voice a sleepy rumble.

She was dazed; his fingers came to play a searing symphony at her nipples, plying them, drawing at them. "I… I want you. I'm not trying to p-prove anything."

"Let me look at you, Libby."

Libby pulled the pink sweater off over her head, stood perfectly still as Jess dispensed with her bra and then stepped back a little way to admire her.

He outlined one blushing nipple with the tip of his finger, progressed to wreak the same havoc on the other. Then, with strong hands, he lifted Libby up onto a counter, so that her breasts were on a level with his face.

She gasped as he took languid, tentative suckle at one peak, then trailed a path with the tip of his tongue to the other, conquering it with lazy ease.

She was desperate now. "Make love to me," she whispered again in broken tones.

"Make love to me, *Jess*," he prompted, nibbling now, driving her half-wild with the need of him.

Libby swallowed hard, closed her eyes. His teeth were scraping gently at her nipple now, rousing it to obedience. "Make love to me, Jess," she repeated breathlessly.

He withdrew his mouth, cupping her in his hands, letting his thumbs do the work his lips and teeth had done before. "Open your eyes," he commanded in a hoarse rumble. "Look at me, Libby."

Dazed, her very soul spinning within her, Libby obeyed.

"Tell me," he insisted raggedly, "that you're not seeing Stacey or your misguided ex-husband. Tell me that you see *me,* Libby."

"I do, Jess."

He lifted her off the counter and into his arms, and his mouth came down on hers, cautious at first, then almost harshly demanding. Libby was electrified by the kiss, by the searching fierceness of his tongue, by the moan of need that came from somewhere deep inside him. Finally he ended the kiss, and his eyes were smiling into hers.

Feeling strangely giddy, Libby laughed. "Is this the part where you make love to me?"

"This is it," he replied, and then they were moving through the house toward the stairs. Lightning crackled and flashed above the skylights, while thunder struck a booming accompaniment.

"The earth is moving already," said Libby into the Jess-scented wool of his sweater.

Jess took the stairs two at a time. "Just wait," he replied.

In the bedroom, which was lit only by the lightning that was sundering the night sky, he set Libby on her feet. For a moment they just stood still, looking at each other. Libby felt as though she had become a part of the terrible storm that was pounding at the tall windows, and she grasped Jess's arms so that she wouldn't be blown away to the mountaintops or flung beyond the angry clouds.

"Touch me, Libby," Jess said, and somehow, even over the renewed rage of the storm, she heard him.

Cautiously she slid her hands beneath his sweater, splaying her fingers so that she could feel as much of him as possible. His chest was hard and broad and softly furred, and he groaned as she found masculine nipples and explored them.

Libby moved her hands down over his rib cage to the sides of his waist, up his warm, granite-muscled back. *I love you,* she thought, and then she bit her lower lip lest she actually say the words.

At some unspoken urging from Jess, she caught his sweater in bunched fists and drew it up over his head. Silver-blue lightning scored the sky and danced on the planes of his bare chest, his magnificent face.

Libby was drawn to him, tasting one masculine nipple with a cautious tongue, suckling the other. He moaned and tangled his fingers in her hair, pressing her close, and she knew that he was experiencing the same keen pleasure she had known.

Presently he caught her shoulders in his hands and held her at arm's length, boldly admiring her bare breasts. "Beautiful," he rasped. "So beautiful."

Libby had long been ashamed of her body, thinking it inadequate. Now, in this moment of storm and fury, she was proud of every curve and hollow, every pore and freckle. She removed her jeans and panties with graceful motions.

Jess's reaction was a low, rumbling groan, followed

by a gasp of admiration. He stood still, a Western Adonis, as she undid his jeans, felt the hollows of his narrow hips, the firmness of his buttocks. Within seconds he was as naked as Libby.

She caught his hands in her own, drew him toward the bed. But instead of reclining with her there, he knelt at the side, positioned Libby so that her hips rested on the edge of the mattress.

His hands moved over every part of her—her breasts, her shoulders, her flat, smooth stomach, the insides of her trembling thighs.

"Jess..."

"Shh, it's all right."

"But..." Libby's back arched and a spasm of delight racked her as he touched the curls sheltering the core of her passion, first with his fingers, then with his lips. "Oh...wait...oh, Jess, no..."

"Yes," he said, his breath warm against her. And then he parted her and took her fully into his mouth, following the instinctive rising and falling of her hips, chuckling at the soft cry she gave.

A violent shudder went through Libby's already throbbing body, and her knees moved wide of each other, shaking, made of no solid substance.

Frantic, she found his head, tangled her fingers in his hair. "Stop," she whimpered, even as she held him fast.

Jess chuckled again and then went right on consuming her, his hands catching under her knees, lifting them higher, pressing them farther apart.

Libby was writhing now, her breath harsh and burning, her vision blurred. The storm came inside the room and swept her up, up, up, beyond the splitting skies. She cried out in wonder as she collided with the moon and bounced off, to be enfolded by a waiting sun.

When she came back inside herself, Jess was beside her on the bed, soothing her with soft words, stroking away the tears that had somehow gathered on her face.

"I've never read..." she whispered stupidly. "I didn't know..."

Jess was drawing her up, so that she lay full on the bed, naked and sated at his side. "Look it up," he teased, kissing her briefly, tenderly. "I think it would be under O."

Libby laughed, and the sound was a warm, soft contrast to the tumult of the storm. "What an ego!"

With an index finger, Jess traced her lips, her chin, the moist length of her neck. Small novas flashed and flared within her as her pulsing senses began to make new demands.

When his mouth came to her breast again, Libby arched her back and whimpered. "Jess... Jess..."

He circled the straining nipple with a warm tongue. "What, babe?"

No coherent words would come to Libby's beleaguered mind. "I don't know," she managed finally. "I don't know!"

"I do," Jess answered, and then he suckled in earnest.

Powerless under the tyranny of her own body, Libby gave herself up to sensation. It seemed that no part of her was left untouched, unconquered or unworshiped.

When at last Jess poised himself above her, strong and fully a man, his face reflected the flashing lightning that seemed to seek them both.

"I'm Jess," he warned again in a husky whisper that betrayed his own fierce need.

Libby drew him to her with quick, fevered hands. "I know," she gasped, and then she repeated his name like some crazy litany, whispering it first, sobbing it when he thrust his searing magnificence inside her.

He moved slowly at first, and the finely sculptured planes of his face showed the cost of his restraint, the conflicting force of his need. "Libby," he pleaded. "Oh, God… Libby…"

She thrust her hips upward in an instinctive, unplanned motion that shattered Jess's containment and caused his great muscular body to convulse once and then assert its dominance in a way that was at once fierce and tender. It seemed that he sought some treasure within her, so deeply did he delve, some shimmering thing that he would perish without.

His groans rose above the sound of thunder, and as his pace accelerated and his passion was unleashed, Libby moved in rhythm with him, one with him, his.

Their bodies moved faster, agile in their quest, each glistening with the sheen of sweet exertion, each straining toward the sun that, this time, would consume them both.

The tumult flung them high, tore them asunder, fused them together again. Libby sobbed in the hot glory of her release and heard an answering cry from Jess.

They clung together, struggling for breath, for a long time after the slow, treacherous descent had been made. Twice, on the way, Libby's body had paused to greedily claim what had been denied it before.

She was flushed, reckless in her triumph. "I did it," she exalted, her hands moving on the slackened muscles in Jess's back. "I did it… I responded…"

Instantly she felt those muscles go taut, and Jess's

head shot up from its resting place in the curve where her neck and shoulder met.

"What?"

Libby stiffened, knowing now, too late, how grave her mistake had been. "I mean, *we* did it…" she stumbled lamely.

But Jess was wrenching himself away from her, searching for his clothes, pulling them on. "Congratulations!" he yelled.

Libby sat up, confused, wildly afraid. Dear God, was he going to walk out now? Was he going to hate her for a few thoughtless words?

"Jess, wait!" she pleaded, clutching the sheet to her chest. "Please!"

"For what, Libby?" he snapped from the top of the stairs. "Exhibit B? Is there something else you want to prove?"

"Jess!"

But he was storming down the stairs, silent in his rage, bent on escaping her.

"Jess!" Libby cried out again in fear, tears pouring down her face, her hands aching where they grasped the covers.

The only answer was the slamming of the front door.

Chapter 7

Ken Kincaid looked up from the cards in his hand as the lights flickered, went out, came on again. Damn, this was a hell of a storm—if the rain didn't let up soon, the creeks would overflow and they'd have range calves drowning right and left.

Across the table, Cleave Barlowe laid down his own hand of cards. "Quite a storm, eh?" he asked companionably. "Jess bring your truck back yet?"

"I don't need it," said Ken, still feeling uneasy.

Lightning creased the sky beyond the kitchen window, and thunder shook the old house on its sturdy foundations. Cleave grinned. "He's with Libby, then?"

"Yup," said Ken, smiling himself.

"Think they know the sky's turning itself inside out?"

There was an easing in Ken; he laughed outright. "Doubt it," he replied, looking at his cards again.

For a while the two men played the two-handed poker they had enjoyed for years, but it did seem that luck wasn't running with either one of them. Finally they gave up the effort and Cleave went home.

With his old friend gone, Ken felt apprehensive again. He went around the house making sure all the windows were closed against the rain, and wondered why one storm should bother him that way, when he'd seen a thousand and never found them anything more than a nuisance.

He was about to shut off the lamp in the front room when he saw the headlights of his own truck swing into the driveway. Seconds later, there was an anxious knock at the door.

"Jess?" Ken marveled, staring at the haggard, rain-drenched man standing on the front porch. "What the hell...?"

Jess looked as though he'd just taken a first-rate gut punch. "Could I come in?"

"That's a stupid question," retorted Ken, stepping back to admit his unexpected and obviously distraught visitor. "Is Libby okay?"

Jess's haunted eyes wouldn't quite link up with Ken's. "She's fine," he said, his hands wedged into the pockets of his jeans, his hair and sweater dripping rainwater.

Ken arched an eyebrow. "What'd you do, anyway—ride on the running board of that truck and steer from outside?"

Jess didn't answer; he didn't seem to realize that he was wet to the skin. There was a distracted look about him that made Ken ache inside.

In silence Ken led the way into the kitchen, poured

a dose of straight whiskey into a mug, added strong coffee.

"You look like you've been dragged backward through a knothole," he observed when Jess was settled at the table. "What happened?"

Jess closed his hands around the mug. "I'm in love with your daughter," he said after a long time.

Ken sat down, allowed himself a cautious grin. "If you drove over here in this rain just to tell me that, friend, you got wet for nothing."

"You knew?" Jess seemed honestly surprised.

"Everybody knew. Except maybe you and Libby."

Jess downed the coffee and the potent whiskey almost in a single gulp. There was a struggle going on in his face, as though he might be fighting hard to hold himself together.

Ken rose to put more coffee into Jess's mug, along with a lot more whiskey. If ever a man needed a drink, this one did.

"Maybe you'd better put on some dry clothes," the older man ventured.

Jess only shook his head.

Ken sat back in his chair and waited. When Jess was ready to talk, he would. There was, Ken had learned, no sense in pushing before that point was reached.

"Libby's beautiful, you know," Jess remarked presently, as he started on his third drink.

Ken smiled. "Yeah. I've noticed."

Simple and ordinary though they were, the words triggered some kind of emotional reaction in Jess, broke down the barriers he had been maintaining so carefully. His face crumbled, he lowered his head to his arms, and he cried. The sobs were deep and dry and ragged.

Hurting because Jess hurt, Ken waited.

Soon enough, his patience was rewarded. Jess began to talk, brokenly at first, and then with stone-cold reason.

Ken didn't react openly to anything he said; much of what Jess told him about Libby's marriage to Aaron Strand came as no real surprise. He was wounded, all the same, for his daughter and for the devastated young man sitting across the table from him.

The level of whiskey in Ken's bottle went down as the hour grew later. Finally, when Jess was so drunk that his words started getting all tangled up with each other, Ken half led, half carried him up the stairs to Libby's room.

In the hallway, he paused, reflecting. Life was a hell of a thing, he decided. Here was Jess, sleeping fitfully in Libby's bed, all alone. And just up the hill, chances were, Libby was tossing and turning in Jess's bed, just as lonely.

Not for the first time, Ken Kincaid felt a profound desire to get them both by the hair and knock their heads together.

Libby cried until far into the night and then, exhausted, she slept. When she awakened, shocked to find herself in Jess Barlowe's bed, she saw that the world beyond the windows had been washed to a clean sparkle.

The world inside her seemed tawdry by comparison.

Her face feeling achy and swollen, Libby got out of bed, stumbled across the room to the bathroom. Jess was nowhere in the house; she would have sensed it if he were.

As Libby filled the tub with hot water, she wondered

whether she was relieved that he wasn't close by, or disappointed. A little of both, she concluded as she slid into her bath and sat there in miserable reverie.

Facing Jess now would have been quite beyond her. Why, why had she said such a foolish thing, when she might have known how Jess would react? On the other hand, why had *he* made such a big deal out of a relatively innocuous remark?

More confused than ever, Libby finished her bath and climbed out to dry herself with a towel. In short order she was dressed and her hair was combed. Because she had no toothbrush—Jess had forgotten that when he picked up her things—she had to be content with rinsing her mouth.

Downstairs, Libby stood staring at the telephone, willing herself to call her father and confess that she needed a ride home. Pride wouldn't allow that, however, and she had made up her mind to walk the distance when she heard a familiar engine outside, the slam of a truck door.

Jess was back, she thought wildly. Where had he been all night? With Monica? What would she say to him?

The questions were pointless, for when Libby forced herself to go to the front door and open it, she saw her father striding up the walk, not Jess.

Fresh embarrassment stained Libby's cheeks, though there was no condemnation in Ken's weathered face, no anger in his understanding eyes. "Ride home?" he said.

Unable to speak, Libby only nodded.

"Pretty bad night?" he ventured in his concise way when they were both settled in the truck and driving away.

"Dismal," replied Libby, fixing her eyes on the red

Hereford cattle grazing in the green, rain-washed distance.

"Jess isn't in very good shape, either," commented Ken after an interval.

Libby's eyes were instantly trained on her father's profile. "You've seen him?"

"Seen him?" Ken laughed gruffly. "I poured him into bed at three this morning."

"He was drunk?" Libby was amazed.

"He had a nip or two."

"How is he now?"

Ken glanced at her, turned his eyes back to the rutted, winding country road ahead. "Jess is hurting," he said, and there was a finality in his tone that kept Libby from asking so much as one more question.

Jess is hurting. What the devil did that mean? Was he hung over? Had the night been as miserable for him as it had been for her?

Presently the truck came to a stop in front of the big Victorian house that had been "home" to Libby for as long as she could remember. Ken made no move to shut off the engine, and she got out without saying goodbye. For all her brave words of the night before, about not needing her father's approval, she felt estranged from him now, subdued.

After forcing down a glass of orange juice and a slice of toast in the kitchen, Libby went into the studio Cathy and her father had improvised for her and did her best to work. Even during the worst days in New York, she had been able to find solace in the mechanics of drawing her cartoon strip, forgetting her own troubles to create comical dilemmas for Liberated Lizzie.

Today was different.

The panels Libby sketched were awkward, requiring too many erasures, and even if she had been able to get the drawings right, she couldn't have come up with a funny thought for the life of her.

At midmorning, Libby decided that her career was over and paced from one end of the studio to the other, haunted by thoughts of the night before.

Jess had made it clear, in his kitchen, that he didn't want to make love just to let Libby prove that she was "normal." And what had she done? She'd *gloated*.

Shame ached in Libby's cheeks as she walked. *I did it,* she'd crowed, as though she were Edison and the first electric light had just been lit. God, how could she have been so stupid? So insensitive?

"You did have a little help, you know," she scolded herself out loud. And then she covered her face with both hands and cried. It had been partly Jess's fault, that scene—he had definitely overreacted, and on top of that, he had been unreasonable. He had stormed out without giving Libby a chance to make things right.

Still, it was all too easy to imagine how he'd felt. Used. And the truth was that, without intending to, Libby had used him.

Small, strong hands were suddenly pulling Libby's hands away from her face. Through the blur, she saw Cathy watching her, puzzled and sad.

"What's wrong?" her cousin asked. "Please, Libby, tell me what's wrong."

"Everything!" wailed Libby, who was beyond trying to maintain her dignity now.

Gently Cathy drew her close, hugged her. For a moment they were two motherless little girls again, clinging to each other because there were some pains that even Ken, with his gruff, unswerving devotion, couldn't ease.

The embrace was comforting, and after a minute or two Libby recovered enough to step back and offer Cathy a shaky smile. "I've missed you so much, Cathy," she said.

"Don't get sloppy," teased Cathy, using her face to give the toneless words expression.

Libby laughed. "What are you doing today, besides being one of the idle rich?"

Cathy tilted her head to one side. "Did you really stay with Jess last night?" she asked with swift hands.

"Aren't we blunt today?" Libby shot back, both speaking and signing. "I suppose the whole ranch is talking about it!"

Cathy nodded.

"Damn!"

"Then it's true!" exalted Cathy aloud, her eyes sparkling.

Some of Libby's earlier remorse drained away, pushed aside by feelings of anger and betrayal. "Has Jess been bragging?" she demanded, her hands on her hips, her indignation warm and thick in her throat.

"He isn't the type to do that," Cathy answered in slow, carefully formed words, "and you know it."

Libby wasn't so certain—Jess had been very angry, and his pride had been stung. Besides, the only other person who had known was Ken, and he was notoriously tight-lipped when it came to other people's business. "Who told you?" she persisted, narrowing her eyes.

"Nobody had to," Cathy answered aloud. "I was down at the stables, saddling Banjo, and one of the range crews was there—ten or twelve men, I guess.

Anyway, there was a fight out front—Jess punched out one of the cowboys."

Libby could only gape.

Cathy gave the story a stirring finale. "I think Jess would have killed that guy if Ken hadn't hauled him off."

Libby found her voice. "Was Jess hurt? Cathy, did you see if he was hurt?"

Cathy grinned at her cousin's undisguised concern. "Not a scratch. He got into an argument with Ken and left."

Libby felt a strong need to find her father and ask him exactly what had happened, but she knew that the effort would be wasted. Even if she could find Ken, which was unlikely considering the size of the ranch and all the places he could be, he wouldn't explain.

Cathy was studying the messy piece of drawing paper affixed to the art board. "You're not going to work?" she signed.

"I gave up," Libby confessed. "I couldn't keep my mind on it."

"After a night with Jess Barlowe, who could?"

Libby suddenly felt challenged, defensive. She even thought that, perhaps, there was more to the deep closeness between Jess and Cathy than she had guessed. "What do you know about spending the night with Jess?" she snapped before she could stop herself.

Cathy rolled her beautiful green eyes. "*Nothing.* For better or worse, and mostly it's been better, I'm married to Jess's brother—remember?"

Libby swallowed, feeling foolish. "Where is Stacey, anyway?" she asked, more to make conversation than because she wanted to know.

The question brought a shadow of sadness to Cathy's face. "He's away on one of his business trips."

Libby sat down on her art stool, folded her hands. "Maybe you should have gone with him, Cathy. You used to do that a lot, didn't you? Maybe if you two could be alone…talk…"

The air suddenly crackled with Cathy's anger and hurt. "*He* talks!" she raged aloud. "I just move my hands!"

Libby spoke softly, gently. "You could talk to Stacey, Cathy—really talk, the way you do with me."

"No."

"Why not?"

"I know I sound like a record playing on the wrong speed, that's why!"

"Even if that were so, would it matter?" signed Libby, frowning. "Stacey knew you were deaf before he married you, for heaven's sake."

Cathy's head went down. "He must have felt sorry for me or something."

Instantly Libby was off her stool, gripping Cathy's shoulders in firm, angry hands. "He loves you!"

Tears misted the emerald-green eyes and Cathy's lower lip trembled. "No doubt that's why he intends to divorce me and marry you, Libby."

"No," insisted Libby, giving her cousin a slight shake. "No, that isn't true. I think Stacey is confused, Cathy. Upset. Maybe it's this thing about your not wanting to have a baby. Or maybe he feels that you don't need him, you're so independent."

"Independent? Don't look now, Libby Kincaid, but *you're* the independent one! You have a career…you can hear—"

"Will you stop feeling sorry for yourself, dammit!" Libby almost screamed. "I'm so tired of hearing how you suffer! For God's sake, stop whining and fight for the man you love!"

Cathy broke free of Libby's grasp, furious, tears pouring down her face. "It's too late!" she cried. "You're here now, and it's too late!"

Libby sighed, stepped back, stricken by her own outburst and by Cathy's, too. "You're forgetting one thing," she reasoned quietly. "I'm not in love with Stacey. And it would take two of us to start anything, wouldn't it?"

Cathy went to the windows and stared out at the pond, her chin high. Knowing that her cousin needed this interval to restore her dignity and assemble her thoughts, Libby did not approach her.

Finally Cathy sniffled and turned back to offer a shaky smile. "I didn't come over here to fight with you," she said clearly. "I'm going to Kalispell, and I wanted to know if you would like to come with me."

Libby agreed readily, and after changing her clothes and leaving a quick note for Ken, she joined Cathy in the shiny blue Ferrari.

The ride to Kalispell was a fairly long one, and by the time Cathy and Libby reached the small city, they had reestablished their old, easy relationship.

They spent the day shopping, had lunch in a rustic steak house bearing the Circle Bar B brand, and then started home again.

"Are you really going to give that to Jess?" Cathy asked, her eyes twinkling when she cast a look at the bag in Libby's lap.

"I may lose my courage." Libby frowned, wondering what had possessed her to buy a T-shirt with such an outlandish saying printed on it. She supposed she'd hoped that the gesture would penetrate the barrier between herself and Jess, enabling them to talk.

"Take my advice," said Cathy, guiding the powerful car off the highway and onto the road that led to the heart of the ranch. "Give him the shirt."

"Maybe," said Libby, looking off into the sweeping, endless blue sky. A small airplane was making a graceful descent toward the Circle Bar B landing strip.

"Who do you suppose that is?" Libby asked, catching Cathy's attention with a touch on her arm.

The question was a mistake. Cathy, who had not, of course, heard the plane's engine, scanned the sky and saw it. "Why don't we find out?"

Libby scrunched down in her seat, sorry that she had pointed out the airplane now. Suppose Stacey was aboard, returning from his business trip, and there was another uncomfortable scene at the airstrip? Suppose it was Jess, and he either yelled at Libby or, worse yet, pretended that she wasn't there?

"I'd rather go home," she muttered.

But Cathy's course was set, and the Ferrari bumped and jostled over the road to the landing strip as though it were a pickup truck.

The plane came to a smooth stop as Cathy parked at one side of the road and got out of the car, shading her eyes with one hand, watching. Libby remained in her seat.

She had, it seemed, imagined only part of the possible scenario. The pilot was Jess, and his passenger was a wan, tight-lipped Stacey.

"Oh, God," said Libby, sinking even farther into the car seat. She would have kept her face hidden in her hand forever, probably, if it hadn't been for the crisp, insistent tap at her window.

Having no other choice, she rolled the glass down and squinted into Jess Barlowe's unreadable, hard-lined face. "Come with me," he said flatly.

Libby looked through the Ferrari's windshield, saw Stacey and Cathy standing nearby, a disturbing distance between them. Cathy was glaring angrily into Stacey's face, and Stacey was casting determined looks in Libby's direction.

"They need some time alone," Jess said, his eyes linking fiercely, warningly, with Libby's as he opened the car door for her.

Anxious not to make an obviously unpleasant situation any worse, Libby gathered up her bags and her purse and got out of the car, following along behind Jess's long strides. His truck, which she hadn't noticed before, was parked close by.

Without looking back at Stacey and Cathy, Libby slid gratefully into the dusty front seat and closed her eyes. Not until the truck was moving did she open them, and even then she couldn't quite bring herself to look at the man behind the wheel.

"That was touching," he said in a vicious rasp.

Libby stiffened in the seat, staring at Jess's rock-hard profile now. "What did you say?"

The powerful shoulders moved in an annoying shrug. "Your wanting to meet Stacey on his triumphant return."

It took Libby a moment to absorb what he was implying. When she had, she slammed him with the paper bag that contained the T-shirt she'd bought for him in Kalispell and hissed, "You bastard! I didn't know Stacey was going to be on that plane, and if I had, I certainly wouldn't have been there at all!"

"Sure," he drawled, and even though he was grinning and looking straight ahead at the road, there was contempt in his tone and a muscle pulsing at the base of his jaw.

Libby felt tears of frustration rise in her eyes. "I thought you believed me," she said.

"I thought I did, too," Jess retorted with acid amusement. "But that was before you showed up at the landing strip at such an opportune moment."

"It was Cathy's idea to meet the plane!"

"Right."

The paper bag crackled as Libby lifted it, prepared to swing.

"Do that again and I'll stop this car and raise blisters on your backside," Jess warned, without so much as looking in her direction.

Libby lowered the bag back to her lap, swallowed miserably, and turned her attention to the road. She did not believe Jess's threat for one moment, but she felt childish for trying to hit him with the bag. "Cathy told me there was a fight at the stables this morning," she dared after a long time. "What happened?"

Another shrug, as insolent as the first, preceded his reply. "One of Ken's men said something I didn't like."

"Like what?"

"Like didn't it bother me to sleep with my brother's mistress."

Libby winced, sorry for pressing the point. "Oh, God," she said, and she was suddenly so tired, so broken, and so frustrated that she couldn't hold back her tears anymore. She covered her face with both hands and turned her head as far away from Jess as she could, but the effort was useless.

Jess stopped the truck at the side of the road, turned Libby easily toward him. Through a blur, she saw the Ferrari race past.

"Let go of me!"

Jess not only didn't let go, he pulled her close. "I'm sorry," he muttered into her hair. "God, Libby, I don't know what comes over me, what makes me say things to hurt you."

"Garden-variety hatred!" sniffled Libby, who was already forgiving him even though it was against her better judgment.

He chuckled. "No. I couldn't ever hate you, Libby."

She looked up at him, confused and hopeful. Before she could think of anything to say, however, there was a loud *pop* from beneath the hood of the truck, followed by a sizzle and clouds of steam.

"Goddammit!" rasped Jess.

Libby laughed, drunk on the scent of him, the closeness of him, the crazy paradox of him. "This crate doesn't exactly fit your image, you know," she taunted. "Why don't you get yourself a decent car?"

He turned from glowering at the hood of the truck to smile down into her face. "If I do, Kincaid, will you let me make love to you in the backseat?"

She shoved at his immovable chest with both hands, laughing again. "No, no, a thousand times no!"

Jess nibbled at her jawline, at the lobe of her ear, chuckled huskily as she tensed. "How many times no?"

"Maybe," said Libby.

Just when she thought she would surely go crazy, Jess drew back from his brazen pursuits and smiled lazily. "It is time I got a new car," he conceded, with an evil light glistening in his jade eyes. "Will you come to Kalispell and help me pick it out, Libby?"

A thrill skittered through Libby's body and flamed in her face. "I was just there," she protested, clutching at straws.

"It shouldn't—" Jess bent, nipped at the side of her neck with gentle teeth "—take long. A couple of days at the most."

"A couple of days!"

"And nights." Jess's lips were scorching their way across the tender hollow of her throat. "Think about it, Lib. Just you and me. No Stacey. No Cathy. No problems."

Libby shivered as a knowledgeable hand closed over one of her breasts, urging, reawakening. "No p-problems?" she echoed.

Jess undid the top button of her blouse.

Libby's breath caught in her throat; she felt heat billowing up inside her, foaming out, just as it was foaming out of the station wagon's radiator. "Wh-where would we s-stay?"

Another button came undone.

Jess chuckled, his mouth on Libby's collarbone now, tasting it, doing nothing to cool the heat that was pounding within her. "How about—" the third button gave way, and Libby's bra was displaced by a gentle hand "—one of those motels…with the…vibrating beds?"

"Tacky," gasped Libby, and her eyes closed languidly and her head fell back as Jess stroked the nipple he'd just found to pebble-hard response.

"My condo, then," he said, and his lips were sliding

down from her collarbone, soft, soft, over the upper rounding of her bare breast.

Libby gasped and arched her back as his lips claimed the distended, hurting peak. "Jess...oh, God...this is a p-public road!"

"Umm," Jess said, lapping at her now with the tip of his tongue. "Will you go with me, Libby?"

Wild need went through her as he stroked the insides of her thighs, forcing her blue-jeaned legs apart. And all the while he plied her nipple into a panic of need. "Yes!" she gasped finally.

Jess undid the snap of her jeans, slid his hand inside, beneath the scanty lace of her panties.

"Damn you," Libby whispered hoarsely, "s-stop that! I said I'd go—"

He told her what else she was about to do. And one glorious, soul-scoring minute later, she did.

Red in the face, still breathing heavily, Libby closed her jeans, tugged her bra back into place, buttoned her blouse. God, what if someone had come along and seen her letting Jess...letting him play with her like that?

All during the ride home, she mentally rehearsed the blistering diatribe he deserved to hear. He could just go to Kalispell by *himself,* she would tell him. If he thought for one damned minute that he was going to take her to his condo and make love to her, he was sadly mistaken, she would say.

"Be ready in half an hour," Jess told her at her father's front door.

"Okay," Libby replied.

After landing the Cessna in Kalispell and making arrangements to rent a car, which turned out to be a temperamental cousin to Jess's truck, they drove through the small city to an isolated tree-dense property beyond. There were at least a million stars in the sky, and as the modest rental rattled over a narrow wooden bridge spanning a creek, Libby couldn't help giving in a little to the romance of it all.

Beyond the bridge, there were more trees—towering ponderosa pines; whispering, shiny-leaved birches. They stopped in the driveway of a condominium that stood apart from several others. Jess got out of the car, came around to open Libby's door for her.

"Let's get rid of the suitcases and go out for something to eat," he said.

Libby's stomach rumbled inelegantly, and Jess laughed as he caught her hand in his and drew her up the darkened walk to the front door of the condominium. "That shoots my plans for a little fun before dinner," he teased.

"There's always after," replied Libby, lifting her chin.

Chapter 8

The inside of the condominium was amazingly like Jess's house on the ranch. There was a loft, for instance, this one accessible by both stairs and, of all things, a built-in ladder. Too, the general layout of the rooms was much the same.

The exceptions were that the floors were carpeted rather than bare oak, and the entire roof was made of heavy glass. *When we make love here, I'll be able to look up and see the stars,* Libby mused.

"Like it?" Jess asked, setting the suitcases down and watching her with discerning, mirthful green eyes.

Libby was uncomfortable again, doubting the wisdom of coming here now that she was faced with the realities of the situation. "Is this where you bring all your conquests?"

Jess smiled, shrugged.

"Well?" prodded Libby, annoyed because he hadn't even had the common decency to offer a denial.

He sat down on the stone ledge fronting the fireplace, wrapped his hands around one knee. "The place does happen to be something of a love nest, as a matter of fact."

Libby was stung. Dammit, how unchivalrous could one man be? "Oh," she said loftily.

"It's my father's place," Jess said, clearly delighting in her obvious curiosity and the look of relief she couldn't quite hide.

"Your father's?"

Jess grinned. "He entertains his mistress here, from time to time. In his position, he has to be discreet."

Libby was gaping now, trying to imagine the sedate, dignified Senator Barlowe cavorting with a woman beneath slanted glass roofs, climbing ladders to star-dappled lofts.

Jess's amused gaze had strayed to the ladder. "It probably puts him in mind of the good old days—climbing into the hayloft, and all that."

Libby blushed. She was still quite disturbed by that ladder, among other things. "You did ask the senator's permission to come here, didn't you?"

Jess seemed to know that she had visions of Cleave Barlowe carrying some laughing woman over the threshold and finding the place already occupied. "Yes," he assured her in a teasing tone, rising and coming toward her. "I said, 'Mind if I take Libby to your condo, dear old dad, and take her to bed?' And he said—"

"Jess!" Libby howled, in protest.

He laughed, caught her elbows in his hands, kissed her playfully, his lips sampling hers, tugging at them in soft entreaty. "My father is in Washington," he said. "Stop worrying."

Libby pulled back, her face hot, her mind spinning. "I'm hungry!"

"Umm," replied Jess, "so am I."

Why did she feel like a sixteen-year-old on the verge of big trouble? "Please...let's go now."

Jess sighed.

They went, but they were back, arms burdened with cartons of Chinese food, in less than half an hour.

While Jess set the boxes out on the coffee table, Libby went to the kitchen for plates and silverware. Scribbled on a blackboard near the sink, she saw the surprising words: "Thanks, Ken. See you next week. B."

A soft chuckle simmered up into Libby's throat and emerged as a giggle. Could it be that her father, her serious, hardworking father, had a ladyfriend who visited him here in this romantic hideaway? Tilting her head to one side, she considered, grinned again. "Naaaah!"

But Libby's grin wouldn't fade as she carried plates, forks, spoons and paper napkins back into the living room.

"What's so funny?" Jess asked, trying to hide the hunk of sweet-and-sour chicken he had just purloined from one of the steaming cartons.

"Nothing," said Libby, catching his hand and raising it to his mouth. Sheepishly he popped the tidbit of chicken onto his tongue and chewed.

"You lie," Jess replied, "but I'm too hungry to press the point."

While they ate, Libby tried to envision what sort of woman her father would be drawn to—tall, short? Quiet, talkative?

"You're mulling over more than the chow mein," accused Jess presently in a good-natured voice. "Tell me, what's going on in that gifted little head?"

Libby shrugged. "Romance."

He grinned. "That's what I like to hear."

But Libby was thinking seriously, following her thoughts through new channels. In all the years since her mother's death, just before Cathy had come to live on the ranch, she had never imagined Ken Kincaid caring about another woman. "It isn't as though he's old," she muttered, "or unattractive."

Jess set down his plate with a mockingly forceful thump. "That does it. Who are you talking about, Kincaid?" he demanded archly, his wonderful mouth twitching in the effort to suppress a grin.

She perused him with lofty disdain. "Am I correct in assuming that you are jealous?"

"Jealous as hell," came the immediate and not-so-jovial response.

Libby laughed, laid a hand on his knee. "If you must know, I was thinking about my father. I've always kept him in this neat little cubicle in my mind, marked 'Dad.' If you can believe it, it has just now occurred to me that he's a man, with a life, and maybe even a love, of his own."

Mirth danced in Jess's jade eyes, but if he knew anything about Ken's personal life, he clearly wasn't going to speak of it. "Pass the eggroll," he said diplomatically.

When the meal was over, Libby's reflections began to shift to matters nearer the situation at hand.

"I don't know what I'm doing here," she said pensively as she and Jess cleared the coffee table and started toward the kitchen with the debris. "I must be out of my mind."

Jess dropped the cartons and the crumpled napkins into the trash compactor. "Thanks a lot," he said, watching her attentively as she rinsed the plates and silverware and put them into the dishwasher.

Wearing tailored gray slacks and a lightweight teal-blue sweater, he was devastatingly attractive. Still, the look Libby gave him was a serious, questioning one. "What is it with us, Jess? What makes us behave the way we do? One minute, we're yelling at each other, or not speaking at all, and the next we're alone in a place like this."

"Chemistry?"

Libby laughed ruefully. "More like voodoo. So what kind of car are you planning to buy?"

Jess drew her to him; his fingertips were butterfly-light on the small of her back. "Car?" he echoed, as though the word were foreign.

There was a soft, quivering ache in one corner of Libby's heart. Why couldn't things always be like this between them? Why did they have to wrangle so fiercely before achieving this quiet accord? "Stop teasing me," she said softly. "We did come here to buy a car, you know."

Jess's hands pulled her blouse up and out of her slacks, made slow-moving, sensuous circles on her bare back. "Yes," he said in a throaty rumble. "A car. But there are lots of different kinds of cars, aren't there, Libby? And a decision like this can't be made in haste."

Libby closed her eyes, almost hypnotized by the slow, languid meter of his words, the depth of his voice. "N-no," she agreed.

"Definitely not," he said, his mouth almost upon hers. "It could take two—or three—days to decide."

"Ummm," agreed Libby, slipping deeper and deeper under his spell.

Jess had pressed her back against a counter, and his body formed an impassable barricade, leaning, hard and fragrant, into hers. He was tracing the length of her neck with soft, searing lips, tasting the hollow beneath her ear.

Finally he kissed her, first with tenderness, then with fervor, his tongue seeking and being granted sweet entry. This preliminary joining made Libby's whole entity pulse with an awareness of the primitive differences between his body and her own. Where she was soft and yielding, he was fiercely hard. Her nipples pouted into tiny peaks, crying out for his attention.

Seeming to sense that, Jess unbuttoned her blouse with deft, brazen fingers that felt warm against her skin. He opened the front catch on her bra, admired the pink-tipped lushness that seemed to grow richer and rounder under his gaze.

Idly he bent to kiss one peak into ferocious submission, and Libby groaned, her head falling back. Etched against the clear roof, she saw the long needles of ponderosa pines splintering the spring moonlight into shards of silver.

After almost a minute of pleasure so keen that Libby was certain she couldn't bear it, Jess turned to the other breast, kissing, suckling, nipping softly with his teeth. And all the while, he worked the opposite nipple skillfully with his fingers, putting it through delicious paces.

Libby was almost mindless by the time she felt the snap and zipper of her jeans give way, and her hands were still tangled in his dark hair as he knelt. Down came the jeans, her panties with them.

She could manage no more than a throaty gasp as his hands stroked the smooth skin of her thighs, the V of curls at their junction. She felt his breath there, warm, promising to cherish.

Libby trembled as he sought entrance with a questioning kiss, unveiled her with fingers that would not await permission.

As his tongue first touched the tenderness that had been hidden, his hands came to Libby's hips, pressing her down onto this fiery, inescapable glory. Only when she pleaded did he tug her fully into his mouth and partake of her.

Jess enjoyed Libby at his leisure, demanding her essence, showing no mercy even when she cried out and shuddered upon him in a final, soaring triumph. When her own chants of passion had ceased, she was conscious of his.

Jess still knelt before her, his every touch saying that he was worshiping, but there was sweet mastery in his manner, too. After one kiss of farewell, he gently drew her jeans and panties back into place and stood.

Libby stared at him, amazed at his power over her. He smiled at her wonder, though there was a spark of that same emotion deep in his eyes, and then lifted her off her feet and into his arms.

Say "I love you," Libby thought with prayerful fervor.

"I need you," he said instead.

And, for the moment, it was enough.

Stars peeked through the endlessly varied patterns the fallen pine needles made on the glass roof, as if to see and assess the glory that glowed beneath. Libby preened under their celestial jealousy and cuddled closer to Jess's hard, sheet-entangled frame.

"Why didn't you ever marry, Jess?" she asked, tracing a soft path across his chest with her fingers.

The mattress shifted as he moved to put one arm around Libby and draw her nearer still. "I don't know. It always seemed that marriage could wait."

"Didn't you even come close?"

Jess sighed, his fingers moving idly in her hair. "A couple of times I seriously considered it, yes. I guess it bothered me, subliminally, that I was looking these women over as though they were livestock or something. This one would have beautiful children, that one would like living on the ranch—that sort of thing."

"I see."

Jess stiffened slightly beneath the patterns she was making in the soft swirls of hair on his chest, and she felt the question coming long before he uttered it.

"What attracted you to Aaron Strand?"

Libby had been pondering that mystery herself, ever since her marriage to Aaron had begun to dissolve. Now, suddenly, she was certain that she understood. Weak though he might be, Aaron Strand was tall, dark-haired, broad in the shoulders. He had given the impression of strength and self-assurance, qualities that any woman would find appealing.

"I guess I thought he was strong, like Dad," she said, because she couldn't quite amend the sentence to a full truth and admit that she had probably superimposed Jess's image over Aaron's in the first place.

"Ummm," said Jess noncommittally.

"Of course, he is actually very weak."

Jess offered no comment.

"I guess my mistake," Libby went on quietly, "was in seeing myself through Aaron's eyes. He made me feel so worthless...."

"Maybe that made him feel better about himself."

"Maybe. But I still hate him, Jess—isn't that awful? I still hate him for leaving Jonathan in the lurch like that, especially."

"It isn't awful, it's human. It appears that you and Jonathan needed more than he had to give. Unconsciously, you probably measured him against Ken, and whatever else he is, your dad is a hard act to follow, Libby."

"Yes," said Libby, but she was thinking: *I didn't measure Aaron against Dad. God help me, Jess, I measured him against you.*

Jess turned over in a graceful, rolling motion, so that he was above her, his head and shoulders blocking out the light of the stars. "Enough heavy talk, woman. I came here to—"

"Buy a car?" broke in Libby, her tone teasing and full of love.

He nuzzled his face between her warm, welcoming breasts. "My God," he said, his voice muffled by her satin flesh, "what an innocent you are, Libby Kincaid!" One of his hands came down, gentle and mischievous, to squeeze her bottom. "Nice upholstery."

Libby gasped and arched her back as his mouth slid up over the rounding of her breast to claim its peak. "Not much mileage," she choked out.

Jess laughed against the nipple he was tormenting so methodically. "A definite plus." His hand moved between her thighs to assert an ancient mastery, and his breath quickened at Libby's immediate response. "Starts easily," he muttered, sipping at her nipple now, tugging it into an obedient little point.

Libby was beyond the game now, rising and falling on the velvet swells of need he was stirring within her. "I… Oh, God, Jess…what are you…ooooh!"

Somehow, Jess managed to turn on the bedside lamp without interrupting the searing pace his right hand was setting for Libby's body. "You are a goddess," he said.

The fevered dance continued, even though Libby willed herself to lie still. Damn him, he was watching her, taking pleasure from the unbridled response she could not help giving. Her heart raced with exertion, blood boiled in every vein, and Jess's lazy smile was lost in a silver haze.

She sobbed out his name, groping for his shoulders with her hands, holding on. Then, shuddering violently, she tumbled into some chasm where there was no sound but the beat of her own heart.

"You like doing that, don't you?" she snapped when she could see again, breathe again.

"Yes," replied Jess without hesitation.

Libby scrambled into a sitting position, blue eyes shooting flames. "Bastard," she said.

He met her gaze placidly. "What's the matter with you?"

Libby wasn't quite sure of the answer to that question. "It just…it just bothers me that you were…you were looking at me," she faltered, covering her still-pulsing breasts with the bedclothes.

With a deliberate motion of his hands, Jess removed the covers again, and Libby's traitorous nipples puckered in response to his brazen perusal. "Why?" he asked.

Libby's cheeks ached with color, and she lowered her eyes. Instantly Jess caught her chin in a gentle grasp, made her look at him again.

"Sweetheart, you're not ashamed, are you?"

Libby couldn't reply, she was so confused.

His hand slid, soothing, from Libby's chin to the side of her face. "You were giving yourself to me, Libby, trusting me. Is there shame in that?"

She realized that there wasn't, not the way she loved this brazen, tender, outlandish man. If only she dared to tell him verbally what her body already had.

He kissed her softly, sensing her need for greater reassurance. "Exquisite," he said. "Even ordinarily, you are exquisite. But when you let me love you, you go beyond that. You move me on a level where I've never even been touched before."

Say it now, Libby urged silently, *say you love me.*

But she had to be satisfied with what he had already said, for it was immediately clear that there would be no poetic avowals of devotion forthcoming. He'd said she was exquisite, that she moved him, but he'd made no declaration.

For this reason, there was a measure of sadness in the lovemaking that followed.

Long after Jess slept, exhausted, beside her, Libby lay awake, aching. She wanted, needed more from Jess than his readily admitted lust. So much more.

And yet, if a commitment were offered, would Libby want to accept it? Weren't there already too many conflicts complicating their lives? Though she tried to shut out the memory, Libby couldn't forget that Jess had believed her capable of carrying on with his brother and hurting her cousin and dearest friend in the process. Nor could she forget the wedge that had been driven between them the first time they'd made love, when she'd slipped and uttered words that had made him feel as though she'd used him to prove herself as a woman.

Of course, they had come together again, despite these things, but that was of no comfort to Libby. If they were to achieve any real closeness, more than just their bodies would have to be in accord.

After several hours, Libby fell into a fitful, dream-ridden sleep. When morning came, casting bright sunlight through the expanse of glass overhead, she was alone in the tousled bed.

"Lib!"

She went to the edge of the loft, peering down over the side. "What?" she retorted, petulant in the face of Jess's freshly showered, bright-and-shiny good cheer.

He waved a cooking spatula with a flourish. "One egg or two?"

"Drop dead," she replied flatly, frowning at the ladder.

Jess laughed. "Watch it. You'll get my hopes up with such tender words."

"What's this damned ladder for, anyway?"

"Are you this grouchy every morning?" he countered.

"Only when I've engaged in illicit sex the night before!" Libby snapped, scowling. "I believe I asked you about the ladder?"

"It's for climbing up and down." Jess shrugged.

Libby's head throbbed, and her eyes felt puffy and

sore. "Given time, I probably could have figured out that much!"

Jess chuckled and shook his head, as if in sympathy.

Libby grasped the top of the peculiar ladder in question and gave it a vigorous shake. It was immovable. Her puzzlement made her feel even more irritable and, for no consciously conceived reason, she put out her tongue at Jess Barlowe and whirled away from the edge of the loft, out of his view.

His laughter rang out as she stumbled into the bathroom and turned on the water in the shower stall.

Once she had showered and brushed her teeth, Libby began to feel semihuman. With this came contrition for the snappish way she had greeted Jess minutes before. It wasn't his fault, after all, that he was so nauseatingly happy in the mornings.

Grinning a mischievous grin, Libby rummaged through the suitcase she had so hastily packed and found the T-shirt she had bought for Jess the day before, when she'd come to Kalispell with Cathy. She pulled the garment on over her head and, in a flash of daring, swung over the loft to climb down the ladder.

Her reward was a low, appreciative whistle.

"Now I know why that ladder was built," Jess said. "The view from down here is great."

Libby was embarrassed; she'd thought Jess was in the kitchen and thus unable to see her novel descent from the loft. Reaching the floor, she whirled, her face crimson, to glare at him.

Jess read the legend printed on the front of the T-shirt, which was so big that it reached almost to her knees, and laughed explosively. "'If it feels good, do it'?" he marveled.

Libby's glare simply would not stay in place, no matter how hard she tried to sustain it. Her mouth twitched and a chuckle escaped her and then she was laughing as hard as Jess was.

Given the situation, his words came as a shock.

"Libby, will you marry me?"

She stared at him, bewildered, afraid to hope. "What?"

The jade eyes were gentle now, still glistening with residual laughter. "Don't make me repeat it, princess."

"I think the eggs are burning," said Libby in tones made wooden by surprise.

"Wrong. I've already eaten mine, and yours are congealing on your plate. What's your answer, Kincaid?"

Libby's throat ached; something about the size of her heart was caught in it. "I... What..."

"I thought you only talked in broken sentences at the height of passion. Are you really as surprised as all that?"

"Yes!" croaked Libby after a struggle.

The broad shoulders, accentuated rather than hidden by a soft yellow sweater, moved in a shrug. "It seemed like a good solution to me."

"A solution? To what?"

"All our separate and combined problems," answered Jess airily. Persuasively. "Think about it, Lib. Stacey couldn't very well hassle you anymore, could he? And you could stay on the ranch."

Despite the companionable delivery, Jess's words made Libby's soul ache. "Those are solutions for me. What problems would marriage solve for you?"

"We're good in bed," he offered, shattering Libby with what he seemed to mean as a compliment.

"It takes more than that!"

"Does it?"

Libby was speechless, though a voice inside her kept screaming silly, sentimental things. *What about love? What about babies and leftover meatloaf and filing joint tax returns?*

"You dad would be happy," Jess added, and he couldn't have hurt Libby more if he'd raised his hand and slapped her.

"My dad? My *dad?*"

Jess turned away, seemingly unaware of the effect his convoluted proposal was having on Libby. He looked like exactly what he was: a trained, skillful attorney pleading a weak case. "You want children, don't you? And I know you like living on the ranch."

Libby broke in coldly. "I guess I meet all the qualifications. I do want children. I do like living on the Circle Bar B. So why don't you just hog-tie me and brand me a Barlowe?"

Every muscle in Jess's body seemed to tense, but he did not turn around to face her. "There is one other reason," he offered.

For all her fury and hurt, hope sang through Libby's system like the wind unleashed on a wide prairie. "What's that?"

He drew a deep breath, his hands clasped behind him, courtroom style. "There would be no chance, for now at least, of Cathy being hurt."

Cathy. Libby's knees weakened; she groped for the sofa behind her, fell into it. Good God, was his devotion to Cathy so deep that he would marry the woman he considered a threat to her happiness, just to protect her?

"I am so damned tired of hearing about Cathy," she

said evenly, tugging the end of the T-shirt down over her knees for something to do.

Now Jess turned, looked at her with unreadable eyes.

Even though Libby felt the guilt she always did whenever she was even mildly annoyed with Cathy, she stood her ground. "A person doesn't have to be handicapped to hurt, you know," she said in a small and rather uncertain voice.

Jess folded his arms and the sunlight streaming in through the glass ceiling glittered in his dark hair. "I know that," he said softly. "And we're all handicapped in some way, aren't we?"

She couldn't tell whether he was reprimanding her or offering an olive branch. Huddling on the couch, feeling foolish in the T-shirt she had put on as a joke, Libby knotted her hands together in her lap. "I suppose that remark was intended as a barb."

Jess came to sit beside her on the couch, careful not to touch her. "Libby, it wasn't. I'm tired of exchanging verbal shots with you—that was fine when we had to ride the same school bus every day, but we're adults now. Let's try to act as such."

Libby looked into Jess's face and was thunderstruck by how much she cared for him, needed him. And yet, even a week before, she would have said she despised Jess and meant it. All that rancor they'd borne each other—had it really been passion instead?

"I don't understand any of this."

Jess took one of her hands into both of his. "Do you want to marry me or not?"

Both fear and joy rose within Libby. In order to look inward at her own feelings, she was forced to look away from him. She did love Jess, there was absolutely no doubt of that, and she wanted, above all things, to be his wife. She wanted children and, at thirty-one, she often had the feeling that time was getting short. Dammit, why couldn't he say he loved her?

"Would you be faithful to me, Jess?"

He touched her cheek, turning her face without apparent effort, so that she was again looking into those bewitching green eyes. "I would never betray you."

Aaron had said those words, too. Aaron had been so very good with words.

But this was Jess, Libby reminded herself. Jess, not Aaron. "I couldn't give up my career," she said. "It's a crazy business, Jess, and sometimes there are long stretches of time when I don't do much of anything. Other times, I have to work ten-or twelve-hour days to meet a deadline."

Jess did not seem to be dissuaded.

Libby drew a deep breath. "Of course, I'd go on being known as Libby Kincaid. I never took Aaron's name and I don't see any sense in taking yours—should I agree to marry you, that is."

He seemed amused, but she had definitely touched a sore spot. That became immediately obvious. "Wait a minute, lady. Professionally, you can be known by any name you want. Privately, however, you'll be Libby Barlowe."

Libby was secretly pleased, but because she was angry and hurt that he didn't love her, she lifted her chin and snapped, "You have to have that Circle Bar B brand on everything you consider yours, don't you?"

"You are not a thing, Libby," he replied rationally, "but I want at least that much of a commitment. Call it male ego if you must, but I want my wife to be Mrs. Barlowe."

Libby swallowed. "Fair enough," she said.

Jess sat back on the sofa, folded his arms again. "I'm waiting," he said, and the mischievous glint was back in his eyes.

"For what?"

"An answer to my original question."

Fool, fool! Don't you ever learn, Libby Kincaid? Don't you ever learn? Libby quieted the voice in her mind and lifted her chin. Life was short, and unpredictable in the bargain. Maybe Jess would learn to love her the way she loved him. Wasn't that kind of happiness worth a risk?

"I'll marry you," she said.

Jess kissed her with an exuberance that soon turned to desire.

Jess frowned at the sleek showroom sports car, his tongue making one cheek protrude. "What do you think?" he asked.

Libby assessed the car again. "It isn't you."

He grinned, ignoring the salesman's quiet disappointment. "You're right."

Neither, of course, had the last ten cars they had looked at been "him." The sports cars seemed to cramp his long legs, while the big luxury vehicles were too showy.

"How about another truck?" Libby suggested.

"Do you know how many trucks there already are on the ranch?" he countered. "Besides, some yokel would probably paint on the family logo when I wasn't looking."

Libby deliberately widened her eyes. "That would be truly terrible!"

He made a face at her, but when he spoke, his words were delivered in a touchingly serious way. "We could get a van and fill the seats with kids and dogs."

Libby smiled at the image. "A grungy sort of heaven," she mused.

Jess laughed. "And of course there would be lots of room to make love."

The salesman cleared his throat and discreetly walked away.

Chapter 9

"I think you shocked that salesman," observed Libby, snapping the seat belt into place as Jess settled behind the wheel of their rental car.

Jess shrugged. "By wanting a van?" he teased.

"By wanting *me* in the van," clarified Libby.

Jess turned the key in the ignition and shifted gears. "He's lucky I didn't list all the other places I'd like to have you. The hood, for instance. And then there's the roof...."

Libby colored richly as they pulled into the slow traffic. "Jess!"

He frowned speculatively. "And, of course, on the ladder at the condo."

"The ladder?"

Jess flung her a brazen grin. "Yeah. About halfway up."

"Don't you think about anything but sex?"

"I seem to have developed a fixation, Kincaid—just since you came back, of course."

She couldn't help smiling. "Of course."

Nothing more was said until they'd driven through the quiet, well-kept streets to the courthouse. Jess parked the car and turned to Libby with a comical leer. "Are you up to a blood test and a little small-town bureaucracy, Kincaid?"

Libby felt a wild, twisting thrill in the pit of her stomach. A marriage license. He wanted to get a marriage license. In three short days, she could be bound to Jess Barlowe for life. At least, she *hoped* it would be for life.

After drawing a deep breath, Libby unsnapped her seat belt and got out of the car.

Twenty minutes later, the ordeal was over. The fact that the wedding itself wouldn't take nearly as long struck Libby as an irony.

On the sidewalk, Jess caught her elbow in one hand and helped her back into the car. While he must have noticed that she was preoccupied, he was chivalrous enough not to say so.

"Stop at that supermarket!" Libby blurted when they'd been driving for some minutes.

Jess gave her a quizzical look. "Supermarket?"

"Yes. They sell food there, among other necessary items."

Jess frowned. "Why can't we just eat in restaurants? There are several good ones—"

"Restaurants?" Libby cried with mock disdain. "How can I prove what a great catch I am if I don't cook something for you?"

Jess's right hand left the steering wheel to slide languorously up and down Libby's linen-skirted thigh.

"Relax, sweetheart," he said in a rather good imitation of Humphrey Bogart. "I already know you're good in the kitchen."

The obvious reference to last night's episode in that room unsettled Libby. "You delight in saying outrageous things, don't you?" she snapped.

"I delight in *doing* outrageous things."

"You'll get no argument on that score, fella," she retorted acidly.

The car came to a stop in front of the supermarket, which was in the center of a small shopping mall. Libby noticed that Jess's gaze strayed to a jewelry store down the way.

"I'll meet you inside," he said, and then he was gone.

Though Libby told herself that she was being silly and sentimental, she was pleased to think that Jess might be shopping for a ring.

The giddy, romantic feeling faded when she selected a shopping cart inside the supermarket, however. She was wallowing in gushy dreams, behaving like a seventeen-year-old virgin. Of *course* Jess would buy a ring, but only because it would be expected of him.

Glumly Libby went about selecting items from a mental grocery list she had been composing since she'd checked the refrigerator and cupboards at the condominium and found them all but empty.

Taking refuge in practical matters, she frowned at a display of cabbage and wondered how much food to buy. Jess hadn't said how long they would be staying in Kalispell, beyond the time it would take to find the car he wanted.

Shrugging slightly, Libby decided to buy provisions for three days. Because that was the required waiting period for a marriage license, they would probably be in town at least that long.

She looked down at her slacks and brightly colored top. The wedding ceremony was going to be an informal one, obviously, but she would still need a new dress, and she wanted to buy a wedding band for Jess, too.

She pushed her cart along the produce aisle, woodenly selecting bean sprouts, fresh broccoli, onions. Her first wedding had been a quiet one, too, devoid of lace and flowers and music, and something within her mourned those things.

They hadn't even discussed a honeymoon, and what kind of ceremony would this be, without Ken, without Cathy, without Senator Barlowe and Marion Bradshaw, the housekeeper?

A box seemed to float up out of the cart, but Libby soon saw that it was clasped in a strong sun-browned hand.

"I hate cereals that crunch," Jess said, and his eyes seemed to be looking inside Libby, seeing the dull ache she would rather have kept hidden. "What's wrong, love?"

Libby fought back the sudden silly tears that ached in her throat and throbbed behind her eyes. "Nothing," she lied.

Jess was not fooled. "You want Ken to come to the wedding," he guessed.

Libby lowered her head slightly. "He was hurt when Aaron and I got married without even telling him first," she said.

There was a short silence before a housewife, tagged by two preschoolers, gave Libby's cart a surreptitious bump with her own, tacitly demanding access to the cereal display. Libby wrestled her groceries out of the way and looked up at Jess, waiting for his response.

He smiled, touched her cheek. "Tell you what. We'll call the ranch and let everybody know we're getting married. That way, if they want to be there, they can. And if you want frills and flash, princess, we can have a formal wedding later."

The idea of a second wedding, complete with the trimmings, appealed to Libby's romantic soul. She smiled at the thought. "You would do that? You would go through it all over again, just for show?"

"Not for show, princess. For you."

The housewife made an appreciative sound and Libby started a little, having completely forgotten their surroundings.

Jess laughed and the subject was dropped. They walked up one aisle and down another, dropping the occasional pertinent item into the cart, arguing good-naturedly about who would do the cooking after they were married.

The telephone was ringing as Libby unlocked the front door of the condo, so she left Jess to carry in their bags of groceries and ran to answer it, expecting to hear Ken's voice, or Marion Bradshaw's, relaying some message from Cathy.

A cruel wave of déjà vu washed over her when she heard Aaron's smooth, confident greeting. "Hello, Libby."

"What do you want?" Libby rasped, too stunned to hang up. How on earth had he gotten that number?

"I told you before, dear heart," said Aaron smoothly. "I want a child."

Libby was conscious of Jess standing at her elbow,

the shopping bags clasped in his arms. "You're insane!" she cried into the receiver.

"Maybe so, but not insane enough to let my grandmother hand over an empire to someone else. She has doubts, you know, about my dependability."

"I wonder why!"

"Don't be sarcastic, sugarplum. My request isn't really all that unreasonable, considering all I stand to lose."

"It is unreasonable, Aaron! In fact, it's sick!" At this point Libby slammed down the receiver with a vengeance. She was trembling so hard that Jess hastily shunted the grocery bags onto a side table and took her into his arms.

"What was that all about?" he asked when Libby had recovered herself a little.

"He's horrible," Libby answered, distracted and very much afraid. "Oh, Jess, he's a monster—"

"What did he say?" Jess pressed quietly.

"Aaron wants me to have his baby! Jess, he actually had the gall to ask me to come back, just so he can produce an heir and please his grandmother!"

Jess's hand was entangled in her hair now, comforting her. "It's all right, Lib. Everything will be all right."

Then why am I so damned scared? Libby asked herself, but she put on a brave face for Jess and even managed a smile. "Let's call my dad," she said.

Jess nodded, kissed her forehead. And then he took up the grocery bags again and carried them into the kitchen while Libby dialed her father's telephone number.

There was no answer, which was not surprising, considering that it was still early. Ken would be working, and because of the wide range of his responsibilities, he could be anywhere on the 150,000 acres that made up the Circle Bar B.

Sounds from the kitchen indicated that Jess was putting the food away, and Libby wandered in, needing to be near him.

"No answer?" he asked, tossing a package of frozen egg rolls into the freezer.

"No answer," confirmed Libby. "I should have known, I guess."

Jess turned, gave her a gentle grin. "You did know, Libby. But you needed to touch base just then, and going through the motions was better than nothing."

"When did you get so smart?"

"Last Tuesday, I think," he answered ponderously. "Know something? You look a little tired. Why don't you climb up that ladder that bugs you so much and take a nap?"

Libby arched one eyebrow. "While you do what?"

His answer was somewhat disappointing. "While I go back to town for a few hours," he said. "I have some things to do."

"Like what?"

He grinned. "Like picking up some travel brochures, so we can decide where to take our honeymoon."

Libby felt a rush of pleasure despite the weariness she was suddenly very aware of. Had it been there all along, or was she tired simply because this subtle hypnotist had suggested it to her? "Does it matter where we honeymoon?"

"Not really," Jess replied, coming disturbingly close, kissing Libby's forehead. "But I like having you all to myself. I can't help thinking that the farther we get from home right now, the better off we're going to be."

A tremor of fear brushed against Libby's heart, but it was quickly stilled when Jess caught her right earlobe between gentle teeth and then told her in bluntly erotic terms what he had wanted to do to her on the supermarket checkout counter.

When he'd finished, Libby was wildly aroused and, at the same time, resigned to the fact that when she crawled into that sun-washed bed up in the loft, she would be alone. "Rat," she said.

Jess swatted her backside playfully. "Later," he promised, and then calmly left the condo to attend to his errands.

Libby went obediently up to the bedroom, using the stairs rather than the ladder, and yawned as she stripped down to her lacy camisole and panties. She shouldn't be having a nap now, she told herself, when she had things of her own to do—choosing Jess's ring, for one thing, and buying a special dress, for another....

She was asleep only seconds after slipping beneath the covers.

Libby stirred, indulged in a deliciously lazy stretch. Someone was trailing soft, warm kisses across her collarbone—or was she dreaming? Just in case she was, she did not open her eyes.

Cool air washed over her breasts as the camisole was gently displaced. "Ummm," she said.

"Good dream?" asked Jess, moistening one pulsing nipple to crisp attention with his tongue.

"Oooooh," answered Libby, arching her back slightly, her eyes still closed, her head pressed into the silken pillow in eager, soft surrender. "Very good."

Jess left that nipple to subject its twin to a tender

plundering that caused Libby to moan with delight. Her hips writhed slightly, calling to their powerful counterpart.

Jess heard their silent plea, slid the satiny panties down, down, away. "You're so warm, Libby," he said in a ragged whisper. "So soft and delicious." The camisole was unlaced, laid aside reverently, like the wrapping on some splendid gift. Kisses rained down on Libby's sleep-warmed, swollen breasts, her stomach, her thighs.

At last she opened her eyes, saw Jess's wondrous nakedness through a haze of sweet, sleepy need. As he ventured nearer and nearer to the silk-sheltered sanction of her womanhood, she instinctively reached up to clasp the brass railings on the headboard of the bed, anchoring herself to earth.

Jess parted the soft veil, admired its secret with a throaty exclamation of desire and a searing kiss.

A plea was wrenched from Libby, and she tightened her grasp on the headboard.

For a few mind-sundering minutes Jess enjoyed the swelling morsel with his tongue. "More?" he asked, teasing her, knowing that she was already half-mad with the need of him.

"More," she whimpered as his fingers strayed to the pebblelike peaks of her breasts, plying them, sending an exquisite lacelike net of passion knitting its way through her body.

Another tormenting flick of his tongue. "Sweet," he said. And then he lifted Libby's legs, placing one over each of his shoulders, making her totally, beautifully vulnerable to him.

She cried out in senseless delirium as he took his pleasure, and she was certain that she would have been flung beyond the dark sky if not for her desperate grasp on the headboard.

Even after the highest peak had been scaled, Libby's sated body convulsed again and again, caught in the throes of other, smaller releases.

Still dazed, Libby felt Jess's length stretch out upon her, seeking that sweetest and most intimate solace. In a burst of tender rebellion, she thrust him off and demanded loving revenge.

Soon enough, it was Jess who grasped the gleaming brass railings lest he soar away, Jess who chanted a desperate litany.

Wickedly, Libby took her time, savoring him, taking outrageous liberties with him. Finally she conquered him, and his cry of joyous surrender filled her with love almost beyond bearing.

His breathing still ragged, his face full of wonder, Jess drew Libby down, so that she lay beside him. With his hands he explored her, igniting tiny silver fires in every curve and hollow of her body.

This time, when he came to her, she welcomed him with a ferocious thrust of her hips, alternately setting the pace and following Jess's lead. When the pinnacle was reached, each was lost in the echoing, triumphant cry of the other, and bits of a broken rainbow showered down around them.

Sitting cross-legged on the living-room sofa, Libby twisted the telephone cord between her fingers and waited for her father's response to her announcement.

It was a soft chuckle.

"You aren't the least bit surprised!" Libby accused, marveling.

"I figured anybody that fought and jawed as much as you two did had to end up hitched," replied Ken Kincaid in his colorful way. "Did you let Cleave know yet?"

"Jess will, in a few minutes. Will you tell Cathy for me, please?"

Ken promised that he would.

Libby swallowed hard, gave Jess a warning glare as he moved to slide an exploring hand inside the top of her bathrobe. "Aren't you going to say that we're rushing into this or something like that? Some people will think it's too soon—"

"It was damned near too late," quipped Ken. "What time is the ceremony again?"

There were tears in Libby's eyes, though she had never been happier. "Two o'clock on Friday, at the courthouse."

"I'll be there, dumplin'. Be happy."

The whole room was distorted into a joyous blur. "I will, Dad. I love you."

"I love you, too," he answered with an ease that was typical of him. "Take care and I'll see you Friday."

"Right," said Libby, sniffling as she gently replaced the receiver.

Jess chuckled, touched her chin. "Tears? I'm insulted."

Libby made a face and shoved the telephone into his lap. "Call your father," she said.

Jess settled back in the sofa as he dialed the number of the senator's house in Washington, balancing the telephone on one blue-jeaned knee. While he tried to talk to his father in normal tones, Libby ran impudent fingertips over his bare chest, twining dark hair into tight curls, making hard buttons of deliciously vulnerable nipples.

With a mock-glare and a motion of his free arm, Jess tried to field her blatant advances. She simply knelt astraddle of his lap and had her way with him, her fingers tracing a path of fire around his mouth, along his neck, over his nipples.

Jess caught the errant hand in a desperate hold, only to be immediately assaulted by the other. Mischief flashed in his jade eyes, followed by an I'll-get-you-for-this look. "See you then," he said to his father, his voice a little deeper than usual and very carefully modulated. There was a pause, and then he added, "Oh, don't worry, I will. In about five seconds, I'm going to lay Libby on the coffee table and kiss her in all the best places. Yes, sir, by the time I get through with her, she'll be—"

Falling into the trap, Libby colored, snatched the receiver out of Jess's hand and pressed it to her ear. The line was, of course, dead.

Jess laughed as she assessed him murderously. "You deserved that," he said.

Libby moved to struggle off his lap, still crimson in the face, her heart pounding with embarrassment. But Jess's hands were strong on her upper arms, holding her in place.

"Oh, no you don't, princess. You're not getting out of this so easily."

"What—"

Jess smiled languidly, still holding her fast with one hand, undoing his jeans with the other. "You let this horse out of the barn, lady. Now you're going to ride it."

Libby gasped as she felt him prod her, hard and insistent, and fierce needs surged through her even as she raged at the affront. She was powerless, both physically and emotionally, to break away from him.

Just barely inside her, Jess reached out and calmly untied her bathrobe, baring her breasts, her stomach, her captured hips. His green eyes glittered as he stroked each satiny expanse in turn, allowing Libby more and more of him until she was fully his.

Seemingly unmoved himself, Jess took wicked delight in Libby's capture and began guiding her soft, trim hips up and down, endlessly up and down, upon him. All the while, he used soft words to lead her through flurries of silver snow to the tumultuous release beyond.

When her vision cleared, Libby saw that Jess had been caught in his own treachery. She watched in love and wonder as he gave himself up to raging sensation—his head fell back, his throat worked, his eyes were sightless.

Gruffly Jess pleaded with Libby, and she accelerated the up-and-down motion of her hips until he shuddered violently beneath her, stiffened and growled her name.

"Mess with me, will you?" she mocked, grinning down at him.

Jess began to laugh, between rasping breaths. When his mirth had subsided and he didn't have to drag air into his lungs, he caressed her with his eyes. In fact, it was almost as though he'd said he loved her.

Libby was still incredibly moved by the sweet spectacle she had seen played out in his face as he submitted to her, and she understood then why he so loved to watch her respond while pleasuring her.

Jess reached up, touched away the tear that tickled on her cheek. It would have been a perfect time for those three special words she so wanted to hear, but he did not say them.

Hurt and disappointed, Libby wrenched her bathrobe closed and tried to rise from his lap, only to be easily thwarted. Jess's hands opened the robe again, his eyes perused her and then came back to her face, silently daring her to hide any part of her body or soul from him.

With an insolent finger he brushed the pink buttons at the tips of her full breasts, smiled as they instantly obeyed him. Apparently satisfied with their pert allegiance, Jess moved on to trace patterns of fire on Libby's stomach, the rounding of her hips, the sensitive hollow at the base of her throat.

Jess seemed determined to prove that he could subdue Libby at will, and he only smiled at the startled gasp she gave when it became apparent that all his prowess had returned in full and glorious force.

He slid her robe off her shoulders then and removed it entirely. They were still joined, and Libby shivered as he toyed idly with her breasts, weighing them in his hands, pressing them together, thumbing their aching tips until they performed for him.

Presently Jess left his sumptuous playthings to tamper elsewhere, wreaking still more havoc, eliciting little anxious cries from a bedazzled Libby.

"What do you want, princess?" he asked in a voice of liquid steel.

Libby was wild upon him, her hands clutching desperately at his shoulders, her knees wide. "I want to be…under you. Oh, Jess…under you…"

In a swift and graceful motion, he turned her, was upon her. The movement unleashed the passion Jess had been able to contain until then, and he began to move over her and within her, his thrusts deep and powerful, his words ragged and incoherent.

As their very souls collided and then fused together, imitating their bodies, it was impossible to tell who had prevailed over whom.

Libby awakened first, entangled with Jess, amazed that they could have slept the whole night on that narrow couch.

A smile lifted one corner of her mouth as she kissed Jess's temple tenderly and then disengaged herself, careful not to disturb him. Heaven knew, he had a right to be tired.

Twenty minutes later, when Libby returned from her shower, dressed in sandals, white slacks and a lightweight yellow sweater, Jess was still sleeping. She could empathize, for her own slumber had been fathomless.

"I love you," she said, and then she went to the kitchen and wrote a quick note on the blackboard there, explaining that she had gone shopping and would be back within a few hours.

Getting into the rented car, which was parked in the gravel driveway near the front door, Libby spotted a cluster of colorful travel brochures fanned out on the opposite seat. Each one touted a different paradise: Acapulco, the Bahamas, Maui.

As Libby slid the key into the ignition and started the car, she grinned. She had it on good authority that paradise was only a few yards away, on the couch where Jess lay sleeping.

The day was a rich mixture of blue and green, set off by the fierce green of pine trees and the riotous blooms of crocuses and daffodils in quiet front yards. Downtown, Libby found a parking place immediately, locked the car and hurried on about her business.

Her first stop was a jewelry store, and while she had anticipated a great quandary, the decision of which wedding band to buy for Jess proved an easy one. Her eyes were immediately drawn to one particular ring, forged of silver, inset with polished chips of turquoise.

Once the jeweler had assured her the band could be resized if it didn't fit Jess's finger, Libby bought it.

In an art-supply store she purchased a sketching pad and a gum eraser and some charcoal pencils. Sweet as this interlude with Jess had been, Libby missed her work and her fingers itched to draw. Too, there were all sorts of new ideas for the comic strip bubbling in her mind.

From the art store, Libby pressed on to a good-sized department store. None of the dresses there quite struck her fancy, and she moved on to one boutique and then another.

Finally, in a small and wickedly expensive shop, she found that special dress, that dress of dresses, the one she would wear when she married Jess Barlowe.

It was a clingy creation of burgundy silk, showing off her figure, bringing a glow of color to her cheeks. There were no ruffles of lace or fancy buttons—only a narrow belt made of the same fabric as the dress itself. It was the last word in elegant simplicity, that garment, and Libby adored it.

Carrying the dress box and the heavy bag of art supplies, she hurried back to the car and locked her purchases inside. It was only a little after ten, and Libby wanted to find shoes that would match her dress.

The shoes proved very elusive, and only after almost an hour of searching did she find a pair that would do.

Tired of shopping and anxious to see Jess again, Libby started home.

Some intuitive feeling made her uneasy as she drove toward the elegant condominium hidden in the tall trees. After crossing the wooden bridge and making the last turn, she knew why—Stacey's ice-blue Ferrari was parked in the driveway.

Don't be silly, Libby reprimanded herself, but she still felt alarmed. What if Stacey had come to try to talk her out of marrying Jess? What if Cathy was with him, and there was an unpleasant scene?

Determined not to let her imagination get the upper hand, Libby gathered up her loot from the shopping trip and got out of the car. As she approached the house, she caught sight of a familiar face at the window and was surprised all over again. Monica! What on earth was she doing here? Hadn't she left for Washington, D.C., with the senator?

Now Libby really hesitated. She remembered the proprietary looks the woman had given Jess as he swam that day in the pool at the main ranch house. Looks that had implied intimacy.

Libby sighed. So what if Jess and Monica had slept together? She could hardly have expected a man like him to live like a monk, and it wasn't as if Libby hadn't had a prior relationship herself, however unsatisfactory.

Despite the cool sanity of this logic, it hurt to imagine Jess making love with Monica—or with any other woman, for that matter.

Libby grappled with her purchases at the front door, reached for the knob. Before she could clasp it, the door opened.

Jess was standing there, shirtless, wearing jeans,

his hair and suntanned chest still damp from a recent shower. Instead of greeting Libby with a smile, let alone a kiss, he scowled at her and stepped back almost grudgingly, as though he had considered refusing her entrance.

Bewildered and hurt, Libby resisted a primal instinct urging her to flee and walked in.

Monica had left the window and was now seated comfortably on the couch, her shapely legs crossed at the knee, a cocktail in her hand.

Libby took in the woman's sleek designer suit and felt shabby by comparison in her casual attire. "Hello, Monica."

"Libby," replied Monica with a polite nod.

The formalities dispensed with, Libby flung a hesitant look at Jess. Why was he glaring at her like that, as though he wanted to do her bodily harm? Why was his jawline so tight, and why was it that he clenched the towel draped around his neck in white-knuckled hands?

Before Libby could voice any of her questions, Stacey came out of the kitchen, raked her with guileless caramel eyes and smiled.

"Hello," he said, as though his very presence, under the circumstances, was not an outrage.

Libby only stared at him. She was very conscious of Jess, seething somewhere on the periphery of her vision, and of Monica, taking in the whole scene with detached amusement.

Suddenly Stacey was coming toward Libby, speaking words she couldn't seem to hear. Then he had the outright gall to kiss her, and Libby's inertia was broken.

She drew back her hand and slapped him, her dress box, purse and bag of art supplies falling to the floor.

Stacey reached out for her, caught her waist in his hands. She squirmed and flung one appealing look in Jess's direction.

Though he looked anything but chivalrous, he did intercede. "Leave Libby alone, Stacey."

Stacey paled. "I've left Cathy," he said, as though that settled everything. "Libby, we can be together now!"

Libby stumbled backward, stunned. Only when she came up against the hard barrier of Jess's soap-scented body did she stop. Wild relief went through her as he enclosed her in a steel-like protective embrace.

"Get out," he said flatly, addressing his brother.

Stacey hesitated, but then he reddened and left the condo in a huff, pulling Monica Summers behind him.

Chapter 10

Furious and shaken, Libby turned to glare at Jess. It was all too clear what had happened—Stacey had been telling more of his outrageous lies and Jess had believed them.

For a few moments he stubbornly returned her angry regard, but then he spread his hands in a gesture of concession and said, "I'm sorry."

Libby was trembling now, but she stooped to pick up her dress box, and the art-store bag. She couldn't look at Jess or he would see the tears that had clouded her eyes. "After all we've done and planned, how could you, Jess? How could you believe Stacey?"

He was near, very near—Libby was conscious of him in every sense. He moved to touch her, instantly stopped himself. "I said I was sorry."

Libby forgot that she'd meant to hide her tears and

looked him full in the face. Her voice shook with anger when she spoke. "Sometimes being sorry isn't enough, Jess!" She carried the things she'd bought across the room, tossed them onto the couch. "Is this what our marriage is going to be like? Are we going to do just fine as long as we aren't around Stacey?"

Jess was standing behind her; his hands came to rest on her shoulders. "What can I say, Libby? I was jealous. That may not be right, but it's human."

Perhaps because she wanted so desperately to believe that everything would turn out all right, that a marriage to this wonderful, contradictory man would succeed, Libby set aside her doubts and turned to face Jess. The depth of her love for this erstwhile enemy still staggered her. "What did Stacey tell you?"

Jess drew in an audible breath, and for a moment there was a tightness in his jaw. Then he sighed and said, "He was sharing the glorious details of your supposed affair. And he had a remarkable grasp on what you like in bed, Libby."

The words were wounding, but Libby was strong. "Did it ever occur to you that maybe all women like essentially the same things?"

Jess didn't answer, but Libby could see that she had made her mark, and she rushed on.

"Exactly what was Monica's part in all this?" she demanded hotly. "Was she here to moderate your sexual discussion? Why the hell isn't she in Washington, where she belongs?"

Jess shrugged, obviously puzzled. "I'm not sure why she was here."

"I am! Once you were diverted from your disastrous

course—marrying me—she was going to take you by the hand and lead you home!"

One side of Jess's mouth lifted in a grin. "I'm not the only one who is prone to jealousy, it appears."

"You were involved with her, weren't you?"

"Yes."

The bluntness of the answer took Libby unawares, but only for a moment. After all, had Jess said no, she would have known he was lying and that would have been devastating. "Did you love Monica?"

"No. If I had, I would have married her."

The possible portent of those words buoyed Libby's flagging spirits. "Passion wouldn't be enough?" she ventured.

"To base a marriage on? Never. Now, let's see what you bought today."

Let's see what you bought today. Libby's frustration knew no bounds, but she was damned if she was going to pry those three longed-for words out of him—she'd fished enough as it was. "I bought a wedding dress, for your information. And you're not going to see it until tomorrow, so don't pester me about it."

He laughed. "I like a woman who is loyal to her superstitions. What else did you purchase, milady?"

Libby's sense of financial independence, nurtured during the insecure days with Aaron, chafed under the question. "I didn't use your money, so what do you care?" she snapped.

Jess arched one eyebrow. "Another touchy subject rears its ugly head. I was merely curious, my love—I didn't ask for a meeting with your accountant."

Feeling foolish, Libby made a great project of opening the art-store bag and spreading its contents out on the couch.

Jess was grinning as he assessed the array of pencils, the large sketchbook. "Have I been boring you, princess?"

Libby pulled a face at him. "You could be called many things, Jess Barlowe, but you are definitely not boring."

"Thank you—I think. Shall we brave the car dealers of Kalispell again, or are you going to be busy?" The question was guileless, indicating that Jess would have understood if she wanted to stay and block out some of the ideas that had come to her.

After Aaron, who had viewed her cartooning as a childish hobby, Jess's attitude was a luxury. "I think I'd rather go with you," she said with a teasing smile. "If I don't you might come home with some motorized horror that has horns on its hood."

"Your faith in my good taste is positively underwhelming," he replied, walking toward the ladder, climbing its rungs to the loft in search of a shirt.

"You were right!" Libby called after him. "The view from down here is marvelous!"

During that foray into the jungle of car salesmen and gasoline-fed beasts, Libby spent most of her time in the passenger seat of Jess's rented car, sketching. Instead of drawing Liberated Lizzie, her cartoon character, however, she found herself reproducing Jess's image.

She imagined him looking out over the stunning view of prairies and mountains at home and drew him in profile, the wind ruffling his hair, a pensive look to his eyes and the set of his face. Another sketch showed him laughing, and still another, hidden away in the middle of the drawing pad, not meant for anyone else to see, mirrored the way Jess looked when he wanted her.

To field the responses the drawing evoked in her, Libby quickly sketched Cathy's portrait, and then Ken's. After that, strictly from memory, she drew a picture of Jonathan, full face, as he'd looked before his illness, then, on the same piece of paper, in a profile that revealed the full ravages of his disease.

She supposed it was morbid, including this aspect of the child, but to leave out his pain would have meant leaving out his courage, and Jonathan deserved better.

Touching his charcoal image with gentle, remembering fingers, Libby heard the echo of his voice in her mind. *Naturally I'm brave,* he'd told her once, at the end of a particularly difficult day. *I'm a Jedi knight, like Luke Skywalker.*

Smiling through a mist of tears, Libby added another touch to the sketch—a tiny figure of Jonathan, well and strong, wielding a light saber in valiant defense of the Rebel Alliance.

"That's terrific," observed a gentle voice.

Libby looked up quickly, surprised that she hadn't heard Jess get into the car, hadn't sensed his presence somehow. Because she couldn't speak just yet, she bit her lower lip and nodded an acknowledgment of the compliment.

"Could I take a closer look? Please?"

Libby extended the notebook and it was a gesture of trust, for these sketches were different from the panels for her comic strip. They were large pieces of her soul.

Jess was pensive as he examined the portraits of himself, Cathy, Ken. But the study of Jonathan was clearly his favorite, and he returned to it at intervals, taking in each line, each bit of shading, each unspo-ken cry of grief.

Finally, with a tenderness that made Libby love him even more than she had before, Jess handed the sketch-book back to her. "You are remarkably talented," he said, and then he had the good grace to look away while Libby recomposed herself.

"D-did you find a car you like?" she asked finally.

Jess smiled at her. "Actually, yes. That's why I came back—to get you."

"Me? Why?"

"Well, I don't want to buy the thing without your checking it out first. Suppose you hated it?"

It amazed Libby that such a thing mattered to him. She set the sketchbook carefully in the backseat and opened her car door to get out. "Lead on," she said, and the clean spring breeze braced her as it touched her face.

The vehicle in question was neither car nor truck, but a Land Rover. It was perfectly suited to the kind of life Jess led, and Libby approved of it with enthusiasm.

The deal was made, much to the relief of a salesman they had been plaguing, on and off, since the day before.

After some discussion, it was decided that they would keep the rental car until after the wedding, in case Libby needed it. Over a luncheon of steak and salad, which did much to settle her shaky nerves, Jess suggested that they start shopping all over again, for a second car.

Practical as it was, the thought exhausted Libby.

"You'll need transportation," Jess argued.

"I don't think I could face all those plaid sport jack-ets and test drives again," Libby replied with a sigh.

Jess laughed. "But you would like to have a car, wouldn't you?"

Libby shrugged. In New York, she had depended on taxis for transportation, but the ranch was different, of course. "I suppose."

"Aren't you choosy about the make, model—all that?"

"Wheels are wheels," she answered with another shrug.

"Hmmmm," Jess said speculatively, and then the subject was changed. "What about our honeymoon? Any place in particular you'd like to go?"

"Your couch," Libby said, shocked at her own audacity.

Again Jess laughed. "That is patently unimaginative."

"Hardly, considering the things we did there," Libby replied, immediately lifting a hand to her mouth. What was wrong with her? Why was she suddenly spouting these outlandish remarks?

Jess bent forward, conjured up a comical leer. "I wish we were on the ranch," he said in a low voice. "I'd take you somewhere private and make violent love to you."

Libby felt a familiar heat simmering inside her, melting through her pelvis. "Jess."

He drew some bills from his wallet, tossed them onto the table. "Let's get out of here while I can still walk," he muttered.

Libby laughed. "I think it's a good thing we're driving separate cars today," she teased, though secretly she was just as anxious for privacy as Jess was.

He groaned. "One more word, lady, and I'll spread you out on this table."

Libby's heart thudded at the bold suggestion and

pumped color over her breasts and into her face. She tried to look indignant, but the fact was that she had been aroused by the remark and Jess knew it—his grin was proof of that.

As they left the restaurant, he bent close to her and described the fantasy in vivid detail, sparing nothing. And later, on the table in the condo's kitchen, he turned it into a wildly satisfying reality.

That afternoon, Libby took another nap. Due to the episode just past, her dreams were deliciously erotic.

As he had before, Jess awakened her with strategic kisses. "Hi," he said when she opened her eyes.

She touched his hair, noted that he was wearing his brown leather jacket. "You've been out." She yawned.

Jess kissed the tip of her nose. "I have indeed. Bought you a present or two, as a matter of fact."

The glee in Jess's eyes made Libby's heart twist in a spasm of tenderness; whatever he'd purchased, he was very pleased with. She slipped languid arms around his neck. "I like presents," she said.

Jess drew back, tugged her camisole down so that her breasts were bared to him. Almost idly he kissed each dusty-rose peak and then covered them again. "Sorry," he muttered, his mouth a fraction of an inch from hers. "I couldn't resist."

That strange, magical heat was surging from Libby's just-greeted breasts to her middle, down into her thighs and even her knees. She felt as though every muscle and bone in her body had melted. "You m-mentioned presents?"

He chuckled, kissed her softly, groaned under his

breath. "I was momentarily distracted. Get out of bed, princess. Said presents await."

"Can't you just...bring them here?"

"Hardly." Jess withdrew from the bed to stand at its side and wrench back the covers. His green eyes smoldered as he took in the sleep-pinkened glow of her curves, and he bent to swat her satin-covered backside. "Get up," he repeated.

Libby obeyed, curious about the gifts but disappointed that Jess hadn't joined her in the bed, too. She found a floaty cotton caftan and slipped it on.

Jess looked at her, made a low growling sound in his throat, and caught her hand in his. "Come on, before I give in to my baser instincts," he said, pulling her down the stairs.

Libby looked around curiously as he dragged her across the living room but saw nothing out of the ordinary.

Jess opened the front door, pulled her outside. There, beside his maroon Land Rover, sat a sleek yellow Corvette with a huge rosette of silver ribbon affixed to its windshield.

Libby gaped at the car, her eyes wide.

"Like it?" Jess asked softly, his mouth close to her ear.

"Like it?" Libby bounded toward the car, heedless of her bare feet. "I love it!"

Jess followed, opened the door on the driver's side so that Libby could slide behind the wheel. When she did that, she got a second surprise. Taped to the gearshift knob was a ring of white gold, and the diamond setting formed the Circle Bar B brand.

"I'll hog-tie you later," Jess said.

Libby's hand trembled as she reached for the ring; it blurred and shifted before her eyes as she looked at it. "Oh, Jess."

"Listen, if you hate it…"

Libby ripped away the strip of tape, slid the ring onto her finger. "Hate it? Sacrilege! It's the most beautiful thing I've ever seen."

"Does it fit?"

The ring was a little loose, but Libby wasn't ready to part with it, not even to let a jeweler size it. "No," she said, overwhelmed, "but I don't care."

Gently Jess lifted her chin with his hand, bent to sample her mouth with his. Beneath the hastily donned caftan and her camisole, Libby's nipples hardened in pert response.

"There's only one drawback to this car," Jess breathed, his lips teasing Libby's, shaping them. "It would be impossible to make love in it."

Libby laughed and pretended to shove him. "Scoundrel!"

"You don't know the half of it," he replied hoarsely, drawing Libby out of the beautiful car and back inside the house.

There she gravitated toward the front windows, where she could alternately admire her new car and watch the late-afternoon sun catch in the very special ring on her finger. Standing behind her, Jess wrapped his arms around her waist and held her close, bending to nip at her earlobe.

"Thank you, Jess," Libby said.

He laughed, and his breath moved in Libby's hair and sent warm tingles through her body. "No need for thanks. I'll nibble on your ears anytime."

"You know what I meant!"

His hands had risen to close over her breasts, fully possessing them. "What? What did you mean?" he teased in a throaty whisper.

Libby could barely breathe. "The car...the ring..."

Letting his hands slip from her breasts to her elbows, Jess ushered Libby over to face the mirror above the fireplace. As she watched his reflection in wonder, he undid the caftan's few buttons and slid it slowly down over her shoulders. Then he drew the camisole up over her head and tossed it away.

Libby saw a pink glow rise over her breasts to shine in her face, saw the passion sparking in her dark blue eyes, saw Jess's hands brush upward over her rib cage toward her breasts. The novelty of watching her own reactions to the sensations he was stirring inside her was erotic.

She groaned as she saw—and felt—masculine fingers rise to her waiting nipples and pluck then gently to attention.

"See?" Jess whispered at her ear. "See how beautiful you are, Libby? Especially when I'm loving you."

Libby had never thought of herself as beautiful, but now, looking at her image in the mirror, seeing how passion darkened her eyes to indigo and painted her cheeks with its own special apricot shade, she felt ravishing.

She tilted her head back against the hard breadth of Jess's shoulder, moaned as he softly plundered her nipples.

He spoke with a gruff, choked sort of sternness. "Don't close your eyes, Libby. Watch. You're beautiful— so beautiful—and I want you to know it."

It was hard for Libby not to close her eyes and give

herself up to the incredible sensations that were raging through her, but she managed it even as Jess came from behind her to bend his head and take suckle at one breast.

Watching him do this, watching the heightened color in her own face, gave a new intensity to the searing needs that were like storm winds within Libby. Her eyes were fires of ink-blue, and there was a proud, even regal lift to her chin as she watched herself pleasing the man she loved.

Jess drank deeply of one breast, turned to the other. It was an earthy communion between one man and one woman, each one giving and taking.

Presently Jess's mouth slid down over Libby's slightly damp stomach, and then he was kneeling, no longer visible in the magic mirror. "Don't close your eyes," he repeated, and Libby felt her satiny panties sliding slowly down over her hips, her knees, her ankles.

The wide-eyed sprite in the mirror gasped, and Libby was forced to brace herself with both hands against the mantelpiece, just to keep from falling. Her breathing quickened to a rasp as Jess ran skilled hands over her bare bottom, her thighs, the backs of her knees. He heightened her pleasure by telling her precisely what he meant to do.

And then he did it.

Libby's release was a maelstrom of soft sobs that finally melded together into one lusty cry of pleasure. Jess was right, she thought, in the midst of all this and during the silvery descent that followed: she *was* beautiful.

Standing again, Jess lifted Libby up into his arms. Still feeling like some wanton Gypsy princess, she let her head fall back and gloried in the liberties his mouth took with the breasts that were thrust into easy reach.

Libby was conscious of an otherworldly floating sensation as she and Jess glided downward, together, to the floor.

Rain pattered and danced on the glass ceiling above the bed, a dismal heralding of what promised to be the happiest day of Libby Kincaid's life.

Jess slept beside her, beautifully naked, his breathing deep and even. If he hadn't actually spoken of his love, he had shown it in a dozen ways. So why did the pit of Libby's stomach jiggle, as though something awful was about to happen?

The insistent ringing of the doorbell brought Jess up from his stomach, push-up style, grumbling. His dark hair hopelessly rumpled, his eyes glazed, he stumbled around the bedroom until he found his robe and managed to struggle into it.

Libby laughed at him as he started down the stairs. "So much for being happy in the mornings, Barlowe," she taunted.

His answer was a terse word that Libby couldn't quite make out.

She heard the door open downstairs, heard Senator Barlowe's deep laugh and exuberant greeting. The sounds eased the feeling of dread that had plagued Libby earlier, and she got out of bed and hurried to the bathroom for a shower.

Periodically, as Libby shampooed her hair and washed, she laughed. Having his father arrive unexpectedly from Washington, probably with Ken and Cathy soon to follow, would certainly throw cold water on any plans the groom might have had for prenuptial frolicking.

When Libby went downstairs, her hair blown dry, her makeup in place, she was delighted to see that Cathy was with the senator. They were both, in fact, seated comfortably on the couch, drinking coffee.

"Where's Dad?" Libby asked when hugs and kisses had been exchanged.

Cleave Barlowe, with his elegant, old-fashioned manners, waited for Libby to sit down before returning to his own seat near Cathy. "He'll be here in time for the ceremony," he said. "When we left the ranch, he was heading out with that bear patrol of his."

Libby frowned and fussed with her crisp pink sundress, feeling uneasy again. Jess had gone upstairs, and she could hear the water running in the shower. "Bear patrol?"

"We've lost a few calves to a rogue grizzly," Cleave said easily, as though such a thing were an everyday occurrence. "Ken and half a dozen of his best men have been tracking him, but they haven't had any luck so far."

Cathy, sitting at her father-in-law's elbow, seemed to sense her cousin's apprehension and signed that she wanted a better look at Libby's ring.

The tactic worked, but as Libby offered her hand, she at last looked into Cathy's face and saw the ravages of her marital problems. There were dark smudges under the green eyes, and a hollow ache pulsed inside them.

Libby reprimanded herself for being so caught up in her own tumultuous romance with Jess as to forget that during his visit the day before, Stacey had said he'd left Cathy. It shamed Libby that she hadn't thought more about her cousin, made it a point to find out how she was.

"Are you all right?" she signed, knowing that Cathy was always more comfortable with this form of communication than with lip reading.

Cathy's responding smile was real, if wan. She nodded and with mischievous interest assessed the ring Jess had had specially designed.

Cleave demanded a look at this piece of jewelry that was causing such an "all-fired" stir and laughed with appreciation when he saw his own brand in the setting.

Cathy lifted her hands. "I want to see your dress."

After Jess had come downstairs, dressed in jeans and the scandalous T-shirt Libby had given him, the two women went up to look at the new burgundy dress.

The haunted look was back in Cathy's eyes as she approved the garment. "I can hardly believe you're marrying Jess," she said in the halting, hesitant voice she would allow only Libby to hear.

Libby sat down on the rumpled bed beside her cousin. "That should settle any doubts you might have had about my relationship with Stacey," she said gently.

Cathy's pain was a visible spasm in her face. "He's living at the main house now," she confessed. "Libby, Stacey says he wants a divorce."

Libby's anger with Stacey was equal only to her sympathy for his wife. "I'm sure he doesn't mean any of the things he's been saying, Cathy. If only you would talk to him..."

The emerald eyes flashed. "So Stacey could laugh at me, Libby? No, thanks!"

Libby drew a deep breath. "I can't help thinking that this problem stems from a lack of communication and trust," she persisted, careful to face toward her cousin. "Stacey loves you. I know he does."

"How can you be so sure?" whispered Cathy. "How, Libby? Marriages end every day of the week."

"No one knows that better than I do. But some things are a matter of instinct, and mine tells me that Stacey is doing this to make you notice him, Cathy. And maybe because you won't risk having a baby."

"Having a baby would be pretty stupid, wouldn't it? Even if I wanted to take the risk, as you call it. After all, my husband moved out of our house!"

"I'm not saying that you should rush back to the ranch and get yourself pregnant, Cathy. But couldn't you just talk to Stacey, the way you talk to me?"

"I told you—I'd be embarrassed!"

"Embarrassed! You are married to the man, Cathy— you share his bed! How can you be embarrassed to let him hear your voice?"

Cathy knotted her fingers together in her lap and lowered her head. From downstairs Libby could hear Jess and the senator talking quietly about the vote Cleave had cast before coming back to Montana for the wedding.

Finally Cathy looked up again. "I couldn't talk to anyone but you, Libby. I don't even talk to Jess or Ken."

"That's your own fault," Libby said, still angry. "Have you kept your silence all this time—all during the years I've been away?"

Cathy shook her head. "I ride up into the foothills sometimes and talk to the wind and the trees, for practice. Do you think that's silly?"

"No, and stop being so afraid that someone is going to think you're silly, dammit! So what if they do? What do you suppose people thought about me when I stayed with a man who had girlfriends?"

Cathy's mouth fell open. "Girlfriends?"

"Yes," snapped Libby, stung by the memory. "And don't tell my dad. He'd faint."

"I doubt it," replied Cathy. "But it must have hurt terribly. I'm so sorry, Libby."

"And I'm sorry if I was harsh with you," Libby answered. "I just want you to be happy, Cathy—that's all. Will you promise me that you'll talk to Stacey? Please?"

"I… I'll try."

Libby hugged her cousin. "That's good enough for me."

There was again a flash of delight in Cathy's eyes, indicating an imminent change of subject. "Is that car outside yours?"

Libby's answer was a nod. "Isn't it beautiful?"

"Will you take me for a ride in it? When the wedding is over and you're home on the ranch?"

"You know I will. We'll be the terror of the back roads—legends in our own time!"

Cathy laughed. "Legends? We'll be memories if we aren't careful."

Libby rose from her seat on the bed, taking up the pretty burgundy dress, slipping it carefully onto a hanger, hanging it in the back of the closet.

When that was done, the two women went downstairs together. By this time Jess and his father were embroiled in one of their famous political arguments.

Feeling uneasy again, Libby went to the telephone with as much nonchalance as she could and dialed Ken's number. There was no answer, of course—she had been

almost certain that there wouldn't be—but the effort itself comforted her a little.

"Try the main house," Jess suggested softly from
just behind her.

Libby glanced back at him, touched by his perception. Consoled by it. "How is it," she teased in a whisper, "that you managed to look elegant in jeans and a
T-shirt that says 'If it feels good, do it'?"

Jess laughed and went back to his father and Cathy.

Libby called the main house and got a somewhat flus-
tered Marion Bradshaw. "Hello!" barked the woman.

"Mrs. Bradshaw, this is Libby. Have you seen my
father this morning?"

There was a long sigh, as though the woman was
relieved to learn that the caller was not someone else.
"No, dear, I haven't. He and the crew are out looking for
that darned bear. Don't you worry, though—Ken told
me he'd be in town for your wedding in plenty of time."

Libby knew that her father's word was good. If he
said he'd be there, he would, come hell or high water.
Still, something in Mrs. Bradshaw's manner was disturbing. "Is something the matter, Marion?"

Another sigh, this one full of chagrin. "Libby, one of
the maids told me that a Mr. Aaron Strand called here,
asking where you could be reached. Without so much
as a by-your-leave, that woman came right out and told
him you were in Kalispell and gave him the number.
I'm so sorry."

So that was how Aaron had known where to call.
Libby sighed. "It's all right, Marion—it wasn't your
fault."

"I feel responsible all the same," said the woman
firmly, "but I'll kick myself on my own time. I just

wanted to let you know what happened. Did Miss Cathy and the senator get there all right?"

Libby smiled. "Yes, they're here. Any messages?"

"No, but I'd like a word with Jess, if it's all right."

Libby turned and gestured to the man in question. He came to the phone, took the receiver, greeted Marion Bradshaw warmly. Their conversation was a brief one, and when Jess hung up, he was laughing.

"What's so funny?" the senator wanted to know

Jess slid an arm around Libby and gave her a quick squeeze. "Dare I say it in front of the creator of Liberated Lizzie, cartoon cave-woman? I just got Marion's blessing—she says I branded the right heifer."

Chapter 11

Libby stood at a window overlooking the courthouse parking lot, peering through the gray drizzle, anxiously scanning each vehicle that pulled in.

"He'll be here," Cathy assured her, joining Libby at the rain-sheeted window.

Libby sighed. She knew that Ken would come if he possibly could, but the rain would make the roads hazardous, and there was the matter of that rogue grizzly bear. "I hope so," she said.

Cathy stood back a little to admire the flowing silken lines of Libby's dress. "You look wonderful. Here—let's see if the flowers match."

"Flowers?" Libby hadn't thought about flowers, hadn't thought about much at all, beyond contemplating the wondrous event about to take place. Her reason said that it was insanity to marry again, especially to marry Jess Barlowe, but her heart sang a very different song.

Cathy beamed and indicated a cardboard box sitting on a nearby table.

At last Libby left her post at the window, bemused. "But I didn't…"

Cathy was already removing a cellophane-wrapped corsage, several boutonnieres, an enormous bouquet made up of burgundy rosebuds, baby's breath, and white carnations. "This is yours, of course."

Libby reached out for her bridal bouquet, pleased and very surprised. "Did you order these, Cathy?"

"No," replied Cathy, "but I did nudge Jess in the florist's direction, after seeing what color your dress was."

Moved that such a detail had been taken into consideration, Libby hugged her cousin. "Thank you."

"Thank Jess. He's the one that browbeat the florist into filling a last-minute order." Cathy found a corsage labeled with her name. "Pin this on, will you?"

Libby happily complied. There were boutonnieres for Jess and the senator and Ken, too, and she turned this last one wistfully in her hands. It was almost time for the ceremony to begin—where was her father?

A light tap at the door made Libby's heart do a jittery flip. "Yes?"

"It's me," Jess said in a low, teasing voice. "Are the flowers in there?"

Cathy gathered up the boutonnieres, white carnations wrapped in clear, crackly paper, made her way to the door. Opening it just far enough to reach through, she held out the requested flowers.

Jess chuckled but made no move to step past the barrier and see his bride before the designated moment. "Five minutes, Libby," he said, and then she heard him walking away, his heels clicking on the marble court-house floor.

Libby went back to the window, spotted a familiar truck racing into the parking lot, lurching to a stop. Two men in rain slickers got out and hurried toward the building.

Ken had arrived, and at last Libby was prepared to join Jess in Judge Henderson's office down the hall. She saw that august room through a haze of happiness, no-ticing a desk, a flag, a portrait of George Washington. In front of the rain-beaded windows, with their heavy, threadbare velvet draperies, stood Jess and his father.

Everyone seemed to move in slow motion. The judge took his place, and Jess, looking quietly magnificent in a tailored three-piece suit of dark blue, took his. His eyes caressed Libby, even from that distance, and some-how drew her toward him. At his side stood the senator, clearly tired from his unexpected cross-country trip, but proud and pleased, too.

Like a person strolling through a sweet dream, Libby let Jess draw her to him. At her side was Cathy, stand-ing up very straight, her green eyes glistening with joyous tears.

Libby's sense of her father's presence was so strong that she did not need to look back and confirm it with her eyes. She tucked her arm through Jess's and the ceremony began.

When all the familiar words had been said, Jess bent toward Libby and kissed her tenderly. The haze lifted and the bride and groom turned, arm in arm, to face their few but much-loved guests.

Instead of congratulations, they met the pain-filled

stares of two cowboys dressed in muddy jeans, sodden shirts and raincoats.

Suddenly frantic, Libby scanned the small chamber for her father's face. She'd been so sure that he was there; he had seemed near enough to touch.

"Where—" she began, but her question was broken off because Jess left her side to stride toward the emissaries from the ranch, the senator close behind him.

"The bear..." said one of them in answer to Jess's clipped question. "We had him cornered and—" the cowboy's Adam's apple moved up and down in his throat "—and he was a mean one, Mr. Barlowe. Meaner'n the devil's kid brother."

Libby knew what was coming and the worn courthouse carpeting seemed to buckle and shift beneath her high-heeled burgundy sandals. Had it not been for Cathy, who gripped her elbow and maneuvered her into a nearby chair, she would have fallen.

"Just tell us what happened!" Jess rasped.

"The bear worked Ken over pretty good," the second cowboy confessed.

Libby gave a strangled cry and felt Cathy's arm slide around her shoulders.

"Is Ken dead?" demanded Cleave Barlowe, and as far as Libby was concerned, the whole universe hinged on the answer to that question.

"No, sir—we got Mr. Kincaid to the hospital fast as we could. But...but."

"But what?" hissed Jess.

"The bear got away, Mr. Barlowe."

Jess came slowly toward Libby, or at least it seemed so to her. As he crouched before her chair and took her chilled hands into his, his words were gentle. "Are you all right?"

Libby was too frightened and sick to speak, but she did manage a nod. Jess helped her to her feet, supported her as they left the room.

She was conscious of the cowboys, behind her, babbling an account of the incident with the bear to Senator Barlowe, of Cathy's quiet sobs, of Jess's steel arm around her waist. The trip to the hospital, made in the senator's limousine, seemed hellishly long.

At the hospital's admissions desk, they were told by a harried, soft-voiced nurse that there was no news yet and directed to the nearest waiting room.

Stacey was there, and Cathy ran to him. He embraced her without hesitation, crooning to her, smoothing her hair with one hand.

"Ken?" barked the senator, his eyes anxious on his elder son's pale face.

"He's in surgery," replied Stacey. And though he still held Cathy, his gaze shifted, full of pain and disbelief, to Libby. "It's bad," he said.

Libby shuddered, more afraid than she'd ever been in her life, her arms and legs useless. Jess was holding her up—Jess and some instinct that had lain dormant within her since Jonathan's death. "Were you there when it happened, Stacey?" she asked dully.

Stacey was rocking Cathy gently in his arms, his chin propped in her hair. "Yes," he replied.

Suddenly rage surged through Libby—a senseless, shrieking tornado of rage. "You had guns!" she screamed. "I know you had guns! Why didn't you stop the bear? Why didn't you kill it?"

Jess's arm tightened around her. "Libby—"

Stacey broke in calmly, his voice full of compassion even in the face of Libby's verbal attack. "There was too much chance that Ken would be hit," he answered. "We hollered and fired shots in the air and that finally scared the grizzly off." There was a hollow look in Stacey's eyes as they moved to his father's face and then Jess's, looking for the same understanding he had just given to Libby.

"What about the bear?" the senator wanted to know.

Stacey averted his eyes for a moment. "He got away," he breathed, confirming what one of the cowboys had said earlier at the courthouse. "Jenkins got him in the hind flank, but he got away. Ran like a racehorse, that son of a bitch. Anyway, we were more concerned with Ken at the moment."

The senator nodded, but Jess tensed beside Libby, his gaze fierce. "You sent men after the grizzly, didn't you?"

Stacey looked pained and his hold on Cathy tightened as her sobs ebbed to terrified little sniffles. "I... I didn't think—"

"You didn't think?" growled Jess. "Goddammit, Stacey, now we've got a wounded bear on the loose—"

The senator interceded. "I'll call the ranch and make sure the grizzly is tracked down," he said reasonably. "Stacey got Ken to the hospital, Jess, and that was the most important thing."

An uncomfortable silence settled over the waiting room then. The senator went to the window to stand, hands clasped behind his back, looking out. The cowboys went back to the ranch, and Stacey and Jess maneuvered their stricken wives into chairs.

The sounds and smells peculiar to a hospital were a

torment to Libby, who had endured the worst minutes, hours, days, and weeks of her life in just such a place. She had lost Jonathan in an institution like this one— would she lose Ken, too?

"I can't stand it," she whispered, breaking the awful silence.

Jess took her chin in his hand, his eyes locking with hers, sharing badly needed strength. "Whatever happens, Libby, we'll deal with it together."

Libby shivered violently, looked at Jess's tailored suit, her own dress, the formal garb of Cathy and the senator. Only Stacey, in his muddy jeans, boots, shirt and sodden denim jacket, seemed dressed for the horrible occasion. The rest of the party was at ludicrous variance with the situation.

My father may be dying, she thought in quiet hysteria, *and we're wearing flowers.* The smell of her bouquet suddenly sickened Libby, bringing back memories of Jonathan's funeral, and she flung it away. It slid under a couch upholstered in green plastic and cowered there against the wall.

Jess's grip tightened on her hand, but no one made a comment.

Presently the senator wandered out, returning some minutes later with cups of vending-machine coffee balanced on a small tray. "Ken is my best friend," he announced in befuddled tones to the group in general.

The words brought a startling cry of grief from Cathy, who had been huddled in her chair until that moment, behind a curtain of tangled, rain-dampened hair. "I won't let him die!" she shrieked, to the open-mouthed amazement of everyone except Libby.

Stacey, draped over the arm and back of Cathy's

chair, stared down at her, his throat working. "Cathy?" he choked out.

Because Cathy was not looking at him, could not see her name on his lips, she did not answer. Her small hands flew to cover her face and she wept for the man who had loved her as his own child, raised her as his own, been her strength as well as Libby's.

"She can't hear you," Libby said woodenly.

"But she talked!" gasped Jess.

Libby lifted one shoulder in a broken shrug. "Cathy has been talking for years. To me, anyway."

"Good God," breathed the senator, his gaze sweeping over his shattered daughter-in-law. "Why didn't she speak to any of us?"

Libby was sorry for Stacey, reading the pain in his face, the shock. Of course, it was a blow to him to realize that his own wife had kept such a secret for so long.

"Cathy was afraid," Libby explained quietly. "She is very self-conscious about the way her voice sounds to hearing people."

"That's ridiculous!" barked Stacey, looking angry now, paler than before. He bolted away from Cathy's chair to stand at the windows, his back to the room. "For God's sake, I'm her husband!"

"Some of us had a few doubts about that," remarked Jess in an acid undertone.

Stacey whirled, full of fury, but the senator stepped between his two sons before the situation could get out of hand. "This is no time for arguments," he said evenly but firmly. "Libby and Cathy don't need it, and neither do I."

Both brothers receded, Stacey lowering his head a little, Jess averting a gaze that was still bright with anger. Libby watched a muscle leap in her husband's jaw and stifled a crazy urge to touch it with her finger, to still it.

"Was Dad conscious when you brought him here?" she asked of Stacey in a voice too calm and rational to be her own.

Stacey nodded, remembering. "He said that bear was almost as tough as a Mexican he fought once, down in Juarez."

The tears Libby had not been able to cry before suddenly came to the surface, and Jess held her until they passed. "Ken is strong," he reminded her. "Have faith in him."

Libby tried to believe the best, but the fact remained that Ken Kincaid was a mortal man, strong or not. And he'd been mauled viciously by a bear. Even if he survived, he might be crippled.

It seemed that Jess was reading her mind, as he so often did. His hand came up to stroke away her tears, smooth her hair back from her face. "Don't borrow trouble," he said gently. "We've got enough now."

Trying to follow this advice, Libby deliberately reviewed pleasant memories: Ken cursing a tangle of Christmas-tree lights; Ken sitting proudly in the audience while Cathy and Libby accepted their high school diplomas; Ken trying, and somehow managing, to be both mother and father.

More than two hours went by before a doctor appeared in the waiting room doorway, still wearing a surgical cap, his mask hanging from his neck. "Are you people here for Ken Kincaid?" he asked, and the simple words had the electrifying effect of a cattle prod on everyone there.

Both Libby and Cathy stiffened in their chairs, unable to speak. It was Jess who answered the doctor's question.

"Mr. Kincaid was severely injured," the surgeon said, "but we think he'll be all right, if he rests."

Libby was all but convulsed by relief. "I'm his daughter," she managed to say finally. "Do you think I could see him, just for a few minutes?"

The middle-aged physician smiled reluctantly. "He'll be in Recovery for some time," he said. "Perhaps it would be better if you visited your father tomorrow."

Libby was steadfast. It didn't matter that Ken was still under anesthetic; if she could touch his hand or speak to him, he would know that she was near. Another vigil had taught her the value of that. "I must see him," she insisted.

"She won't leave you alone until you say yes," Jess put in, his arm tight around Libby's shoulders.

Before the doctor could answer, Cathy was gripping Libby's hands, searching her cousin's face. "Libby?" she pleaded desperately. "Libby?"

It was clear that Cathy hadn't discerned the verdict on Ken's condition, and Libby's heart ached for her cousin as she freed her hands, quickly motioned the reassurances needed.

When that was done, Libby turned back to the doctor. "My cousin will want to see my father, too."

"Now, just a minute…"

Stubbornly Libby lifted her chin.

Three hours later, Ken Kincaid was moved from the recovery room to a bed in the intensive-care unit. As soon as he had been settled there, Cathy and Libby were allowed into his room.

Ken was unconscious, and there were tubes going into his nostrils, an IV needle in one of his hands. His chest and right shoulder were heavily bandaged, and there were stitches running from his right temple to his neck in a crooked, gruesome line.

"Oh, God," whimpered Cathy.

Libby caught her cousin's arm firmly in her hand and faced her. "Don't you *dare* fall apart in here, Cathy Barlowe," she ordered. "He would sense how upset you are, and that would be bad for him."

Cathy trembled, but she squared her shoulders, drew a deep breath and then nodded. "We'll be strong," she said.

Libby went to the bedside, barely able to reach her father for all the equipment that was monitoring and sustaining him. "I hear you beat up on a bear," she whispered.

There was no sign that Ken had heard her, of course, but Libby knew that humor reached this man as nothing else could, and she went on talking, berating him softly for cruelty to animals, informing him that the next time he wanted to waltz, he ought to choose a partner that didn't have fur.

Before an insistent nurse came to collect Ken's visitors, both Libby and Cathy planted tender kisses on his forehead.

Stacey, Jess and Cleave were waiting anxiously when they reached the waiting room again.

"He's going to live," Libby said, and then the room danced and her knees buckled and everything went dark.

She awakened to find herself on a table in one of the hospital examining rooms, Jess holding her hand.

"Thanks for scaring the hell out of me," he said softly, a relieved grin tilting one corner of his mouth. "I needed that."

"Sorry," Libby managed, touching the wilting boutonniere that was still pinned to the lapel of his suit jacket. "Some wedding day, huh, handsome?"

"That's the wild west for you. We like excitement out here. How do you feel, princess?"

Libby tried to sit up, but the room began to swirl, so she fell back down. "I'm okay," she insisted. "Or I will be in a few minutes. How is Cathy?"

Jess smiled, kissed her forehead. "Cathy reacted a little differently to the good news than you did."

Libby frowned, still worried. "How do you mean?"

"After she'd been assured that you had fainted and not dropped dead of a coronary, she lit into Stacey like a whirlwind. It seems that my timid little sister-in-law is through being mute—once and for all."

Libby's eyes rounded. "You mean she was yelling at him?"

"Was she ever. When they left, he was yelling back."

Despite everything, Libby smiled. "In this case, I think a good loud argument might be just what the doctor ordered."

"I agree. But the condo will probably be a war zone by the time we get there."

Libby remembered that this was her wedding night, and with a little help from Jess, managed to sit up. "The condo? They're staying there?"

"Yes. The couch makes out into a bed, and Cathy wants to be near the hospital."

Libby reached out, touched Jess's strong face. "I'm sorry," she said.

"About what?"

"About everything. Especially about tonight."

Jess's green eyes laughed at her, gentle, bright with understanding. "Don't worry about tonight, princess. There will be plenty of other nights."

"But—"

He stilled her protests with an index finger. "You are in no condition to consummate a marriage, Mrs. Barlowe. You need to sleep. So let's go home and get you tucked into bed—with a little luck, Stacey and Cathy won't keep us awake all night while they throw pots and pans at each other."

Jess's remark turned out to be remarkably apt, for when they reached the condo, Stacey and his wife were bellowing at each other and the floor was littered with sofa pillows and bric-a-brac.

"Don't mind us," Jess said with a companionable smile as he ushered his exhausted bride across the war-torn living room. "We're just mild-mannered honeymooners, passing through."

Jess and Libby might have been invisible, for all the notice they got.

"Maybe we should have stayed in a motel," Libby yawned as she snuggled into Jess's strong shoulder, minutes later, in the loft bed.

Something shattered downstairs, and Jess laughed. "And miss this? No chance."

Cathy and Stacey were yelling again, and Libby winced. "You don't think they'll hurt each other, do you?"

"They'll be all right, princess. Rest."

Too tired to discuss the matter further, Libby sighed and fell asleep, lulled by Jess's nearness and the soft sound of rain on the glass roof overhead. She awakened once, in the depths of the night, and heard the sounds of another kind of passion from the darkened living room. A smile curved her lips as she closed her eyes.

Cathy was blushing as she tried to neaten up the demolished living room and avoid Libby's gaze at the same time. Stacey, dead to the world, was sprawled out on the sofa bed, a silly smile shaping his mouth.

Libby made her way to the telephone in silence, called the hospital for a report on her father. He was still unconscious, the nurse on duty told her, but his vital signs were strong and stable.

Cathy was waiting, wide-eyed, when Libby turned away from the telephone.

Gently Libby repeated what the nurse had told her. After that, the two women went into the kitchen and began preparing a quick breakfast.

"I'm sorry about last night," Cathy said.

Standing at the stove, spatula in hand, Libby waited for her cousin to look at her and then asked, "Did you settle anything?"

Cathy's cheeks were a glorious shade of hot pink. "You heard!" she moaned.

Libby had been referring to the fight, not the lovemaking that had obviously followed, but there was no way she could clarify this without embarrassing her cousin further. She bit her lower lip and concentrated on the eggs she was scrambling.

"It was crazy," Cathy blurted, remembering. "I was *yelling* at Stacey! I wanted to hurt him, Libby—I really wanted to hurt him!"

Libby was putting slices of bread into the toaster and

she offered no comment, knowing that Cathy needed to talk.

"I even threw things at him," confessed Cathy, taking orange juice from the refrigerator and putting it in the middle of the table. "I can't believe I acted like that, especially when Ken had just been hurt so badly."

Libby met her cousin's gaze and smiled. "I don't see what one thing has to do with the other, Cathy. You were angry with your husband—justifiably so, I'd say—and you couldn't hold it in any longer."

"I wasn't even worried about the way I sounded," Cathy reflected, shaking her head. "I suppose what happened to Ken triggered something inside me—I don't know."

"The important thing is that you stood up for yourself," Libby said, scraping the scrambled eggs out of the pan and onto a platter. "I was proud of you, Cathy."

"Proud? I acted like a fool!"

"You acted like an angry woman. How about calling those lazy husbands of ours to breakfast while I butter the toast?"

Cathy hesitated, wrestling with her old fear of being ridiculed, and then squared her shoulders and left the kitchen to do Libby's bidding.

Tears filled Libby's eyes at the sound of her cousin's voice. However ordinary the task was, it was a big step forward for Cathy.

The men came to the table, Stacey wearing only jeans and looking sheepish, Jess clad in slacks and a neatly pressed shirt, his green eyes full of mischief.

"Any word about Ken?" he asked.

Libby told him what the report had been and loved

him the more for the relief in his face. He nodded and then executed a theatrical yawn.

Cathy blushed and looked down at her plate, while Stacey glared at his brother. "Didn't you sleep well, Jess?" he drawled.

Jess rolled his eyes.

Stacey looked like an angry little boy; Libby had forgotten how he hated to be teased. "I'll fight with my wife if I want to!" he snapped.

Both Libby and Jess laughed.

"Fight?" gibed Jess good-naturedly. "Was that what you two were doing? Fighting?"

"*Somebody* had to celebrate your wedding night," Stacey retorted, but then he gave in and laughed, too.

When the meal was over, Cathy and Libby left the dirty dishes to their husbands and went off to get ready for the day.

They were allowed only a brief visit with Ken, and even though his doctor assured them that he was steadily gaining ground, they were both disheartened as they returned to the waiting room.

Senator Barlowe was there, with Jess and Stacey, looking as wan and worried as either of his daughters-in-law. Unaware of their approach, he was saying, "We've got every available man tracking that bear, plus hands from the Three Star and the Rocking C. All we've found so far is paw-prints and dead calves."

Libby was brought up short, not by the mention of the bear but by the look on Jess's face. He muttered something she couldn't hear.

Stacey sliced an ironic look in his brother's direction. "I suppose you think you can find that son of Satan when the hands from three of the biggest ranches in the state can't turn up a trace?"

"I know I can," Jess answered coldly.

"Dammit, we scoured the foothills, the ranges…"

Jess's voice was low, thick with contempt. "And when you had the chance to bring the bastard down, you let him trot away instead—wounded."

"What was I supposed to do? Ken was bleeding to death!"

"Somebody should have gone after the bear," Jess insisted relentlessly. "There were more than enough people around to see that Ken got to the hospital."

Stacey swore.

"Were you scared?" Jess taunted. "Did the big bad bear scare away our steak-house cowboy?"

At this, Stacey lunged toward Jess and Jess bolted out of his chair, clearly spoiling for a fight.

Again, as he had before, the senator averted disaster. "Stop it!" he hissed. "If you two have to brawl, kindly do it somewhere else!"

"You can bank on that," Jess said bitterly, his green gaze moving over Stacey and then dismissing him.

"What's gotten into the two of you?" Senator Barlowe rasped in quiet frustration. "This is a hospital! And have you forgotten that you're brothers?"

Libby cleared her throat discreetly, to let the men know that she and Cathy had returned. She was disturbed by the barely controlled hostility between Jess and his brother, but with Ken in the condition that he was, she had no inclination to pursue the issue.

It was later, in the Land Rover, when she and Jess were alone, that Libby voiced a subject that had been bothering her. "You plan to go looking for that bear, don't you?"

Jess appeared to be concentrating on the traffic, but a muscle in his cheek twitched. "Yes."

"You're going back to the ranch and track him down," Libby went on woodenly.

"That's right."

She sank back against the seat and closed her eyes. "Let the others do it."

There was a short, ominous silence. "No way."

Libby swallowed the sickness and fear that roiled in her throat. God in heaven, wasn't it enough that she'd nearly lost her father to that vicious beast? Did she have to risk losing her husband, too? "Why?" she whispered miserably. "Why do you want to do this?"

"It's my job," he answered flatly, and Libby knew that there was no point in trying to dissuade him.

She squeezed her eyes even more tightly shut, but the tears escaped anyway. When they reached the condo again, Stacey's car and Cleave's pulling in behind them, Jess turned to her, brushed the evidence of her fear from her cheeks with gentle thumbs and kissed her.

"I promise not to get killed," he said softly.

Libby stiffened in his arms, furious and full of terror. "That's comforting!"

He kissed the tip of her nose. "You can handle this alone, can't you? Going to the hospital, I mean?"

Libby bit her lower lip. Here was her chance. She could say that she needed Jess now, she could keep him from hunting that bear. She did need him, especially now, but in the end, she couldn't use weakness to hold him close. "I can handle it."

An hour later, when Stacey and the senator left for

the ranch, Jess went with them. Libby was now keeping two vigils instead of one.

Understanding Libby's feelings but unable to help, Cathy built a fire in the fireplace, brewed cocoa, and tried to interest her cousin in a closed-caption movie on television.

Libby watched for a while, then got out her sketchbook and began to draw with furious, angry strokes: Jess on horseback, a rifle in the scabbard of his saddle; a full-grown grizzly, towering on its hind legs, ominous muscles rolling beneath its hide, teeth bared. Try though she did, Libby could not bring herself to put Jess and that bear in the same picture, either mentally or on paper.

That evening, when Libby and Cathy went to the hospital, Ken was awake. He managed a weak smile as they came to his bedside to bestow tearful kisses.

"Sorry about missin' the wedding," he said, and for all his obvious pain, there was mirth in his blue eyes.

Libby dashed away the mist from her own eyes and smiled a shaky smile, shrugging. "You've seen one, cowboy, you've seen them all."

Ken laughed and the sound was beautiful.

Chapter 12

Having assured herself that Ken was indeed recovering, Cathy slipped out to allow Libby a few minutes alone with her father.

"Thanks for scaring me half to death," she said.

Ken tried to shrug, winced instead. "You must have known I was too mean to go under," he answered. "Libby, did they get the bear?"

Libby stiffened. The bear, the bear—she was so damned sick of hearing about the bear! "No," she said after several moments, averting her eyes.

Ken sighed. He was pale and obviously tired. "Jess went after him, didn't he?"

Libby fought back tears of fear. Was Jess face to face with that creature even now? Was he suffering injuries like Ken's, or even worse? "Yes," she admitted.

"Jess will be all right, Libby."

"Like you were?" Libby retorted sharply, without thinking.

Ken studied her for a moment, managed a partial grin. "He's younger than I am. Tougher. No grizzly in his right mind would tangle with him."

"But this grizzly isn't in his right mind, is he?" Libby whispered, numb. "He's wounded, Dad."

"All the more reason to find him," Ken answered firmly. "That bear was dangerous before, Libby. He's deadly now."

Libby shuddered. "You'd think the beast would just crawl off and die somewhere."

"That would be real handy, but he won't do it, Lib. Grizzlies have nasty dispositions as it is—their eyesight is poor and their teeth hurt all the time. When they're wounded, they can rampage for days before they finally give out."

"The Barlowes can afford to lose a few cows!"

"Yes, but they can't afford to lose people, Lib, and that's what'll happen if that animal isn't found."

There was no arguing that; Ken was proof of how dangerous a bear could be. "The men from the Three Star and the Rocking C are helping with the hunt, anyway," Libby said, taking little if any consolation from the knowledge.

"That's good," Ken said, closing his eyes.

Libby bent, kissed his forehead and left the room.

Cathy was pacing the hallway, her lower lip caught in her teeth, her eyes wide. Libby chastised herself for not realizing that Stacey was probably hunting the bear too, and that her cousin was as worried as she was.

When Libby suggested a trip to the Circle Bar B, Cathy agreed immediately.

During the long drive, Libby made excuses to herself. She wasn't going just to check on Jess—she absolutely was not. She needed her drawing board, her pens and inks, jeans and blouses.

The fact that she could have bought any or all of these items in Kalispell was carefully ignored.

By the time Libby and Cathy drew the Corvette to a stop in the wide driveway of the main ranch house, the sun was starting to go down. There must have been fifty horsemen converging on the stables, all of them looking tired and discouraged.

Libby's heart wedged itself into her throat when she spotted Jess. He was dismounting, wrenching a high-powered rifle from the scabbard on his saddle.

She literally ran to him, but then she stopped short, her shoes encased in the thick, gooey mud Montanans call gumbo, her vocal cords no more mobile than her feet.

"Ken?" he asked in a hoarse whisper.

Libby was quick to reassure him. "Dad's doing very well."

"Then what are you doing here?"

Libby smiled, pried one of her feet out of the mud, only to have it succumb again when she set it down. "I had to see if you were all right," she admitted. "May I say that you look terrible?"

Jess chuckled, rubbed the stubble of beard on his chin, assessed the dirty clothes he wore in one downward glance. "You should have stayed in town."

Libby lifted her chin. "I'll go back in the morning," she said, daring him to argue.

Jess surrendered his horse to one of the ranch hands,

but the rifle swung at his side as he started toward the big, well-lighted house. Libby slogged along at his side.

"Is that gun loaded?" she demanded.

"No," he replied. "Any more questions?"

"Yes. Did you see the bear?"

They had reached the spacious screened-in porch, where Mrs. Bradshaw had prudently laid out newspapers to accommodate dozens of mud-caked boots.

"No," Jess rasped, lifting his eyes to some distant thing that Libby could not see. "That sucker might as well be invisible."

Libby watched as Jess kicked off his boots, flung his sodden denim jacket aside, dispensed with his hat. "Maybe he's dead, Jess," she blurted out hopefully, resorting to the optimism her father had tacitly warned her against. "Maybe he collapsed somewhere—"

"Wrong," Jess bit out. "We found more cattle."

"Calves?"

"A bull and two heifers," Jess answered. "And the hell of it is, he didn't even kill them to eat. He just ripped them apart."

Libby shivered. "He must be enormous!"

"The men that were with Stacey and Ken said he stood over eight feet," Jess replied, and his green eyes moved wearily over Libby's face. "I don't suppose I need to say this, but I will. I don't like having you here, not now. For God's sake, don't go wandering off by yourself—not even to walk down to the mailboxes. The same goes for Cathy."

It seemed ludicrous that one beast could restrict the normal activities of human beings—in fact, the bear didn't seem real to Libby, even after what had happened to Ken. Instead, it was as though Jess was telling one of the delicious, scary stories he'd loved to terrify Libby with when they were children.

"That means, little one," he went on sternly, "that you don't go out to the barn and you don't go over to Ken's to sit and moon by that pond. Am I making myself clear?"

"Too clear," snapped Libby, following him as he carried the rifle through the kitchen, down a long hallway and into the massive billiard room where the gun cabinets were.

Jess locked the weapon away and turned to his wife. "I'm a little bit glad you're here," he confessed with a weary grin.

"Even tough cowboys need a little spoiling now and then," she replied, "so hie thyself to an upstairs bathroom, husband of mine, and get yourself a shower. I'll bring dinner to your room."

"And how do you know where my room is, Mrs. Barlowe?"

Libby colored a little. "I used to help Marion Bradshaw with the cleaning sometimes, remember?"

"I remember. I used to watch you bending over to tuck in sheets and smooth pillows and think what a great rear end you had."

She arched one eyebrow. "Had?"

Jess caught her bottom in strong hands, pressed her close to him. "Have," he clarified.

"Go take your shower!" Libby huffed, suddenly conscious of all the cowboys that would be gathering in the house for supper that night.

"Join me?" drawled Jess, persistent to the end.

"Absolutely not. You're exhausted." Libby broke away, headed toward the kitchen.

"Not *that* exhausted," Jess called after her.

Libby did not respond, but as she went in to prepare a dinner tray for her husband, she was smiling.

Minutes later, entering Jess's boyhood bedroom, she set the tray down on a long table under a line of windows. The door of the adjoining bathroom was open and steam billowed out like the mist in a spooky movie.

Presently Libby heard the shower shut off, the rustling sound of a towel being pulled from a rack. She sat down on the edge of Jess's bed and then bounded up again.

"Libby?"

She went cautiously to the doorway, looked in. Jess was peering into a steamy mirror, trying to shave. "Your dinner is getting cold," she said.

After flinging one devilish look at his wife, Jess grabbed the towel that had been wrapped around his hips and calmly used it to wipe the mirror. "I'll hurry," he replied.

Libby swallowed hard, as stunned by the splendor of his naked, muscle-corded frame as she had been on that first mantelpiece night when they'd made love in the bedroom at Jess's house, the fevered motions of their bodies metered by the raging elements outside.

Jess finished shaving, rinsed his face, turned toward Libby like a proud savage. She could not look away, even though she wanted to. Her eyes were fixed on the rising, swelling shaft of his manhood.

Jess laughed. "I used to fantasize about this."

"What?" Libby croaked, her throat tight.

"Bringing the foreman's pretty daughter up here and having my way with her."

Libby's eyes were, at last, freed, and they shot upward to his face. "Oh, yeah?"

"Yeah."

"I thought you liked Cathy then."

He nodded. "I did. But even before she married Stacey, I thought of her as a sister."

"And what, pray tell, did you think of me as?"

"A hellion. But I wanted to be your lover, all the same. Since I didn't dare, I settled for making your life miserable."

"How very chivalrous of you!"

Jess was walking toward her now, holding her with the scorching assessment of those jade-green eyes even before his hands touched her. "Teenage boys are not chivalrous, Libby."

Libby closed her eyes as he reached her, drew her close. "Neither are men," she managed to say.

Her blouse was coming untucked from her jeans, rising until she felt the steamy air on her stomach and back. Finally it was bunched under her arms and Jess was tracing a brazen finger over the lines of her scanty lace bra. Beneath the fabric, her nipples sprang into full bloom, coy flowers offering their nectar.

"Y-your dinner," she reminded Jess, floating on the sensations he was stirring within her, too bedazzled even to open her eyes.

The bra slipped down, just on one side, freeing a hard-peaked, eager breast. "Yes," Jess breathed evilly, "my dinner."

"Not that. I mean—"

His mouth closed over the delicate morsel, drawing at it softly. With a pleased and somewhat triumphant chuckle, Jess drew back from the tender treat and Libby's eyes flew open as he began removing her blouse and then her bra, leaving her jeans as they were.

He led her slowly to the bed, but instead of laying her down there, as she had expected, Jess stretched out on his back and positioned her so that she was sitting up, astraddle of his hips.

Gripping her waist, he pulled her forward and lifted, so that her breasts were suspended within easy reach of his mouth.

"The age-old quandary," he breathed.

Libby was dazed. "What qu-quandary?"

"Which one," Jess mused. "How like nature to offer two when a man has only one mouth."

Libby blushed hotly as Jess nuzzled a knotted peak, a peak that ached to nourish him. "Oh, God, Jess," she whispered. "Take it...take it!"

He chuckled, flicked the nipple in question with an impertinent tongue. "I love it when you beg."

Both rage and passion moved inside Libby. "I'm... not...begging!" she gasped, but even as she spoke she was bracing herself with her hands, brushing her breast back and forth across Jess's lips, seeking admission.

"You will," he said, and then he caught the pulsing nipple between careful teeth, raking it to an almost unendurable state of wanting.

"Not on your wretched life!" moaned Libby.

"We'll see," he replied.

The opposite breast was found and thoroughly teased and Libby had to bite her lower lip to keep from giving in and pleading senselessly for the suckling Jess promised but would not give. He played with her, using his tongue and his lips, delighting in the rocking motion of her body and the soft whimpers that came from her throat.

The sweet torment became keener, and Libby both loved and hated Jess for being able to drive her to such lengths. "Make love to me...oh, Jess...make love...to me."

The concession elicited a hoarse growl from Jess, and Libby found herself spinning down to lie flat on the bed. Her remaining clothes were soon stripped away, her legs were parted.

Libby gasped and arched her back as he entered her in one ferocious, needing thrust. After gaining this warm and hidden place, Jess paused, his hard frame shuddering with restraint.

As bedazzled as she was, Libby saw her chance to set the pace, to take command, and she took it. Acting on an age-old instinct, she wrapped her legs around his hips in a fierce claiming and muttered, "Give me all of you, Jess—all of you."

He groaned in lusty surrender and plunged deep within her, seeking solace in the velvety heat of her womanhood. They were locked together for several glittering moments, each afraid to move. Soon enough, however, their bodies demanded more and began a desperate, swift rhythm.

Straining together, both moaning in fevered need, Libby and Jess reached their shattering pinnacle at the same moment, crying out as their two souls flared as one golden fire.

Twice after Jess lay still upon her, his broad back moist beneath her hands, Libby convulsed softly, whimpering.

"Some people are really greedy," he teased when,

at last, her body had ceased its spasmodic clenching and unclenching.

Libby stretched, sated, cosseted in delicious appeasement. "More," she purred.

"What did I tell you?" Jess sighed. "The lady is greedy."

"Very."

He rolled, still joined with Libby, bringing her with him so that she once again sat astraddle of him. They talked, in hushed and gentle voices, of very ordinary things.

After some minutes had passed, however, Libby began to trace his nipples with feather-light fingertips. "I've always wanted to have my way with the boss's son," she crooned, teasing him as he had teased her earlier.

She bent forward, tasted those hardening nipples, each in turn, with only the merest flick of her tongue. Jess groaned and grew hard within her, by degrees, as she continued to torment him.

"How like nature," she gibed tenderly, "to offer two when a woman has only one mouth."

Jess grasped her hips in inescapable hands and thrust his own upward in a savage demand.

Libby's release came swiftly; it was soft and warm, rather than violent, and its passing left her free to bring Jess to exquisite heights. She set a slow pace for him, delighting in the look in his eyes, the back-and-forth motion of his head on the pillow, the obvious effort it took for him to lie still beneath her.

He pleaded for release, but Libby was impervious, guiding him gently, reveling in the sweet power she held over this man she so completely loved. "I'm going to love you in my own way," she told him. "And in my own time."

His head pressed back into the pillows in magnificent surrender, Jess closed his eyes and moaned. His control was awesome, but soon enough it slipped and he began to move beneath Libby, slowly at first and then quickly. Finally, his hands tangling in her hair, he cried out and his body spasmed as she purposely intensified his pleasure. His triumph seemed endless.

When Jess was still at last, his eyes closed, his body glistening with perspiration, Libby tenderly stroked a lock of hair back from his forehead and whispered, "Some people are really greedy."

Jess chuckled and was asleep before Libby withdrew from him to make her way into the bathroom for a shower of her own.

The dream was very sexy. In it, a blue-gray dawn was swelling at the bedroom windows and Libby's breast was full in Jess's hand, the nipple stroked to a pleading state.

She groaned as she felt his hard length upon her, his manhood seeking to sheathe itself in her warmth. Jess entered her, and his strokes were slow and gentle, evoking an immediate series of tremulous, velvet-smooth responses.

"Good," she sighed, giving herself up to the dream. "So good…"

The easy strokes became demanding thrusts. "Yes," said the dream Jess gruffly. "Good."

"Ooooooh," moaned Libby, as a sudden and piercing release rocked her, thrusting her into wakefulness.

And Jess was there, upon her, his face inches from

her own. She watched in wonder and in love as his features grew taut and his splendid body flexed, more rapidly now. She thrust herself up to receive the fullness of his love.

Libby's hands clasped Jess's taut buttocks as he shuddered and delved deep, his manhood rippling powerfully within her, his rasping moan filling Libby's heart.

Minutes later, a languid, hazy sleep overtook Libby and she rolled over onto her stomach and settled back into her dreams. She stirred only slightly when Jess patted her derriere and left the bed.

Hours later, when she awakened fully, Libby was not entirely certain that she hadn't dreamed the whole gratifying episode. As she got out of bed, though, to take a bath and get dressed, Libby knew that Jess had loved her—the feeling of lush well-being she enjoyed was proof of that.

The pampered sensation was short-lived. When Libby went downstairs to search out a light breakfast, she found Monica Summers sitting in the kitchen, sipping coffee and reading a weekly newsmagazine.

Even though Monica smiled, her dark gray eyes betrayed her malice. "Hello… Mrs. Barlowe."

Libby nodded uneasily and opened the refrigerator to take out an apple and a carton of yogurt. "Good morning," she said.

"I was very sorry to hear about your father," Monica went on, the tone of her voice totally belying her expression. "Is he recovering?"

Libby got a spoon for her yogurt and sat down at the table. "Yes, thank you, he is."

"Will you be staying here with us, or going back to Kalispell?"

There was something annoyingly proprietary in the way Monica said the word "us," as though Libby were somehow invading territory where she didn't belong. She lifted her chin and met the woman's stormy-sky gaze directly. "I'll be going back to Kalispell," she said.

"You must hate leaving Jess."

The pit of Libby's stomach developed an unsettling twitch. She took a forceful bite from her apple and said nothing.

"Of course, I'll be happy to…look after him," sighed Monica, striking a flame to the fuse she had been uncoiling. "It's an old habit, you know."

Libby suppressed an unladylike urge to fly over the table, teeth bared, fists flying. "Sometimes old habits have to be broken," she said, sitting very still, reminding herself that she was a grown woman now, not the foreman's little brat. Furthermore, she was Jess's wife and she didn't have to take this kind of subtle abuse in any case.

Monica arched one perfect eyebrow. "Do they?"

Libby leaned forward. "Oh, yes. You see, Ms. Summers, if you mess with my husband, I'll not only break the habit for you, I'll break a few of your bones for good measure."

Monica paled, muttered something about country girls.

"I am not a girl," Libby pointed out. "I'm a woman, and you'd better remember it."

"Oh, I will," blustered Monica, recovering quickly. "But will Jess? That's the question, isn't it?"

If there was one thing in the world Libby had absolutely no doubts about, at that moment anyway, it was her ability to please her husband in the way Monica was referring to. "I don't see how he could possibly forget," she said, and then she finished her apple and her yogurt, dropped the remnants into the trash, and left the room.

Marion Bradshaw was sweeping away residual dried mud when Libby reached the screened porch, hoping for one glimpse of Jess before she had to go back to Kalispell.

He was nowhere in sight, of course—Libby had not really expected him to be.

"How's Ken getting on?" Marion asked.

Libby smiled. "He's doing very well."

The housekeeper sighed, leaning on her broom. "Thank the good Lord for that. Me and Ken Kincaid run this place, and I sure couldn't manage it alone!"

Libby laughed and asked if Cathy was around.

Sheer delight danced in Mrs. Bradshaw's eyes. "She's where she belongs—upstairs in her husband's bed."

Libby blushed. She had forgotten how much this astute woman knew about the goings-on on the ranch. Did she know, too, why Jess had never gotten around to eating his dinner the night before?

"No shame in loving your man," Mrs. Bradshaw twinkled.

Libby swallowed. "Do you know if Stacey went with the others this morning?"

"He did. You go ahead and wake Miss Cathy right now, if you want to."

Libby was grateful for an excuse to hurry away.

Finding Stacey's room from memory, in just the way she'd found Jess's, she knocked briskly at the closed door, realized the foolishness of that, and turned the knob.

Cathy was curled up like a kitten in the middle of a

bed as mussed and tangled as the one Libby had shared with Jess.

Libby bent to give Cathy's bare shoulder a gentle shake. Her cousin sat up, mumbling, her face lost behind a glistening profusion of tangled hair. "Libby? What...?"

Libby laughed and signed, "I'm going back to town as soon as I pick up some of my things at the other house. Do you want to go with me?"

Cathy's full lips curved into a mischievous smile and she shook her head.

"Things are going well between you and Stacey, then?"

Cathy's hands moved in a scandalously explicit answer.

"I'm shocked!" Libby signed, beaming. And then she gave her cousin a quick kiss on the forehead, promised to call Mrs. Bradshaw if there was any sort of change in Ken's condition, and left the room.

In Jess's room she found paper and a pen, and probably because of the tempestuous night spent in his bed, dared to write, "Jess. I love you. Sorry I couldn't stay for a proper goodbye, but I've got to get back to Dad. Take care and come to me if you can. Smiles and sunshine, Libby."

On the way downstairs, Libby almost lost her courage and ran back to rip up the note. Telling Jess outright that she loved him! What if he laughed? What if he was derisive or, even worse, pitying?

Libby denied herself the cowardice of hiding her feelings any longer. It was time she took responsibility for her own emotions, wasn't it?

The weather was crisp and bright that day, and Libby

hummed as she drove the relatively short distance to her father's house, parked her car behind his truck and went in to get the things she needed.

Fitting extra clothes and her special set of pens and inks into the back of the Corvette proved easy enough, but the drawing board was another matter. She turned it this way and that way and it just wouldn't fit.

Finally Libby took it back inside the house and left it there. She would just have to make do with the kitchen table at the condo for the time being.

Libby was just passing the passenger side of Ken's truck when she heard the sound; it was a sort of shifting rustle, coming from the direction of the lilac hedge on the far side of the yard. There followed a low, ominous grunt.

Instinctively Libby froze, the hair tingling on the nape of her neck. Dear God, it couldn't be... Not here— not when there were men with rifles searching every inch of the ranch....

She turned slowly, and her heart leapt into her throat and then spun back down into the pit of her stomach. The bear stood within ten feet of her, on its hind legs.

The beast growled and lolled its massive head to one side. Its mangy, lusterless hide seemed loose over the rolling muscles beneath, and on its flank was a blood-crusted, seeping wound.

In that moment, it was as though Libby became two people, one hysterically afraid, one calm and in control. Fortunately, it was this second Libby that took command. Slowly, ever so slowly, she eased her hand back behind her, to the door handle, opened it. Just as the bear lunged toward her, making a sound more horrifying than she could ever have imagined, she leapt inside the truck and slammed the door after her.

The raging beast shook the whole vehicle as it flung its great bulk against its side, and Libby allowed herself the luxury of one high-pitched scream before reaching for Ken's CB radio under the dashboard.

Again and again, the furious bear pummeled the side of the truck, while Libby tried frantically to make the CB radio work. She knew that the cowboys would be carrying receivers, in order to communicate with each other, and they were her only hope.

Fingers trembling, Libby finally managed to lift the microphone to her mouth and press the button. Her mind skittered over a series of movies she'd seen, books she'd read. *Mayday,* she thought with triumphant terror. *Mayday!* But the magic word would not come past her tight throat.

Suddenly a giant claw thundered across the windshield, shattering it into a glittering cobweb of cracks. One more blow, just one, and the bear would reach her easily, even though she was now crouching on the floorboard.

At last she found her voice. "Cujo!" she screamed into the radio receiver. "Cujo!" She closed her eyes, gasping, tried to get a hold on herself. *This is not a Stephen King movie,* she reminded herself. *This is reality. And that bear out there is going to tear you apart if you don't do something!*

"Libby!" the radio squawked suddenly. "Libby, come in!"

The voice was Jess's. "Th-the bear," she croaked, remembering to hold in the button on the receiver when she talked. "Jess, the bear!"

"Where are you?"

Libby closed her eyes as the beast again threw itself against the truck. "My dad's house—in his truck."

"Hold on. Please, baby, hold on. We're not far away."

"Hurry!" Libby cried, as the bear battered the windshield again and tiny bits of glass rained down on her head.

Another voice came in over the radio, this one belonging to Stacey. "Libby," he said evenly, "honk the horn. Can you do that?"

Libby couldn't speak. There were tears pouring down her face and every muscle in her body seemed inert, but she did reach up to the center of the wheel and press the truck's horn.

The bear bellowed with rage, as though the sound had hurt him, but he stopped striking the truck and withdrew a little way. Libby knew he wasn't gone, for she could hear him lumbering nearby, growling in frustration.

Jess's men converged with Stacey's at the end of the rutted country road leading to Ken's house. When the pickup truck was in sight, they reined in their horses.

"He's mine," Jess breathed, reaching for the rifle in his scabbard, drawing it out, cocking it. He was conscious of the other men and their nervous, nickering horses, but only vaguely. Libby was inside that truck—his whole being seemed to focus on that one fact.

The bear rose up in full view suddenly, its enormous head visible even over the top of the pickup's cab. Even over the repeated honking of the truck's horn, the beast's hideous, echoing growl was audible.

"Sweet Jesus," Stacey whispered.

"Easy," said Jess, to himself more than the men around him, as he lifted the rifle, sighted in carefully, pulled back the trigger.

The thunderous shot struck the bear in the center of its nose, and the animal shrieked as it went down. The impact of its body was so solid that it seemed to shake the ground.

Instantly Jess was out of the saddle. "Make sure he's dead," he called over one shoulder as he ran toward the truck.

Stacey and several of his men reached the bear just as Jess wrenched open the door on the driver's side.

Libby scrambled out from under the steering wheel, her hair a wild, glass-spattered tangle, to fling herself, sobbing, into his arms. Jess cradled her in his arms, carried her away from the demolished truck and inside the house. His own knees suddenly weak, he fell into the first available chair and buried his face in Libby's neck.

"It's over, sweetheart," he said. "It's over."

Libby shuddered and wailed with terror.

When she was calmer, Jess caught her chin in his hand and lifted it. "What the hell did you mean, yelling 'Cujo! Cujo!'"

Libby sniffled, and the fight was back in her eyes, a glorious, snapping blue. "There was this book about a mad dog...and then there was a movie..."

Jess lifted his eyebrows and grinned.

"Oh, never mind!" hissed Libby.

Chapter 13

Libby froze in the doorway of Ken's room in the intensive-care unit, her mouth open, her heart racing as fast as it had earlier, when she'd been trapped by the bear.

"Where is he?" she finally managed to whisper. "Oh, Jess, where is my father?"

Standing behind Libby, Jess lifted his hands to her shoulders and gently ushered her back into the hallway, out of sight of the empty bed. "Don't panic," he said quietly.

Libby trembled, looked frantically toward the nurses' station. "Jess, what if he...?"

There was a gentle lecture forming in Jess's features, but before he could deliver it, an attractive red-headed nurse approached, trim in her uniform. "Mrs. Barlowe?"

Libby nodded, holding her breath.

"Your father is fine. We moved Mr. Kincaid to another floor earlier today, since he no longer needs such careful monitoring. If you will just come back to the desk with me, I'll be happy to find out which room he's in."

Libby's breath escaped in one long sigh. What with spending perilous minutes cowering inside a truck, with a rogue bear doing its best to get inside and tear her to bits, and then rushing to the hospital to find her father's bed empty, she had had more than enough stress for one day. "Thank you," she said, giving Jess a relieved look.

He got rather familiar during the elevator ride down to the second floor, but desisted when the doors opened again.

"You're incorrigible," Libby whispered, only half in anger.

"Snatching my wife from the jaws of death has that effect on me," he whispered back. "I keep thinking that I might never have gotten the chance to touch you like that again."

Libby paused, in the quest for Room 223, to search Jess's face. "Were you scared?"

"Scared? Sweet thing, I was *terrified.*"

"You seemed so calm!"

He lifted one eyebrow. "Somebody had to be."

Libby considered that and then sighed. "I don't suppose we should tell Dad what actually happened. Not yet, at least."

Jess chuckled. "We'll tell a partial truth—that the bear is dead. The rest had better wait until he's stronger."

"Right," agreed Libby.

When they reached Ken's new room, another surprise was in store. A good-looking dark-haired woman was there plumping the patient's pillows, fussing with his covers. She wore well-cut jeans and a Western shirt trimmed with a rippling snow-white fringe, and the way she laughed, low in her throat, said more about her relationship with Ken Kincaid than all her other attentions combined.

"Hello, Becky," said Jess, smiling.

Becky was one of those people, it seemed, who smile not just with the mouth but with the whole face. "Jess Barlowe," she crowed, "you black-hearted son-of-a-gun! Where ya been?"

Libby drew a deep breath and worked up a smile of her own. Was this the woman who had written that intriguing farewell on the condo's kitchen blackboard?

Deliberately she turned her attention on her father, who looked downright rakish as he favored his startled daughter with a slow grin and a wink.

"Who's this pretty little gal?" demanded Becky, giving Libby a friendly once-over.

For the first time, Ken spoke. "This is my daughter, Libby. Libby, Becky Stafford."

"I'll be!" cried Becky, clearly delighted. "Glad to meet ya!"

Libby found the woman's boisterous good nature appealing, and despite a few lingering twinges of surprise, she responded warmly.

"Did you get that bear?" Ken asked of Jess, once the women had made their exchange.

"Yes," Jess replied, after one glance at Libby.

Ken gave a hoot of delight and triumph. "Nail that son-of-a...nail that devil's hide to the barn door for me, will you?"

"Done," answered Jess with a grin.

A few minutes later, Jess and the energetic Becky left the room to have coffee in the hospital cafeteria. Libby lifted her hands to her hips, fixed her father with a loving glare and demanded, "Is there something you haven't told me?"

Ken laughed. "Maybe. But I'll wager that there are a few things you haven't told me, either, dumplin'."

"Who is Becky, exactly?"

Ken thought for a moment before speaking. "She's a good friend of mine, Libby. An old friend."

For some reason, Libby was determined to find something to dislike about Becky Stafford, difficult as it was. "Why does she dress like that? Is she a rodeo performer or something?"

"She's a cocktail waitress," Ken replied patiently.

"Oh," said Libby. And then she couldn't sustain her petty jealousy any longer, because Becky Stafford was a nice person and Ken had a right to like her. He was more than just her father, after all, more than just Senator Barlowe's general foreman. He was a man.

There was a brief silence, which Ken broke with a very direct question. "Do you like Becky, Lib?"

Like her? The warmth and humor of the woman still lingered in that otherwise dreary room, as did the earthy, unpretentious scent of her perfume. "Sure I do," said Libby. "Anybody with the perception to call Jess Barlowe a 'black-hearted son-of-a-gun' is okay in my book!"

Ken chuckled, but there was relief in his face, and his expression revealed that he knew how much Libby loved her husband. "How's Cathy?" he asked.

Remembering that morning's brief conversation with

her cousin, Libby grinned. "She's doing fine, as far as I can tell. Bad as it was, your tussle with that bear seems to have brought Cathy and Stacey both to a point where they can open up to each other. Cathy actually talked to him."

Ken did not seem surprised by this last; perhaps he'd known all along that Cathy still had use of her voice. "I don't imagine it was peaceable," he observed drily.

"Not in the least," confirmed Libby, "but they're communicating and…and, well, let's just say they're closer."

"That's good," answered Ken, smiling at his daughter's words. "That's real good."

Seeing that her father was getting very tired, Libby quickly kissed him and took her leave. When she reached the cafeteria, Becky was sitting alone at a table, staring sadly into her coffee cup.

Libby scanned the large room for Jess and failed to see him, but she wasn't worried. Probably he had gone back to Ken's room and missed seeing Libby on the way. Noticing the pensive look on Becky's face, she was glad for a few minutes alone with the woman her father obviously liked and perhaps even loved.

"May I sit down?" she asked, standing behind the chair that had probably been Jess's.

Becky looked up, smiled. "Sure," she said, and there was surprise in her dark eyes.

Libby sat down with a sigh. "I hate hospitals," she said, filled to aching with the memory of Jonathan's confinement.

"Me too," answered Becky, but her eyes were watchful. Hopeful, in a touchingly open way.

Libby swallowed. "My...my father has been very lonely, and I'm glad you're his friend."

Becky's smile was almost cosmic in scope. "That's good to hear," she answered. "Lordy, that man did scare the life out of me, going a round with that damned bear that way."

Libby thought of her own chance meeting with the creature and shivered. She hoped that she would never know that kind of numbing fear again.

Becky's hand came to pat hers. "It's all right now, though, isn't it? That hairy booger is dead, thanks to Jess."

Libby laughed. Indeed, that "hairy booger" was dead, and she did have Jess to thank for her life. When she'd tried to voice her gratitude earlier, he had brushed away her words and said that she was his wife and, therefore, saving her from bears, fire-breathing dragons and the like was just part of the bargain.

As if conjured by her thoughts of him, Jess appeared to take Libby home.

The coming days were happy ones for Libby, if hectic. She visited her father morning and evening and worked on her cartoon strip and the panels for the book between times, her drawing board having been transported from the ranch by Jess and set up in the middle of the condo's living room.

Jess commuted between Kalispell and the ranch; many of Ken's duties had fallen to him. Instead of being exhausted by the crazy pace, however, he seemed to thrive on it and his reports on the stormy reconciliation taking place between Cathy and Stacey were encouraging. It appeared that, with the help of the marriage counselor they were seeing, their problems might be worked out.

The irrepressible Becky Stafford rapidly became Libby's friend. Vastly different, the two women nevertheless enjoyed each other—Libby found that Becky could draw her out when she became too burrowed down in her work, and just as quickly drive her back if she tried to neglect it.

"You did what?" Jess demanded archly one early-summer evening as he and Libby sat on the living-room floor consuming the take-out Chinese food they both loved.

Libby laughed with glee and a measure of pride. "I rode the mechanical bull at the bar where Becky works," she repeated.

Jess worked up an unconvincing scowl. "Hanging around bars these days, are you?" he demanded, waving a fortune cookie for emphasis.

Libby batted her eyelashes demurely. "Don't you worry one little bit," she said, feigning a musical Southern drawl. "Becky guards mah virtue, y'all."

Jess's green eyes slipped to the V neck of Libby's white sweater, which left a generous portion of cleavage in full and enticing view. "Does she now? And where is she, at this very moment, when said virtue is in immediate peril?"

An anticipatory thrill gyrated in the pit of Libby's stomach and warmed her breasts, which were bare beneath her lightweight sweater. Jess had loved her often, and well, but he could still stir that sweet, needing tension with remarkable ease. "What sort of peril am I in, exactly?"

Jess grinned and hooked one finger in the V of her

sweater, slid it downward into the warmth between her breasts. "Oh, the most scandalous sort, Mrs. Barlowe."

Libby's breath quickened, despite stubborn efforts to keep it even. "Your attentions are quite unseemly, Mr. Barlowe," she replied.

He moved the wanton finger up and down between the swelling softness that was Libby, and sharp responses ached in other parts of her. "Absolutely," he said. "I mean to do several unseemly things to you."

Libby tensed with delicious sensation as Jess's exploring finger slid aside, explored a still-hidden nipple.

"I want to see your breast, Libby. This breast. Show it to me."

The outrageous request made Libby color slightly, but she knew she would comply. She was a strong, independent person, but now, in this sweet, aching moment, she was Jess's woman. With one motion of her hand, she tugged the sweater's neckline down and to one side, so that it made a sort of sling for the breast that had been softly demanded.

Not touching the rounded pink-tipped treasure in any way, Jess admired it, rewarding it with an approving smile when the confectionlike peak tightened into an enticing point.

Libby was kneeling now, resting on her heels, the cartons littering the coffee table completely forgotten. She was at once too proud to plead for Jess's mouth and too needing of it to cover herself.

Knowing that, Jess chuckled hoarsely and bent to flick at the exposed nipple with just the tip of his tongue. Libby moaned and let her head fall back, making the captured breast even more vulnerable.

"Unseemly," breathed Jess, nibbling, drawing at the straining morsel with his lips.

Libby felt the universe sway in time with his tender plundering, but she bit down hard on the garbled pleas that were rising in her throat. They escaped through her parted lips, all the same, as small gasps.

Her heartbeat grew louder and louder as Jess finally took suckle; it muffled the sounds of his greed, of the cartons being swept from the surface of the coffee table in a motion of one of his arms.

The coolness of the air battled with the heat of Libby's flesh as she was stripped of her sweater, her white slacks, her panties. Gently he placed her on the coffee table.

Entranced, Libby allowed him to position her legs wide of each other, one on one side of the low table, one on the other. Beyond the glass roof, in the dark, dark sky, a million silvery stars surged toward her and then melted back into the folds of heaven, becoming pinpoints.

Jess found the silken nest of her passion and attended it lovingly, stroking, kissing, finding, losing. Libby's hips moved wildly, struggling even as she gave herself up.

And when she had to have this singular gratification or die, Jess understood and feasted unreservedly, his hands firm under her bottom, lifting her, the breadth of his shoulders making it impossible for her to deny him what he would have from her.

At last, when the tumult broke on a lusty cry of triumph from Libby, she saw the stars above plummet toward her—or had she risen to meet them?

"Of course you're going to the powwow!" cried Becky, folding her arms and leaning over the platter of french fries in front of her. "You can't miss that and call yourself a Barlowe!"

Libby shrank down a little in the benchlike steakhouse seat. As this restaurant was a part of the Barlowe chain, the name drew immediate attention from all the waiters and a number of the other diners, too. "Becky," she began patiently, "even though Dad's getting out of the hospital this afternoon, he won't be up to something like that, and I wouldn't feel right about leaving him behind."

"Leaving Ken behind?" scoffed Becky in a more discreet tone of voice. "You just try keeping him away—he hasn't missed a powwow in fifteen years."

Libby's memories of the last powwow and all-day rodeo she had attended were hardly conducive to nostalgia. She remembered the dust, the hot glare of the summer sun, the seemingly endless rodeo events, the revelers draped over the hoods of parked cars and sprawled on the sidewalks. She sighed.

"Jess'll go," Becky prodded.

Libby had no doubt of that, and having spent so much time away from Jess of late, what with him running the ranch while she stayed in Kalispell, she was inclined to attend the powwow after all.

Becky saw that she had relented and beamed. "Wait'll you see the Sioux doing their war dances," she enthused. "There'll be Blackfoot, too, and Flathead."

Libby consoled herself with the thought of the dances and the powwow finery of feathers and buckskin and beads. She could take her sketchbook along and draw, at least.

Becky wasn't through with her conversation. "Did

you tell Jess how you rode that electric bull over at the Golden Buckle?"

Libby tried to look dignified in the wake of several molten memories. "I told him," she said shyly.

Her friend laughed. "If that wasn't a sight! I wish I woulda took your picture. Maybe you should enter some of the events at the powwow, Libby." Her face took on a disturbingly serious expression. "Maybe barrel racing, or women's calf roping—"

"Hold it," Libby interceded with a grin. "Riding a mechanical bull is one thing and calf roping is quite another. The only sport I'm going to take part in is stepping over drunks."

"Stepping over what?" inquired a third voice, masculine and amused, from the table side.

Libby looked and saw Stacey. "What are you doing here?"

He laughed, turning his expensive silver-banded cowboy hat in both hands. "I own the place, remember?"

"Where's Cathy?" Becky wanted to know. As she had become Libby's friend, she had also become Cathy's—she was even learning to sign.

Stacey slid into the bench seat beside Libby. "She's seeing the doctor," he said, and for all his smiling good manners, he seemed nervous.

Libby elbowed her brother-in-law lightly. "Why didn't you stay there and wait for her?"

"She wouldn't let me."

Just then Becky stood up, saying that she had to get to work. A moment later, eyes twinkling over some secret, she left.

Libby felt self-conscious with Stacey, though he hadn't made any more advances or disturbing comments. She wished that Becky had been able to stay a little longer. "What's going on? Is Cathy sick?"

"She's just having a checkup. Libby…"

Libby braced herself inwardly and moved a little closer to the wall of the enclosed booth, so that Stacey's thigh wasn't touching hers. "Yes?" she prompted when he hesitated to go on.

"I owe you an apology," he said, meeting her eyes. "I acted like a damned fool and I'm sorry."

Knowing that he was referring to the rumors he'd started about their friendship in New York, Libby chafed a little. "I accept your apology, Stacey, but I truly don't understand why you said what you did in the first place."

He sighed heavily. "I love Cathy very much, Libby," he said. "But we do have our problems. At that time, things were a lot worse, and I started thinking about the way you'd leaned on me when you were going through all that trouble in New York. I liked having somebody need me like that, and I guess I worked the whole thing up into more than it was."

Tentatively Libby touched his hand. "Cathy needs you, Stacey."

"No," he answered gruffly, looking at the flickering bowl candle in the center of the table. "She won't allow herself to need me. After some of the things I've put her through, I can't say I blame her."

"She'll trust you again, if you're worthy of it," Libby ventured. "Just be there for Cathy, Stace. The way you were there for me when my whole life seemed to be falling apart. I don't think I could have gotten through those days without you."

At that moment Jess appeared out of nowhere and

slid into the seat Becky had occupied before. "Now, that," he drawled acidly, "is really touching."

Libby stared at him, stunned by his presence and by the angry set of his face. Then she realized that both she and Stacey were sitting on the same side of the booth and knew that it gave an impression of intimacy. "Jess…"

He looked down at his watch, a muscle dancing furiously in his jaw. "Are you going to pick your father up at the hospital, or do you have more interesting things to do?"

Stacey, who had been as shocked by his brother's arrival as Libby had, was suddenly, angrily vocal. The candle leapt a little when he slammed one fist down on the tabletop and hissed, "Dammit, Jess, you're deliberately misunderstanding this!"

"Am I?"

"Yes!" Libby put in, on the verge of tears. "Becky and I were having lunch and then Stacey came in and—"

"Stop it, Libby," Stacey broke in. "You didn't do anything wrong. Jess is the one who's out of line here."

The long muscle in Jess's neck corded, and his lips were edged with white, but his voice was still low, still controlled. "I came here, Libby, because I wanted to be with you when you brought Ken home," he said, and his green eyes, dark with passion only the night before, were coldly indifferent now. "Are we going to collect him or would you rather stay here and carry on?"

Libby was shaking. "Carry on? *Carry on?*"

Stacey groaned, probably considering the scandal a scene in this particular restaurant would cause. "Couldn't we settle this somewhere else?"

"We'll settle it, all right," Jess replied.

Stacey's jaw was rock-hard as he stood up to let a shaken Libby out of the booth. "I'll be on the ranch," he said.

"So will I," replied Jess, rising, taking a firm grip on Libby's arm. "See you there."

"Count on it."

Jess nodded and calmly propelled Libby out of the restaurant and into the bright sunlight, where her shiny Corvette was parked. Probably he had seen the car from the highway and known that she was inside the steak house.

Now, completely ignoring her protests, he dragged her past her car and thrust her into the Land Rover beside it.

"Jess—damn you—will you *listen* to me?"

Jess started the engine, shifted it into Reverse with a swift motion of his hand. "I'm afraid storytime will have to wait," he informed her. "We've got to go and get Ken, and I don't want him upset."

"Do you think I do?"

Jess sliced one menacing look in her direction but said nothing.

Libby felt a need to reach him, even though, the way he was acting, he didn't deserve reassurances. "Jess, how can you...after last night, how could you..."

"Last night," he bit out. "Yes. Tell me, Libby, do you do that trick for everybody, or just a favored few?"

It took all her determination not to physically attack him. "Take me back to my car, Jess," she said evenly. "Right now. I'll pick Dad up myself, and we'll go back to his house—"

"Correction, Mrs. Barlowe. *He* will go to his house. You, my little vixen, will go to mine."

"I will not!"

"Oh, but you will. Despite your obvious attraction to my brother, you are still my wife."

"I am not attracted to your brother!"

They had reached the hospital parking lot, and the Land Rover lurched to a stop. Jess smiled insolently and patted Libby's cheek in a way so patronizing that it made her screaming mad. "That's the spirit, Mrs. Barlowe. Walk in there and show your daddy what a pillar of morality you are."

Going into that hospital and pretending that nothing was wrong was one of the hardest things Libby had ever had to do.

Preparations for Ken's return had obviously been going on for some time. As Libby pulled her reclaimed Corvette in behind Jess's Land Rover, she saw that the front lawn had been mowed and the truck had been repaired.

Ken, still not knowing the story of his daughter, his truck, and the bear, paused after stepping out of Jess's Land Rover, his arm still in a sling. He looked his own vehicle over quizzically. "Looks different," he reflected.

Jess rose to the occasion promptly, smoothly. "The boys washed and waxed it," he said.

To say the very least, thought Libby, who would never forget, try though she might, how that truck had looked before the repair people in Kalispell had fixed and painted it. She opened her mouth to tell her father what had happened, but Jess stopped her with a look and a shake of his head.

The inside of the house had been cleaned by Mrs.

Bradshaw and her band of elves; every floor and stick of furniture had been either dusted or polished or both. The refrigerator had been stocked and a supply of the paperback Westerns Ken loved to read had been laid in.

As if all this wasn't enough to make Libby's services completely superfluous, it turned out that Becky was there, too. She had strung streamers and dozens of brightly colored balloons from the ceiling of Ken's bedroom.

Her father was obviously pleased, and Libby's last hopes of drumming up an excuse to stay the night, at least, were dashed. Becky, however, was delighted with her surprise.

"I thought you were working!" Libby accused.

"I lied," replied Becky, undaunted. "After I left you and Stacey at the steak house, I got a friend to bring me out here."

Libby shot a glance in Jess's direction, knew sweet triumph as she saw that Becky's words had registered with him. After only a moment's chagrin, however, he tightened his jaw and looked away.

While Becky was getting Ken settled in his room and generally spoiling him rotten, Libby edged over to her husband. "You heard her," she whispered tersely, "so where's my apology?"

"Apology?" Jess whispered back, and there was nothing in his face to indicate that he felt any remorse at all. "Why should I apologize?"

"Because I was obviously telling the truth! Becky said—"

"Becky said that she left you and Stacey at the steak house. It must have been a big relief when she did."

Heedless of everything but the brutal effect of Jess's unfair words, Libby raised one hand and slapped him, hard.

Stubbornly, he refused her the satisfaction of any response at all, beyond an imperious glare, which she returned.

"Hey, do you guys...?" Becky's voice fell away when she became aware of the charged atmosphere of the living room. She swallowed and began again. "I was going to ask if you wanted to stay for supper, but maybe that wouldn't be such a good idea."

"You can say that again," rasped Jess, catching Libby's arm in a grasp she couldn't have broken without making an even more embarrassing scene. "Make our excuses to Ken, will you, please?"

After a moment's hesitation and a concerned look at Libby, Becky nodded.

"You overbearing bastard!" Libby hissed as her husband squired her out of the house and toward his Land Rover.

Jess opened the door, helped her inside, met her fiery blue gaze with one of molten green. Neither spoke to the other, but the messages flashing between them were all too clear anyway.

Jess still believed that Libby had been either planning or carrying on a romantic tryst with Stacey, and Libby was too proud and too angry to try to convince him otherwise. She was also too smart to get out of his vehicle and make a run for hers.

Jess would never hurt her, she knew that. But he would not allow her a dramatic exit, either. And she couldn't risk a screaming fight in the driveway of her father's house.

Because she was helpless and she hated that, she began to cry.

Jess ignored her tears, but he too was considerate of Ken—he did not gun the Land Rover's engine or back out at a speed that would fling gravel in every direction, as he might have at another time.

When they passed his house, with its window walls, and started up a steep road leading into the foothills beyond, Libby was still not afraid. For all his fury, this man was too tender a lover to touch her in anger.

"Where are we going?" she demanded.

He ground the Land Rover into a low gear and left the road, now little more than a cow path, for the rugged hillside. "On our honeymoon, Mrs. Barlowe."

Libby swallowed, unnerved by his quiet rage and the jostling, jolting ascent of the Land Rover itself. "If you take me in anger, Jess Barlowe, I'll never forgive you. Never. That would be rape."

The word "rape" got through Jess's hard armor and stung him visibly. He paled as he stopped the Land Rover with a lurch and wrenched on the emergency brake. "Goddammit, you *know* I wouldn't do anything like that!"

"Do I?" They were parked at an almost vertical angle, it seemed to Libby. Didn't he realize that they were almost straight up and down? "You've been acting like a maniac all afternoon!"

Jess's face contorted and he raised his fists and brought them down hard on the steering wheel. "Dammit it all to hell," he raged, "you drive me crazy! Why the devil do I love you so much when *you drive me crazy?*"

Libby stared at him, almost unable to believe what she had heard. Not even in their wildest moments of passion had he said he loved her, and if he had found that note she'd left for him, betraying her own feelings, the day the bear was killed, he'd never mentioned it.

"What did you say?"

Jess sighed, tilted his head back, closed his eyes. "That you drive me crazy."

"Before that."

"I said I loved you," he breathed, as though there was nothing out of the ordinary in that.

"Do you?"

"Hell, yes." The muscles in his sun-browned neck corded as he swallowed, his head still back, his eyes still closed. "Isn't that a joke?"

The words tore at Libby's heart. "A joke?"

"Yes." The word came, raw, from deep within him, like a sob.

"You idiot!" yelled Libby, struggling with the door, climbing out of the Land Rover to stalk up the steep hillside. She trembled, and tears poured down her face, and for once she didn't care who saw them.

At the top of the rise, she sat down on a huge log, her vision too blurred to take in the breathtaking view of mountains and prairies and an endless, sweeping sky.

She sensed Jess's approach, tried to ignore him.

"Why am I an idiot, Libby?"

Though the day was warm, Libby shivered. "You're too stupid to know when a woman loves you, that's why!" she blurted out, sobbing now. "Damn! You've had me every way but hanging from a chandelier, and you still don't know!"

Jess straddled the log, drew Libby into his arms and held her. Suddenly he laughed, and the sound was a shout of joy.

Chapter 14

The powwow of the Sioux, Flathead and Blackfoot was a spectacle to remember. Held annually in the same small and otherwise unremarkable town, the meeting of these three tribes was a tradition that reached back to days of mist and shadow, days recorded on no calendar.

Now, on a hot July morning, the erstwhile cow pasture and ramshackle grandstands were churning with activity, and Libby Barlowe's fingers ached to make use of the sketchbook and pencils she carried.

Craning her neck to see the authentic tepees and their colorfully clad inhabitants, she could hardly stand still long enough for the plump woman at the admission gate to stamp her hand.

There was so much noise—laughter, the tinkle of change in the coin box, the neighing and nickering of horses that would be part of the rodeo. Underlying all this was the steady beat of tom-toms and guttural chants of the singers.

"Enjoy yourself now, honey," enjoined the woman tending the cashbox, and Libby jumped, realizing that she was holding up the line behind her. After one questioning look at the hat the woman wore, which consisted of panels cut from various beer cans and crocheted together, she hurried through the gate.

Jess chuckled at the absorbed expression on Libby's face. There was so much to see that a person didn't know where to look first.

"I think I see a fit of creativity coming on," he said.

Libby was already gravitating toward the tepees, plotting light angles and shading techniques as she went. In her heart was a dream, growing bigger with every beat of the tom-toms. "I want to see, Jess," she answered distractedly. "I've got to *see*."

There was love in the sound of Jess's laughter, but no disdain. "All right, all right—but at least let me get you a hat. This sun is too hot for you to go around bareheaded."

"Get me a hat, get me a hat," babbled Libby, zeroing in on a group of small children as they sat watching fathers, uncles and elder brothers perform the ancient rites for rain or success in warfare or hunting.

Libby was taken with the flash of their coppery skin, the midnight black of their hair, the solemn, stalwart expressions in their dark eyes. Flipping open her sketchbook, she squatted in the lush summer grass and began to rough in the image of one particular little boy.

Her pencil flew, as did her mind. She was thinking in terms of oil paints—vivid shades that would do justice to the child's coloring and the peacock splendor of his headdress.

"Hello," she said when the dark eyes turned to her in dour question. "My name is Libby, what's yours?"

"Jimmy," the little boy responded, but then he must have remembered the majesty of his ancestry, for he squared his small shoulders and amended, "Jim Little Eagle."

Libby made a hasty note in the corner of his sketch. "I wish I had a name like that," she said.

"You'll have to settle for 'Barlowe,'" put in a familiar voice from behind her, and a lightweight hat landed on the top of her head.

Libby looked up into Jess's face and smiled. "I guess I can make do with that," she answered.

Jess dropped to his haunches, assessed the sketch she'd just finished with admiring eyes. "Wow," he said.

Libby laughed. "I love it when you're profound," she teased. And then she took off the hat he'd given her and inspected it thoroughly. It was a standard Western hat, made of straw, and it boasted a trailing tangle of turquoise feathers and crystal beads.

Jess took the hat and put it firmly back on, then arranged the feathers so that they rested on her right shoulder, tickling the bare, sun-gilded flesh there in a pleasant way. "Did you wear that blouse to drive me insane, or are you trying to set a world record for blistering sunburns?" he asked unromantically.

Libby looked down at the brief white eyelet suntop and wondered if she shouldn't have worn a Western shirt, the way Becky and Cathy had. The garment she had on had no shoulders or sleeves; it was just a series of ruffles falling from an elasticized band that fitted around her chest, just beneath her collarbone. Not even wanting to think about the tortures of a sunburn, she had liberally applied sunblock to her exposed skin. Not wanting to give Jess the satisfaction, though, she crinkled her nose and said, "I wore it to drive you insane, of course."

Jess was going to insist on being practical; she saw it in his face. "They're selling T-shirts on the fairway—buy one."

"Now?" complained Libby, not wanting to leave the splendors of the recreated Native American village even for a few minutes.

Jess looked down at his watch. "Within half an hour," he said flatly. "I'm going to find Ken and the others in the grandstands, Rembrandt. I'll see you later."

Libby squinted as he rose against the sun, towering and magnificent even in his ordinary jeans and worn cowboy shirt. "No kiss?"

Jess crouched again, kissed her. "Remember. Half an hour."

"Half an hour," promised Libby, turning to a fresh page in her sketchbook and pondering a little girl with coal-black braids and a fringed buckskin shift. She took a new pencil from the case inside her purse and began to draw again, her hand racing to keep up with the pace set by her heart.

When the sketch was finished, Libby thought about what she meant to do and how the syndicate that carried her cartoon strip would react. No doubt they would be furious.

"Portraits!" her agent would cry. "Libby, Libby, there is no *money* in portraits."

Libby sighed, biting her lower lip. Money wasn't a

factor really, since she had plenty of that as it was, not only because she had married a wealthy man but also because of prior successes in her career.

She was tired of doing cartoons, yearning to delve into other mediums—especially oils. She wanted color, depth, nuance—she wanted and needed to grow.

"Where the hell is that T-shirt I asked you to buy?"

Libby started, but the dream was still glowing in her face when she looked up to meet Jess's gaze. "Still on the fairway, I would imagine," she said.

His mouth looked very stern, but Jess's eyes were dancing beneath the brim of his battered western hat. "I don't know why I let you out of my sight," he teased. And then he extended a hand. "Come on, woman. Let's get you properly dressed."

Libby allowed herself to be pulled through the crowd to one of the concession stands. Here there were such thrilling offerings as ashtrays shaped like the state of Montana and gaudy scarves commemorating the pow-wow itself.

"Your secret is out," she told Jess out of the corner of her mouth, gesturing toward a display of hats exactly like her own. The colors of their feather-and-bead plumage ranged from a pastel yellow to deep, rich purple. "This hat is not a designer original!"

Jess worked up an expression of horrified chagrin and then laughed and began rifling through a stack of colorful T-shirts. "What size do you wear?"

Libby stood on tiptoe, letting her breath fan against his ear, delighting as that appendage reddened visibly. "About the size of the palm of your hand, cowboy."

"Damn," Jess chuckled, and the red moved out from his ear to churn under his suntan. "Unless you want me to drag you off somewhere and make love to you right now, you'd better not make any more remarks like that."

Suddenly Libby was as pink as the T-shirt he was measuring against her chest. Coming from Jess, this was no idle threat—since their new understanding, reached several weeks before on the top of the hill behind his house, they had made love in some very unconventional places. It would be like him to take her to one of the small trailers brought by some of the cowboys from the Circle Bar B and follow through.

Having apparently deemed the pink T-shirt appropriate, Jess bought it and gripped Libby's hand, fairly dragging her across the sawdust-covered fairgrounds. From the grandstands came the deafening shouts and boot-stompings of more than a thousand excited rodeo fans.

Reaching the rest rooms, which were housed in a building of their own, Jess gave an exasperated sigh. There must have been a hundred women waiting to use the facilities, and he clearly didn't want to stand around in the sun just so Libby could exchange her suntop for a T-shirt.

Before she could offer to wait alone so that Jess could go back and watch the rodeo, he was hauling her toward the nest of Circle Bar B trailers at such a fast pace that she had to scramble to keep up with him.

Thrusting her inside the smallest, which was littered with boots, beer cans and dirty clothes, he ordered, "Put on the shirt."

Libby's color was so high that she was sure he could see it, even in the cool darkness of that camper-trailer. "This is Jake Peterson's camper, isn't it? What if he comes back?"

"He won't come back—he's entered in the bull-riding competition. Just change, will you?"

Libby knew only too well what would happen if she removed that suntop. "Jess…"

He closed the camper door, flipped the inadequate-looking lock. Then he reached out, collected her be-feathered hat, her sketchbook, her purse. He laid all these items on a small, messy table and waited.

In the distance, over the loudspeaker system, the rodeo announcer exalted, "This cowboy, folks, has been riding bulls longer'n he's been tying his shoes."

There was a thunderous communal cry as the cowboy and his bull apparently came out of their chute, but it was strangely quiet in that tiny trailer where Jess and Libby stood staring at each other.

Finally, in one defiant motion of her hands, Libby wrenched the suntop off over the top of her head and stood still before her husband, her breasts high and proud and completely bare. "Are you satisfied?" she snapped.

"Not yet," Jess retorted.

He came to stand very close, his hands gentle on her breasts. "You were right," he said into her hair. "You just fit the palms of my hands."

"Oh," said Libby in sweet despair.

Jess's hands continued their tender work, lulling her. It was so cool inside that trailer, so intimate and shadowy.

Presently Libby felt the snap on her jeans, and then the zipper, give way. She was conscious of a shivering heat as the fabric glided downward. Protesting was quite beyond her powers now; she was bewitched.

Jess laid her on the narrow camper bed, joining her

within moments. Stretched out upon her, he entered her with one deft thrust.

Their triumph was a simultaneous one, reached after they'd both traveled through a glittering mine field of physical and spiritual sensation, and it was of such dizzying scope that it seemed natural for the unknowing crowd in the grandstands to cheer.

Furiously Libby fastened her jeans and pulled on the T-shirt that had caused this situation in the first place. She gathered up her things, plopped her hat onto her head, and glared into Jess's amused face.

He dressed at a leisurely pace, as though they weren't trespassing.

"If Jake Peterson ever finds out about his, I'll die," Libby said, casting anxious, impatient looks at the locked door.

Jess pulled on one boot, then the other, ran a hand through his rumpled hair. His eyes smoldering with mischief and lingering pleasure, he stood up, pulled Libby into his arms and kissed her. "I love you," he said. "And your shameful secret is safe with me, Mrs. Barlowe."

Libby's natural good nature was overcoming her anger. "Sure," she retorted tartly. "All the same, I think you should know that every man who had ever compromised me in a ranch hand's trailer has said that self-same thing."

Jess laughed, kissed her again, and then released her. "Go back to your drawing, you little hellion. I'll find you later."

"That's what I'm afraid of," Libby tossed back over one shoulder as she stepped out of the camper into the

bright July sunshine. Almost before her eyes had ad-
justed to the change, she was sketching again.

Libby hardly noticed the passing of the hours, so intent was she on recording the scenes that so fascinated
her: men festooned with colorful feathers, doing their
war and rain dances; women in their worn buckskin
dresses, demonstrating the grinding of corn or making their beaded belts and moccasins; children playing
games that were almost as old as the distant mountains
and the big sky.

Between the residual effects of that scandalous bout
of lovemaking in the trailer and the feast of color and
sound assaulting her now, Libby's senses were reeling.
She was almost relieved when Cathy came and signed
that it was time to leave.

As they walked back to find the others in the still-
dense crowd, Libby studied her cousin out of the corner of
her eye. Cathy and Stacey were living together again, but
there was a wistfulness about Cathy that was disturbing.

There would be no chance to talk with her now—
there were too many distractions for that—but Libby
made a mental vow to get Cathy alone later, perhaps
during the birthday party that was being held on the
ranch for Senator Barlowe that evening, and find out
what was bothering her.

As the group made plans to stop at a favorite café
for an early supper, Libby grew more and more uneasy
about Cathy. What was it about her that was different,
besides her obviously downhearted mood?

Before Libby could even begin to work out that complex question, Ken and Becky were off to their truck,
Stacey and Cathy to their car. Libby was still staring
into space when Jess gently tugged at her hand.

She got into the Land Rover, feeling pensive, and laid her sketchbook and purse on the seat.

"Another fit of creativity?" Jess asked quietly, driving carefully through a maze of other cars, staggering cowboys and beleaguered sheriff's deputies.

"I was thinking about Cathy," Libby replied. "Have you noticed a change in her?"

He thought, shook his head. "Not really."

"She doesn't talk to me anymore, Jess."

"Did you have an argument?"

Libby sighed. "No. I've been so busy lately, what with finishing the book and everything, I haven't spent much time with her. I'm ashamed to say that I didn't even notice the change in her until just a little while ago."

Jess gave her a gentle look. "Don't start beating yourself up Libby. You're not responsible for Cathy's happiness or unhappiness."

Surprised, Libby stared at him. "That sounds strange, coming from you."

They were pulling out onto the main highway, which was narrow and almost as choked with cars as the parking area had been. "I'm beginning to think it was a mistake, our being so protective of Cathy. We all meant well, but I wonder sometimes if we didn't hurt her instead."

"Hurt her?"

One of Jess's shoulders lifted in a shrug. "In a lot of ways, Cathy's still a little girl. She's never had to be a grown-up, Libby, because one of us was always there to fight her battles for her. I think she uses her deafness as an excuse not to take risks."

Libby was silent, reflecting on Cathy's fear of being a mother.

As though he'd looked into her mind, Jess went on

to say, "Both Cathy and Stacey want children—did you know that? But Cathy won't take the chance."

"I knew she was scared—she told me that. She's scared of so many things, Jess—especially of losing Stacey."

"She loves him."

"I know. I just wish she had something more—something of her own so that her security as a person wouldn't hinge entirely on what Stacey does."

"You mean the way your security doesn't hinge on what I do?" Jess ventured, his tone devoid of any challenge or rancor.

Libby turned, took off her hat and set it down between them with the other things. "I love you very, very much, Jess, but I could live without you. It would hurt unbearably, but I could do it."

He looked away from the traffic only long enough to flash her one devilish grin. "Who would take shameful liberties with your body, if it weren't for me?"

"I guess I would have to do without shameful liberties," she said primly.

"Thank you for sidestepping my delicate male ego," he replied, "but the fact of the matter is, there's no way a woman as beautiful and talented as you are would be alone for very long."

"Don't say that!"

Jess glanced at her in surprise. "Don't say what?"

It was his meaning that had concerned Libby, not his exact words. "I don't even want to think about another man touching me the way you do."

Jess's attention was firmly fixed on the road ahead. "If you're trying to make me feel secure, princess, it's working."

"I'm not trying to make you feel anything. Jess, before

we made love that first time, when you said I was really a virgin, you were right. Even the books I've read couldn't have prepared me for the things I feel when you love me."

"It might interest you to know, Mrs. Barlowe, that my feelings toward you are quite similar. Before we made love, sex was just something my body demanded, like food or exercise. Now it's magic."

She stretched to plant a noisy kiss on her husband's cheek. "Magic, is it? Well, you're something of a sorcerer yourself, Jess Barlowe. You cast spells over me and make me behave like a wanton."

He gave an exaggerated evil chuckle. "I hope I can remember the hex that made you give in to me back there at the fairgrounds."

Libby moved the things that were between them into the backseat and slid closer, taking a mischievous nip at his earlobe. "I'm sure you can," she whispered.

Jess shuddered involuntarily and snapped, "Dammit, Libby, I'm driving."

She was exploring the sensitive place just beneath his ear with the tip of her tongue. "Umm. You like getting me into situations where I'm really vulnerable, don't you, Jess?" she breathed, sliding one hand inside his shirt. "Like today, for instance."

"Libby…"

"Revenge is sweet."

And it was.

Shyly Libby extended the carefully wrapped package that contained her personal birthday gift to Senator Barlowe. She had not shown it to anyone else, not even Jess, and now she was uncertain. After all, Monica had given Cleave gold cufflinks and Stacey and Cathy planned to present him with a bottle of rare wine. By comparison, would her offering seem tacky and homemade?

With the gentle smile that had won him so many hearts and so many votes over the years, he took the parcel, which was revealingly large and flat, and turned it in his hands. "May I?" he asked softly, his kind eyes twinkling with affection.

"Please do," replied Libby.

It seemed to take Cleave forever to remove the ribbons and wrapping paper and lift the lid from the box inside, but there was genuine emotion in his face when he saw the framed pen-and-ink drawing Libby had been working on, in secret, for days. "My sons," he said.

"That's us, all right," commented Jess, who had appeared at the senator's side. "Personally, I think I'm considerably handsomer than that."

Cleave was examining the drawing closely. It showed Jess looking forward, Stacey in profile. When the senator looked up, Libby saw the love he bore his two sons in his eyes. "Thank you," he said. "This is one of the finest gifts I've ever received." He assessed the drawing again, and when his gaze came back to meet hers, it was full of mischief. "But where are my daughters? Where are you and Cathy?"

Libby smiled and kissed his cheek. "I guess you'll have to wait until your *next* birthday for that."

"In that case," rejoined the senator, "why not throw in a couple of grandchildren for good measure?"

Libby grinned. "I might be able to come up with one, but a couple?"

"Cathy will just have to do her part," came the immediate reply. "Now, if you'll excuse me, I want to take this picture around and show all my guests what a talented daughter-in-law I have."

Once his father had gone, Jess lifted his champagne glass and one eyebrow. "*Talented* is definitely the word," he said.

Libby knew that he was not referring to her artwork and hastily changed the subject. "You look so splendid in that tuxedo that I think I'd like to dance with you."

Jess worked one index finger under the tight collar of his formal shirt, obviously uncomfortable. "Dance?" he echoed drily. "Lead me to the organ grinder and we're in business."

Laughing, Libby caught at his free hand and dragged him into the spacious living room, which had been prepared for dancing. There was a small string band to provide the music.

Libby took Jess's champagne glass and set it aside, then rested both hands on his elegant satin lapels. The other guests—and there were dozens—might not have existed at all.

"Dance with me," she said.

Jess took her into his arms, his eyes never leaving hers. "You know," he said softly, "you look so wonderful in that silvery dress that I'm tempted to take you home and make damned sure my father gets that grandchild he wants."

"When we start a baby," she replied seriously, "I want it to be for us."

Jess's mouth quirked into a grin and his eyes were alight with love. "I wasn't going to tape a bow to the little stinker's head and hand it over to him, Libby."

Libby giggled at the picture this prompted in her mind. "Babies are so funny," she dreamed aloud.

"I know," Jess replied. "I love that look of drunken wonder they get when you lift them up high and talk to them. About that time, they usually barf in your hair."

Before she could answer, Ken and Becky came into the magical mist that had heretofore surrounded Libby and Jess.

"All right if I cut in?" Ken asked.

"How soon do you want a grandchild?" Jess countered.

"Sooner the better," retorted Ken. "And, Jess?"

"What?" demanded his son-in-law, eyes still locked with Libby's.

"The music stopped."

Jess and Libby both came to a startled halt, and Becky was so delighted by their expressions that her laughter pealed through the large room.

When the band started playing again, Libby found herself dancing with her father, while Jess and Becky waltzed nearby.

"You look real pretty," Ken said, beaming down at her.

"You're pretty fancy yourself," Libby answered. "In fact, you look downright handsome in that tuxedo."

"She says that to everybody," put in Jess, who happened to be whirling past with Becky.

Ken's laugh was low and throaty. "He never gets too far away from you, does he?"

"About as far as white gets from rice. And I like it that way."

"That's what I figured. Libby…"

The serious, tentative way he'd said her name gave Libby pause. "Yes?"

"Becky and I are going to get married," he blurted out, without taking a single breath.

Libby felt her eyes fill. "You were afraid to tell me that? Afraid to tell me something wonderful?"

Ken stopped, his arms still around his daughter, his blue eyes bright with relief and delight. Then, with a raucous shout that was far more typical of him than tuxedos and fancy parties, her father lifted her so high that she was afraid she would fall out of the top of her dress.

"That was certainly rustic," remarked Monica, five minutes later, at the refreshment table.

Libby saw Jess approaching through the crowd of guests and smiled down at the buttery crab puff in her fingers. "Are you making fun of my father, Ms. Summers?"

Monica sighed in exasperation. "This *is* a formal party, after all—not a kegger at the Golden Buckle. I don't know why the senator insists on inviting the help to important affairs."

Slowly, and with great deliberation, Libby tucked her crab puff into Monica's artfully displayed cleavage. "Will you hold this, please?" she trilled, and then walked toward her husband.

"The foreman's brat strikes again," Jess chuckled, pulling her into another waltz.

Cathy was sitting alone in the dimly lit kitchen, her eyes fixed on something far in the distance. Libby was careful to let her cousin see her, rather than startle her with a touch.

"Hi," she said.

Cathy replied listlessly.

Libby took a chair opposite Cathy's and signed, "I'd like to help if I can."

Cathy's face crumbled suddenly and she gave a soft

cry that tore at Libby's heart. Her hands flew as she replied, "Nobody can help me!"

"Don't I even get to try?"

A tendril of Cathy's hair fell from the soft knot at the back of her head and danced against a shoulder left bare by her Grecian evening gown. "I'm pregnant," she whispered. "Oh, Libby, I'm pregnant!"

Libby felt confusion and just a touch of envy. "Is that so terrible? I know you were scared before, but—"

"I'm still scared!" Cathy broke in, her voice unusually loud.

Libby drew a deep breath. "Why, Cathy? You're strong and healthy. And your deafness won't be the problem you think it will—you and Stacey can afford to hire help, if you feel it's necessary."

"All of that is so easy for you to say, Libby!" Cathy flared with sudden and startling anger. "You can hear! You're a whole person!"

Libby felt her own temper, always suppressed when dealing with her handicapped cousin, surge into life. "You know something?" she said furiously. "I'm sick of your 'Poor Cathy' number! A child is just about the best thing that can happen to a person and instead of rejoicing, you're standing here complaining!"

"I have a reason to complain!"

Libby's arms flew out from her side in a gesture of wild annoyance. "All right! You're deaf, you can't hear! Poor, poor Cathy! Now, can we get past singing your sad song? Dammit, Cathy, I know how hard it must be to live in silence, but can't you look on the positive side for once? You're married to a successful, gentle-hearted man who loves you very much. You have everything!"

"Said the woman who could hear!" shouted Cathy.

Libby sighed and sat back in her chair. "We're all handicapped in some way—Jess told me that once, and I think it's true."

Cathy was not going to be placated. "What's your handicap, Libby?" she snapped. "Your short fingernails? The fact that you freckle in the summer instead of getting tan?"

The derisive sarcasm of her cousin's words stung Libby. "I'm as uncertain of myself at times as you are, Cathy," she said softly. "Aaron—"

"Aaron!" spouted Cathy with contempt. "Don't hand me that, Libby! So he ran around a little—I had to stand by and watch my husband adore my own cousin for months! And I'll bet Jess has made any traumas you had about going to bed with a man all better!"

"Cathy, please…"

Cathy gave a guttural, furious cry of frustration. "I'm so damned tired of you, Libby, with your career and your loving father and your…"

Libby was mad again, and she bounded to her feet. "And my what?" she cried. "I can't help that you don't have a father—Dad tried to make up for that and I think he did a damned good job! As for a career—don't you dare hassle me about that! I worked like a slave to get where I am! If you want a career, Cathy, get off your backside and start one!"

Cathy stared at her, stunned, and then burst into tears. And, of course, Jess chose exactly that moment to walk in.

Giving Libby one scalding, reproachful look, he gathered Cathy into his arms and held her.

Chapter 15

After one moment of feeling absolutely shattered, Libby lifted her chin and turned from Jess's annoyance and Cathy's veiled triumph to walk out of the kitchen with dignity.

She encountered a worried-looking Marion Bradshaw just on the other side of the door. "Libby... Mrs. Barlowe...that man is here!"

Libby drew a deep breath. "What man?" she managed to ask halfheartedly.

"Mr. Aaron Strand, that's who!" whispered Marion. "He had the nerve to walk right up and ring the bell...."

Libby was instantly alert, alive in every part of her being, like a creature being stalked in the wilds. "Where is he now?"

"He's in the senator's study," answered the flushed, quietly outraged housekeeper. "He says he won't leave till he talks with you, Libby. I didn't want a scene, what with all these people here, so I didn't argue."

Wearily Libby patted Marion's shoulder. Facing Aaron Strand, especially now, was the last thing in the world she wanted to do. But she knew that he would create an awful fuss if his request was denied, and besides, what real harm could he do with so many people in the house? "I'll talk to him," she said.

"I'll get Jess," mused Mrs. Bradshaw, "and your daddy, too."

Libby shook her head quickly, and warm color surged up over her face. Jess was busy lending a strong shoulder to Cathy, and she was damned if she was going to ask for his help now, even indirectly. And though Ken was almost fully recovered from his confrontation with the bear, Libby had no intention of subjecting him to the stress that could result from a verbal round with his former son-in-law. "I'll handle this myself," she said firmly, and then, without waiting for a reply, she started for the senator's study.

Aaron was there, tall and handsome in his formal clothes.

"At least when you crash a party, you dress for it," observed Libby drily from the doorway.

Aaron set down the paperweight he had been examining and smiled. His eyes moved over her in a way that made her want to stride across the room and slap him with all her might. "That dress is classy, sugarplum," he said in acid tones. "You're definitely bunkhouse-calendar material."

Libby bit her lower lip, counted mentally until the urge to scream passed. "What do you want, Aaron?" she asked finally.

"Want?" he echoed, pretending pleasant confusion.

"Yes!" hissed Libby. "You flew two thousand miles—you must want something."

He sighed, leaned back against the senator's desk, folded his arms. "Are you happy?"

"Yes," answered Libby with a lift of her chin.

Again he assessed her shiny silver dress, the hint of cleavage it revealed. "I imagine the cowboy is pretty happy with you, too," he said. "Which Barlowe is it, Libby? The steak-house king or the lawyer?"

Libby's head began to ache; she sighed and closed her eyes for just a moment. "What do you want?" she asked again insistently.

His shoulders moved in a shrug. "A baby," he answered, as though he was asking for a cup of coffee or the time of day. "I know you're not going to give me that, so relax."

"Why did you come here, then?"

"I just wanted a look at this ranch. Pretty fancy spread, Lib. You do know how to land on your feet, don't you?"

"Get out, Aaron."

"Without meeting your husband? Your paragon of a father? I wouldn't think of it, Mrs. Barlowe."

Libby was off balance, trying to figure out what reason Aaron could have for coming all the way to Montana besides causing her added grief. Incredible as it seemed, he had apparently done just that. "You can't hurt me anymore, Aaron," she said. "I won't let you. Now, get out of here, please."

"Oh, no. I lost everything because of you—everything. And I'll have my pound of flesh, Libby—you can be sure of that."

"If your grandmother relieved you of your company responsibilities, Aaron, that's your fault, not mine. I should think you would be glad—now you won't have anything to keep you from your wine, women and song."

Aaron's face was tense. Gone was his easy, gentlemanly manner. "With the company went most of my money, Libby. And let's not pretend, sweetness—I can make your bright, shiny new life miserable, and we both know it."

"How?" asked Libby, poised to turn and walk out of the study.

"By generating shame and scandal, of course. Your father-in-law is a prominent United States senator, isn't he? I should think negative publicity could hurt him very badly—and you know how good I am at stirring that up."

Rage made Libby tremble. "You can't hurt Cleave Barlowe, Aaron. You can't hurt me. Now, get out before I have you thrown out!"

He crossed the room at an alarming speed, had a hold on Libby's upper arms before she could grasp what was happening. He thrust her back against the heavy door of the study and covered her mouth with his own.

Libby squirmed, shocked and repulsed. She tried to push Aaron away, but he had trapped her hands between his chest and her own. And the kiss went on, ugly and wet, obscene because it was forced upon her, because it was Aaron's.

Finally he drew back, smirking down at her, grasping her wrists in both hands when she tried to wriggle away from him. And suddenly Libby was oddly detached, calm even. Mrs. Bradshaw had been right when she'd wanted to let Jess know that Aaron was here, so very right.

Libby had demurred because of her pride, because she was mad at Jess; she'd thought she could handle Aaron Strand. Pride be damned, she thought, and then she threw back her head and gave a piercing, defiant scream.

Aaron chuckled. "Do you think I'm afraid of your husband, Libby?" he drawled. Incredibly, he was about to kiss her again, it appeared, when he was suddenly wrenched away.

Libby dared one look at Jess's green eyes and saw murder flashing there. She reached for his arm, but he shook her hand away.

"Strand," he said, his gaze fixed on a startled but affably recovering Aaron.

Aaron gave a mocking half-bow. It didn't seem to bother him that Jess was coldly furious, that half the guests at the senator's party, Ken Kincaid included, were jammed into the study doorway.

"Is this the part," Aaron drawled, "where we fight over the fair lady?"

"This is the part," Jess confirmed icily.

Aaron shrugged. "I feel honor-bound to warn you," he said smugly, "that I am a fifth-degree black belt."

Jess spared him an evil smile, but said nothing.

Libby was afraid; again she grasped at Jess's arm. "Jess, he really is a black belt."

Jess did not so much as look at Libby; he was out of her reach, and not just physically. She felt terror thick in her throat, and flung an appealing look at Ken, who was standing beside her, one arm around her waist.

Reading the plea in his daughter's eyes, he denied it with an almost imperceptible shake of his head.

Libby was frantic. As Jess and Aaron drew closer to each other, circling like powerful beasts, she struggled to free herself from her father's restraining arm. For all his weaknesses of character, Aaron Strand was agile and strong, and if he could hurt Jess, he would, without qualms of any kind.

"Jess, no!" she cried.

Jess turned toward her, his jaw tight with cold annoyance, and Aaron struck in that moment. His foot came up in a graceful arc and caught Jess in the side of the neck. Too sick to stand by herself or run away, Libby buried her face in Ken's tuxedo jacket in horror.

There were sounds—terrible sounds. Why didn't someone stop the fight? Why were they all standing around like Romans thrilling to the exploits of gladiators? Why?

When the sounds ceased and Libby dared to look, Jess was still standing. Aaron was sitting on the floor, groaning theatrically, one corner of his lip bleeding. It was obvious that he wasn't badly hurt, for all his carrying on.

Rage and relief mingled within Libby in one dizzying sweep. "Animals!" she screamed, and when she whirled to flee the ugliness, no one moved to stop her.

Libby sat on the couch in the condo's living room, her arms wrapped around her knees, stubbornly ignoring the ringing of the telephone. She had turned off the answering machine, but she couldn't help counting the rings—that had become something of a game in the two days since she'd left the ranch to take refuge here. Twenty-six rings. It was a record.

She stood up shakily, made her way into the kitchen, where she had been trying to sketch out the panels for her cartoon strip. "Back to the old drawing board," she said to the empty room, and the stale joke fell flat because there was no one there to laugh.

The telephone rang again and, worn down, Libby reached out for the receiver affixed to the kitchen wall and snapped, "Hello!"

"Lib?" The voice belonged to her father, and it was full of concern. "Libby, are you all right?"

"No," she answered honestly, letting a sigh carry the word. "As a matter of fact, I'm not all right. How are you?"

"Never mind me—why did you run off like that?"

"You know why."

"Are you coming back to the ranch?"

"Why?" countered Libby, annoyed. "Am I missing some bloody spectacle?"

Ken gave a gruff sigh. "Dammit, Libby, do you love Jess Barlowe or not?"

Tears stung her eyes. Love him? These two days away from him had been hell, but she wasn't about to admit that. "What does it matter?" she shot back. "He's probably so busy holding Cathy's hand that he hasn't even noticed I'm gone."

"That's it. Cathy. Standing up for her is a habit with Jess, Lib—you know that."

Libby did know; in two days she'd had plenty of time to come to the conclusion that she had overreacted in the kitchen the night of the party when Jess had seemed to take Cathy's part against her. She shouldn't have walked out that way. "There is still the fight—"

"You screamed, Libby. What would you have done, if you'd been in Jess's place?" Without waiting for an answer, her father went on, "You're just being stubborn, and so is Jess. Do you love him enough to make the first move, Lib? Do you have the gumption?"

Libby reached out for a kitchen chair, sank into it. "Where is he?"

There was a smile in her father's voice. "Up on that ridge behind your place," he answered. "He's got a camp up there."

Libby knew mild disappointment; if Jess was camping, he hadn't been calling. She had been ignoring the telephone for two days for nothing. "It's nice to know he misses me so much," she muttered petulantly.

Having said his piece, Ken was silent.

"He does miss me, doesn't he?" demanded Libby.

"He misses you," chuckled Ken. "He wouldn't be doing his hermit routine if he didn't."

Libby sighed. "The ridge, huh?"

"The ridge," confirmed Ken with amusement. And then he hung up.

I shouldn't be doing this in my condition, Libby complained to herself as she made her way up the steep hillside. *But since the mountain won't come to me...*

She stopped, looked up. The smoke from Jess's campfire was curling toward the sky; the sun was hot and bright. What the devil did he need with a fire, anyway? It was broad daylight, for heaven's sake.

Muttering, holding on to her waning courage tenaciously, Libby made her way up over the rise to the top of the ridge. Jess was standing with his back to her, looking in the opposite direction, but the stiffness of his shoulders revealed that he knew she was there.

And suddenly she was furious. Hadn't she climbed up this cursed mountain, her heart in her throat, her pride God-only-knew-where? Wasn't the current situation as much his fault as her own? Hadn't she found out, the very day after she'd left him, that she was going to have his baby?

"Damn you, Jess Barlowe," she hissed, "don't you dare ignore me!"

He turned very slowly to face her. "I'm sorry," he said stiffly and with annoying effort.

"For what?" pressed Libby. Damned if she was going to make it easy!

Jess sighed, idly kicked dirt over his campfire with one booted foot. There was a small tent pitched a few feet away, and a coffeepot sat on a fallen log, along with a paperback book and a half-eaten sandwich. "For assuming that the scene with Cathy was your fault," he said.

Libby huffed over to the log, which was a fair distance from Jess, and sat down, folding her arms. "Well, praise be!" she murmured. "What about that stupid fistfight in your father's study?"

His green eyes shot to her face. "You'll grow horns, lady, before you hear me apologize for that!"

Libby bit her lower lip. Fighting wasn't the ideal way to settle things, it was true, but she couldn't help recalling the pleasure she herself had taken in stuffing that crab puff down the front of Monica Summers's dress at the party. If Monica had made one move to retaliate, she would have gladly tangled with her. "Fair enough," she said.

There was an uncomfortable silence, which Libby finally felt compelled to break. "Why did you have a fire going in the middle of the day?"

Jess laughed. "I wanted to make damned sure you found my camp," he replied.

"Dad told you I was coming!"

He came to sit beside her on the log and even though he didn't touch her, she was conscious of his nearness in every fiber of her flesh and spirit. "Yeah," he admitted, and he looked so sad that Libby wanted to cry.

She eased closer to him. "Jess?"

"What?" he asked, looking her squarely in the eyes now.

"I'm sorry."

He said nothing.

Libby drew a deep breath. "I'm not only sorry," she went on bravely, "I'm pregnant, too."

He was quiet for so long that Libby feared she'd been wrong to tell him about their child—at least for now. It was possible that he wanted to ask for a separation or even a divorce, but he might stay with her out of duty now that he knew. To hold him in that manner would break Libby's heart.

"When did you find out?" he asked finally, and the lack of emotion in his face and in his voice made Libby feel bereft.

"Day before yesterday. After Cathy said she was pregnant, I got to thinking and realized that I had a few symptoms myself."

Jess was silent, looking out over the trees, the ranges, the far mountains. After what seemed like an eternity, he turned to her again, his green eyes full of pain. "You weren't going to tell me?"

"Of course I was going to tell you, Jess. But, well, the time didn't seem to be right."

"You're not going to leave, are you?"

"Would I have climbed a stupid mountain, for pity's sake, if I wanted to leave you?"

A slow grin spread across Jess's face, and then he gave a startling hoot of delight and shot to his feet, his hands gripping Libby's and pulling her with him. If he hadn't caught her in his arms and held her, she would probably have fallen into the lush summer grass.

"Is it safe to assume you're happy about this announcement?" Libby teased, looking up at him and loving him all the more because there were tears on his face.

He lifted her into his arms, kissed her deeply in reply.

"Excuse me, sir," she said when he drew back, "but I was wondering if you would mind making love to me. You see, I'd like to find out if I'm welcome here."

In answer, Jess carried her to the tent, set her on her feet. "My tent is your tent," he said.

Libby blushed a little and bent to go inside the small canvas shelter. Since there wasn't room enough to stand, she sat on the rumpled sleeping bag and waited as Jess joined her.

She was never sure exactly how it came about, but within moments they were both lying down, facing each other. The weight of his hand was bliss on her breast, and so were the hoarse words he said.

"I love you, Libby. I need you. No matter how mad I make you, please don't leave me again."

Libby traced the strong lines of his jaw with a fingertip. "I won't, Jess. I might scream and yell, but I won't leave. I love you too much to be away from you—if I learned anything in the last two days, it was that."

He was propped up on one elbow now, very close, and he was idly unbuttoning her blouse. "I want you."

Libby feigned shock. "In a tent, sir?"

"And other novel places." He paused, undid the front catch of her bra.

Libby sighed, then gasped as the warmth of his mouth closed over the straining peak of her breast. The sensation was exquisite, sweeping through her, pushing away the weariness and confusion and pain. She tangled her fingers in his rumpled hair, holding him close.

Jess finally left the breast he had so gently plundered to remove his clothes, and then, more slowly, Libby's. When she lay naked before him in the cool shadows of the tiny tent, he took in her waiting body with a look of rapt wonder. "Little enchantress," he breathed, "let me worship you."

Libby could not bear to be separate from him any longer. "Be close to me, Jess," she pleaded softly, "be part of me."

With a groan, he fell to her, his mouth moist and commanding upon hers. His tongue mated with Libby's and his manhood touched her with fire, prodding, taking only partial shelter inside her.

At last Jess broke the kiss and lifted his head, and Libby saw, through a shifting haze, that he was savoring her passion as well as his own. She was aware of every muscle in his body as he struggled to defy forces that do not brook the rebellion of mere mortals.

Finally these forces prevailed, and Jess was thrust, with a raspy cry, into Libby's depths. They moved to-

gether wildly, seeking and reaching and finally breaking through the barriers that divide this world from the
glories of the next.

Cathy assessed the large oil painting of Jim Little
Eagle, the child Libby had seen at the powwow months
before, her hands resting on her protruding stomach.

Libby, whose stomach was as large as Cathy's, was
wiping her hands on a rag reserved for the purpose. The
painting was a personal triumph, and she was proud
of it. "What do you think?" she signed, after setting
aside the cloth.

Cathy grinned. "What do I think?" she asked aloud,
sitting down on the tall stool behind Libby's drawing
board. "I'll tell you what I think. I think you should
sell it to me instead of letting that gallery in Great Falls
handle it. After all, they've got your pen-and-ink drawings and the other paintings you did."

Libby tried to look stern. "Are you asking for special
favors, Cathy Barlowe?"

Cathy laughed. "Yes!" Her sparkling green eyes fell
to the sketch affixed to Libby's drawing board and she
exclaimed in delighted surprise. "This is great!"

Libby came to stand behind her, but her gaze touched
only briefly on the drawing. Instead, she was looking
out at the snow through the windows of her studio in
Ken and Becky's house.

"What are you going to do with this?" Cathy demanded, tugging at Libby's arm.

Libby smiled, looking at the drawing. It showed her
cartoon character, given over to the care of another art-
ist now. Liberated Lizzie was in an advanced state of
pregnancy, and the blurb read, "If it feels good, do it."

"I'm going to give it to Jess," she said with a slight blush. "It's a private joke."

Cathy laughed again, then assessed the spacious, well-equipped studio with happy eyes. "I'm surprised you work down here at your dad's place. Especially with Jess home almost every day, doing paperwork and things."

Libby's mouth quirked in a grin. "That's *why* I work down here. If I tried to paint there, I wouldn't get anything done."

"You're really happy, aren't you?"

"Completely."

Cathy enfolded her in a hug. "Me, too," she said. And when her eyes came to Libby's face, they were dancing with mischief. "Of course, you and Jess have to understand that you will never win the Race. Stacey and I are ahead by at least a nose."

Libby stood straight and tried to look imperious. "We will not concede defeat," she said.

Before Cathy could reply to this, Stacey came into the room, pretending to see only Libby. "Pardon me, pudgy person," he began, "but has my wife waddled by lately?"

"Is she kind of short, with long, pretty hair and big green eyes and a stomach shaped rather like a watermelon?"

Stacey snapped his fingers and a light seemed to go on in his face. "That's a pretty good description."

"Haven't seen her," said Libby.

Cathy gave her a delighted shove and flung herself at her husband, laughing. A moment later they were on their way out, loudly vowing to win what Jess and Stacey had dubbed the Great Barlowe Baby Race.

Through with her work for the day and eager to get home to Jess, Libby cleaned her brushes and put them away, washed her hands again, and went out to find her coat. The first pain struck just as she was getting into the car.

At home, Jess was standing pensively in the kitchen, staring out at the heavy layer of snow blanketing the hillside behind the house. Libby came up as close behind him as her stomach would allow and wrapped her arms around his lean waist.

"I've just had a pretty good tip on the Baby Race," she said.

The muscles beneath his bulky woolen sweater tightened, and he turned to look down at her, his jade eyes dark with wonder. "What did you say?"

"We're on the homestretch, Jess. I need to go to the hospital. Soon."

He paled, this man who had hunted wounded bears and fire-breathing dragons. "My God!" he yelled, and suddenly they were both caught up in a whirlwind of activity. Phone calls were made, suitcases were snatched from the coat-closet floor, and then Jess was dragging Libby toward his Land Rover.

"Wait, I'm sure we have time—"

"I'm not taking any chances!" barked Jess, hoisting her pear-shaped and unwieldy form into the car seat.

"Jess," Libby scolded, grasping at his arm. "You're panicking!"

"You're damned right I'm panicking!" he cried, and then they were driving over the snowy, rutted roads of the ranch at the fastest pace he dared.

When they reached the airstrip, the Cessna had been brought out of the small hangar where it was kept and fuel was being pumped into it. After wrestling Libby into the front passenger seat, Jess quickly checked the engine and the landing gear. These were tasks, she had learned, that he never trusted to anyone else.

"Jess, this is ridiculous!" she protested when he scrambled into the pilot's seat and began a preflight test there. "We have plenty of time to drive to the hospital."

Jess ignored her, and less than a minute later the plane was taxiing down the runway. Out of the corner of one eye Libby saw a flash of ice blue.

"Jess, wait!" she cried. "The Ferrari!"

The plane braked and Jess craned his neck to see around Libby. Sure enough, Stacey and Cathy were running toward them, if Cathy's peculiar gait could be called a run.

Stacey leapt up onto the wing and opened the door. "Going our way?" he quipped, but his eyes were wide and his face was white.

"Get in," replied Jess impatiently, but his eyes were gentle as they touched Cathy and then Libby. "The race is on," he added.

Cathy was the first to deliver, streaking over the finish line with a healthy baby girl, but Libby produced twin sons soon after. Following much discussion, the Great Barlowe Baby Race was declared a draw.

* * * * *

For additional books by *New York Times*
bestselling author Brenda Jackson,
visit her website, www.brendajackson.net.

A WIFE
FOR A WESTMORELAND

Brenda Jackson

Chapter 1

Lucia Conyers's heart was beating like crazy as she made a sharp turn around the curve while the wheels of her SUV barely gripped the road. She knew she should slow down, but couldn't. The moment she'd heard that Derringer Westmoreland had been taken to the emergency room due to an injury he sustained after being thrown from a horse, a part of her had nearly died inside.

It didn't matter that most of the time Derringer acted as though he didn't know she existed or that he had a reputation in Denver as a ladies' man—although she doubted the women he messed around with could really be classified as ladies. Derringer was one of Denver's heartthrobs, a hottie if ever there was one.

But what did matter, although she wished otherwise, was that she loved him and would probably always love him. She'd tried falling out of love with him several times and just couldn't do it.

Not even four years of attending a college in Florida had changed her feelings for him. The moment she had returned to Denver and he had walked into her father's paint store to make a purchase, she'd almost passed out from a mixture of lust and love.

Surprisingly, he had remembered her. He'd welcomed her back to town and asked her about school. But he hadn't asked her out, or offered to share a drink somewhere for old time's sake. Instead, he had gathered up the merchandise he'd come to the store to buy and left.

Her obsession with him had started back in high school when she and his sister Megan had worked on a science project together. Lucia would never forget the day that Megan's brother had come to pick them up from the library. She'd almost passed out when she first laid eyes on the handsome Derringer Westmoreland.

She thought she'd died and gone to heaven, and when they were introduced, he smiled at her, showing a pair of dimples that should be outlawed on anyone, especially a man. Her heart had melted then and there and hadn't solidified since. That introduction had taken place a few months after her sixteenth birthday. Now she was twenty-nine and she still got goose bumps whenever she thought about that first meeting.

Ever since her best friend, Chloe, had married Derringer's brother Ramsey, she saw more of Derringer, but nothing had changed. Whenever he saw her he was always nice to her. But she knew he really didn't see her as a woman he would be interested in.

So why wasn't she getting on with her life? Why was

she risking it now by taking the roads to his place like a madwoman, needing to see for herself that he was still in one piece? When she'd gotten the news, she'd rushed to the hospital only to receive word from Chloe that he'd been released and was now recuperating at home.

He would probably wonder why she, of all people, was showing up at his place to check on him. She wouldn't be surprised if some woman was already there waiting on him hand and foot. But at the moment it didn't matter. Nothing mattered but to make sure for herself that Derringer was okay. Even the threat of possible thunderstorms this evening hadn't kept her away. She hated thunderstorms, and yet she had left her home to check on a man who barely knew she was alive.

It was a really stupid move, but she continued to speed down the road, deciding she would consider the foolishness of her actions later.

The loud sound of thunder blasting across the sky practically shook the house and awakened Derringer. He immediately felt a sharp pain slice through his body, the first since he'd taken his pain medication, which meant it was time to take more.

Wrenching at the pain, he slowly pulled himself up in bed, reached across the nightstand and grabbed the pills his sister Megan had laid out for him. She'd said not to take more before six, but a quick glance at his clock said that it was only four and he needed the relief now. He was aching all over and his head felt as if it had split in two. He felt sixty-three instead of a mere thirty-three.

He had been on Sugar Foot's back less than three minutes when the mean-spirited animal had sent him flying. More than his ego had gotten bruised, and each and every time he breathed against what felt like broken ribs he was reminded of it.

Derringer eased back down onto the bed and laid flat on his back. He stared at the ceiling, waiting for the pain pills to kick in.

Derringer's Dungeon.

Lucia slowed her truck when she came to the huge wooden marker in the road. Any other time she would have found it amusing that each of the Westmorelands had marked their property with such fanciful names. Already she had passed Jason's Place, Zane's Hideout, Canyon's Bluff, Stern's Stronghold, Riley's Station and Ramsey's Web. She'd heard when each Westmoreland reached the age of twenty-five they inherited a one-hundred-acre tract of land in this part of the state. That was why all the Westmorelands lived in proximity to each other.

She nervously gnawed on her bottom lip, finally thinking she might have made a mistake in coming here when she pulled into the yard and saw the huge two-story structure. This was her first time at Derringer's Dungeon and from what she'd heard, most women only came by way of an invite.

So what was she doing here?

She brought her car to a stop and cut off the engine and just sat there a moment as reality set in. She had acted on impulse and of course on love, but the truth of the matter was that she had no business being here. Derringer was probably in bed resting. He might even be on medication. Would he be able to come to the door? If he did, he would probably look at her as if she had two heads for wanting to check on him. In his book they were acquaintances, not even friends.

She was about to back out and leave, when she noticed the rain had started to come down harder and a huge box that had been left on the steps of the porch was getting wet. The least she could do was to move it to an area on the porch where the rain couldn't touch it.

Grabbing her umbrella out the backseat, she hurriedly got out of the truck and ran toward the porch to move the box closer to the door. She jumped at the sound of thunder and drew in a sharp breath when a bolt of lightning barely missed the top of her head.

Remembering what Chloe had once told her about how the Westmoreland men were notorious for not locking their doors, she tried the doorknob and saw what her best friend had said was true. The door was not locked.

Slowly opening the door, she stuck her head in and called out in a whisper in case he was downstairs sleeping on the sofa instead of upstairs. "Derringer?"

When he didn't answer, she decided she might as well bring the box inside. The moment she entered the house, she glanced around, admiring his sister Gemma's decorating skills. Derringer's home was beautiful, and the floor-to-ceiling windows took full advantage of the mountain view. She was about to ease back out the door and lock it behind her when she heard a crash followed by a bump and then a loud curse.

Acting on instinct, she took the stairs two at a time and stumbled into several guest bedrooms before entering what had to be the master bedroom. It was decorated in a more masculine theme than all the others. She glanced around and then she saw him lying on the floor as if he'd fallen out of bed.

"Derringer!"

She raced over to him and knelt down beside him, trying to ignore the fact that the only clothing he had on was a pair of black briefs. "Derringer? Are you all right?" she asked, a degree of panic clearly in her voice. "Derringer?"

He slowly opened his eyes and she couldn't stop the fluttering of her heart when she gazed down into the gorgeous dark depths. The first thing she noticed was they were glassy, as if he'd taken one drink too many... or probably one pill too many. She then took a deep breath when a slow smile touched the corners of his lips and those knock-a-girl-off-her-feet dimples appeared in his cheeks.

"Well, now, aren't you a pretty thing," he said in slurred speech. "What's your name?"

"Puddin' Tame," she replied smartly. His actions confirmed he'd evidently taken one pill too many since he was acting as if he'd never seen her in his life.

"That's a real nice name, sweetheart."

She rolled her eyes. "Whatever you say, cowboy. Would you like to explain why you're down here and not up there?" She motioned toward his bed.

"That's easy enough to answer. I went to the bathroom and when I got back, someone moved the bed and I missed it."

She tried keeping the smile from her face. "You sure did miss it. Come on and hold on to me while I help you back into it."

"Someone might move it again."

"I doubt it," she said, grinning, while thinking even when he was under the influence of medication, the deep, husky sound of his voice could do things to her. Make the nipples of her breasts strain against her damp shirt. "Come on, you have to be hurting something awful."

He chuckled. "No, in fact I feel good. Good enough to try riding Sugar Foot again."

She shook her head. "Not tonight you won't. Come on, Derringer, let me help you up and get you back in bed."

"I like it down here."

"Sorry, pal, but you can't stay down here. You either let me help you up or I'll call one of your brothers to help you."

Now it was he who shook his head. "I don't want to see any of them again for a while. All they know how to say is, I told you so."

"Well maybe next time you'll listen to them. Come on."

It took several attempts before she was able to help Derringer to his feet. It wasn't easy to steer him to the bed, and she suddenly lost her balance and found herself tumbling backward onto his bed with him falling on top of her.

"I need you to shift your body a little to get off me, Derringer," she said when she was able to catch her breath.

He flashed those sexy dimples again and spoke in a voice throaty with arousal. "Um, why? I like being on top of you, Puddin'. You feel good."

She blinked and then realized the extent of her situation. She was in bed—Derringer's bed—and he was sprawled on top of her. It didn't take much to feel the bulge of his erection through his briefs that was connecting with the area between her legs. A slow burn began inching from that very spot and spreading all through her, entering her bloodstream and making her skin burn all over. And if that wasn't bad enough, the nipples of her breasts, which were already straining, hardened like pebbles against his bandaged chest.

As if sensing her body's reaction to their position, he lifted his face to stare down at her and the glassy eyes that snagged hers were so drenched with desire that her breath got caught in her throat. Something she'd never felt before, a pooling of heat, settled between her legs, wetting her panties, and she watched his nostrils flare in response to her scent.

The air between them was crackling more than the thunder and lightning outside, and his chest seemed to rise and fall with each and every beat of her heart.

Fearing her own rapid reaction to their predicament, she made an attempt to gently shove him off her, but found she was no match for his solid weight.

"Derringer..."

Instead of answering her, he reached up and cupped her face into his hands as if her mouth was water he needed to sip, and before she could turn her mouth away from his, with perfect aim, he lowered his mouth and began devouring hers.

Derringer figured he had to be dreaming, and if he was, then this was one delusion he didn't care to ever wake up from. Feasting on Puddin' Tame's lips was the epitome of sensual pleasure. Molded perfectly, they were hot and moist. And the way he had plunged his tongue inside her mouth, devouring hers was the sort of fantasy wet dreams were made of.

Somewhere in the back of his lust-induced mind he

remembered getting thrown off a horse; in that case, his body should be in pain. However, the only ache he was feeling was the one in his groin that signaled a need so great his body was all but trembling inside.

Who was this woman and where did she come from? Was he supposed to know her? Why was she enticing him to do things he shouldn't do? A part of him felt that he wasn't in his right mind, but then another part didn't give a damn if he was in his wrong mind. The only thing he knew for sure was that he wanted her. He could eat her alive and wouldn't mind testing that theory to see if he really could.

He shifted his body a little and brought her in the center of the bed with him. He lifted his mouth only slightly off hers to whisper huskily against her moist lips, "Damn, Puddin', you feel good."

And then his mouth was back on hers, sucking on her tongue as if he was a man who needed to taste her as much as he needed to breathe, and what was so shocking to him at that moment was that he was convinced that he did.

Lucia knew she had to put a stop to what she and Derringer were doing. He was delirious and didn't even know who she was. But it was hard to stop him when her body was responding to everything he was doing to it. Her mouth had never been kissed like this before. No man had consumed her with so much pleasure for her not to think straight. Never had she known a woman could want a man with such magnitude as she wanted Derringer. She had always loved him, but now she wanted him with a need that had been foreign to her.

Until now.

"I want you, Puddin'..."

She blinked as he slightly leaned up off her and the reality of the moment hit her. Although he was delusional, Lucia realized that the honorable part of Derringer would not force her into doing anything she didn't want to do. Now was her chance to slide from beneath him and leave. Chances were, he wouldn't even remember anything about tonight.

But something wouldn't let her flee. It kept her rooted in place as she stared up at him, caught in a visual exchange that not only entrapped her sight but also her mind. A part of her knew this would be the one and only time she would have his attention like this. Sadly, it would be the one and only time he would want her. She pushed to the back of her mind that it had taken an overdose of pain medication to get him to this state.

If she didn't love him so much, she probably would have been able to fight this sexual pull, but love combined with lust was a force she couldn't fight, and a part of her truly didn't want to. She would be thirty in ten months and as of yet, she hadn't experienced how it would feel to be with a man. It was about time she did and it might as well be with the one and only man she'd ever loved.

She would take tonight into her soul, cradle it in her heart and keep it safe in the deep recesses of her brain. And when she saw him again she would have a secret he wouldn't know about, although he would have been the main person responsible for making it happen.

Captured by his deep, dark gaze, she knew it was only a matter of minutes before he took her silence as consent. Now that she'd made up her mind about what she wanted to do, she didn't want to wait even that long.

And as more liquid heat coiled between her legs, she lifted her arms to wrap around his neck and tilted her mouth to his. The moment she did, pleasure between them exploded and plunged her into a mirage of sensations that she'd never even dreamed about.

He began kissing her senseless and in her lust-induced mind she was barely aware of him pulling her blouse over her head and removing her lace bra from her body. But she knew the exact moment he latched on to a nipple and eased it between heated lips and began sucking on it as though it was just for his enjoyment.

Waves of pleasures shot through every part of her as if she'd been hit with an atomic missile that detonated on impact. She caught his head between her hands to keep his mouth from going anywhere but on her. Several moans she hadn't known she was capable of making eased from her lips and she couldn't help but writhe the lower part of her body against him, needing to feel the hardness of his erection between her thighs.

As if he wanted more, she knew the moment his fingers eased up her skirt and tracked their way to the part of her that was burning more than any other part—her moist, hot center. He slid one hand beneath the edge of her panties and, as if his finger knew exactly what it was after, it slowly and diligently trekked toward her throbbing clitoris.

"Derringer!"

Her entire body began trembling and with all the intent of a man on a mission he began stroking her with fingers that should be outlawed right along with his dimples. Her womanly core was getting more attention than it had ever gotten before, and she could feel sensations building up inside her at such a rapid rate she was feeling dizzy.

"I want you," he said in a low, guttural tone. And then he kissed her again in a deep, drugging exchange that had him sliding his tongue all over her mouth, tasting her as if doing so was his right. Just the thought made her powerless to do anything other than accept his seduction with profound pleasure.

She was so into the kiss that she hadn't realized he had worked his briefs down his legs and had removed her panties, until she felt them flesh to flesh. His skin felt hot against hers and the iron-steel feel of his thighs resting over hers was penetrating through to every pore in her body.

And when he broke the kiss to ease his body over hers, she was so overcome with desire that she was rendered powerless to stop him.

He lowered his eyes to her breasts and smiled before his eyes slowly returned to her face and snagged her gaze. The look he gave her at that moment was so sexual that she was willing to convince herself that she was the only woman on earth he'd ever given it to. And she was just that far gone to believe it.

Then he leaned down and captured her mouth at the same time he thrust into her body. She couldn't help but cry out from the pain and, as if he sensed what had happened and just what it meant, his body went completely still. He eased his mouth away from hers and glanced down at her while still deeply embedded within her. Not sure just what thoughts were going through his mind about her virginal state and not really wanting to know, she reached up and wrapped her arms around him. And when she began using her tongue to kiss him the way he'd done to her earlier, she felt his body tremble slightly before he began moving inside her. The first time he did so, she thought she would come apart, but as his body began thrusting into hers, smoldering heat from him was being transferred to her, building a fire she could not contain any longer.

He released her mouth long enough for her to call his name. "Derringer!"

He was devouring her in a way she'd never been devoured before and she couldn't help but cry out as his tongue took over. The lower part of him was sending waves of pleasure crashing through her that had her sucking in sharp breaths.

She had heard—mainly from Chloe during one of their infamous girl chats—that making love to a man, especially one you loved, was a totally rewarding and satisfying experience. But no one told her that it could be so mind-consuming and pleasurable. Or that it could literally curl your toes. Maybe Chloe had told her these things and she hadn't believed her. Well, now she believed. And with each hard plunge into her body, Derringer was making all the fantasies she'd ever had of him a reality.

He released her mouth to look down at her while he kept making love to her, riding her the way he rode those horses he tamed. He was good. And he was also greedy. To keep up with him, she kept grinding her hips against his as sensations within her intensified to a degree that she knew she couldn't handle much longer. She cried out again and again as sensations continued to spiral through her.

And then something happened that had never happened to her before and she knew what it was the moment she felt it. He drove deeper and deeper into her, riding her right into a climax of monumental proportions. He lifted his head and met her gaze and the dark orbs gazing at her pushed her even more over the edge.

And when he whispered the name Puddin', thinking it was hers, she accepted it because it had sounded so good coming from him, and it was all she needed to hear to push her into her very first orgasm.

"Derringer!"

He lowered his head again and his tongue slid easily inside her mouth. She continued to grind against him, accepting everything he was giving. Moments later, after breaking off the kiss, he threw his head back and whispered the name again in a deep guttural tone, and he continued to stroke her into sweet oblivion.

Lucia slowly opened her eyes while wondering just how long she'd slept. The last thing she remembered was dropping her head onto the pillow. She'd been weak, spent and totally and thoroughly satisfied after making love to the sexiest man to walk the face of the earth.

He was no longer on top of her, but was asleep beside her. She missed the weight of him pressing down on her. She missed how his heart felt beating against hers, but most of all she missed the feel of him being inside her.

Remnants of ecstasy were still trickling through her when she thought of what they'd done and all they'd shared. Being gripped in the throes of orgasm after orgasm for several long moments was enough to blow anybody's mind and it had certainly done a job on her. And the way he had looked down at her—during those times he wasn't kissing her—had sent exquisite sensation after exquisite sensation spiraling through her. Even with the bandages covering his chest and parts of his back, she had felt him—the hardness of his shoulders and the way the muscles in his back had flexed beneath her fingertips.

There was no way she could or would forget tonight. It would always be ingrained in her memory despite the fact that she knew he probably would not remember a single thing. That thought bothered her and she fought back the tears that threatened her eyes. They should be tears of joy and not of sorrow, she thought. She had loved him for so long, but at least she had these memories to cherish.

The rain had stopped and all was quiet except the even, restful sound of Derringer's breathing. Day was breaking and she had to leave. The sooner she did so the better. She could just imagine what he would think if he woke and found her there in bed with him. Whatever words he might say would destroy the beautiful memories of the night she intended to keep.

And her guess was that someone—any one of his brothers, sisters or cousins—might show up any minute to check up on him. They, too, would be shocked as heck to find her there.

She slowly eased out of bed, trying not to wake him, and glanced around for her clothes. She found all the items she needed except for her panties. He had taken them off her while she was in bed, so chances were they were somewhere under the covers.

She slowly lifted the covers and saw the pair of pink panties were trapped beneath his leg. It would be easy enough to wake him and ask him to move his leg so she could get them, but there was no way she could do such a thing. She stood there a moment, hoping he would stir just a little so she could pull them free.

Lucia nervously gnawed on her bottom lip, knowing she couldn't just stand there forever, so she quietly began getting dressed. And only when the sun began peeking over the horizon did she accepted that she had to leave quickly…without her panties.

Glancing around the room to make sure that was the only thing she would be leaving behind, she slowly tiptoed out of the room, but not before glancing over her shoulder one last time to look at Derringer. So this was how he looked in the early mornings. With his shadowed face showing an unshaven chin while lying on the pillow, he looked even more handsome than he'd been last night.

He would probably wonder whose panties were left in his bed, but then he might not. He bedded so many women that it wouldn't matter that one had left a pair of their panties behind. To him it might not be any big deal. Probably wouldn't be.

Moments later while driving away, she glanced back in her rearview mirror at Derringer's home, remembering all that had taken place during the night in his bedroom. She was no longer a virgin. She had given him something she had never given another man, and the only sad part was that he would never, ever know it.

Chapter 2

Some woman had been in his bed.

The potent scent of sex brought Derringer awake, and he lifted his lids then closed them when the sunlight coming through his bedroom window nearly blinded him. He shifted his body and then flinched when pain shot up one of his legs at the same time his chest began aching.

He slowly lifted his head from the pillow, thinking he needed to take some more pain pills, and dropped it back down when he remembered he might have taken one too many last night. Megan would clobber him for taking more than he should have, but at least he'd slept through the night.

Or had he?

He sniffed the air and the scent of a woman's perfume and of sex was still prevalent in his nostrils. Why?

And why were clips of making love to a woman in this very bed going through his brain? It was the best dream he'd had in years. Usually a dream of making love to a woman couldn't touch the reality, but with the one he'd had last night, he would beg to differ. He could understand dreaming about making love to a woman because it had been a while for him. Getting the horse business off the ground with his brother Zane, his cousin Jason and their newfound relatives, those Westmorelands living in Georgia, Montana and Texas, had taken up a lot of his time lately. But his dream had felt so real. That was one hell of an illusion.

Nevertheless, he thought, stretching his body then wishing he hadn't when he felt another pain, it had been well worth the experience.

He reached down to rub his aching thigh, when his hand came in contact with a lacy piece of material. He brought up his hand and blinked when he saw the pair of lace bikini panties that carried the feminine scent he had awakened to.

Pulling himself up in bed, he studied the underthings he held in his hand. Whose were they? Where had they come from? He sniffed the air. The feminine scent was not only in the panties but all over his bed as well. And the indention on the pillow beside him clearly indicated another head had been there.

Monumental panic set in. Who the hell had he made love to last night? Since now there was no doubt in his mind he'd made love to someone. All that pleasure hadn't been a figment of his imagination, but the real thing. But who had been the woman?

He closed his eyes and tried to come up with a face and couldn't. It had to have been someone he knew;

otherwise, who would have come to his house and gotten into his bed? He had messed around with some pretty brazen women in his lifetime, but none would have dared.

Hell, evidently one had.

He opened his eyes and stared at the wall, trying to recall everything he could about yesterday and last night. He remembered the fall off Sugar Foot's back; there was no way he could forget that. He even remembered Zane and Jason rushing him to the emergency room and how he'd gotten bandaged up and then sent home.

He definitely recalled how his brother and cousin kept saying over and over, "We told you so." He remembered that after he'd gotten into bed, Megan had stopped by on her way to the hospital where she worked as an anesthesiologist.

He recalled when she'd given him his pain medicine with instructions of when to take it. The pain had come back sometime after dark and he'd taken some of the pills.

Hell, how much of the stuff had he taken? He distinctly recalled the E.R. physician's warning that the painkillers were pretty potent stuff and had to be taken when instructed. So much for that.

Okay, so he had taken more pain medicine than he was supposed to. But still, what gave some woman the right to enter his home and take advantage of him? He thought of several women who it could have been; anyone who might have heard about his fall and decided to come over and play nursemaid. Only Ashira would have been bold enough to do that. Had he slept with her last night? Hell, he sure hoped not. She might try to pull something and he wasn't in the market of being any baby's daddy any time soon. Besides, what he'd shared with his mystery woman had been different from anything he'd ever shared with Ashira. It had been more profound with one hell of a lasting effect.

He then remembered something vital. The woman he'd slept with had been a virgin—although it was hard to believe he could remember that, he did. And it was pretty far-fetched to think there were still any of them around in this day and time. But there was no way in hell he could have imagined her innocent state even with a mind fuzzy with painkillers. And he knew for certain the woman could not have been Ashira since she didn't have a virginal bone in her body. Besides, he had a steadfast rule to leave innocents alone.

Derringer sighed deeply and wished, for his peace of mind, that he could remember more in-depth details about last night, including the face of the woman whose virginity he had taken. The thought of that made him cringe inside because he knew for certain he hadn't used a condom. Was last night a setup and the result would be a baby just waiting to be born nine months from now?

The thought of any woman taking advantage of him that way—or any way—made his blood boil. And anger began filling him to a degree he hadn't known was possible. If the woman thought she had gotten the best of him she had another thought coming. She had not only trespassed on his private property, but she had invaded his privacy and taken advantage of him when he'd been in a weakened, incoherent state.

If he had to turn over every stone in Denver, he would find out the identity of the woman who'd had the nerve to pull one over on him. And when he found her, he would definitely make her pay for her little stunt.

"Lucia, are you all right?"

It was noon and Lucia was sitting behind the desk of her office at the Denver branch of *Simply Irresistible*, the magazine designed for today's up-and-coming woman.

The magazine, Chloe's brainchild, had started out as a regional publication in the Southeast a few years ago. When Chloe had made the decision to expand to the West and open a Denver office, she had hired Lucia to manage the Denver office.

Lucia loved her job as managing editor. Chloe was editor in chief, but since her baby—a beautiful little girl named Susan—was born six months ago, Chloe spent most of her time at home taking care of her husband and daughter. Lucia had earned a business-management degree in college, but when Chloe had gotten pregnant she had encouraged Lucia to go back to school and get a master's degree in mass communications to further her career at *Simply Irresistible*. Lucia only needed a few more classes to complete that degree.

Lucia figured it would only be a matter of time before Chloe and Ramsey decided they would want another baby, and the running of *Simply Irresistible's* Denver office would eventually fall in her lap.

"Lucia!"

She jumped when Chloe said her name with a little more force, getting her attention. "What? You scared me."

Chloe couldn't help but smile. It had been a long time since she'd seen her best friend so preoccupied. "I was asking you a question."

Lucia scrunched up her face. "You were?"

"Yes."

"Oh, what was your question?"

Chloe shook her head, smiling. "I asked if you were all right. You seem preoccupied about something and I want to know what. Things are looking good here. We doubled our print run for April's issue since the president is on the cover, so that shouldn't cause you any concern. What's going on with you?"

Lucia nibbled on her bottom lip. She needed to tell someone about what happened last night and since Chloe was her best friend, she would be the logical person. However, there was a problem with that. Chloe was married to Ramsey, who was Derringer's oldest brother. There was no doubt in Lucia's mind Chloe would keep her mouth closed about anything if she asked her to, but still…

"Okay, Lucia, I'm only going to ask you one more time. What's wrong with you? You've been acting spaced out since I got here, and I doubt you were listening to anything Barbara was saying during the production meeting. So what's going on with you?"

Lucia breathed in deeply. "It's Derringer."

Frowning, Chloe stared. "What about Derringer? Ramsey called and checked on him this morning and he was doing fine. All he needed was a dose of pain medication and a good night's sleep."

"I'm sure he got the dose of pain medication, but I don't know about the good night's sleep," Lucia said drily, before taking a long sip of cappuccino.

"And why don't you think he got a good night's sleep?"

Lucia shrugged, started to feign total ignorance to

Chloe's question and then decided to come clean. She looked up and met her friend's curious gaze.

"Because I spent the night with him and I know for certain we barely slept at all."

She could tell from the look that suddenly appeared on Chloe's face that she had shocked her friend witless. Now that she had confessed her sins, she was hoping they could move on and talk about something else, but she should know better than to think that.

"You and Derringer finally got together?" Chloe asked. The shocked expression had been replaced by a smile.

"Depends on what you mean by got together. I'm no longer a virgin, if that's what you mean," Lucia said evenly. "But he was so over the top on painkillers he probably doesn't remember a thing."

The smile dropped from Chloe's lips. "You think so?"

"I know so. He looked right in my face and asked me for my name."

She took the next ten minutes and told Chloe everything, including the part about the panties she had left behind. "So that's the end of it," Lucia finished her tale by saying.

Chloe shook her head. "I really don't think so for two reasons, Lucia. First, you're in love with Derringer and have been for a very long time. I don't see that coming to an end any time soon. In fact, now that the two of you have been intimate, you're going to see him in a whole new light. Whenever you run into him, your hunger for him will automatically kick in."

Chloe's expression became even more serious when she said, "And you better hope Derringer doesn't find your panties. If he does find them and can't remember the woman he took them off of, he will do everything in his power to track her down."

Lucia preferred not hearing that. She gripped the handle of her cup tightly in her hand. Turning away to look out the window to view downtown Denver, she drew in a deep ragged breath before taking a sip of her coffee. She hoped Chloe was wrong. The last thing she needed was to worry about that happening.

"With his reputation with women it will be like looking for a needle in a haystack."

"Possibly. But what happens if he finds that needle?"

Lucia didn't want to think about that. She had loved Derringer secretly for so long, she wasn't sure she wanted that to change, especially when he didn't love her back.

"Lucia?"

She turned and looked at Chloe. There was a serious expression on her best friend's face. "I don't know what will happen. I don't want to think that far. I want to believe he won't remember and let it go."

A few moments passed. "What I said earlier was true. Whenever you see Derringer, you're going to want him," Chloe said softly.

She shrugged. "I've always wanted him, Clo."

"Now it will be doubly so."

Lucia opened her mouth to deny Chloe's words and decided not to waste her time because she knew Chloe was probably right. She had thought about him all that day, barely getting any work done. She kept playing over and over in her mind just what the two of them had done together. "I will fight it," she finally said.

Chloe bristled at her words. "It won't be that simple."

She could believe that. Nothing regarding Derringer had ever been simple for her. "Then what do you suggest I do?" Lucia said with resignation in her voice.

"Come out of hiding once and for all and go after him."

She wasn't surprised Chloe would advise her to do something like that. Her best friend was the daring one. She never hesitated in going after anything she wanted and she'd always envied Chloe for being so bold and brave.

Chloe must have seen the wistful look in her eyes and kept pushing. "Go after him, Lucia. Go ahead and take Derringer on. After last night, don't you think it's about time you did?"

A week later, Jason Westmoreland glanced over at his cousin and grinned. "Was that supposed to be a trick question or something?"

Derringer shook his head as he eased back in the chair. He'd done nothing over the past few days but stay on his pain medication and get plenty of sleep. Each time he awoke he would reach under his pillow and pull out the panties he had placed there just to make sure he hadn't dreamed the whole thing. They proved that he hadn't. And the name Puddin' Tame, the alias the woman had given him, kept going through his mind.

This morning he woke feeling a whole lot better and decided to lay off the pills. He hoped clearing his head would trigger something in his memory about what happened a week ago. So far it hadn't.

Jason had dropped by to check on him and the two were sharing early-morning coffee at the kitchen table. "No, it's not a trick question. I figured I'd ask you first before moving on to Riley, Zane, Canyon and Stern. Afterward, I'll compare everybody's answers."

Jason inclined his head with the barest hint of a nod. "Okay, I'll give your question a shot, so go ahead and repeat it to make sure I heard you right."

Derringer rolled his eyes and then leaned closer to the table. His expression was serious. "What can you tell about a woman from the panties she wears, both style and color?"

Jason rubbed his chin a moment. "I would have to say nothing in particular unless they are white, granny-style ones."

"They aren't." He hadn't told Jason why he was asking, and Jason, the easygoing Westmoreland, wouldn't ask... There was no doubt in Derringer's mind that everyone else would.

"Then I really don't know," Jason said, taking a sip of his coffee. "I think some pieces of clothing are supposed to convey messages about people. I picked white because it usually means innocence. But then again, Fannie Nelson had on a pair of low-riding jeans one day that showed her white panties, and she is a long way from being innocent."

"Aren't you curious as to why I want to know?"

"Yes, I'm curious, but not enough to ask. I figure you have your reasons and I don't want to come close to thinking what they might be."

Derringer nodded, understanding why Jason felt that way. His cousin knew his history with women. And what Jason said was true. He had his reasons, all right.

"So what do you plan to do today now that you've returned to the world of the living? I heard the E.R. doc tell you to take it easy for at least a week or so to recuperate, so you're still under restrictions," Jason reminded him.

"Yes, but I'm not restricted from driving. I'm going to hang around here and take it easy for a few more days before venturing out anywhere."

"I'm glad you're following the doc's advice. Although things could have been worse, that was still a nasty fall you took. And as far as your question regarding women's undergarments, I suggest you talk to Zane when he gets back from Boulder." Jason chuckled and then added, "And be prepared to take notes."

Two days later Derringer left home for the first time since his accident and drove to Zane's Hideout. He was glad to see his brother's truck parked in the yard, which meant he was back. Jason was right. He should have been prepared to take notes. Zane, who was only fourteen months older but a heck of a lot wiser where women were concerned, had no qualms about telling him what he wanted to know.

According to Zane, the color and style of a woman's panties said a lot about her. Sexually liberated women wore thongs or barely-there panties, all colors except white, and they rarely wore pastel colors. Most of them preferred black.

Zane further went on to say that women who liked to tease men wore black lace. Women who preferred lace to any other design were women who liked to look and feel pretty. And bikini panties weren't as popular these days as thongs and hipsters, so a woman still wearing bikini panties weren't as sexually liberated as others.

Derringer smiled when Zane, with a serious look on his face, advised him to steer clear of women who wore granny panties. Zane furthermore claimed that women who wore red panties gave the best blow jobs. Those with yellow panties the majority of the time weren't afraid to try anything and were pretty good with a pair of handcuffs. Blue panties–wearing women were loyal to a fault—although they had a tendency to get possessive sometimes, and those who preferred wearing green were only after your money, so the use of double condoms was in order.

It had taken his brother almost an hour to make it to pink panties and, according to the Laws of Zane, women who wear pink panties were the ones you needed to stay away from because they had the word *marriage* written all over them, blasting like neon lights. They were a cross between innocent and a woman with an inner hunger for getting laid. But in the end she would still want a wedding ring on her finger.

"Okay, now that you've taken up more than an hour of my time, how about telling me why you're so interested in a woman's panties," Zane said, eyeing him curiously.

For a moment Derringer considered not telling his brother anything, but then thought better of it. He, his five brothers and all his cousins were close, but there was a special bond between him, Zane and Jason. Besides, it was evident that Zane knew a lot more about women than he did, so maybe his brother could give him some sound advice about how to handle what had occurred that night, just in case he had been set up.

"Some woman came over to my place the night I was injured and let herself in. I can't remember who she was, but I do remember making love to her."

Zane stared at him intently for a moment. "Are you absolutely sure you made love to her and didn't imagine the whole thing? When we took you home from the hospital—right before I had to take off for the airport—you were pretty high on those pain meds. Megan figured that you would probably sleep through most of the night, although she set out more medicine for you to take later."

Derringer shook his head. "Yeah, I was pretty drugged up, but I remember making love to her, Zane. And to prove I didn't dream the whole thing, I found her panties in bed with me the next morning." What he decided not to say was that as far as he was concerned, it had been the best lovemaking he'd ever experienced with a woman.

Zane drew in a deep breath and then said on a heavy sigh. "You better hope it wasn't Ashira. Hell, man, if you didn't use a condom she would love to claim you're her new baby's daddy."

Derringer rubbed the ache that had suddenly crept into his temples at the thought. "It wasn't Ashira, trust me. This woman left one hell of an impression. I've never experienced lovemaking like it before. It was off the charts. Besides, Ashira called a few days after hearing about the accident. She left town to go visit her sick grandmother in Dakota the day before the accident and won't be back for a few weeks."

"You do know there's a way for you to find out the identity of your uninvited visitor, don't you?" Zane asked.

Derringer glanced over at him. "How?"

"Did you forget about the video cameras we had installed on your property to protect the horses, the week before your fall? Anyone pulling into your yard would be captured on film if they got as far as your front porch."

Derringer blinked when he remembered the video camera and wondered why he hadn't recalled it sooner. He got up from Zane's table and swiftly strode to the door. "I need to get home and check out that tape," he said without looking back.

"What happens when you find out who she is?" Zane called out.

He slowed to a stop and glanced over his shoulder. "Whoever she is, she will be sorry." He then turned and continued walking.

He meant what he said. Thanks to Zane, the mystery might have been solved. But once Derringer discovered the woman's identity, her nightmare for what she'd done would just be beginning, he thought, getting into his truck and driving away. He had a feeling his nightmare would continue until he found her—their night together had been so good, it haunted his dreams.

He made it back to Derringer's Dungeon in record time, and once inside his house he immediately went to his office to log on to his computer. The technician who had installed the video camera had told him he had access to the film from any computer anywhere with his IP address. This would be the first time he had reason to view the footage since the cameras had been installed.

A year ago his Westmoreland cousins from Montana had expanded their very successful horse-breeding and training business and had invited him, Jason and Zane to join as partners. Since all three were fine horsemen—although you couldn't prove how good he was, considering what had happened on Monday—they had jumped at the chance to be included. In anticipation of the horses that would be arriving, they had decided to install cameras on all three of their properties to make sure horse thieves, which were known to pop up every so often in these parts, didn't get any ideas about stealing from a Westmoreland.

Derringer hauled in a deep breath when the computer came to life and he typed in the code to get him to the video-camera channel and almost held his breath as he searched for the date he wanted. He then sat there, with his gaze glued to the computer screen, and waited with bated breath for something to show up.

It seemed it took forever before the lights of a vehicle came into view. The time indicated it wasn't early afternoon, not quite dark, but there had been a thunderstorm brewing. He then recalled it had been raining something awful with thunder and lightning flashing all around. At one point the intensity of it had awakened him.

He squinted at the image, trying to make out the truck that turned into his yard in the torrential rain. It seemed the weather worsened and rain started to pour down on the earth the moment the vehicle pulled into his yard.

It took only a second to recall whose SUV was in focus and he could only lean back in his chair, not believing what he was seeing. The woman who got out of her truck, battling the weather before tackling the huge box on his porch by dragging it inside his place was none other than Lucia Conyers.

He shook his head trying to make heads or tails of what he was seeing. Okay, he had it now. He figured, for whatever reason, Lucia had come by—probably as a favor to Chloe—to check on him and had been kind enough to bring the box inside the house, out of the rain.

He sat there watching the computer screen, expecting her to come back out at any minute and then get in her truck and pull off. He figured once she left, another vehicle would drive up, and the occupant of that car would be the woman he'd slept with. But as he sat there for another twenty minutes or so viewing the screen, Lucia never came back out.

Lucia Conyers was his Puddin' Tame?

Derringer shook his head, thinking that there was no way. He then decided to fast-forward the tape to five o'clock the next morning. His eyes narrowed suspiciously when a few minutes later he watched his front door open and Lucia ease out of it as if she was sneaking away from the scene of some crime. And she was wearing the same clothes she had on when she'd first arrived the night before. It was obvious she had dressed hurriedly and was moving rather quickly toward her SUV.

Damn. He couldn't believe it. He wouldn't believe it if he wasn't seeing it for himself. She was the one woman he would never have suspected, not in a million years. But from the evidence he'd gotten off his video camera, Lucia was the woman he had slept with. Lucia, his sister-in-law's best friend. Lucia was innocent—at least his assumption of that had been right. His mystery lover had been Lucia, the woman who would shy away from him and act skittish whenever he came around her.

Last month he recalled hearing Chloe and his sisters tease her about this being the last year of her twenties and challenge her to write a list of everything she wanted to do before hitting the big three-oh. He couldn't help wondering if she had added something outlandish like getting pregnant before her biological clock stopped ticking or ridding herself of her virginity.

Anger filled him, seeped through every pore in his body. Lucia Conyers had a hell of a lot of explaining to do. She better have a good reason for getting into bed with him that night two weeks ago.

He pulled his cell phone out of his pocket and punched in the number to his sister-in-law's magazine.

"*Simply Irresistible,* may I help you?"

"Yes, I'd like to speak to Lucia Conyers, please," he said, trying to control his anger.

"Sorry, but Ms. Conyers just stepped out for lunch."

"Did she say where she was going?" he asked.

The receptionist paused and then asked. "Who may I ask is calling?"

"This is Mr. Westmoreland."

"Oh, Mr. Westmoreland, how are you? Your wife and baby were here a couple of days ago, and your daughter looks just like you."

Derringer shook his head. Evidently the woman thought he was Ramsey, which was okay with him if he could get the information he wanted out of her.

"I take that as a compliment. Did Lucia say where she was going for lunch?"

"Yes, sir. She's dining at McKay's today."

"Thanks."

"You're welcome, sir."

Derringer hung up the phone and leaned back in his chair as an idea formed in his mind. He wouldn't let her know he had found out the truth about her visit. He would let her assume that she had gotten away with it and that he didn't have a clue that she was the woman who'd taken advantage of him that night.

And then when she least expected it, he would play his hand.

Chapter 3

Something, Lucia wasn't sure exactly what, made her glance over her menu and look straight into the eyes of Derringer Westmoreland. She went completely still as he moved in fluid precision toward her, with an unreadable expression on his face.

Staring at him, taking him all in, all six-three of him, while broad shoulders flexed beneath a blue Western shirt, and a pair of jeans clung to him like a second layer of skin and showed the iron muscles in his thighs. And then there was his face, too handsome for words, with his medium-brown skin tone, dark coffee-colored eyes and firm and luscious-looking lips.

For the moment she couldn't move; she was transfixed. A part of her wanted to get up quickly and run in another direction, but she felt glued to the chair. But that didn't stop liquid heat from pooling between her thighs when her gaze locked onto his face and she looked at the same features she had seen almost two weeks ago in his bed.

Why was he here and approaching her table? Had he found her panties and figured out she was the woman who had left them behind? She swallowed, thinking there was no way he could have discovered her identity, but then she asked herself why else would he seek her out?

He finally came to a stop at her table and she nervously moistened her lips with the tip of her tongue. She could swear his gaze was following her every movement. She swallowed again, thinking she had to be imagining things, and opened her mouth to speak. "Derringer? What are you doing here? Chloe mentioned you had taken a nasty fall a couple of weeks ago."

"Yes, but a man has to eat sometime. I was told McKay's serves the best potpie on Thursdays for lunch and there's always a huge crowd. I saw you sitting over here alone and thought the least we can do is help the place out," he said.

She was trying hard to follow him and not focus on the way his Adam's apple moved with every word he said, as if it was on some sensuous beat. She lifted a brow. "Help the place out in what way?"

He gave her a smooth smile. "Freeing up a table by us sharing one."

Lucia was trying really hard not to show any emotion—especially utter astonishment and disbelief—as well as not to let the menu she was holding fall to the floor. Had he just suggested that they share a table during lunch? Breathe the same air?

She was tempted to pick up the glass filled with

ice water and drink the whole thing in one gulp. Instead, she drew in a deep breath to stop her heart from pounding so hard in her chest. How could spending only one night in his bed cause her to want to let go of her sensibilities and play out these newfound urges at the sight of him?

Of course, there was no way she would do something like that. In fact, a part of her was shaking inside at the thought he wanted to join her for lunch. She quickly wondered how Chloe would handle the situation if she was in her place. The answer came easy, but then she wasn't Chloe. However, she had to keep her cool and respond with the confidence Chloe possessed. The confidence that she lacked.

Lucia forced a smile to her lips. "I think that's a good idea, Derringer."

His lips eased into a smile right before her eyes. "Glad you agree," he said, taking the chair across from her.

She forced herself to breathe and belatedly realized just what she'd done. She had agreed to let him sit at her table. What on earth would they have to talk about? What if she let something slip and said something really stupid like, "*Oh, by the way, when can I drop by and get the panties I left behind the other night?*"

She sighed heavily. For all she knew, he might have figured things out already. Seriously, why else would he give a royal flip whether or not McKay's was crowded for lunch? That in itself was suspect because he'd never sought out her attention before.

She glanced over at him and he smiled at her, flashing those same dimples that he'd flashed that night she almost melted in her chair. He looked the same, only thing was that his eyes no longer had a hungover look. Today his gaze was as clear as glass.

The waitress saved them from talking when she walked up to take both their lunch orders. When she left, Lucia wished she had a mirror to see how she looked. She would die if she didn't at least look halfway decent. Absently, she ran a finger through her hair and pressed her lips together. She was grateful to feel her lipstick still in place, although she was tempted to get the tube of lipstick from her purse and apply a fresh coat.

"I understand you're back in school."

She was watching his mouth and his lips moved. She realized he'd said something. "Excuse me?"

He smiled again. "I said I heard you were back in school."

"Yes, I am. How did you know?"

"Chloe mentioned it."

"Oh." She wondered why Chloe would mention such a thing unless he'd asked about her. Had he? She shook her head, finding the idea unlikely. Her name must have popped up for conversational purposes and nothing more than that. If there had been anything more, Chloe definitely would have told her.

"Yes, I'm back at school taking night classes to get my master's degree in mass communications." Then, without missing a beat, she said, "You seem to be doing well from your fall." No sooner had the words left her mouth than she wished she could take them back. Why on earth would she bring up anything relating to that day?

"Yes, but I'm doing better now. I've been taking it

easy for the past week or so and sleeping most of the time. It helped. I feel in pretty good shape now."

She didn't know how to tell him that as far as she was concerned, he'd been in pretty good shape that night as well. His movements hadn't been hindered in any way. The thought of all he'd done to her sent heat soaring all through her body.

"So, what else have you been up to lately?"

Lucia felt her heart give a loud thump in her chest and wondered if he'd heard it. Dragging her gaze from her silverware, she thought that she could remember in vivid detail just what she'd been up to lately with him. Sitting across from her was the man who'd taken her virginity. The man who'd introduced her to the kind of pleasure she'd only read about in romance novels, and the man whom she'd loved forever. And knowing he probably had no idea of any of those things was the epitome of insane. But somehow she would fake it and come off looking like the most poised person that ever existed.

"Not a whole lot," she heard herself saying. "School and the magazine keep me pretty busy, but because I enjoy doing both I won't complain. What about you?" His gaze seemed to linger on her lips.

He chuckled. "Other than making a fool of myself with Sugar Foot, I haven't been up to a whole lot either."

She inclined her head. "What on earth would entice you to ride that horse? I think everyone has heard how mean he is."

He chuckled and the sound was a low, sexy rumble that made goose bumps form on her arms. "Ego. I figured if Casey could do it then so could I."

She knew his cousin Casey and her husband, along

with his cousin Durango and his wife, Savannah, had come visiting a few weekends ago. She'd heard everyone had been amazed at the ease with which Casey had gotten on Sugar Foot's back and held on even when the horse had been determined to get her off.

"I'm a pretty good horseman," Derringer said, breaking into her thoughts. "Although I'd be the first to admit I wasn't personally trained by the renowned and legendary Sid Roberts like Casey and her brothers while growing up."

Lucia nodded. His cousins Casey, Cole and Clint were triplets, and she had heard that they had lived with Roberts, their maternal uncle, while growing up. "We can all learn from the mistakes we make," she said, taking a sip of her water to cool off.

"Yes, we sure can."

Deciding she needed to escape, if only for a short moment, Lucia stood. "Would you excuse me for a moment? I need to go to the ladies' room."

"Sure, no problem," he said, standing.

Lucia drew in a deep breath, wishing she was walking out the restaurant door with no intention of returning and not just escaping to the ladies' room. And as she continued walking, she could actually feel Derringer staring at her back.

Derringer watched Lucia leave, thinking she looked downright sexy in her below-the-knee skirt and light blue pullover sweater. And then he couldn't help but admire her small waistline and the flare of her hips in the skirt as she walked. Standing about five-seven, she had a pair of nice-looking black leather boots on her feet, but he could recall just what a nice pair of legs she had and remembered how those legs had felt wrapped around him the night they'd made love.

He would be the first to admit that he'd always thought Lucia was pretty, with her smooth brown skin and lustrous shoulder-length black hair that she usually wore pulled back in a ponytail. Then there were her hazel eyes, high cheekbones, cute chin and slim nose. And he couldn't forget her luscious-looking mouth, one that could probably do a lot of wicked things to a man.

He leaned back in his chair remembering how years ago when she'd been about eighteen—about to leave home for college—and he had been in the process of moving back home from university, she had caught his eye. In memory of his parents and his aunt and uncle, who'd died together in a plane crash while he was in high school, the Westmorelands held a charity ball every year to raise money for the Westmoreland Foundation, which had been founded to aid various community causes. Lucia had attended the ball that year with her parents.

He had been standing by the punch bowl when she had arrived, and the sight of her in the dress she'd been wearing that night had rendered him breathless. He hadn't been able to take his eyes off her all evening. Evidently others had noticed his interest, and one of those had been her father, Dusty Conyers.

Later that same night the older man had pulled him aside and warned him away from his daughter. He let Derringer know in no uncertain terms that he would not tolerate a Westmoreland sniffing behind his daughter, creating the kind of trouble that Carl Newsome was having with Derringer's cousin Bane.

Bane had had the hots for Crystal Newsome since

junior high school, and since Bane had a penchant for getting into trouble, Newsome hadn't wanted him anywhere near his daughter. Unfortunately, Crystal had other ideas and had been just as hot for Bane as he'd been for her, and Crystal and Bane managed to get into all kinds of naughty trouble together. Once, they'd even tried their hand at eloping before Carl Newsome had found his daughter and shipped her off to heaven knows where. A brokenhearted Bane had decided to take charge of his life by going into the Navy.

Derringer knew that although he didn't have Bane's badass reputation, he was still a Westmoreland, and a lot of mamas and daddies were dead set on protecting their daughters from what they thought was a Westmoreland heartbreak just waiting to happen. A part of him couldn't fault Dusty Conyers for being one of them; especially since Derringer had made it known far and wide that he had no plans to settle down with any one woman. A wife was the last thing on his mind then as well as now. Making a success of the horse-training business he'd just started was his top priority.

"I'm back."

He glanced up and stood for her to sit and thought that Lucia was even more beautiful up close. She had a nervous habit of licking her lips with her tongue. He would do just about anything to replace her tongue with his the next time she did it. And he also liked the sound of her voice. She spoke in a quiet yet sexy tone that did things to his insides, and he decided to keep her talking every chance he got.

"Tell me about the classes you're taking at the university and why you decided to go back and get your master's degree."

She lifted a brow and then her lips curved into one of her smiles again. Evidently, he'd hit on a subject she liked talking about. "Although Chloe hasn't made any announcements about anything, I can see her spending less and less time with *Simply Irresistible.* Whenever she does come into the office she has the baby with her, and it's obvious that she prefers being home with Susan and Ramsey."

He nodded, thinking he'd had that same impression as well. Whenever he paid Ramsey and Chloe a visit, they appeared to be a content and very happy couple who thoroughly enjoyed being parents. He'd heard from his other brothers that already Ramsey and Chloe were thinking about having another child.

"And I want to be prepared if she decides to take a leave of absence for a while," Lucia continued. "She and I talked about it, and because my bachelor's degree was in business, we thought it would be a good idea for me to get a degree in communications as well."

The waitress chose that moment to return with their food, and once the plates had been placed in front of them, she left.

"I understand Gemma is adjusting to life in Australia."

He couldn't help but smile. Although he missed his sister, it seemed from all the phone calls they got that she *was* adjusting to life in Australia. He'd known Callum, the man who used to be the manager of Ramsey's sheep farm, had loved Gemma for a while, even if his sister had been clueless. He'd always known Callum's feelings for Gemma had been the real thing and not for the sole purpose of getting her into bed. He'd wholeheartedly approved of Gemma and Callum's relationship.

"Yes, I talked to her a few days ago. She and Callum are planning to come home for the Westmoreland Charity Ball at the end of the month." He wondered if she planned to go and if so, if she already had a date.

"Are you dating anyone seriously?" he decided to ask and set his plan into motion.

She looked over at him after popping a strawberry into her luscious mouth, chewed on it a moment, and then she swallowed it before replying. "The only dates I have these days are with my schoolbooks."

"Um, what a pity, that doesn't sound like a lot of fun. How about a movie this weekend?"

She cocked a surprised eyebrow. "A movie?"

He could tell his suggestion had surprised her. "Yes, a movie. Evidently, you're not spending enough time having fun, and everyone needs to let loose now and then. There's a new Tyler Perry movie coming out this weekend that I want to see. Would you like to go with me?"

Lucia's heart began pounding in her chest as she quickly reached the conclusion that Derringer had to have figured out that she was the woman who'd brazenly shared his bed. What other reason could he have for asking her out? Why the sudden interest in her when he'd never shown any before?

Their eyes held for what seemed like several electrifying moments before she finally broke eye contact with him. But what if he *didn't* know, and asking her out was merely a coincidence? There was only one way to find out. She glanced back over at him and saw he was still staring at her with that unreadable expression of his. "Why do you want to take me out, Derringer?"

He gave her a smooth smile. "I told you. You're spending too much time studying and working and need to have a little fun."

She still wasn't buying it. "We've known each other for years. Yet you've never asked me out before. In fact, you've never shown any interest."

He chuckled. "It wasn't that I didn't want to show an interest, Lucia, but I love my life and all my body parts."

She raised a brow and paused with the fork halfway to her mouth. "What do you mean?"

He took a sip of his iced tea and then his mouth curved ruefully. "I was warned away from you early on and took the warning seriously."

She nearly dropped the fork from her hand and had to tighten her grip to place it back down. "What do you mean you were warned away from me?" That was impossible. She'd never had a boyfriend jealous enough to do such a thing.

A grin flashed across his face. "Your dad knows how to scare a man off, trust me."

Her head began spinning at the same time her heart slammed hard against her rib cage. "My dad warned you away from me?"

He smiled. "Yes, and I took him seriously. It was the summer you were about to leave for college. You were eighteen and I was twenty-two and returning home from university. You attended the Westmoreland Charity Ball with your parents before you left. He saw me checking you out, probably thought my interest wasn't honorable, and pulled me aside and told me to keep my eyes to myself or else…"

Lucia swallowed. She knew her dad. His bark was

worse than his bite, but most people didn't know that.
"Or else what?"

"Or else my eyes, along with another body part I'd
rather not mention, would get pulled from their sockets.
The last thing he would put up with was a Westmoreland dating his daughter."

Lucia didn't know whether to laugh or cry. She could
see her father making a threat like that because he was
overprotective of her. But she doubted Derringer knew
how much his words thrilled her. He had been checking her out when she was eighteen?

She nervously moistened her lips with the tip of her
tongue and couldn't help noticing the movement of
his gaze to her mouth. Her skin began burning at the
thought that he had been attracted to her even when she
hadn't had a clue. But still…

"Aw, come on, Derringer, that was more than ten
years ago," she said in a teasing tone.

"Yes, but you probably don't recall a few years ago I
dropped by the paint store to make a purchase and you
were working behind the counter and waited on me."

*Oh, she definitely remembered that day, and three
years later hadn't been able to forget it. But of course
she couldn't tell him that.* "That was a long time ago,
but I think I remember that day. You needed a can of
paint thinner." She could probably tell him what brand
it was and exactly how much he'd paid for it.

"Yes, well, I had planned to ask you out then, but
Mr. Conyers gave me a look that reminded me of the
conversation we'd had years before and that his opinion of me pursuing you hadn't changed."

She couldn't help but laugh and it felt good. He had

actually wanted to talk to her then, too. "I can't believe you were afraid of Dad."

"Believe it, sweetheart. He can give you a look that lets you know he means business. And it didn't help that he and Bane had had a run-in a few years before when Bane swiped a can of paint on display in front of the store and used it to paint some not-so-nice graffiti all over the front of Mr. Milner's feed store and signed off by saying it was a present from your father."

Lucia wiped tears of laughter from her eyes. "I was away at college, but I heard about that. Mom wrote and told me all the details. You're right, Dad was upset and so was Mr. Milner. Your cousin Bane had a reputation for getting into all kinds of trouble. How are things going with him and the Navy?"

"He's doing fine at the Naval Academy. It's hard to believe he's been gone for almost two years already, but he has."

"And he hasn't been back since he left?"

Derringer shook his head sadly. "No, not even once. He refuses to come back knowing Crystal isn't here, and he's still angry that he doesn't know where she is. The Newsomes made sure of that before they moved away. We are hoping he'll eventually forget her and move on, but so far he hasn't."

In a way, she knew how Bane felt. She hadn't looked forward to returning to Denver either, knowing she was still harboring feelings for Derringer. It was hard running into him while he was dating other girls and wishing they were her. And now to find out they could have been her. Her father had no idea what he'd done and the sad thing was that she couldn't get mad at him. Bane hadn't been the only Westmoreland with a reputation that had made it hard on the other family members. Derringer's younger brothers—the twins, Adrian and Aidan—as well as his baby sister Bailey had been Bane's sidekicks and had gotten into just as much trouble.

Needless to say, it had gotten to the point everyone in town would get up in arms when they saw any Westmoreland headed their way. But she had heard her father say more than once lately that considering everything, he thought Dillon and Ramsey had done a pretty good job in raising their siblings and in keeping the family together, and that he actually admired them for it. She knew that several people in town did. All the Westmorelands were college-educated and in some sort of business for themselves or holding prestigious jobs. And together they were the wealthiest family in the county and the largest landowners. People no longer feared them, they highly respected them.

"Just look how things turned out, Derringer," she heard herself say. "The twins are at Harvard. Bailey will be finishing up her studies at the university here in a year, and Bane is in the hands of Uncle Sam. Ramsey mentioned that Bane wants to become a Navy SEAL. In that case, he has to learn discipline, among other things."

Derringer chuckled. "For Bane, even with Uncle Sam, that won't be easy to do." He picked up his glass to take a sip of his iced tea. "So do we have a date for Saturday night or what?"

A date with Derringer Westmoreland...

She couldn't stop herself from feeling all giddy inside. She almost trembled at the thought. But at the same time she knew she had to be realistic. He would take her out on Saturday night and probably some other girl on Sunday. He'd asked her out to the movies, not a trip to Vegas to get married.

She would take the date for what it was and not put too much stock in it. She hadn't been born yesterday and she knew Derringer's reputation around town. He dated a lot, but let it be known that he didn't like women who clung or got too possessive.

Still, she couldn't help but smile at the thought that he was attracted to her and had been since she was eighteen. Didn't that account for something? She decided that it did.

"Yes, I'd love to go to the movies with you Saturday night, Derringer."

Chapter 4

Derringer frowned the moment he pulled into his yard and saw his sister Bailey's car parked there. The last thing he needed was for her to drop by to play nursemaid again. Megan was bad enough, but his baby sister Bailey was worse. She had only been seven when their parents had gotten killed. Now at twenty-two, she attended college full-time, and when she didn't have her nose stuck in some book it was stuck in her five brothers' personal affairs. She liked making it her business to know anything and everything about their comings and goings. Now that Ramsey was married, she'd given him some slack, but she hadn't let up with him, Zane and the twins.

He wondered how long she'd been there waiting on him and figured she probably wouldn't like the fact that he hadn't been home and had driven into town. Since she wasn't out on the porch, that meant she had let herself inside, which wouldn't be a hard thing to do since he never locked his doors. His sister flung open the door the moment his foot touched the step. The look on her face let him know he was in trouble. She was there when the doctor restricted him from doing almost anything, other than breathing and eating, for two weeks.

"Just where have you been, Derringer Westmoreland, in your condition?"

He walked past her to put his hat on the rack. "And what condition is that, Bailey?"

"You're injured."

"Yes, but I'm not dead."

He regretted the words the moment they left his mouth when he saw the expression that suddenly appeared on her face. He and his brothers knew the real reason Bailey was so overprotective of them was that she was afraid of losing them the way she'd lost their parents.

But he could admit to having the same fears, and if he were to analyze things further, he would probably conclude that Zane had them as well. All of them had been close to their parents, aunt and uncle. Everyone had taken their deaths hard. The way Derringer had managed to move on, and not look back, was by not getting too attached to anyone. He had his cousins and his siblings. He loved them, and they were all he needed. If he were to fall in love, give his heart to a woman, and then something were to happen to her—there was no telling how he'd handle it, or even if he could. He liked things just the way they were. And, for that reason, he doubted he would ever marry.

He crossed the room and placed a hand on her shoulder when he saw her trembling. "Hey, come on, Bail, it wasn't that bad. You were there at the hospital and heard what Dr. Epps said. It's been almost two weeks now and I'm fine."

"But I also heard him say that it could have been worse, Derringer."

"But it wasn't. Look, unless you came to cook for me or do my laundry, you can visit some other time. I'm going to take a nap."

He saw the sad look on her face turn mutinous and knew his ploy had worked. She didn't like it when he bossed her around or came across as if she was at his beck and call. "Cook your own damn meals and do your own laundry, or get one of those silly girls who fawn all over you to do it."

"Whatever. And watch your mouth, Bailey, or I'll think you're slipping back to your old ways and I'll have to wash your mouth out with soap."

She grabbed the remote off the table, dropped down on the sofa and began watching television, ignoring him. He glanced at his watch and fought to hide his smile. "So, how long are you staying?" he asked. Because she hadn't yet inherited her one hundred acres, she had a tendency to spend time at any of their places. Most of the time she stayed with Megan, which suited all her brothers just fine because Bailey had a tendency to drop in unannounced at the most inconvenient times.

Like now.

She didn't even look over at him when she finally answered his question. "I'm staying until I'm ready to leave. You have a problem with it?"

"No."

"Good," she said, using the remote to flip to another

channel. "Now go take your nap and I hope when you wake up you're in a lot better mood."

He chuckled as he leaned down and planted a brotherly kiss on her forehead. "Thanks for worrying about me so much, kid," he said softly.

"If me, Megan and Gemma don't do it, who will? All those silly girls you mess around with are only after your money."

He lifted a brow in mock surprise. "You think so?"

She glanced up at him and rolled her eyes. "If you don't know the truth about them then you're in real trouble, Derringer."

Derringer chuckled again thinking yes, he knew the truth about them…especially one in particular. Lucia Conyers. He didn't think of her as one of those "silly girls" and knew Bailey wouldn't either. He would be taking Lucia to the movies Saturday night. He intended to return her panties to her then. He looked forward to the moment her mouth fell open and she realized he knew what she'd done and had known all this time. He couldn't wait to see what excuse she would come up with for what she had done.

Before heading up the stairs, he decided to feel his sister out about something. "I ran into Lucia Conyers a few moments ago at McKay's."

Bailey didn't take her gaze off the television and for a moment he thought that possibly she hadn't heard him, but then she responded. "And?"

He smiled. "And we shared a table since McKay's was crowded." He paused a moment. "She's pretty. I never realized just how pretty she is." The latter he knew wasn't true, because he'd always known how pretty she was.

He watched as Bailey slowly turned toward him with a frown on her face. "I hope you're not thinking what I think you're thinking."

He smiled. "Oh, I don't know. What do you think I'm thinking?"

"That you plan to hit on Lucia."

He grinned. "If by 'hit on her' you mean ask her out, I've already done so. We have a date to go to the movies this Saturday night."

Bailey's eyes widened. "Are you crazy? That's Chloe's best friend."

Now it was his turn. "And?"

"And everybody around these parts knows how most of the single male Westmorelands operate. You're used to those silly girls and wouldn't know how to appreciate a woman with sense like Lucia."

"You don't think so?"

"I know so and if you end up doing something stupid like hurting her, Chloe would never forgive you for it."

He shrugged at the thought. Chances were, Chloe had no idea what her best friend had pulled that night. And as far as what Bailey said about Lucia's having sense, he didn't doubt that, which made him uneasy about just what she would gain from tumbling into bed with him.

"Lucia is an adult. She can handle me," he said. He wouldn't break it down and tell her that Lucia *had* handled him and had done a real good job doing so. He got a hard-on every time he thought about that night.

"I'm still warning you, Derringer. And besides being Chloe's best friend, Megan, Gemma and I like her as well."

He cocked an amused brow. "I guess that means a

lot. The three of you never like any of the girls I date. I'll have to keep that in mind."

Without giving his kid sister time to say anything else, he quickly moved up the stairs for his nap.

Lucia couldn't wait to get back to her office to give Chloe a call and tell her about her date on Saturday night with Derringer.

"I'm happy for you," Chloe said with a smile in her voice that Lucia heard. "Falling off that horse must have knocked some sense into him. At least you know why he never approached you before. I can see your dad warning him off. I heard the Westmorelands had quite a reputation back in the day."

Lucia nodded. "And you think I did the right thing in agreeing to go out with him?"

"Come on, Lucia, don't you dare ask me that. You've loved the guy forever. You've even gone so far as to sleep with him."

She drew in a deep, ragged breath. "But he doesn't know that. At least I don't think he does."

"You honestly think he doesn't know?"

"I assumed he did and that was the only reason he wanted to share my table."

She heard Chloe bristle at that assumption. "Why do you continue to think you're no match for Derringer when you're classier than all those other women he messes around with?"

"But that's just it, Chloe. I'm not the kind of woman he prefers, the kind he has a history of dating. I can't hold a candle to someone like Ashira Lattimore. And everyone knows she has been vying for his attention for years."

"I've met her and she's spoiled, self-centered, possessive and clingy. Definitely not wife material."

"Wife material?" Lucia laughed. "A wife is the furthest thing from Derringer's mind. You know that as well as I do."

"Yes, but I'm sure a lot of people said the same thing about Ramsey before I arrived on the scene. So that means a man's mind can change with the right woman. All you have to do is convince Derringer you're the right woman."

Lucia cringed at the thought of trying to do that. She wouldn't even know where to begin. "That's easy for you to say and do, Chloe. You've always been sure of yourself in everything you did."

"In that case, maybe you ought to try it for yourself. Just think, Lucia. Evidently Derringer is on your hook and now you have the chance to reel him right on in. You know how I feel about missed opportunities. How would things have turned out had I accepted Ramsey's refusal to be on the cover of my magazine? I saw what I wanted and decided to go after it. I think you should use that same approach."

"I don't know," Lucia said on a heavy sigh. This wasn't the first time Chloe had made that suggestion. A part of her knew her friend was right, but what she was suggesting was easier said than done. At least for her it was.

"Think about it. Saturday is only two days away and if I were you, when Derringer arrived at my place to pick me up I'd make sure he would take one look at me and know he would enjoy every minute of his time in my presence. Now's your chance, Lucia. Don't let it go by without taking advantage of it."

A few moments later, after hanging up the phone with Chloe, indecisiveness weighed heavy in her chest. More than anything she would love to pique Derringer's interest, but what if she failed in her efforts to do so? What if she couldn't get the one man she loved to want to love her back? Was there a possibility that she was wrong about the type of women Derringer actually preferred?

One thing Chloe had said was true. No one would have figured that Ramsey Westmoreland would have fallen for any woman. The man had been set in his ways for years and the last woman he'd attempted to marry had announced she was pregnant from another man in the middle of the wedding. Yet, he had fallen in love with Chloe, whether he had wanted to or not. So maybe there was hope for all those other single Westmorelands; but especially for Derringer.

"I've heard you're interested in women's undergarments these days, Derringer. Is there a reason why?"

Derringer slowly turned away from the pool table with a cue stick in his hand to gaze at each man in the dimly lit room inside his basement. Now that he knew who his late-night visitor had been, he wouldn't tell anyone, not even Zane, her identity.

"No reason," he answered his cousin Canyon who was four years younger.

Canyon smiled. "Well, you never got around to asking me anything, but just so you know, the women I date don't wear underwear."

Derringer shook his head and chuckled. He didn't find that hard to believe. He studied the other men who had gone back to sipping their beers while waiting their turn at shooting pool—his brother Zane and his cousins Jason, Riley, Canyon and Stern. They were as close as brothers. Zane knew more than the others about the situation with him and the underwear, but Derringer was confident his brother wouldn't say anything.

"So, what's this I hear about you going on a date with Lucia? I thought old man Conyers pretty much scared you off her years ago," Jason said, chuckling.

Derringer couldn't help but smile. "He did, but like you said, it was years ago. Lucia isn't a kid anymore. She's an adult and old enough to make her own decisions about who she wants to date."

"True, but she's not your type and you know it," Riley piped in.

Derringer lifted a brow. That was the same thing Bailey had alluded to earlier that day. "And what, supposedly, is my type?"

"Women who wear black panties," Canyon said, chuckling.

"Or no panties at all," Riley added, laughing.

"Hmm, for all you all know, my taste in women might have changed," he said, turning back to the pool table.

Zane snorted. "Since when? Since you got thrown off Sugar Foot's back and hit your head?"

Derringer frowned as he turned back around. "I didn't hit my head."

"Makes us wonder," Riley said. "First you're going around asking about women's underwear and now you're taking Lucia Conyers out on a date. You better treat her right or Chloe will come gunning for you."

"Hell, we'll all come gunning for you," Zane said, taking a sip of his beer. "We like her."

Derringer turned back to the pool table and proceeded to chalk his stick. At the moment, he didn't give a royal flip how his family felt about Lucia. He still planned to deal with her in his own way and if they didn't like the outcome that was too bad.

Chapter 5

By the time seven o'clock came around on Saturday night, Lucia was almost a nervous wreck. She had pulled her father aside that week to verify what Derringer had told her. With a sheepish grin on his face, Dusty Conyers hadn't denied a thing, and had laughingly agreed he had intentionally put the fear of God in Derringer. He didn't regret doing so and was glad it had worked.

He did agree that now she was old enough to handle her own business and wouldn't butt in again. She had ended up giving him a kiss on his bald head after telling him how much she loved him, and that he was the best dad in the whole wide world.

His confirmation meant that what Derringer had said the other day was true. He had shown interest in her years ago, but her father had discouraged him. Although she knew she would always wonder how things might have gone if her father hadn't intervened, she was a firm believer that things happened for a reason. Besides, at eighteen she doubted she would have been able to handle the likes of Derringer Westmoreland and was even doubtful she could have at twenty-two. She wasn't even confident she had the ability to handle him now, but was determined to try. She was convinced there was a reason she had shared his bed that night.

She just wished she had a clue what that reason was.

She was grateful that one didn't have anything to do with the other. The reason he had asked her out had nothing to do with them sleeping together and she felt good about that. She had played the details of their night together over and over in her mind so many times that she knew practically every single movement by heart.

All week she had found herself going to bed but unable to sleep until she replayed in her mind every sensation she'd felt that night. It didn't take much to remember how it felt to grip his iron-steel shoulders beneath her fingers while he thrust in and out of her. The thought of making love with a man like Derringer sent sensuous chills up her spine.

She knew the exact moment Derringer pulled into her driveway. From the smooth hum of the engine she could tell he was driving his two-seater sports car instead of his truck. That meant the car's interior would be that much cozier. The thought of being in such proximity to Derringer stirred all kinds of feelings inside.

She had spoken to Chloe earlier and her best friend had said the Westmorelands were torn as to whether or not her dating Derringer was a good idea, considering his history with women. Bottom line was that no one wanted to see her get hurt. But what they didn't know was that she had loved Derringer so long that to her tonight was really a dream come true. And if he never asked her out again that would be fine because she would always have memories of tonight to add to those she had of that Monday night. Not that she expected things would get as heated tonight as they had in his bedroom, mind you. But she couldn't wait to see what was in store for her tonight. Just knowing she was Derringer's date made her feel good inside, and knowing he had no ulterior motive in taking her out made it that much more special.

Derringer smiled when he pulled into Lucia's driveway, thinking her house was the brightest on the block with floodlights in every corner, the porch light on and a light pole shining in the front of the yard. He thought it was a real nice neighborhood with beautiful trees on both sides of the street and the silhouette of mountains in the background. But he felt crowded. One of the pitfalls of being a Westmoreland was that because each of them owned a hundred acres of land, living anywhere else would seem restrictive and too confining.

As he walked up to the porch, he felt as if he was under the bright lights and wouldn't be surprised if some of her neighbors were watching him. In fact, he was certain he saw the front curtain move in the house across the street. He chuckled, thinking if she could deal with her nosy neighbors then he certainly could.

Besides, he had enough on his plate dealing with his own nosy relatives. Maybe it had been a bad idea to mention his date to Bailey. She hadn't wasted time spreading the word. He'd gotten a number of calls warning him he had best behave tonight—whatever that meant. And yet, the one call he'd expected, the one from Chloe, had never come. That made him wonder if she knew a lot more than he thought she did.

He glanced at his watch before ringing Lucia's doorbell. It was seven-thirty exactly. He'd made good time and since he'd already reserved tickets online, they wouldn't have to stand in line at the theater. He had thought of everything, including when would be the best time to drop the bomb on her about that night. He had decided that they would enjoy the movie first before dealing with any unpleasantness.

He heard the lock turn on her door and then seconds later she was standing there, illuminated in the doorway. He blinked in surprise when he gazed down at her. She looked different. She'd always been a pretty girl, but tonight she looked absolutely stunning.

Gone was the ponytail. Instead, her hair was curled and fell in feathered waves to her shoulders. And she had done something with her eyes that made them look more striking and the entire look somehow showcased her dazzling sophistication.

And then there was the outfit she was wearing. Not too daring, but enough to keep him on the edge all evening. Her sweater dress was a plum color and she had black suede boots on her feet. She wasn't overly dressed for the movie and he thought her attire was perfect... and it fit her just that way, emphasizing her small waist, and falling above the knees, it definitely showed off a beautiful pair of thighs encased in tights.

A second passed and then several before he was able to open his mouth to speak, and from the smile that touched her lips she was well aware of the effect she

was having on him. He couldn't help but smile back.
She had definitely pulled one over on him. Gone was
just the "pretty" Lucia and in her place stood a creature
so gorgeous that she took his breath away.

"Derringer."

He exhaled an even breath. At least he tried to. "Lucia."

"I just need to get my jacket. Would you like to come
in for a second?" she asked.

He felt another smile pull at his lips. She was inviting him in. "Sure."

When he brushed by her, he almost buckled to his
knees when he took a whiff of her perfume. It was the
same scent he had awakened to that Tuesday morning. The same scent that was all in his head. She was
the one woman who had him sleeping each night with
her panties under his pillow. He took in a deep breath
to pull more of the fragrance into his nostrils. There
was just something potent about the scent of a woman.

"Would you like a drink before we leave?"

"No, but thanks for the offer," he said, glancing
around her living room.

"It won't take but a minute to grab my jacket."

"Take your time," he said, watching as she walked
away, appreciating her movements in the dress, especially how it fit her from behind. He forced his gaze
away from her when she entered her bedroom and continued his study of her house, thinking it was small
but just the right size for her. And it was tidy, not a
single thing out of place, even the magazines on the
table seemed to lie in a perfect position. He liked her
fireplace and could imagine how it would look with a
fire blazing in it. He could imagine her on the floor,

stretched out in front of it on one of those days that was cold, snowy and dreary outside.

On the drive over, he did notice that this particular subdivision was centrally located to just about everything; shopping, fast-food places, grocery stores and a dry cleaner. That had to be pretty advantageous to her. He rolled his eyes wondering why the heck he cared if it was or not.

"I'm ready now, Derringer."

He turned and glanced back at her. She was standing beside a floor lamp and the lighting totally captured her beauty. For a moment he just stood there and stared, unable to tear his gaze away from her. What the hell was wrong with him? He knew the answer when he felt blood rush straight to his groin. It would be so easy for him to suggest that they forget about the movie and hang here instead. But he knew he couldn't do that.

However, there was something he could do, something he definitely felt compelled to do at that moment. He slowly moved toward her with his heart pounding hard in his chest with every step he took. And when he stood directly in front of her, he said the only words he could say at that moment. Words he knew were totally true. "You look simply beautiful tonight, Lucia."

Lucia didn't know what to say. His compliment caused soothing warmth to spread all through her. In the back of her mind something warned her that the man was smooth, sophisticated and experienced. Like most men, he would say just about anything to score. But at that moment she didn't care. The compliment had come from Derringer Westmoreland and to her that meant everything.

"Thank you, Derringer."

He lowered his head a little, bent low to murmur in her ear, "You're so very welcome."

He kept his head lowered to that angle and she knew without a shadow of a doubt that he intended to kiss her. And that knowledge caused several heated antici-patory sensations to flow from the toes of her feet to the crown of her head.

"Lucia?"

The throaty tone of his voice seemed to stroke every-thing within her and was doing so effortlessly.

"Yes?"

He lifted his hand to cradle her chin and tilt her face up to his. Her pulse rate increased when a slow smile touched his lips the moment their eyes connected. "I need to kiss you." And before she could draw her next breath, he lowered his mouth to hers.

He had kissed her that night numerous times in the throes of passion, but she immediately thought this kiss was different. The passion was still there, but unlike before it wasn't flaming out of control. What he was doing was slowly and deliberately robbing her senses of any and all control.

His tongue eased between her lips on a breathless moan and he seemed in no hurry to do anything but stand there, feed on every angle of her mouth, every nook and cranny. His kiss burned her in its wake, shar-ing its heat. He tasted like the peppermint candy he'd obviously been sucking on earlier.

But now he was sucking on her—her tongue at least; and he wasn't letting up as he probed deeply, gently but thoroughly, plunging her into an oasis of sensations as his tongue continued to sweep over her mouth.

She felt something roll around in her belly at the same time he moved his body closer, and automatically the cradle of her thighs nestled the hard erection pressing against her, causing an ache that was so engaging she couldn't do anything but moan.

This was the sort of kiss most men left a girl with after a date and not before the start of their evening. But evidently no one told that to Derringer and he was showing her there was no particular order in the way he did things. He made his own rules, set his own parameters. Now she knew why he was so high in demand with women, and why fathers warned him not to pursue their daughters. And why heat could resonate off his body like nobody's business.

But tonight he was making it her *business.*

He shifted the intensity of the kiss without warning and the hands that were already wrapped around her waist tightened in a possessive grip. The probing of his tongue deepened and she could only stand there and continue to moan while her pulse throbbed erratically in her throat. Her hips moved instinctively against his and the heat that spread lower all through her belly didn't slow down any.

There was no telling how long they would have stood there, going at each other's mouths, if she hadn't pulled back for air. She closed her eyes and took a deep breath, licking her lips and and tasting him on her tongue. The pleasure she felt just being kissed by him was almost unbearable. She slowly opened her eyes to calm the turbulent emotions inside her.

For the second time that night, his hand lifted to capture her chin, lifting her face to meet his gaze. The look in his eyes was dark, intense, sexually hungry. At that moment, he looked as rugged as the landscape in which he lived. Westmoreland country. She never realized until now just how much that had defined him. She continued to hold his gaze. Mesmerized. Falling deeper and deeper in love.

"You, Lucia Conyers, are more than I bargained for," he said in a deep, husky tone that sounded intimate and overwhelming at the same time.

She chuckled unevenly while wondering if this was how a kiss could easily get out of hand. Was this how a couple could take a kiss to another level without realizing they'd done so until it was too late to do anything about it?

"Is being more than you bargained for a good thing or a bad thing, Derringer?" she asked him.

He laughed softly at her question and released her chin, but not before lowering his head and brushing his lips across hers. "I'll let you decide that later," he whispered hotly against her lips. "Come on. Let's get out of here while we can."

Tonight was not going the way he'd planned, Derringer thought. Even the smell of popcorn couldn't get rid of her scent. His nostrils were inflamed with it. This was their first date and he had fully intended for it to be their last.

But…

And there was a *but* in there someplace. For him there were probably several and each of them were messing with his mind. Making him not want to end their evening together. Or to spoil just how good things were going between them.

After the movie he suggested they go to Torie's for

coffee. She was everything a man could appreciate in a date, while at the same time not fully what a man expected—but in a positive way. She had the ability to ease into a conversation that wasn't just about her. And as he maneuvered his sports car through downtown Denver, he quickly reached the conclusion that he liked the sound of her voice and in the close confines of the car, her scent continued to overtake his senses.

Derringer couldn't help but wonder if there was something with this "scent of a woman" theory that men often talked about behind closed doors and in dimly lit, whiskey-laden poolrooms. Over his lifetime he had encountered a lot of women who smelled good, but the one sitting next to him right now, whose eyes were closed as she took in the sound of John Legend on his CD player, not only smelled good but was good to smell. And he decided then and there that there was a difference. He chuckled and shook his head at his conclusion.

"Um, what's so funny?" she asked, opening her eyes and turning her head to glance over at him.

"I was just thinking about the movie," he lied, knowing there was no way he would tell her what really had amused him.

She laughed lazily. "It was good, wasn't it?"

When the car slowed in traffic, he gave her a sidelong glance. "Yes, it was. Are you comfortable?"

"Yes. And thanks. This car is nice."

"Glad you like it." He was certain his smile flashed in the dimly lit interior. He appreciated any woman who liked his car. A number of his former dates had complained that although his car was sleek and fast, it was not roomy enough.

"Can you believe they are expecting snow next weekend?"

He chuckled. "Hey, this is Denver. Snowstorms are always expected." They passed a moment in silence. "Did you enjoy living in Florida those four years?"

She nodded. "Immensely."

"Then why did you return to Denver?"

She didn't answer right away. "Because I couldn't imagine living anywhere else," she said finally.

He nodded, understanding completely. Although he had enjoyed living in Phoenix while attending college, he never could wait to return home...to see her again. He hadn't been back a week when Ramsey had sent him into town to pick up a can of paint thinner and he'd seen her again.

At first he'd been taken aback, nearly not recognizing her. She had gone from the gangly young girl to a twentysomething-year-old woman who had grown into a beauty that he had noticed right away. It was a good thing her father had been on guard and had intervened again, because there was no telling where his lustful mind would have led him that day. She had gotten spared from being added to the list as one of Derringer's Pleasers. When he'd returned home it seemed women had come out of the woodwork vying for his attention.

They soon arrived at Torie's, an upscale coffee shop that was known for its signature award-winning coffee and desserts. He helped her out of his sports car, very much aware of the looks they were getting. But now, unlike the other times, he wasn't so sure the focus was on his specially-designed Danish car and not on the woman he was helping out of it. For the first time since he could remember, he relinquished the car to the valet without giving the young man a warning look and strict instructions to be careful on how his prize was handled.

"Mr. Westmoreland, it's nice to see you," the maître d' greeted when they entered the coffee shop.

"Thanks, Pierre. And I'd like a private table in the back."

"Most certainly."

He cupped Lucia's arm as they were led to a table that overlooked the mountains and a lake. The fire that was blazing in the fireplace added the finishing touch. A romantic setting that for even someone like him—a man who probably didn't have a romantic bone in his body until it suited him—was clearly defined. "We can have just coffee if you like, but their strawberry cheesecake is good," he said, smiling when they were seated.

Lucia chuckled. "I'm going to take your word for it and try some."

The waiter came to take their drink order. She ordered a glass of wine and when he ordered only a club soda she glanced over at him curiously. "I'm driving, remember? And I'm still on medication," he said by way of explanation. "And the doctor was adamant about me not consuming alcohol while I'm taking them."

She nodded. "Are you still in pain?"

A rueful smile touched his lips. "Not unless I move too fast. Otherwise, I'm doing fine."

"I guess you won't be getting on Sugar Foot's back again any time soon."

"What makes you say that? In fact, I plan to try him again tomorrow."

Her look of horror and disbelief was priceless, he

thought, and he chuckled as he reached across the table to engulf her hand in his. "Hey, I was just kidding."

She frowned over at him. "I hope so, Derringer, and I certainly hope you've learned your lesson about taking unnecessary risks."

He laughed. "Trust me, I have," he said, although he knew she was a risk and he had a feeling spending too much time with her wasn't a good thing. It was then that he realized he was still holding her hand, and with supreme effort he released it.

He should know better than to get too attached to a woman like Lucia. She was the kind of woman a man could become attached to before he knew it. His attraction to her seemed too natural, but way too binding. She was a woman who seemed to be created just for the purpose of making a man want her in ways he had never wanted a woman before. And that wasn't good.

After their initial drinks, they ordered coffee and then shared a slice of strawberry cheesecake, and while they sat there she had his undivided attention. They conversed about a number of topics. More than once he caught his gaze roaming across her face, studying her features and appreciating her beauty. Whether she knew it or not, her facial bone structure was superb and any man would definitely find her attractive. But he knew there was more to her than just her outside beauty. She was beautiful on the inside as well. Derringer listened as she told him about a number of charities and worthwhile events she supported, and he was impressed.

A couple of hours later while driving her back home, he couldn't help but reflect on how the evening had gone. Certainly not the way he had planned. When the car came to a traffic light, he glanced over at her. Not surprisingly, she had fallen asleep. He thought about all the things he wanted to do to her when he got her back to her place, and knew the only thing he should do was walk her to her door and then leave. Something was going on with him that he didn't understand and he was smart enough to know when to back off.

That thought was still on his mind when he walked her to the door later. For some reason, he was being pulled in another direction and frankly he didn't like it. Her kiss alone had shot his brain cells to hell and back and knocked his carefully constructed plans to teach her a lesson to the wind. Even now the taste from her kiss was lingering in his mouth.

"Thanks again for such a wonderful evening, Derringer. I had a great time."

He'd had a great time, too. "You're welcome." He forced his lips closed to stop from asking her out again. He simply refused to do that. "Well, I guess I'll be going now," he said, trying to get his feet to step back and trying to figure out why they wouldn't budge.

"Would you like to come inside for more coffee?"

He shook his head. "Thanks, but I don't think my stomach can hold much more. Besides, my restrictions are over and I can return to work soon. I'll be helping Zane and Jason with the horses in the morning. I need to get home and get to bed."

"All right."

He made a move to leave but couldn't. Instead, his gaze settled on the face staring at him and he felt something pull at his gut. "Good night, Lucia," he whispered, just seconds before leaning down and brushing a kiss across her lips.

"Good night, Derringer."

He straightened and watched as she let herself inside the house. When the door clicked locked behind her, he turned to move down the walkway toward his car. He opened the door and slid inside. He needed to go home and think about things, regroup and revamp. And he had to figure out what there was about Lucia Conyers that got to him on a level he wasn't used to.

Chapter 6

Zane stopped saddling his horse long enough to glance over at his brother. "What's going on with you, Derringer? Last week you were inquiring about women's panties and now this week you want to know about a woman's scent. Didn't you get that mystery solved by viewing the tape on that video camera?"

Derringer rubbed his hand down his face. He should have known better than to come to Zane, but the bottom line was his brother knew more about women than *he* did and right now he needed answers. After he got them he'd be able to figure out what was going on with him when it came to Lucia. It had been almost a week after their date to the movies and he still didn't have a clue. And he had yet to confront her about being his late-night visitor.

He glanced over at Zane across the horse's back.

"There's nothing going on with me. Just answer the damn question."

Zane chuckled. "Getting kind of testy, aren't you? And how did your date go with Lucia Saturday night? I haven't heard you say."

"And I'm not going to say either, other than we had a nice time."

"For your sake I think that's all you better say or Chloe, Megan and Bailey will be coming down on you pretty hard. You might get a reprieve from Gemma since she's out of the country, but I wouldn't count on it if I were you, because she's coming home later this month for the charity ball."

Derringer grunted. The women in his family ought to stay out of his business and he would tell them so if the topic of Lucia ever came up with any of them again. So far, he'd been lying low this week, and when he had dropped by to see Ramsey, Chloe and baby Susan, the topic of Lucia hadn't come up. He could inwardly admit the reason he'd made himself scarce was his fear of running into her at Ramsey's. It was unheard of for Derringer Westmoreland to avoid any woman.

"So, will you answer my question?"

Zane crossed his arms over his chest. "Only after you answer mine. Did you or did you not watch that video footage?"

He glared over at his brother. "Yes, I watched it."

"And?"

"And I'd rather not discuss it."

A smirk appeared on Zane's face. "I bet you'll be glad to discuss it if you get hit with a paternity suit nine months from now."

Zane's words hit Derringer below the belt with a reminder that Lucia could be pregnant with his child.

They'd had unprotected sex that night. She had to know that as well. Was she not worried about that possibility? He met his brother's intense gaze. "I'll handle it if that were to happen, now answer the question."

Zane smiled. "You're going to have to repeat it. My attention span isn't what it used to be these days."

Like hell it's not, Derringer thought. He knew Zane was trying to get a rise of him and he didn't like it, but since he needed answers he would overlook his brother's bad attitude for now. "I want to know about the scent of a woman."

Zane smiled as he leaned back against the corral post. "Um, that's an easy one. Every woman has her own unique scent and if a man is attentive enough he's able to tell them apart by it. Some men will know their woman's location in a room before setting eyes on her just from her scent alone."

Derringer pulled in a deep breath. He knew all that already. He tilted his Stetson back off his head. "What I want to know is the effect that scent can have on a man."

Zane chuckled. "Well, I know for a fact that a woman's natural scent is a total turn-on for most men. It's all in the pheromones. Remember that doctor I dated last year?"

Derringer nodded. "Yes, what about her?"

"Man, her scent used to drive me crazy, and she damn well knew it. But it didn't bother me one bit when she took that job in Atlanta and moved away," Zane said.

Derringer decided not to remind Zane of the bad mood he'd been in for months after the woman left. "Every woman has her unique scent, but many douse it with cologne," Zane continued. "Then every woman that wears that cologne practically smells the same. But when you make love to a woman, her natural scent will override everything."

Zane paused a minute and then said, "And the effect it can have on a man depends on what degree of an attractant her scent can be. A woman's scent alone can render him powerless."

Derringer lifted his brow. "Powerless?"

"Yes, the scent of a woman is highly potent and sexually stimulating. And some men have discovered their own male senses can detect the woman who was meant to be their mate just from her scent. Animals rely on scent for that purpose all the time, and although some people might differ with that theory, there are some who believe it's true for humans as well. So if the scent of some woman is getting to you, that might be your cue she's your mate."

Derringer studied his brother's gaze, not sure if Zane was handing him a bunch of bull or not. The thought of his future being shared with a woman because of her scent didn't make much sense, but he'd watched enough shows on *Animal Kingdom* to know that was basically true with animals. Was man different from other animals?

"Some woman's scent has gotten to you," Zane taunted.

He didn't answer. Instead, he looked away for a second, wondering about that same thing. When he looked back at Zane moments later, his brother was grinning.

"What the hell do you find amusing?"

"Trust me, you don't want to know."

Derringer frowned. Zane was right; he didn't want to know.

"And you haven't heard from Derringer since your date Saturday night?"

A lump formed in Lucia's throat with Chloe's question. It was Friday night, late afternoon, and she sat curled on her sofa. Although she really hadn't expected Derringer to seek her out again, the notion that he didn't still bothered her, especially because she thought they'd had such a good time. At least she knew for a fact *she* had, and he'd seemed to enjoy himself as well. But she figured when you were Derringer Westmoreland, you could have a different girl every day.

When he had brought her home Saturday night, she had expected him to accept her invitation to come inside for coffee, although she would be the first to admit they had drunk plenty of the stuff at Torie's. He had declined her offer and given her a chaste kiss on the lips then left.

"No, I haven't heard anything, but that's okay. I was able to write in my diary that I had a date with him and that's good."

"One date isn't good when there can be others, Lu. You do know that women don't have to wait for the man to call for a date, we have that right as well."

Yes, but Lucia knew she couldn't be that forward with a man. "I know, but—"

There was a knock at her door. "Someone's at the door, Chloe. It's probably Mrs. Noel from across the street. She bakes on Fridays and uses me as her guinea pig, but I have no complaints. I'll call you back later."

When the knock sounded again, she called out after hanging up the phone. "I'm coming."

She eased off the sofa and headed to the door, thinking she would chow down on Mrs. Noel's sweets and get her romance groove on by watching a romantic movie on Lifetime. If you couldn't have the real thing in your life then she figured a movie was second best.

She nearly choked when she glanced out her peephole. Her caller wasn't her neighbor. It was Derringer. She suddenly felt hot when she realized he was staring at the peephole in the door as if he knew she was watching him. She closed her eyes trying to slow down the beating of her heart. He was the last person she expected to see tonight. In fact, she'd figured he wouldn't appear on her doorstep any time soon, or ever again. She assumed they would get back into the routine of running into each other whenever she visited Chloe, Ramsey and the baby.

Forcing her brain cells to stop scrambling, she turned the doorknob to open the door and there he stood in a pair of jeans, a sweater, a leather jacket and boots. He looked good, but then he always did. He was leaning against a post on her porch with his hands in his pockets.

She cleared her throat. "Derringer, what are you doing here?"

He held her gaze. "I know I should have called first."

She stopped herself from saying that he could appear on her doorstep anytime. The last thing a woman should do is let a man assume she was pining for him... even if she was. "Yes, you should have called first. Is anything wrong?"

"No, I just needed to see you."

She tried to ignore how low his voice had dropped and how he was looking at her. Instead, she tried to focus on what he'd said. *He just needed to see her.*

Yeah, right. She thought he could really do better than that, especially since he hadn't done so much as picked up a phone to call her since their date on Saturday night. Was she to believe needing to see her had brought him to her door? She wondered if his date tonight had canceled and she had been his backup plan. Curious about that possibility, she decided to ask him.

Crossing her arms over her chest, she said. "Um, let me guess, your date stood you up and I was next on the list." After saying the words, she realized her mistake. First, she doubted very seriously that any woman stood him up and she really thought a lot of herself to even assume she was on any list he had.

He tilted his head as if he needed to see her more clearly. "Is that what you think?"

She shook her head. "To be honest with you, Derringer, I really don't know what to think."

He made a slow move and inched closer to her face. He then leaned over and whispered against her ear. "Invite me in and I promise you won't be thinking at all."

And that was what she was afraid of.

She drew in a deep breath, thinking she would be able to handle him. She opened the door and stepped back, hoping at that moment that she could.

What the hell am I doing here? Derringer wondered as he brushed by her. He had caught a whiff of her scent the moment she had opened the door, and as always it was playing hard on his senses.

He turned when he heard her close the door behind him and his gaze studied her. For some reason he didn't have the strength or inclination to tear his eyes away from her. What was wrong with him? When had he ever let a woman affect him this way? She was standing there leaning back against the door in her bare feet and a pair of leggings and a T-shirt. Her hair was back in that signature ponytail. She looked comfortable. She looked sexy. Damn, she looked good enough to eat.

He cleared his throat. "What are your plans for to-night?"

She shrugged. "I didn't have any. I was just going to watch a movie on Lifetime."

He was familiar with that channel, the one that was supposed to be for women that showed romance movies 24/7. His sisters used to be glued to their television sets, and in Bailey's case, sometimes to his.

"How would you like to go roller skating?"

The glow from a table lamp captured the expression of surprise on her face. "You want us to go out again?"

He noted that there was a degree of shock in her voice. There was a note of wariness as well.

"Yes, I know I should have called first, and I am sorry about that. And just to set the record straight, when I left home I didn't have a date. I didn't have any plans for tonight. I got in my car and I ended up here. What I said earlier was true. I needed to see you."

Serious doubt was etched in her features. "Why, Derringer? Why did you need to see me?"

It should be so easy to use this moment and come clean and say because I know who you are. I know you are the woman to whom I made love in what should have been a weak and crazy moment, but it ended up being the one time I slept with a woman that I remember the most. That no matter what I do or where I go, your scent is right there with me. You are responsible for the lust that rages through my body every time I think of you, whenever I see you. Even now there is a throb-bing in my groin that you're causing and I want more than anything to make love to you again.

"Derringer?"

He realized at that moment that he hadn't answered

her. Instead, he had been standing there and staring at her like a lust-crazed maniac. He slowly crossed the floor, pinning her in when he braced his hands on both sides of her head, and leaned in close to her mouth.

"I really don't know why I needed to see you tonight," he whispered huskily against her lips. "I can't explain it. I just needed to see you, be with you and spend time with you. I enjoyed Saturday night and—"

"Could have fooled me."

He noticed her voice had barely been audible, but he'd heard that, and he'd heard the hurt in her tone. He hadn't called her. He should have. He had wanted to. But he had fought the temptation. If only she knew to what degree he had fought it. A part of him knew being here with her now wasn't good; especially when he was thinking of all the things he wanted to do to her right now—against the door, on the floor, on her bed, the table, the sofa, every damn place in her house. But even more important was that he knew more about the situation than she did. He had yet to tell her that he knew about her visit to his home that night.

He had spent the last few days going over the video time and time again. It was evident from viewing the footage and seeing how she had merely stuck her head in the door that initially she'd had no intention of staying. Then she had glanced back at the box and decided to put it inside. She must have heard him fall once she was inside, because this week he remembered that part—missing the bed when he'd gotten up to use the bathroom and falling flat on his behind when he was returning to bed. He remembered someone, his Puddin' Tame, helping him back into bed, and the only thing he remembered after that was making love to a woman.

And the woman he had made love to had been her.

Things were still kind of fuzzy, but he remembered that much now. "I apologize for not calling you this week. I should have," he murmured.

She shook her head. "You didn't have to. I'm the one who should be apologizing. I should not have given you the impression that you should have called, just now."

His heart beat hard in his chest. That statement alone showed how different she was from the other women he messed around with. And that difference, among other things, he was convinced, was what had him here with her now.

"I don't want any apologies from you," he said, leaning in closer, drawing one of her earlobes between his lips. "This is what I want." He then brushed his tongue across her lips and when she gave a sharp intake of breath, he did it again. And again.

"Why, Derringer...why me?" she whispered moments before she began trembling against the door.

"Why not you?" he breathed huskily against her lips before bending close to taste them again. Her flavor as well as her scent was getting to him on a level that made him want to push forward instead of drawing back.

Then deciding they had done enough talking for now, he sidled up closer to her and pressed his mouth to hers.

By rights she should send him away, Lucia's mind screamed over and over again. But it was hard to listen to what her mind was saying when Derringer was causing so much havoc with her body. This was the kind of kiss that could knock the sense out of a woman. It was long, deep and downright greedy. He was eating at her mouth as if it were his last meal, and there was no doubt in her mind this kiss was definitely X-rated.

And if that wasn't bad enough, his erection was pressing into her right at the juncture of her thighs, cradled against her womanly mound as if it had specifically sought out that part of her. And then there were the nipples of her breasts that were piercing his chest through the material of her T-shirt. She couldn't help but remember how it felt when they had been flesh to flesh, skin to skin. If he was seducing her then he was certainly going at it the right way.

He suddenly pulled back. Puzzled as to why, she nervously chewed on her bottom lip—a lip he'd just released from devouring—and stared up at him. He was staring back. "I think we need to take time and think through a few things," he said huskily.

She arched a bemused brow. He evidently was speaking for himself. As far as she was concerned there was nothing to think through. She knew what she wanted and had a feeling that he did, too. So what was the problem? She knew the score. Nothing was forever with Derringer Westmoreland and she was okay with that. Although she was hopelessly in love with the man, she knew her limitations. She had accepted them long ago. She had made more strides within the last twelve days than she'd expected in her entire lifetime. They had made love, for heaven's sake, and he had kissed her senseless a week ago tomorrow.

But still…she was no longer a teenager with fantasies of him marrying her and living happily ever after with each other. She totally understood that was not the way the ball would bounce. She was not entering into anything with him blindly; she had both eyes wide open.

Bottom line was that she didn't have to safeguard her heart. Although she wished otherwise, the man had her heart, lock, stock and barrel, and it was too late to do anything about it but gladly take whatever she could and live the rest of her life on memories.

"I think I need to give you time to get dressed so we can get to the skating rink."

She couldn't help but smile softly. "Do you really want to do that?"

He shook his head. "No, but if you knew what I really want to do you would probably kick me out."

"Try me."

He threw his head back and laughed. "No, I think I'll pass. I'll wait out here until you change clothes."

She moved around him to head down the hall and stopped right before crossing the threshold into her room. "You know it would probably be more fun if we stayed here, don't you?"

He smiled then said in a firm voice, "Go get dressed, Lucia."

Laughing, she entered the bedroom and closed the door behind her. While removing her clothes, Lucia made a decision about something.

For the first time ever she intended to try her luck at seducing a man.

Chapter 7

Derringer glanced over at Lucia, who was across the room standing in line to check out their roller skates. He had two words to describe the jeans she was wearing—snug and tight. And then the first two words that would describe her overall appearance tonight were hot and sexy.

Deciding he needed to stop staring at her every chance he got, he glanced around. He had expected the place to be crowded since it was a Friday night, but why were there more kids than adults? Granted, it had been years since he'd gone skating, but still, he would think it was past these kids' bedtime.

He laughed recalling how some smart-mouthed preteen had come up to him a few minutes ago and said he hoped he and Lucia were fast enough on the skates to keep up and not get in anyone's way. Hell, he and Lucia weren't *that* old.

"What's so funny?"

He glanced down to see Lucia had returned with their skates. He then told her about the smart-mouthed kid and she smiled. "Doesn't this city still have a curfew?" he asked her.

She shook her head. "Not anymore."

He lifted a brow. "When did they do away with it?" He figured she would know because her dad had been a member of Denver's city council for years.

She smiled sweetly up at him. "They did away with it when Bane turned eighteen."

He stared at her for a second, saw she was serious and threw his head back and laughed so hard they couldn't help but get attention. "You're making a scene, Derringer Westmoreland," she whispered.

He shook his head and pulled her closer to him. "Is there anywhere Bane didn't leave his mark?"

"According to my father, the answer to that question is a resounding no. Now, come on, *old man*, or that kid will return and ask us to step aside."

He took her teasing of his age in stride, but still he reached out and grabbed her around the waist. "I'll show you who's old and who's not," he said, and then he took off, pulling her with him.

It was past three in the morning when Derringer returned Lucia home, and he smiled as he escorted her inside her home. It had taken a while, but he'd eventually shown that smart-mouthed kid why he once had earned the reputation of being hell on wheels with roller skates. And then when the kid had found out he was a Westmoreland—a cousin to the infamous Bane Westmoreland—he had to all but sign autographs.

"Can you believe those kids actually think Bane is some kind of hero?" he said, dropping onto Lucia's love seat.

She chuckled as she sat down on the sofa across from him. "Yes, I can believe that. Bane was bold enough to do some of the horrific things they would probably love to try but know that they can't get away with doing. Tell me, who in their right mind would take off in the sheriff's car while he's giving someone a ticket other than Bane? He became something of a legend if you were to read some of the stuff the girls wrote all over the walls in the bathroom at the local high school. He and the twins."

He glanced over at her. "How do you know about those walls? That was after your time."

She smiled as she settled back against the cushions, wrapping her arms across the back. "I have a young cousin who used to have a crush on Aidan and he's all she used to talk about then, in addition to all the trouble Aidan, Adrian and Bane would get into."

Derringer shook his head and chuckled, remembering those times. "And let's not forget Bailey—she was just as bad. At one time we considered sending all four of them to military school, but that would be like giving up on our own, and we knew we couldn't do that."

A serious expression touched his features before he said, "I don't tell Ramsey and Dillon enough how much I appreciate them keeping our family together. Losing my parents and my aunt and uncle at the same time was hard on everyone, but they helped us get through it." Derringer inwardly struggled with what he'd just told her, realizing he had never shared those emotions and feelings with anyone, certainly not any of his women.

"I'm sure they know you appreciate what they did,

Derringer. The proof is in the successful, law-abiding men and women you all became. That's a testimony in itself. The Westmorelands are getting something now the townspeople figured they wouldn't ever get after your parents and aunt and uncle passed away."

He lifted a brow. "And what's that?"

"Respect." A smile touched her lips when she added, "And admiration. I wish you would have noticed the look on that kid's face tonight when he realized you were a Westmoreland."

Derringer snorted. "Yes, but he was admiring me for all the wrong reasons."

"It doesn't matter."

He knew deep down that Lucia was right—it didn't matter, because in the end what Dillon and Ramsey had done was indeed a success story in his book. He stretched his legs out in front of him thinking how throughout the evening he had enjoyed the time he was spending with Lucia. It had been the first time he'd spent with a woman when he'd had honest-to-goodness fun. She had been herself and hadn't gone out of her way to impress him and draw all the attention on her.

Even on the drive to and from the skating arena he had enjoyed their conversation, and although it was hard to believe, they had a lot in common and shared the same interests. They both enjoyed watching Westerns, they enjoyed a good comedy every once in a while and were huge fans of the Wayans brothers, Bill Cosby and Sandra Bullock. She also rode horses and enjoyed going hunting.

But more than anything, he had enjoyed being with her, sharing her space and breathing the same air that she did. And he smiled, thinking she wasn't too bad on roller skates either. He had enjoyed going around the rink with her, often hearing her throaty laugh, looking over at her and seeing the huge smile on her face; and he especially liked wrapping his arms around her waist when they skated together.

"I had a wonderful time tonight, Derringer. I really enjoyed myself."

He glanced over at her. At some point, she had removed her boots and shifted position on the sofa to tuck her jeans-clad legs beneath her. But still, it didn't take much to remember how her long, curvy legs looked in a pair of shorts, a skirt or a dress. But most of all, he could recall those same legs wrapped around his waist while they had made love. The more time he spent with her, the more things were coming back to him that he had forgotten about their night together.

"I enjoyed myself as well," he responded.

"You were pretty good on those skates."

"You weren't so bad yourself." He wondered why he was sitting here making small talk with her when what he really wanted to do was to cross the room and join her on that sofa. His attention was trained directly on her and he could tell by the way she was moving her fingers on her knee he was making her nervous.

"Lucia, does my being here bother you?"

"What makes you think that?"

"Because you're over there and I'm here," he didn't hesitate to say. He watched as she nervously licked her bottom lip, and immediately the lower part of his body—directly behind his zipper—responded in a hard-up way.

"There's nothing keeping you over there, Derringer," she said softly.

He couldn't help but smile at her deduction. She

was right. There was nothing keeping him on this love seat when more than anything he wanted to be on that sofa with her. Knowing what he should do was stand up, thank her again for a good time and head toward the door and leave, never to return again, he remained seated for a minute. But he knew, just as much as he knew that tomorrow would bring another day, he wasn't going to do that.

And he also knew that she didn't know, she didn't have a clue just what she did to him, what being here with her was doing to him. He figured his intense attraction to her had everything to do with the night they had made love. But that wouldn't make sense since he'd made love to a number of women before and none had left the kind of lasting impression that she had. So why had the time with her been different, and why was he so quick to accept that it was?

The answer nearly made him tremble inside. It made his chest clench and made blood rush through his veins. She was deeply embedded in his system and he knew only one way to get her out of there. When they'd made love before, he hadn't been completely coherent and maybe that was the problem. Now he needed to make love to her in his right mind, if for no other reason than to purge her from his thoughts, mind and body. Then he could get on with his life and she could get on with hers. But before it was all over, he intended to let her know he was well aware that she had been his visitor that night.

Deciding he was doing too much thinking and not delivering enough action, he eased off the love seat.

Nowhere to run and nowhere to hide.

Deep down, Lucia knew she didn't want to do either

as she watched Derringer slowly move toward her. Why was she getting all tense and nervous? Hadn't she made up her mind to seduce him tonight? But it seemed as if he had beat her to the punch and he was about to take things into his own hands. Literally.

His visit had been a surprise. She hadn't expected him tonight. He was the most unlikely person to show up at her place tonight or any other time. Not only had he shown up, but he'd taken her out again. Skating. It was their second date and he claimed the reason he was here was because he had needed to see her.

She knew needing to see her had only been a line and men like Derringer were good at saying such things. They said whatever they thought a woman wanted to hear. But that hadn't stopped her from allowing herself to be taken in, relish the moments spent with him and be greedy enough to want more. She would take whatever part of Derringer she could get. Tomorrow she would wake up and hate herself for being such a weakling where he was concerned, but she would also wake wearing the blush of a satisfied woman all over her face.

There was no doubt in her mind that he intended to make love to her. He'd done it before, and from the dark, intense look in his eyes, he planned to do so again. And tonight he wouldn't get any resistance, because she loved him just that much and was secretly grateful for this time with him.

He slid down beside her on the sofa. "There is just something tantalizingly sweet about your scent, Lucia."

Another line, she was sure of it. "Is there?"

"Yes. It makes my body burn for you," he said, wrapping his arms around her shoulders.

She drew in a deep breath, thinking she would love to believe what he was saying, but knew better. However, tonight it was all about make-believe. Besides, it was hard not to melt under the intense look he was giving her and the way his arm felt around her shoulders. And he was sitting so close, every time he spoke his warm breath blew across her lips.

He then pulled back slightly and gazed at her thoughtfully. "You don't believe a word I've said, do you?"

She began nibbling on her bottom lip. She could easily lie and assure him that she did, but deep down she knew she didn't believe him. She tilted her chin upward. "Does it matter whether or not I believe you, Derringer?"

He continued to stare at her for a moment with an unreadable expression on his face, and for a split second she thought he was going to say something but he didn't. Instead, he reached out and cupped her chin with his fingertips before slowly lowering his mouth to hers.

Sensations ripped through her the moment their lips touched. She closed her eyes when his tongue eased into her mouth and he began kissing her with a hunger that had her groaning deep in her throat.

Her heart thundered when he captured her tongue with his and began doing all kinds of erotic things to it, sucking on it as if there was a time limit to get his fill, mating their tongues as if all they had was the here and now. This was the kind of kissing that made a woman forget that she was supposed to be a lady.

She wanted this. She wanted every mind-blowing moment because she knew there *was* a time limit on this fantasy. Everyone around town knew of Derringer's reputation for getting tired of his women quickly. There was only a chosen one or two who were determined to hang in for the long haul no matter what—by their choice and not his. She refused to be one of those women. She would take this and be satisfied.

When he broke off the kiss to shift their positions to press her back against the sofa cushions, she moved willingly with him. She gazed up at him when his body eased on top of hers. She could feel his hard erection between her thighs.

He lowered his head and began nibbling around her throat, taking the tip of his tongue and licking around her chin. "Too many clothes." She heard him utter the word moments before he leaned up and, without warning, pulled the sweater over her head. He tossed it to the floor. He then proceeded to tug her jeans down her legs.

He looked down at her and smiled at her matching red lace bra and panties. She wondered what was going through his mind and why he was so captivated by her lingerie. He then glanced back up at her. "I like a woman who wears lace," he whispered huskily before leaning down and taking her mouth once more.

His lips seemed incredibly hot and he had no problem sliding his tongue where he pleased while kissing her with slow, deep strokes. And when she felt his fingers move toward her breasts, ease under her bra to stroke a nipple, she nearly shot off the sofa when sensations speared through her.

"Derringer..." she whispered in a strained voice.

This was getting to be too much and she began quivering almost uncontrollably, knowing what she'd heard for years was true. Derringer Westmoreland was almost too much for any woman to handle.

She was wrong. It did matter to him that she believed what he said.

That thought raged through Derringer's mind as he continued to kiss her with a hunger he could not understand. What was there about her that made him want to taste her all over, make her groan mercilessly and torture her over and over again before exploding inside her? The mere thought of doing the latter made his groin throb.

He pulled back slightly, wanting her to watch exactly what he was doing. What he was about to do. When he released the front fastener of her bra, his breath quickened when her breasts came tumbling out. They were full, firm and ripe and the nipples were dark and tightened even more into hard nubs before his eyes. And when he swooped his mouth down and captured a peak between his lips, she moaned and closed her eyes. "Keep them open, Lucia. Watch me. I want you to see what I'm doing to you."

He saw her heavy-lidded eyes watch as he tugged a nipple into his mouth and begin sucking on it, and the more he heard her moan the more pressure he exerted with his mouth.

But that wasn't enough. Her scent was getting to him and he needed to touch her, to taste her, to bury himself in a feminine fragrance that was exclusively hers. He left one breast and went to another as he lowered a hand underneath the waistband of her lace bikini panties. And when his fingers ran over the wetness of her feminine folds, she writhed against his hand and let out a deep moan and whispered his name.

He lifted his head to stare down at eyes that were dazed with passion. "Yes, baby? You want something?"

Instead of answering, she began trembling as his fingers slipped inside her and he began stroking her while watching the display of emotions and expressions appear on her face. The breathless wonder drenched with pleasure that he saw in her gaze, in response to his touch, was a sight to behold and the sweetest thing he'd ever seen.

Lust thundered through him with the force of a hurricane and he knew he had to make love to her in the most primitive way. Leaning back, he eased to his feet and continued to hold her gaze while he tugged off his boots, pulled off his socks and unzipped his jeans. He took the time to remove a condom from the back pocket and held it between his teeth while he yanked down his jeans, careful of his engorged erection.

"Derringer…"

If she said his name like that, with that barely-there voice, one more time, he would lose it. The sound was sending splendorous shivers up his spine and there was a chance he would come the minute he got inside her, without making a single thrust. And he didn't want that. He wanted to savor the moment, make it last for as long as he could.

When he was totally naked, he stood before her and watched her gaze roam over him, seeing some parts of him that she probably hadn't seen their other night together. There was no shame in his game, but he knew deep down this wasn't a game with him. He was serious about what was taking place between them.

Thinking he had wasted more than enough time, he bent over her to remove the last item of clothing covering her body. Her panties. He touched the center of her and she sucked in a deep breath. He tossed aside the condom packet he'd been holding between his teeth. "You're drenched, baby," he said in a low, rough voice. "I know you don't believe me, but there is something about you that drives me crazy."

When he began tugging her panties down her legs, he whispered throatily, "Lift your hips and bend your legs for me."

She did, and when he removed her panties, instead of tossing them aside, he rubbed the lacy material over his face before he bent to the floor and tucked them into the back pocket of his jeans. He knew she was watching his every move and was probably wondering what on earth possessed him to do such a thing.

Instead of mounting her now, as he wanted to do, there was something he wanted to do even more. Taste her. He wanted to taste all that sweetness that triggered the feminine aroma he enjoyed inhaling. It was a scent he was convinced he had become addicted to.

He lowered his body to his knees and before she could pull in her next breath, he pressed an open mouth to the wet, hot feminine lips of her sex. She groaned so deep in her throat that her body began trembling. But he kept focused on the pleasure awaiting him as he leisurely stroked her with his tongue, feasting on her with a hunger he knew she could not understand, but that he intended her to enjoy.

Because he was definitely enjoying it.

He'd been of the mind that no other woman had her scent. Now he was just as convinced that no other woman had her taste as well. It was unique. It was hers. And at the moment, as crazy as it sounded, he was also of the mind that it was also *his,* in a possessive way he'd never encountered before with any woman. The mere thought should have scared the hell out of him, but he was too far gone to give a damn.

When heat and lust combined and resonated off his mind he knew he had to be inside her or risk exploding then and there. He tore his mouth from her and threw his head back and released a deep savage groan. He then stared down at her while licking her juices from his lips. He felt as if he was taking part in a scorching-hot, exciting and erotic dream, and it was a dream he was dying to turn into a reality. And there was only one way he knew to do that.

He would take her and now.

Without saying a word, he leaned over and spread her thighs and placed a kiss on each before moving off his knees to shift his body over hers. Instinctively she arched her back and wrapped her arms around his neck. Their gazes held as he eased his body down, the thick head of his shaft finding what it wanted and working its way inside her wet tightness. He paused when he'd made it halfway, glorying in the feel of her muscles clamping down on him, convulsing around him.

He wanted to take things slow, but the feel of her gripping him had him groaning deep in his throat, and when in a naughty, unexpected move she licked out her tongue and flicked his budded nipple before easing it into her mouth with a hungry suck, he took in a sharp breath at the same time he thrust hard into her.

When he heard her cry out, he apologized in a soothing whispered voice. "I'm sorry. I didn't mean to hurt you. Just lie still for a moment."

He used that time to lick around her mouth, nibble at the corners, and when she parted her mouth on a sweet sigh, he eased his tongue inside and sank right into a hungry kiss filled with more urgency and desire than he'd ever known or had ever cared knowing. Until now.

And then he felt the lower part of her body shift beneath the weight of his. He pulled back from the kiss. "That's it, baby," he crooned close to her ear. "Take it. All that you want."

His body remained still as she moved her body, grinding against him, dipping her hips into the sofa cushions before lifting them up again, arching her back in the process. Then she began rotating her hips, pushing up and lowering back down.

Derringer's body froze when he remembered the condom he'd tossed aside and he knew he needed to pull out now. But heaven help him, he couldn't do so. Being inside of her like this felt so darn right. He kept his body immobile until he couldn't stay still any longer and then he joined her, driving his erection deeper into her. He thrust in and out with precise and concentrated strokes that he felt all the way to the soles of his feet.

He had thought their first time together had been off the charts, but nothing, he decided, could compare to this. Nothing could compete with the incredible feeling of being inside her this way. Nothing. Desperate to reach the highest peak with her, he took total possession of her, kissing her with urgency while their bodies mated in the most primitive pleasure known to humankind.

He whispered erotic things in her ear before reaching

down and cupping her face in his hands to stare down at her while his body continued to drive heatedly into hers. Their gazes locked and something happened between them at that moment that nearly threw him off balance. Somewhere in the back of his mind a voice was taunting that this had nothing to do with possessing but everything to do with claiming.

Denial froze hard in his throat and he wanted to scream that it wasn't possible. He claimed no woman. Instead, he grunted savagely as his body exploded, and then he heard her scream as she cried out in ecstasy. He kept thrusting into her, pushing them further and further into sweet oblivion and surging them beyond the stars.

Chapter 8

Lucia moved her head slowly, opened her eyes and then came fully awake when a flash of sunlight through her bedroom window hit her right in the face. It was then that she felt the male body pressed tightly against her back and the heated feel of Derringer's breathing on her neck.

She then remembered.

They had made love on the sofa before moving into her bedroom where they had made love again before drifting off to sleep. Sometime during the wee hours of early morning they had made love again. The entire thing seemed unreal, but Derringer's presence in her bed assured her that it had been real.

Her body felt sore, tender in a number of places, but mostly between her legs, and she wouldn't be surprised if her lips were swollen from all the kissing they had done. Her cheeks flooded with heat thinking about a number of other things they'd gotten into as well. She had proven to him in a very sexual way that she definitely knew how to ride a stallion. He had taunted her to prove it and she'd done so.

Her eyes fluttered closed as she thought how she would handle things from here on out. She knew last night meant more to her than it had to him, and she could handle that. But what she wouldn't be able to handle was letting things go beyond what they'd shared these past few hours. She loved him and for him to ever make love to her again would turn things sexual, into a casual relationship that would tarnish her memories rather than enhance them. She was smart enough to know when to let go and move on. Now was the time.

Tears flooded her eyes. Derringer would always have her heart, but the reality was that she would never have his. And being the type of person that she was, she could never allow herself to become just one in a long line of women vying for his attention. She preferred letting things go back to the way they were between them before they'd become intimate.

The way she saw things, if she never had him then there was no way she could lose him. She couldn't risk a broken heart because of Derringer and she knew her place in his life. She didn't have one. If she began thinking of developing something serious with him knowing the kind of man he was, she was setting herself up for pain from which she might never be able to heal.

She would continue to love him like this—secretly. She had gotten used to doing things that way and, no matter what, she couldn't let their sexual encounters—

no matter how intense they'd been—fill her head and mind with false illusions.

She swallowed when she felt Derringer's penis swell against her backside and tried to convince herself it wouldn't be a good idea to make love to him one last time. But she knew the moment he pulled her closer to his hard, masculine body that she would. This would be saying goodbye to the intimacy between them. She knew it even if he didn't.

"You're awake?" He turned her in his arms to face him.

Desire rippled through her the moment she looked into his face. Propped with his head on her pillow, his eyes had the same desire-glazed look they'd had that first night they'd made love. It was a sexy, drowsy look, complete with a darkened shadow on his chin. No man had a right to look this good in the morning. He looked so untamed, wild and raw. His rumpled look was calling out to her, arousing her and making her want him all over again.

"Sort of," she said, yawning, and couldn't help the anticipation she heard in her voice. And when he gave her a dimpled cowboy smile, sensations shot through her entire body, but especially in the area between her thighs.

"Then let me wake you up the Derringer Westmoreland way." He then captured her mouth at the same time he tossed his leg over hers, adjusting their positions to ease inside her body.

"Oh," she whispered, and when he locked his leg on her and began slowly moving in and out of her and capturing her lips with his, she figured there was nothing wrong with one for the road…even though she knew she would end up in heaven.

* * *

Derringer's smile faded as he buttoned up his shirt and stared at Lucia. "What do you mean we can't ever make love again?"

He saw the flash of regret that came into her eyes before she stopped brushing her teeth long enough to rinse out her mouth. "Just what I said, Derringer. Last night was special and I want to remember it that way."

He was confused. "And you don't think you can if we make love again?"

"No. I know about the women you usually sleep with and, personally, I don't want to be one of them."

He frowned, crossing his arms over his chest, not sure he liked what she'd said. "Then why did you sleep with me last night?"

"I had my reasons."

His frown deepened. He couldn't help but wonder if those reasons were the same ones he had initially suspected her of having. And it didn't help matters to know that every time he had made love to her they had been unprotected. The first time had been a slip-up, and then after that, he'd deliberately chosen not to think about it. Why he'd done such a thing, he didn't know. He usually made it a point to always use protection. Even now, Lucia might be pregnant with his child.

"And just what are those reasons, Lucia?"

"I'd rather not say."

Anger ignited inside him. That response wasn't good enough.

"Oh!" she cried out in surprise when he reached out, snatched her off her feet and tossed her over his shoulders like a sack of potatoes and strode out of the bathroom.

"Derringer! What in the world is wrong with you? Put me down."

He did. Tossing her on the bed and glaring down at her. "I want to hear these reasons."

She glared back. "You don't need to know them. All you need to know is that I won't be sharing a bed with you again."

"Why? Because you think you're pregnant now and that's what this is about?"

Shock leaped into her face. "Pregnant? What are you talking about?"

"Are you on the pill or something?"

He could tell his question had surprised her. "No."

His frown deepened. "There's only one reason I can think of for a woman to let a man come inside her. Are you going to deny that sleeping with me this time around…as well as the last time…has nothing to do with you wanting a Westmoreland baby?"

He saw her throat tighten. "The last?"

"Yes," he said between clenched teeth. "I know all about your little visit that night when I was drugged up on pain medication."

She blinked. "You know?"

"Yes, and I couldn't figure out why you, a virgin, would get into my bed and take advantage of me. And, yes, I do remember you were a virgin even if I couldn't recall your identity."

She angrily reared up on her haunches. "I did not take advantage of you! I was helping you back into bed after you fell. If anything, you're the one who took advantage of me."

"So you say." He could see fury consume her body. and smoke was all but coming out her ears, but he didn't care.

She rolled off the bed and stood in front of him, almost nose to nose. "Are you insinuating I slept with you that night to deliberately get pregnant? And that I only slept with you last night and this morning for the same reason?"

"What am I supposed to think?"

She threw her hair over her shoulders. "That maybe I am different from all those other women you spend your time with, and that I would not have an ulterior motive like that," she all but screamed at him.

"You said you had your reasons."

"Yes, I have my reasons and they have nothing to do with getting pregnant by you, but everything to do with being in love with you. Do you have any idea how it is to fall in love with a man knowing full damn well he won't ever love you back?"

"In love with me," he said in a shocked stupor. "Since when?"

"Since I was sixteen."

"Sixteen!" He shook his head. "Hell, I didn't know."

She placed her hands on her hips and her eyes sparked with fire. "And you weren't *supposed* to know. It was a secret I had planned to take to my grave. Then like a fool I rushed over to your place when I heard you'd gotten hurt. And when you fell, I rushed up the stairs to help you back into bed and you wouldn't get off me."

He lifted a brow. His head was still reeling from her admission of love. "Are you saying I forced myself on you?"

"No, but I would not have gotten into bed with you if you hadn't fallen on top of me. And then, when you began kissing me, I—"

"Didn't want me to stop," he finished for her. Her cheeks darkened and he knew he'd embarrassed her. "Look, Lucia, I—"

"No, *you* look, Derringer. You're right. The thought of pushing you off me only entered my mind for a quick second, but I didn't set out to get pregnant by you that night or any other night."

"But you let me make love to you without any protection." He remembered all too well that he hadn't used a condom this time either.

"Then I can accuse you of the same thing. Trying to *get* me pregnant," she all but snarled.

"And why would I do something like that?"

"I don't know, but if you're willing to think the worst of me, then I can certainly do the same thing with you. You had taken the condom out of your wallet last night, why didn't you put it on?"

Derringer tensed. To say he'd been too carried away with making love to her would be to admit a weakness for her that he didn't want to own up to. "I think this conversation has gotten out of hand."

"You're right. I want you to leave."

He arched his brow. "Leave?"

"Yes. And my front door is that way," she said as she pointed to the door.

He narrowed his eyes. "I know where your door is located and we haven't finished our conversation."

"There's nothing else left to say, Derringer. I've already told you more than I should have and I'm ashamed of doing it. Now that you know how I feel, I won't let you take advantage of those feelings. For me it's even more important to protect my heart more than ever. Nothing has changed from the way you've always looked at me. Most of the time you acted like I didn't exist."

"That's not true. I told you I was attracted to you a few years back."

"Yes, and I honestly thought it meant something and that you were seeking me out after all that time. Now I know you only did so because you knew I was the one who slept with you that night."

She didn't say anything for a moment and then asked, "How did you know? I figured you wouldn't remember anything."

He jammed his hands into his jeans. "Oh, I remembered just fine, and you left a little something behind that definitely jogged my memory. Something pink and lacy. I just couldn't remember who they belonged to. My security system gave me the answers I needed. I had video cameras installed outside my place last month. You were the woman I saw entering my house that evening and the same one I saw sneaking out the next morning with a made-love-all-night-long look all over you."

Lucia tightened her bathrobe around her. "Like I said, that wasn't the purpose of my visit. I just wanted to make sure you were okay."

"It had been storming that night. You hate storms. Yet you came to check on me," he said.

That realization touched something within him. The reason he knew about her aversion to storms was because of something Chloe had once teased her about from their college days in Florida that involved a torrential thunderstorm and her reaction to it.

"Doesn't matter now."

"And what if I say it matters to me?" he all but snarled.

"Then I would suggest you get over it," she snapped back.

"I can't. I want to be with you again."

She narrowed her gaze. "And I told you that we won't be together that way ever again. So get it through that thick head of yours that I won't become just another woman you sleep with. You have enough of those."

Emotions he had never felt before stirred in Derringer's stomach. He should leave and not come back and not care if he ever saw her again, but for some reason she had gotten in his blood and making love to her again hadn't gotten her out. Instead the complete opposite had happened; she was more in his blood than ever before.

"I'll give you time to think about what I said, Lucia." He turned to leave the room knowing she was right on his heels as he moved toward the living room.

"There's nothing to think about," she snapped behind him.

He turned back around after snagging his Stetson off the rack. "Sure there is. We will be making love again."

"No, we won't!"

"Yes, we will," he said, moving toward the door. "You're in my blood now."

"I'm sure so are a number of other women in this town."

There was no point in saying that although he'd had a lot of women in the past, none had managed to get into his blood before. When he got to the door, he put on his hat before turning back to her. "Get some rest. You're going to need it when we make love again."

"I told you that we—"

He leaned forward and swiped whatever words she was about to say from her lips with a kiss, effectively silencing her. He then straightened and smiled at the infuriated face staring back at him and tipped the brim of his hat. "We'll talk later, sweetheart."

He opened the door and stepped outside and it didn't bother him one bit when she slammed the door behind him with enough force to wake up the whole neighborhood.

Chloe leaned forward and kissed Lucia on the cheek. "Hey, cheer up. It might not be so bad."

Lucia covered her face with both hands. "How can you say that, Clo? Now that Derringer knows how I feel, he's going to do everything in his power to find a weakness to get me back in his bed. I should never have told him."

"But you did tell him, so what's next?"

She lowered her hands and narrowed her eyes. "Nothing is next. I know what he's after and it's not happening. And just to think he knew I was the one who slept with him that night, when silly me thought he didn't have a clue. And now he wants to add me to his list."

Chloe raised a brow. "Did he actually say that?"

"He didn't have to. His arrogance was showing and that was enough." She doubted she could forget his exit and his statement about their talking later. She was so angry with him. The only good part about his leaving was the mesmerizing view of his backside before she slammed the door shut on him.

"I've known Derringer a lot longer than you, Chloe,

and he doesn't know the meaning of committing to one woman," she decided to add.

Chloe shrugged. "Maybe he's ready to change his ways."

Lucia rolled her eyes. "Fat chance."

"I don't know," Chloe said, tapping her finger against her chin. "Of the three die-hard-bachelor Westmoreland men who hang tight most of the time—Jason, Zane and Derringer—I think Jason will get married first...then Derringer...and last, Zane." She chuckled. "I can see Zane kicking, screaming and throwing out accusations all the way to the altar."

Lucia couldn't help but smile because she could envision that as well. Zane was more of a womanizer than Derringer. Jason didn't have the reputation the other two had, but he was still considered a ladies' man around town because he didn't tie himself down to any one woman.

"Derringer is so confident he's getting me back into his bed again, but I'm going to show him just how wrong he is."

Chloe took a long sip of her iced tea. She had been out shopping and had decided to drop by Lucia's. Unfortunately, she had found her best friend in a bad mood and it didn't take long for her to get Lucia to spill her guts about everything.

"Now, tell me once more your reason for not wanting to sleep with Derringer again."

Lucia rolled her eyes as she sat back on the sofa. "I know how those Westmoreland brothers and cousins operate with women. I don't want to become one of those females, pining away and sitting by the phone hoping I'm next on the list to call."

"But you've been pining away for Derringer for years anyway."

"I haven't been pining. Yes, I've loved him, but I knew he didn't love me back and I accepted that. I was fine with it. I had a life. I didn't expect him to phone or show up on my doorstep making booty calls."

Chloe laughed. "He didn't make a booty call exactly. He did take you out on a date."

"But that's beside the point."

Chloe leaned forward, grinning. "And what is your point exactly? I warned you that once you had a piece of a Westmoreland you'd become addicted. Now you've had Derringer more than once, so watch out. Staying away from him is going to be easier said than done, Lucia."

Lucia shook her head. "You just don't understand, Chloe."

Chloe smiled sadly. "You're right, I don't. I don't understand how a woman who loves a man won't go after him using whatever means it takes to get him. What are you afraid of?"

Lucia glanced over at Chloe. "Failing. Which will lead to heartbreak." She drew in a deep breath. "I had a cousin who had a nervous breakdown over a man. She was twenty and her parents sent her all the way from Nashville to live with us for a while. She was simply pathetic. She would go to bed crying and wake up doing the same thing. It was so depressing. I hate to say this, but I couldn't wait until she pulled herself together enough to leave."

"How sad for her."

"No, that's the reality of things when you're dealing with a man like Derringer."

Chloe quirked a brow. "I still think you might be wrong about him."

Lucia figured she couldn't change the way her best friend thought; however, she intended to take all the precautions where Derringer was concerned. Now he saw her as a challenge because she was the woman not willing to give him the time of day anymore.

Some men didn't take rejection well and she had a feeling that Derringer Westmoreland was one of them.

Chapter 9

Jason snapped his fingers in front of Derringer's face. "Hey, man, have you been listening to anything I've said?"

Derringer blinked, too ashamed to admit that he really hadn't. The last thing he recalled hearing was something about old man Bostwick's will being read that day. "Sort of," he said, frowning. "You were talking about old man Bostwick's will."

Herman Bostwick owned the land that was adjacent to Jason's. For years, Bostwick had promised Jason if he ever got the mind to sell, he would let Jason make him the first offer. The man died in his sleep and had been laid to rest a couple of days ago. It didn't take much to detect from the look in Jason's eyes that he wanted the land and Hercules, Bostwick's prize stallion. A colt from Hercules would be a dream come true for any horse breeder.

"So who did he leave the land to?" Derringer asked. "I hope it didn't go to his brother. Kenneth Bostwick is one mean son of a gun and will take us to the cleaners if we have to buy the land and Hercules from him."

Jason shook his head and took a sip of his beer. "The old man left everything to his granddaughter. Got Kenneth kind of pissed off about it."

Derringer lifted a brow. "His granddaughter? I didn't know he had one."

"It seems not too many people did. I understand that he and his son had a falling-out years ago, and when he left for college the son never returned to these parts. He married and settled down in the South. He had one child, a girl."

Derringer nodded and took a sip of his own beer. "So this granddaughter got the land and Hercules?"

"Yes. The only good thing is that I heard she's a prissy miss from Savannah who probably won't be moving here permanently. More than likely she'll be open to selling everything, and I want to be ready to buy when she does."

Jason then slid down to sit on the steps across from him, and Derringer looked out across his land. It was late afternoon and he still couldn't get out of his mind what had happened earlier that day with Lucia. If she thought he was done with her then she should think again.

He glanced over at his cousin. "Have you ever met a woman that got in your blood, real good?"

Jason just stared at him for a long moment. It didn't take much to see that Derringer's question had caught his cousin off guard. But he knew Jason; he liked mulling things over—sometimes too damn long.

"No. I'm not sure that can happen. At least not with me. Any woman who gets in my blood will end up being the one I marry. I don't have a problem with settling down and getting married one day, mind you. One day, when I'm ready, I want to start a family. I want to will everything I've built up to my wife and kids. You know what they say, 'You can't take it with you.'"

Jason then studied Derringer. "Why do you ask? Have you met a woman that's gotten deep in your blood?"

Derringer glanced away for a moment and then returned his gaze to Jason. "Yes… Lucia."

"Lucia Conyers?"

"Yeah."

Jason stood, almost knocking over his beer bottle. "Damn, man, how do you figure that? You only had one date with her."

Derringer smiled. "I've had two. We went skating last night." He didn't say anything and wanted to see what Jason had to say. Jason sat back down without opening his mouth.

"She's different," Derringer added after a moment.

Jason glanced over at him. "Of course she's different. You're not talking about one of your usual airheads or Derringer's Pleasers. We're discussing Lucia Conyers for heaven's sake. She used to be one of the smartest girls at her school. Remember when Dillon and Ramsey paid her to tutor Bailey that time so she wouldn't be left back? Lucia was only seventeen then."

Derringer smiled. He had almost forgotten about that time. And if he wanted to believe what she'd told him earlier, she had been in love with him even then. "Yes, I remember."

"And remember the time Megan got her first A on a science project because she was smart enough to team up with Lucia?"

Derringer chuckled, recalling that time as well. "Yeah, I recall that time as well." At least he did now.

"And you actually think someone that smart is destined to be your soul mate?"

"Soul mate?"

"Yes, if a woman is in your blood that much then it means she's destined to be your soul mate. Someone you want to be with all the time. Think about it, Derringer. Like I said, Lucia is not some airhead, she's pretty smart."

He didn't say anything for a moment as he studied his boots, grinning, thinking Jason's question had to be a joke. Then he lifted his gaze to find a serious-looking Jason staring at him, still waiting for a response. So he gave him the only one he knew. "Yes, I'm not exactly a dumb ass, Jason, so what does her being so smart have to do with anything? And as far as being my soul mate if that means sharing a bed with her whenever I want, then I intend to do everything in my power to convince her that she is the one."

Jason rolled his eyes and then rubbed his chin thoughtfully as he stared at Derringer. "So are you saying you've fallen in love with Lucia?"

Derringer looked taken aback. "Fallen in love with her? Are you crazy? I wouldn't go *that* far."

Jason appeared confused. "You have no problem wanting to claim her as your soul mate and sleep with her, but you aren't in love with her?"

"Yes. That's pretty much the shape and size of it."

Jason shook his head, grinning. "I hate to tell you this, but I'm not sure that's how it works."

Derringer finished off his beer and said, "Too bad. That's the way it's going to work for me."

On Monday morning, Lucia stood in the middle of her office refusing to let the huge arrangement of flowers get to her. They were simply gorgeous and she would be the first to admit Derringer had good taste. But she knew just what the flowers represented. He wanted her back in his bed and would try just about anything to get her there. She wished things could go back to how they used to be when he hadn't had a clue about her feelings. But it was too late for that.

Six hours later, Lucia glanced over at the flowers and smiled. They were just as beautiful as they had been when they'd been delivered that morning. She glanced at her watch. She would leave in a couple of hours to go straight to class. Mondays were always her busiest days with meetings and satellite conference calls with the other *Simply Irresistible* offices around the country during the day and class at night.

She kicked off her shoes, leaned back in her chair and closed her eyes. The office would be closing in less than twenty minutes and since she would be there long after that, she figured there was no reason she couldn't grab a quick nap.

With her eyes shut, it didn't surprise her when an image of Derringer came into view. Boy, he was gorgeous. And arrogant. She frowned, thinking he was as arrogant as he was gorgeous Still...

She wasn't sure how long she slept. But she remem

bered she was dreaming of Derringer, and wherever they were, she had whispered for him to kiss her and he had. She heard herself moan as the taste of him registered on her brain, and she couldn't help thinking how real her dream was. And was that really the feel of his fingertips on her chin as he devoured her mouth with plenty of tongue play. She could actually inhale his scent. Hot, robust and masculine.

They continued kissing in her dream and she simply melted while he leisurely explored the depths of her mouth. Nobody could kiss like him, she thought as he probed his tongue deeper. She had dreamed of him kissing her many times before, but for some reason this was different. This was like the real deal.

Her eyes flew open and she squealed when she realized it wasn't a dream! It was the real deal! She jerked forward and pushed him away from her. "Derringer! How dare you come into my office and take advantage of me."

He stood back, licked his lips and smiled. "The way I assume you took advantage of me that night? Just for the record, Lucia, you asked me to kiss you. When I entered your office, you were whispering my name. And I distinctively heard you ask me to kiss you."

"I was dreaming!"

He gave her an arrogant smirk. "Nice to know I'm in your dreams, sweetheart."

She eased out of her chair and crossed her arms over her chest. When she saw where his gaze went—directly to where her blouse dipped to reveal more cleavage than she wanted—she dropped her arms, scowling. "What are you doing here and who let you into my office?"

He jammed his hands into the pockets of his jeans.

"I came to see you and I arrived when your administrative assistant was leaving. She remembered me from Chloe and Ramsey's wedding and let me in."

His smile widened. "She figured I was safe. I did knock on the door a few times before I entered, and would not have come in if I hadn't heard you call out my name."

Lucia swallowed. Had she really called out his name? She ignored that possibility. "Why are you here?"

"To make sure you liked your flowers."

She dragged her gaze from him to the huge floral arrangement she had been admiring all day. In fact, everyone in the office had admired it, and she knew they were wondering who'd sent the flowers. She glanced back at Derringer. Okay, maybe she should have called and thanked him; she hadn't wanted to give him any ideas, but it seemed he'd gotten plenty without her help.

"Yes, they're beautiful. Thank you. Now you can leave."

He shook his head. "I figured while I'm here I might as well drop you off at school. You do have class tonight, right?"

"Yes, but why would I want you to drop me off at school when I can drive myself? I do have a car."

"Yes, but I wouldn't want you to get a ticket. You told me all about your Monday-night professor and how he hates it when anyone is late. You also mentioned that tonight is your final. You're going to be late."

Lucia glanced down at her watch and went still. She wasn't aware she had slept that long. She needed to be in class in twenty minutes and it would take her longer than that to get through town. Professor Turner had already warned the class that he would close his door exactly at seven, and Derringer was right, tonight she was to take her final.

She slipped into her shoes and quickly moved around the desk to grab her purse out of the desk drawer. "And just how are you supposed to get me there any sooner than I can drive myself?" she asked, hurrying out the office door. He was right behind her.

"I have my ways." He then pulled his cell phone out of his back pocket. "Pete? This is Derringer. I need a favor."

She glanced over her shoulder as she was locking the door. He was calling Pete Higgins, one of the sheriff's deputies and also one of his good friends.

"I need escort service from *Simply Irresistible* to the U, and we need to be there in less than fifteen minutes." Derringer smiled. "Okay, we're on our way down."

He glanced over at her when he put his phone in his back pocket. "We'll leave your car here and come back for it after class."

She frowned over at him as they stepped into the elevator. "Why can't I drive my own car and your friend Pete can just give me escort service?"

He shook his head. "It doesn't work that way. He knows I'm trying to impress my girl."

"I am not your girl, Derringer."

"Sure you are. Why else would you moan my name in your sleep?"

Lucia turned her head away from him, deciding that question didn't need an answer. Besides, what response could she give him?

Once they reached the bottom floor, things moved quickly. He took her laptop bag off her shoulder and put it in the backseat of his truck. By the time he escorted her to the passenger side, Pete pulled up in the patrol car with his lights flashing and a huge grin on his face. He nodded at her before giving Derringer a thumbs-up.

Luckily, she got to school in one piece and was able to make it to class on time. An hour or so later, after she'd finished her exam and placed her pencil aside, instead of glancing back over her exam to make sure she didn't need to do any last-minute changes, her mind drifted to Derringer.

Lucia shook her head. What some men wouldn't do for a piece of tail, she thought. Regardless of what Chloe assumed, she knew that was probably all she was to him. Of course he was trying to impress her just to prove a point, and just the thought that he had caught her dreaming about him, and that in her sleep she had asked him to kiss her, was enough for her to wear a brown bag over her head for the rest of the year.

And what was even worse was that he would be picking her up when class was over. She had no choice if she wanted to get home without taking the bus. A part of her steamed at the thought of how things had worked out nicely for him in that regard. He would be driving her to get her car and nothing more. If he thought there would be more, he had another think coming.

The moment she stepped out of the Mass Communications Building, she glanced around. Derringer's truck was parked in a space in a lighted area and he was leaning against it as if he was expecting her, which was odd since he hadn't known when her class would let out. Had he been here the entire time?

She quickly crossed to where he stood. "How did you know I was about to walk out?"

He glanced over at her as he opened the truck door

for her. "I didn't. I figured that you would catch a cab to get your car if I wasn't here, so I thought the best thing to do was to be here when you came out."

She frowned at him before stepping up into the truck. "You've been here the whole time?"

"Yep."

"Don't you have anything better to do?" she asked coolly.

"Nope." He then closed the door and moved around the front of the truck to get into the driver's side.

He closed the door, buckled his seat belt and turned the key in the ignition. "Don't you think you're getting carried away with all this, Derringer?"

He chuckled. "No."

She rolled her eyes. "Seriously. I couldn't have been that great in bed."

His mouth tilted in a slow, ultrasatisfied smile. "Trust me, Lucia. You were."

She crossed her arms over her chest as he pulled out of the parking lot. "So you admit this is only about sex."

"I didn't say that, so I won't be admitting anything. I told you what I wanted."

She glanced over at him. "To sleep with me again."

"Yes, but not just a couple more times. I'm talking about the rest of my life. You're my soul mate." Derringer smiled thinking that sounded pretty darn good and had to thank Jason for putting the idea into his head.

Her mouth dropped. "Soul mate?"

"Yes."

"That's insane," she threw out

"That's reality. Get used to it," he threw back.

She turned around in her seat as much as her seat belt would allow. "It's not reality and I won't get used to it, because it doesn't make sense. If this has anything to do with you thinking I got pregnant from our previous encounters you don't have that to worry about. My monthly visitor arrived this morning."

"That wasn't it, although that would have definitely been important to me if you had gotten pregnant. But like I told you before, you're in my blood now. You were a virgin and I'd never been with a virgin before."

"Whoop-de-do," she said sarcastically. "No big deal."

"For me it is."

She just stared at him, deciding not to argue with him anymore. Doing so would give her a friggin' headache. She shifted positions to sit straight in her seat and closed her eyes, but she wouldn't go to sleep for fear of waking up with her lips locked to his again.

Each time she felt herself being lulled to sleep by the smooth jazz sounds coming from the CD player, she would open her eyes to gaze out the window and study all the buildings they passed. She thought Denver was a beautiful city and there was no other place quite like it.

Due to the lack of traffic, they returned to her office building sooner than she had anticipated. And, she tried convincing herself, not as quickly as she would have liked. But she knew that was a lie. She liked the fact that she was the woman riding in the truck with him tonight. She had been the one he had waited for outside her classroom building. And she was the one for whom he had ordered a special escort service to get her to school on time. Then there were the flowers. A girl could really succumb to him if she wasn't careful.

"How do you think you did on your test tonight?"

His question surprised her and she glanced over

at him when he parked his truck behind her car. She couldn't help but smile. "I think I aced it. I'm almost sure of it. There were a lot of multiple-choice questions, but there was one essay question to test our writing skills."

"I'm happy for you then."

"Thanks."

She watched as he opened his door and then walked around the back of the truck to open the door for her. Once he helped her out, they stood there facing each other. "I appreciate all you did tonight, Derringer. Because of you I got to school on time."

"No problem, baby."

The term of endearment sent sensations rippling through her. "Don't call me that, Derringer."

"What?"

"Baby."

He leaned against his truck. "Why?"

"Because I'm sure I'm not the only woman you've called that."

"No, you're not, but you're the only one I've called that when it meant something."

She shook her head as she walked slowly to her car with him strolling beside her. The April air was cold and everyone was talking about a snowstorm headed their way this weekend. "You just won't give up, will you?"

"No."

"I wish you would."

They came to a stop next to her car. The smile he gave her was slow and sexy. "And I wish you would let me make love to you again, Lucia."

She was certain that irritation showed on her face. "Yet you want me to believe it's not just about sex?"

She shook her head sadly, thinking he just didn't get it. She loved him and now that he knew how she felt, she refused to settle for anything less than being loved in return. She knew for him to fall in love with her was something that wouldn't happen—not in her wildest dreams—so all she wanted to do was get on with her life without him being a part of it. "Good night, Derringer."

He moved out of the way when she got into her car and quickly drove away.

Later that night, Derringer tossed and turned in his bed. Finally, he pulled himself up and reached out to turn on the light. Brightness flooded the room and he rubbed his hands down his face.

Tomorrow would be a busy day for Denver's branch of D&M Horse-Breeding and Training Company. In fact, the rest of the week would be hectic. His cousin Cole would be delivering more than one hundred horses from Texas at the end of the week and they needed to make sure everything was ready. It didn't help matters that a snowstorm was expected this weekend. That made things even more complicated as well as challenging.

He reached behind him and lifted his pillow and smiled when his hand touched the lacy items. He had two pairs of Lucia panties. Added to the pink pair were the red ones he'd taken off her last weekend. He wondered if she'd missed them yet and figured she probably hadn't; otherwise, she would have mentioned it.

And she wasn't pregnant. He'd actually been disappointed when she'd made that announcement. He had gotten used to the idea that perhaps she could be pregnant with his child. He knew that kind of thinking didn't make much sense, but he had.

He settled back down in bed thinking she just wouldn't let up with this "only sex" thing. He had all but told her she was his soul mate so what else did she want?

He knew the answer without thinking much about it. She wanted him to love her, but that wouldn't and couldn't happen. What if she got real sick or something and he couldn't get her to the hospital in time? What if she was in a car accident and didn't survive? What if she got stampeded by a herd of horses? What if…he lost her like he had his parents? His aunt and uncle? They were here one day and had been gone the next. He rubbed his hand down his face, not liking how his thoughts were going. He was freaking out for no reason; especially when he didn't intend to get attached to her like that.

He liked things just the way they were and didn't intend for any woman, not even Lucia, to start messing with his mind…and definitely not with his heart. But he wanted her.

There had to be a middle ground for them, something they could both agree on. It would have to be something that would satisfy them both.

He would come up with a plan. Because, no matter what, he had no intention of giving up on her.

Chapter 10

Lucia closed the lid to her washing machine and leaned back against it thinking that Derringer had not given her back the panties he'd taken off her the other night. The red pair. Now he had two. What was he doing with them? Collecting them as souvenirs?

She strolled to the window and glanced out. It looked totally yucky outside. The forecasters' predictions had been correct. She had awakened to see huge snowflakes falling outside. That's the only thing she missed about the time she lived in Florida. This was the middle of April, spring break in most states and it was hard to believe that in some other place the sun was shining brightly. A week spent on Daytona Beach sounded pretty darn good about now. At least the snow had waited for the weekend and most people didn't have a reason to venture outside.

Her parents had gotten smart and decided to fly to Tennessee for a few weeks to visit her mother's sister. Chloe had called this morning to chat and to tell her how she, Ramsey and the baby were snuggled inside in front of the roaring fireplace and planned to stay that way. Lucia sighed deeply, thinking this was the only time she regretted being an only child. Things could get lonely at times.

She moved away from the window to go into the kitchen to make herself a cup of hot chocolate and watch that movie she had planned to watch last week, and she remembered why she hadn't.

Derringer had dropped by.

She hadn't heard from him since the night he had taken her to school. Maybe he had finally admitted to himself that he only wanted one thing from her and had moved on to some other willing female. The thought of him making love to someone else had her hurting inside, but she could deal with it the way she'd always done. It wasn't the first time she'd known the man she loved was sleeping with others and it wouldn't be the last. But it hurt knowing someone else was the recipient of his smile, his look and his touch. More than anything, a part of her wished she hadn't experienced any of it for herself. But then a part of her was glad that she had and would not trade in a single moment.

Moments later, with a cup of hot chocolate in her hand, she moved toward the living room to watch her movie. She had a fire blazing in the fireplace and it added soothing warmth to the entire room. Why she wanted to watch a romantic movie when she lacked romance in her own life was beyond her. But then, women had their dreams and fantasies, didn't they?

Lucia had settled back against her sofa with a cup in one hand and a remote in the other when the doorbell rang. She frowned, wondering what on earth could get Mrs. Noel to come across the street in this weather, unless her heating unit was on the blink again. Standing, she placed the cup and the remote on the table and headed for the door. She looked out the peephole and caught her breath.

Derringer!

Denying the rush of heat she immediately felt between her thighs, seeing him standing there and looking sexier than any man had a right to look—this time of day and in this horrid weather—she drew in a deep breath and fought the anger escalating in her chest. She would not hear from him for a week or so and then he would show up at her place unannounced. It didn't matter that she had told him to leave her alone. That was beside the point. The only point she could concentrate on was that he evidently thought he could add her to his booty-call list. Well, she had news for him.

She snatched the door open and was about to ask what he was doing there, but wasn't given the chance to do so.

Derringer didn't give Lucia the chance to ask any questions, but leaned in and covered her mouth with his. He not only wanted to silence her, he also wanted the heat from his kiss to inflame her as they stood just inside with a frigid snowstorm raging outside. There was no doubt in his mind the kiss had enough spark, power and electricity to light the entire city of Denver. And he felt it all rush through his body.

She didn't resist him, and at the moment that was

a good thing. He didn't need her resistance, what he needed was this—the taste of her all over his tongue.

He had tried not thinking about her all week. Hell, with the delivery of those horses he'd had enough to keep his mind and time occupied. But things hadn't happened quite that way. She'd still managed to creep into his thoughts most of the time, and he had awakened that morning with a need to see her so intense that he just couldn't understand it. And nothing, not elephant snowflakes nor below-zero-degree temperature would keep him from her. From this.

He finally pulled back from the kiss. Somehow they had made it inside her house and closed the door behind them and that was a good thing. Having an X-rated kiss on her doorstep would definitely have given her neighbors something to talk about for years.

She gazed up at him and he thought at that moment she was the most beautiful person he had ever seen. No other women he'd messed around with before could claim that. He inwardly flinched when he thought of what he'd just done. He had compared her with all the other women in his womanizing life and in essence none could compare to her. In fact, her biggest beef about having an affair with him were those other women in his life. But he knew at that moment he would give them all up for her.

The reality of him willingly doing that hit him below the belt and he nearly tumbled over. Derringer Westmoreland would give up his lifestyle for a woman? Make a commitment to be only with her? He drew in a sharp breath. He'd never made such an allegiance with any female. Had never intended to be dedicated or devoted to one. There were too many out there and

he enjoyed being footloose and fancy-free. Was she
worth all of that? He knew in that instant that she was.

"What are you doing here, Derringer?"

He could tell she had regained control of the senses
they'd both lost when she had opened her door. He had
initiated the kiss, but she had reciprocated, which told
him that although she wished otherwise, she had enjoyed it as much as he had.

"I needed to see you," he said simply.

She rolled her eyes. "That's what you said the last
time."

"And I'm saying it again."

She drew in a deep breath and then turned and
walked toward the sofa. He followed, thinking at least
she hadn't asked him to leave…yet. She sat down on the
couch and he dropped down on the love seat.

"If you had to venture out in this blasted weather,
why not go visit Ashira Lattimore? I'm sure she has a
bed warming for you."

The last thing he needed to do was to admit there
was a strong possibility the woman did. As far as he
knew, Ashira had gotten it into her head that she would
eventually become Mrs. Derringer Westmoreland. He
wouldn't marry Ashira if she was the last woman on
earth. She was too possessive and clingy. On the other
hand, the woman sitting across from him wasn't possessive and clingy enough. Yet she claimed to love him,
when he knew all Ashira wanted was the Westmoreland
name and all his worldly possessions.

"She isn't the woman I want warming a bed for me,"
he said quietly, glancing over at her intently. Not only
did she look good as usual, she smelled good, too. He

was so familiar with her scent that he could probably pick her out of any room even if he was blindfolded.

"Do most men care what woman warms their bed?"

He'd never cared until now.

"Don't answer, Derringer, you might incriminate yourself," she said bitterly.

That should have gotten him off the hook, but he felt a need to respond anyway. "Those who find the woman they want care. Then they are willing to give up all the others."

She lifted a brow and he knew the moment she thought she had boxed him into the perfect corner, one she figured he wouldn't be able to get out of because there was no way he would give up his other women for her. It amazed him that he could discern just how his woman thought.

His woman?

He smiled thinking that yes, she was definitely *his* woman.

"And you want me to believe you're willing to give up all other women for me," she said, chuckling with a look on her face that said the whole idea of him doing such a thing was simply ridiculous.

"Yes, I'd give up all other women for you," he said, meeting her gaze with a look that told her he was dead serious. She almost dropped the cup she was holding in her hand.

She shook her head. "Don't be silly."

"I'm not," he responded. "I'm as serious as a Bugatti Veyron on an open road."

"No, you're not."

"Oh, yes, sweetheart, I am."

She simply stared at him for a moment and then asked in a cautious and quiet tone, "Why?"

"Because you are the only woman I want," he said.

"But love has nothing to do with it?"

He knew he had to be completely honest with her. He didn't want to give her false hope or misguided illusions. "No. Love has nothing to do with it. But we'll have something just as important."

"What?"

"Respect for each other and a sense of caring. I do care for you, Lucia, or I wouldn't be here." There. He'd painted her the picture he intended for her to see. She loved him and had admitted to doing so and he had no reason not to believe her. But he knew a woman's love went deep and things could get rather messy if she expected or anticipated those feelings in return. She wouldn't get them.

"Are you willing to accept being the only woman in my life in a long-term exclusive affair, Lucia?"

She stared at him, not saying anything and then as if to be certain she'd heard him correctly and clearly understood the perimeters of what he'd proposed, she asked, "And during that time you won't be involved with any woman but me?"

"Yes, I give you my word on it. Something I've never given any woman I've been involved with in the past. You are the first woman." It was on the tip of his lips to add, *Just like I was your first man.*

Lucia sat there, staring at Derringer and searching his face for any signs that he was being anything but aboveboard. Was he giving her a line? She drew in a deep breath. He had given her his word, and most peo-

ple knew that the Westmorelands' word meant everything to them. But could it withstand temptation? What
if he got tired of her and was tempted to test the waters
elsewhere with someone else?

"And if you change your mind about this exclusivity thing, you will let me know? I wouldn't find out
from others?"

He shook his head. "No, you wouldn't find out from
others. I wouldn't do you that way, Lucia. If and when
I get ready to end things between us, you will be the
first to know."

He paused for a moment and then inclined his head.
"So, if you fully accept those terms, please come over
here for a second," he murmured in seductive invitation.

She hesitated, still uncertain. She knew there was
sexual chemistry between them, she could feel the snap,
crackle and pop even now with the distance separating
them. On what was probably the coldest day in Denver this year, he was sitting over there looking hotter
than any man had a right to look, and he got finer and
finer each time she saw him. His dark eyes were pulling her in, mesmerizing her down to her panties. And
that luscious mouth of his seemed to be calling out to
her, tempting her in ways she really didn't need to be
tempted; especially when she went to bed each night
dreaming of him.

She would be the first to say that his offer of an exclusive affair surprised her because she knew that's
not how he operated. In fact, that was not how any of
the single Westmorelands handled their business with
women. So why was he treading off the beaten track?

One thing was for certain; his blatant honesty about
the kind of relationship he wanted with her had caught

her off guard. He wasn't promising love, although he was well aware of how she felt about him. Instead of offering her love in return, he was offering her an exclusive affair.

Suddenly something happened that she hoped she didn't live to regret. At that moment, she began listening to her heart and not her mind. Her heart was telling her that she loved him too much not to take him up on the offer he'd laid out to her. She would be entering the affair with both eyes open and no expectations except one. He would give her advance notice when he was ready to end things between them.

That meant that while things lasted she would spend all the time with him she desired. She would be the only woman sharing his bed. The one and only woman claiming Derringer Westmoreland's full attention. She glanced down at her hand and accepted the fact that the only drawback was that he would never put a ring on her finger.

She glanced back up and her gaze returned to the deep, dark eyes that were staring at her. And waiting. And as she returned his stare, she was getting wet just thinking about all the things they would probably spend their time doing together as an exclusive couple.

She moistened her lips with the tip of her tongue and watched his gaze take in her every movement as she slowly stood. And then he stood and at that moment she realized what he was doing. Something she hadn't expected. He was meeting her halfway.

He began walking toward her the moment she began walking toward him and they met in the center. "I wasn't sure you were going to take those steps," he whispered throatily when they stood face-to-face, his mesmerizing dark gaze locked on hers.

"I wasn't sure either."

He then cupped her face in his hands and took possession of her mouth in the way she'd gotten used to him doing.

When Lucia began responding to his kiss that had liquid heat flaming inside him, he knew what they both wanted and needed. And this was the perfect day for it. He broke off the kiss and swept her off her feet and into his arms and purposefully moved toward her bedroom. Wanting her this much was the epitome of insanity, but he might as well get used to it.

He placed her on the bed and stepped back to quickly remove his clothes, sending them flying all over the place. And then for the first time since they'd made love, he took the time to use a condom.

When he returned to the bed, he captured her hand and drew her toward him to remove her clothes, slowly stripping her bare. Today she was wearing a pair of white panties, but they weren't of the granny style. They were bikinis. But the style or color of her undergarments didn't matter to him.

"Nice panties," he said, picking up his jeans and placing the panties in the back pocket.

"Why are you doing that? You have two pairs of mine already. Is there something I should know?" she asked when he tossed his jeans back to the floor and eased down onto the bed to join her.

"Yes," he said, pulling her into his arms. "I go to sleep every night with them under my pillow."

Her mouth dropped. "You're kidding, right?"

He smiled. "No, I'm not kidding, and before you ask, the answer is no. I've never collected the underwear of other women, Lucia. Just yours."

He saw the confused look on her face and thought she could dwell on what he'd confessed at another time. He needed her full concentration for what he intended to do to her right now.

Now that she was his, he wanted to get to know each and every inch of her body. Reaching out, he cradled her chin in his hand, forcing her to meet his gaze again. He could tell she was still trying to understand what he'd said earlier about her panties.

He smiled, thinking this was where he needed to shift her focus.

Lucia saw the sexy-curvy smile that touched Derringer's lips and knew she was in trouble in the most sensual way. For some reason, she knew this lovemaking session would be different, but she didn't know in what way.

"We're staying in all weekend," he whispered in a voice so low and hot that a burning sensation began at the tips of her toes and moved upward through her body.

She was trying to understand what he'd said about staying in all weekend. Was he letting her know that he intended to keep her here, in this bed, the majority of the time? Before she could think further about it, he lifted his hand and went straight to her breasts and his fingers began toying with a darkened nipple.

"I like your breasts. I especially like how well defined they are and how easy they can slip into my mouth. Like this."

He lowered his head and his stiffened tongue laved

the nipple, licking all around it a few times before easing the firm pebble between his lips, and began sucking.

Her eyes fluttered closed as a multitude of sensations pulled at the juncture of her thighs in response to the pulling motion to her breasts. His mouth was like a vacuum, drawing her nipple more and more into his mouth as his hot tongue did all kinds of wicked things to it. He switched breasts, to take on nipple number two, and she watched through hooded eyes as he continued to devour her this way.

Moments later, he drew away to lean back on his haunches to look down at her with a satisfied smile on his lips. It was then that she sensed a need in him, and the thought of him wanting her that much sent a rush of excitement through her bloodstream.

"Now for your pillows," he said, reaching behind her and grabbing both to place under her hips. She didn't have to ask what he was about to do and groaned softly at the vision that flowed through her mind. When he'd gotten her in the position he wanted, with the lower part of her elevated to his liking, he just continued to gaze at that part of her.

"You're beautiful," he whispered. "All over. But especially here," he said, reaching out and gently tracing a hand inside her inner thigh, slowly letting his fingers work their way toward the feminine folds that she knew were wet and ready for his touch.

She couldn't help but respond, and moaned as his fingers continued to lightly skim over her most intimate parts, causing sensuous shivers to flow through her. By the time he inserted two fingers inside her, she let out a deep groan and threw her head back, unable to help the way her hips rolled against the pillows cushioning them. And when he lowered his head, her fingers sank into the blades of his shoulders.

"Scent is closely linked to taste," he whispered, his breath hot against her womanly folds. "You're so wet here," he said softly, and proceeded to blow air through his lips onto her. "Since I can't blow you dry, that means I'm going to have to lap you up."

His words turned every cell in her body into a wild, unrestrained state. Instinctively, she bucked wildly against his mouth and he retaliated by grabbing her hips and diving his tongue between her womanly folds.

"Derringer!"

Her hands left his shoulders to grab hold of his head. Not to push him away, but to keep him there. Right there at that perfect angle, that most sensuous position as his mouth devoured her as if she were the tastiest meal he'd ever consumed.

She continued to cry out his name over and over, but there was no stopping him. He used his mouth to brand the woman he wanted. And the mere thought that that woman was her made her become more and more deeply entranced with every stroke of his tongue.

And when she couldn't take any more and her body began shuddering violently in the wake of one gigantic orgasm, he wouldn't let up, but continued to make love to her this way until the last jolt passed through her body. It was then that he quickly removed the pillows from beneath her body before mounting her.

"Lucia."

Her name was a whispered hunger from Derringer's lips. Hunger that had only slightly been appeased. And when she opened glazed eyes to look up at him the exact moment he slid into her, his nostrils flared and he felt his shaft thicken even more inside her. He knew she felt it the moment that it did.

"Take me, baby, hold me, clench me. Get everything out of me that you want," he prodded in a deep, guttural voice.

And from the way her inner muscles began clenching him, clamping down tight, compressing him, he could only throw his head back, knowing he was about to enjoy the ride of his life. This was one mating he would never forget.

He began moving, thrusting in and out of her, and when she began moving in rhythm with him, the sound of flesh smacking against flesh, he let out a ragged groan. And when she locked her legs around him and rubbed her breasts against his chest, he leaned close to her mouth and captured her lips with his.

There was nothing like kissing a woman while you made love to her, he thought. Knowing your body was planted deep in hers, knowing sensual aches were being satisfied and an earth-shattering climax was on the horizon. And when she moaned deep within his mouth, he pulled back, looked down at her, wanting to see the exact moment an orgasm ripped through her.

He watched in breathless fascination as the pleasure he was giving her contorted her features, made her tremble, almost took her breath away. It was then that he felt his own body explode, and he thrust into her deeper than he'd ever gone before.

"Lucia!"

No woman had ever done this to him; reduce him to a ball of fiery sensations that had him bucking wildly all over the place. He gripped her hips as sensations continued to tear into him, enthrall him, and each desperate thrust only called for another.

And when she came again, he was right there with her and together their bodies quaked violently as unrestrained pleasure took them over the edge.

"How are we going to explain things to your family, Derringer?"

His eyes popped open and he shifted his gaze to look over at Lucia. They had taken a nap after their last lovemaking session and she was leaning down over him, still naked and with strands of her hair hanging in arousing disarray around her shoulders. He glanced beyond her to the window to look outside. Was it getting dark already? He hadn't eaten breakfast or lunch yet.

"Derringer?"

His gaze returned to her and he saw the anxiety in her eyes and the way she was nervously biting her lower lip. "We don't owe them any explanations, Lucia. We're adults."

"I know that, but…"

When she didn't complete what she was going to say, he decided to finish it off for her. "But they're going to think you've lost your mind for getting involved with me."

He knew it was true and really didn't like the way it sounded. His family knew of his reputation more than anyone, and for him to have talked Lucia into an affair wouldn't sit too well with them. But as he'd told her, he and Lucia were adults.

"They're going to think you'll eventually hurt me," she said quietly.

"Then I guess it will be on me to prove otherwise,

because I'm not letting what they think cause a rift between us. Besides, they know we've been out a couple of times, and once they see how taken I am with you, they'll start minding their own business."

And he *was* taken with her, he'd admit that much. He was taken with her in a way no other woman could claim. He couldn't help but smile when he then said, "But I'm not the one they need to be concerned about. Zane's and Canyon's womanizing ways are probably right up there with Raphel's."

"Your great-grandfather? The one who was married to all those women?" she asked.

"Well, we're still trying to figure out what's fact and what's fiction. So far, the women we thought were his first two wives actually weren't. Dillon gave all the records he'd accumulated to Megan. She's determined to find out the truth as to whether Raphel actually lived all those lives," he said, pulling her down to him before he would be tempted to take one of her nipples into his mouth. As much as he loved tasting her, he figured they needed to eat something more nourishing now.

"I think I'll shower and then go into your kitchen to see what I can throw together for us," he said.

She looked surprised. "You're going to feed me?"

He couldn't help but smile, thinking that wasn't all he intended to do to her. "Yes, but trust me, I have a reason for doing so. I meant what I said earlier about keeping you inside all weekend, sweetheart."

And then he leaned down and locked his mouth with hers. This was one snowstorm that he would never forget.

Chapter 11

"So how are things going with you and Derringer?"

Sensations of excitement rippled in Lucia's stomach at the mention of Derringer's name. She and Chloe had decided to do lunch at McKay's, and as soon as the waitress had taken their orders and moved away, Chloe had begun asking Lucia a number of questions.

The weather had started clearing up a little on Sunday night, and Derringer had talked her into going to his ranch and leaving for work on Monday morning from there. He had even helped her pack an overnight bag. What she hadn't expected was his siblings and cousins showing up early Monday morning to check on him because no one had seen or heard from him all weekend. She hadn't missed the look of surprise on their faces when she'd come down the stairs dressed for work, giving everyone a clear idea of how he'd spent those snowed-in hours and with whom.

That had been a couple of weeks ago. "So far, so good. I enjoy spending time with him."

And truly she did. He'd taken her to the movies several times and picked her up from work on several occasions, and had spent the night over at her place a number of times as well.

Chloe beamed. "I'm glad. Ramsey is too. Already he's seen a change in Derringer."

Lucia raised a brow as she took a sip of her iced tea. "What kind of change?"

"Peace. Calm. He seems more focused. Less untamed and wild. Not only Ramsey but the other Westmorelands think you're good for him."

Lucia nervously nibbled at her lower lip. "I hope they aren't getting any ideas. I told you what's between me and Derringer is only temporary. He made sure I understood that, Chloe."

Chloe waved her words away. "All men think nothing is forever at first, only a few have love on their minds initially. Callum was an exception. He knew he loved Gemma before she had a clue."

"But Derringer doesn't love me. He's said as much. I'm in this relationship with both eyes open."

Later, back in her office, she recalled her words to Chloe as she sat staring at the huge arrangement of flowers that was sitting on her desk that had been delivered while she was at lunch. The card had simply said, *I'm thinking of you.*

Just the thought that he was thinking of her made everything inside her rock with anticipation to see him again. It was Friday and they were going skating again tonight and she couldn't wait.

The intercom on her desk went off, almost startling her. "Yes?"

"Someone is here to see you, Ms. Conyers."

Excitement flowed in her stomach. The last time she'd received flowers from Derringer, he had shown up at her office later. Was he here to see her now? "Who is it, Wanda?"

"Ashira Lattimore."

Lucia's throat tightened. Why would Ashira Lattimore be visiting her? There was only one way to find out. "Thanks, Wanda, ask her to come in."

Lucia clicked off her intercom and glanced at the flowers on her desk. Something about them gave her inner strength to deal with what was about to take place. She wasn't exactly sure what would happen, but she figured it had something to do with Derringer.

It wasn't long before the woman knocked on her door. "Come in."

Ashira walked in and just like all the other times Lucia had seen her she looked beautiful. But Lucia knew that beauty was merely on the outside. She had heard a number of stories about the spoiled and reckless woman who had long ago stamped ownership on Derringer. In a way she was surprised Ashira hadn't confronted her before now.

"Ashira, this is a surprise. What can *Simply Irresistible* do for you?" Lucia plastered a smile on her lips.

The woman didn't bother returning her fabricated smile. "I've been gone, Lucia, visiting a sick relative in Dakota, and thought I'd let you know I'm back."

Lucia placed her arms across her chest. "And that's supposed to mean something to me?"

The woman glanced at the flowers on Lucia's desk,

paused a minute and then said, "I think it would where Derringer is concerned. Not sure if he told you, but the two of us have an understanding."

"Do you?"

"Yes. No matter who he dallies with, I'm the one he'll always come back to. I'm sure you've known him long enough to know our history."

"Unfortunately, I don't, and for you to pay me a visit to stake a claim you think you have speaks volumes. It makes me think you're not as confident as you want to claim," she said with more bravado than she actually felt.

"Think whatever you want. Just remember, when he's done with you he'll come back to me. He and I have plans to marry one day."

Lucia's heart dropped at the woman's announcement. "Congratulations on your and Derringer's future plans. Now, if you've said everything you've come here to say, I think you should leave."

It was then that Ashira smiled, but the smile didn't quite reach her eyes. It didn't come close. "Fine, just remember my warning. I'm trying to spare you any heartbreak." The woman then walked out of her office.

Derringer's gaze flickered over Lucia's face. "You okay? You've been quiet most of the evening."

They had gone skating with what he was now beginning to think of as the regular crowd. Most of the kids and teens had gotten used to him and Lucia invading their turf. And now they were back at her place, but he hadn't said a whole lot since he'd picked her up that evening.

She smiled over at him. "Yes, I'm fine. This has been

a busy week at work and I'm just glad it's the weekend. I need it."

He pulled her into his arms. "And I need it as well.
More horses are arriving this week and then all our
relatives start arriving the week after that for the Westmoreland Charity Ball. You are going to the ball with
me, aren't you?"

He watched her features and she seemed surprised
he'd asked. Her next question proved him right. "You
really want to take me?"

"Of course I do."

"Thanks."

He stared down at her for a moment. "Why are you
thanking me?"

"Um, no reason. I just wasn't sure what your plans
would be."

It was on the tip of his tongue to say that whatever
his plans were they would always include her, but he
didn't. Lately, he was encountering feelings and emotions when it came to Lucia that he didn't quite understand and didn't want to dwell on.

"I hear Gemma is coming home in a few days," she
said, cutting into his thoughts.

A smile touched his lips. "Yeah, and I miss her. I'
gotten used to Gemma being underfoot and wasn't sur
how I'd handle her up and moving to Australia. Bu
Callum loves her and we know he's taking good car
of her. Besides, homecomings are good."

"Yes, he does love her."

There was something about her tone of voice tha
sounded contemplative and reflective, as if she wa
wondering, considering just how that would be for

man to love her that way. For a moment he didn't know what to say, so he decided not to say anything.

Instead, he did something he always enjoyed doing to her. He touched her chin, making rotary motions with his thumb on her soft skin before tilting her head back to lower his mouth to kiss her.

The sound of her sensual purr fueled his desire, making him so aroused his erection thickened painfully against the zipper of his jeans. And when she wrapped her arms around his neck as he deepened the kiss, he went crazy with lust for her.

Not able to hold back any longer, he swept her off her feet into his arms and carried her upstairs to the bedroom.

"Why haven't you mentioned Ashira's visit to Derringer, Lucia?"

Lucia glanced over at Chloe. They had just finished a business meeting and she'd known something had been on her best friend's mind all morning. "And how do you know I haven't?"

"Trust me, had you told him, all hell would have broken loose. He's never appreciated Ashira's possessiveness."

Lucia shrugged. "For all I know they could have an understanding just like she claims."

"I can't believe you would think that."

"In all honesty I'm trying not to think about anything regarding Derringer and Ashira. I'm just taking one day at a time."

Chloe frowned. "She would never have come into *my* office with that haughty I'm-Derringer's-real-woman foolishness, trust me."

"Because you know Ramsey loves you, I can't say that for Derringer and me. I know he doesn't love me," she said softly.

Later that night she lay in Derringer's arms with her naked body spooned intimately to his. His arm was thrown over her and he slept with his hand cupping her breast. His warm body and the scent of his musky masculinity surrounded her and she became aroused by it. That was something she couldn't help.

Since becoming sexually involved with Derringer, she had become more aware of herself as a woman, particularly her needs and wants, mainly because he made her feel as if she was the most enticing and alluring woman he'd ever met. And coming from a man like Derringer, that meant a lot.

She then thought about her conversation with Chloe earlier that day. Maybe she should have mentioned Ashira's visit to her office to Derringer. And yet a part of her didn't want to draw him into any women-over-man drama. Besides, time would tell if what the woman said was true.

She knew the moment he'd awakened by the change in his breathing. The other telltale sign was the feel of his erection beginning to swell against her naked backside. And then he began touching her. With the hand that wasn't cupping her breast he started at the dip in her thigh and let his fingers do a little walking, tracing a line toward her waist. It then followed the curve toward the juncture at her inner thighs.

"Shift open your legs for me, baby," he leaned over to whisper in her ear. "I need to touch you there."

She did what he asked and moments later she was moaning at his exploratory touch. And then when th hand cupping her breasts began doing its own thing by torturing her nipples, she clenched her lips to keep from crying out his name.

"You're so passionate," he murmured close to her ear. "You are the most sensuous woman I know."

She wanted so much to believe him. She wanted to believe it was her that he wanted and not Ashira. And when she couldn't take his torture any longer, she cried out for him to make love to her.

"My pleasure."

He then eased her onto her back and straddled her, and before she could draw her next breath, he entered her, melding their bodies as one. And each time he stroked into her and retreated, she ground her body against him ready for his reentry.

Over and over, back and forth, performing the mating dance the two of them had created as he thrust in and out of her and all she could do was continue to groan out her cries of pleasure. And when a guttural moan flowed from Derringer's lips, she knew they had been tossed into the turbulent waves of pure ecstasy.

Incredible.

Derringer pulled in a deep breath. That's how he always thought of making love with Lucia. Each and every time was simply incredible. And she was incredible. He glanced over at her and saw she had fallen asleep with her body spooned against his.

The room was quiet as images flickered in his mind of all the things they'd done together over the past few weeks, and not all of them had been in the bedroom. He enjoyed taking her places, being seen with her and spending time with her. Exclusivity was working, but he knew it was only because the woman was Lucia.

No other woman crossed his mind. He didn't want any other woman but her. And his inner fear of something happening to her lessened more and more each day. When he considered all the possibilities, weighed all his options and thought of what could happen, none of it was more significant than spending time with her, being with her. For the rest of his life. He loved her.

Derringer drew in a sharp breath because at that moment he couldn't imagine being without her.... He wanted to live each day to the fullest with her, loving her completely. She was the only woman he wanted. For his soul mate and then one day for his wife.

His wife.

A smile touched his lips. No other woman deserved that title. And he was determined that Lucia—only Lucia—would wear it. He knew he couldn't rush her. He had to take things slow and believe that one day she would realize she was the only woman who could be a wife for this Westmoreland.

The following days passed quickly and everyone was excited when Gemma returned home and confirmed the rumor that she and Callum would become parents in seven months. It was decided that a cookout was in order to welcome the couple home and to celebrate their good news. Another Westmoreland baby was on the way.

Derringer, his brothers and cousins were playing a friendly game of horseshoes when someone rang the bell letting them know it was time to eat. The men went into Dillon's kitchen to wash up, when Zane leaned over and whispered, "Lucia looks just like she belongs with the Westmorelands, Derringer."

His gaze moved across the yard to where she was helping Chloe and Megan set the table. Zane was right. She did look as if she belonged, mainly because she did belong. In a way, he'd always known that. And now he was waiting patiently for her to realize it as well.

They had been spending a lot of time together lately. It had become his regular routine to go home and shower after working with the horses and then head on over to her place each day. School was out, so she was home most evenings now. They cooked dinner together, on occasion they would go out to take in a movie or shoot pool—something he had shown her how to do. Then on Friday nights they went roller skating. But he also enjoyed those times they would stay inside to cuddle on the sofa and watch videos.

As if she felt him looking at her, she glanced over at him and an intimate connection, as well as sexual chemistry, flowed between them the way it always did. A slow, flirty smile touched his lips and he tipped his hat to her. She returned his smile and nodded before returning to what she was doing.

"I think you like her," Zane said, reminding Derringer he was there.

Derringer smiled at his brother, refusing to let Zane bait him. "Of course I like her. We all do."

"Hey, don't be an ass, Derringer. You're in love with the woman. Admit it."

Derringer only smiled and glanced back to where Lucia was sitting. The women were crowded together on the porch listening to Gemma share stories about her

Australian adventure and how she was settling into her role as Mrs. Callum Austell.

He couldn't help it, but he kept looking at Lucia. Each and every time he saw her, spent time with her, he fell more and more in love with her. Now he understood how Dillon could have left home to investigate all the rumors they'd heard about Raphel and return less than a month later an engaged man. At first he thought his cousin had needed to have his head examined, but once he met Pam and had seen how Dillon would light up around her, he sort of understood. But he'd figured nothing like that would ever happen to him.

He had been proven wrong.

He loved everything about Lucia, including her interaction with his family. But mainly he loved the way she made him feel whenever they were together.

His thoughts were pulled back to the present when Jason took a minute to provide an update on old man's Bostwick's granddaughter from Savannah. Folks were saying the woman was supposed to arrive in town to claim her inheritance in a couple of weeks. Jason was anxious about that and he was hoping his offer for the land and Hercules was the one the woman would accept.

"Looks like we have a visitor," Canyon whispered. "At least, she's *your* visitor, Derringer."

Derringer frowned when he saw the sports car driven by Ashira Lattimore pull up in the yard. He couldn't help wondering what she wanted since he knew she hadn't been invited. Also, Ashira and his sisters didn't get along. But that had never stopped Ashira from thinking her lack of an invite was merely an oversight on someone's part. She was her parents' only child and was spoiled rotten. In contrast, he thought,

Lucia was her parents' only child, yet she was sweet as wine. The difference in the two women was like night and day.

"Hello, everyone," she called out, waving, while glancing around as if she had every right to show up at a family function uninvited. Her face lit up in a huge smile when she saw Derringer, and she immediately headed toward him.

"Derringer, sweetheart, I've missed you." She leaned over, wrapped her arms around his neck and placed a kiss on his lips in full view of everyone.

He took her arms from around his neck and stared down at her. "What are you doing here, Ashira?"

She gave him a pouty look. "I came to see you."

"This is not where I live," he said in an annoyed voice.

"I know, but you weren't home and we need to talk."

"About what?"

She leaned up on tiptoe and whispered close to his ear, "About that horse you're trying to sell Daddy. Since he's buying it for me, I think we need to discuss it, don't you?"

"I'm busy right now, Ashira."

"But you want to make that sale, don't you? Daddy is ready. He wants to see you now, at the ranch."

Derringer knew he needed to put Ashira in her place once and for all, but here was not the place to do it. "Okay, let's go," he said, gripping her hand and pulling her with him toward her car. "I'll be back later," he called over his shoulder to everyone. "I've got some business to take care of."

He was angry. He didn't care about the horse sale as much as Ashira assumed that he did. If she thought it was a carrot she could dangle in front of him to make him do what she wanted then she had another thought coming. What ticked him off more than anything was her underhanded behavior. He should have put her in her place regarding him years ago.

He was so intent on taking her off somewhere to give her a piece of his mind, that he didn't notice the haughty look of victory the woman shot over her shoulder at Lucia.

Chloe drew in a deep breath. "I don't think you should leave, Lucia."

Lucia wiped the tears from her eyes. "There's no reason for me to stay," she said, gathering up her things. "You saw it for yourself. Ashira shows up and he leaves. She wanted to prove what she told me that day was true and she did."

Chloe shook her head. "But I don't think that's the way it was. According to Zane and Jason, Derringer said it was about business and probably had to talk to her about that horse he's trying to sell her father."

"And it couldn't wait? Please don't make excuses for what I saw with my own eyes, Chloe. She snaps her finger and he takes off. He was leading her over to the car and not the other way around. And I truly don't want to be here when they come back."

She reached out and hugged Chloe and whispered in a broken voice, "I'll call you later."

Lucia knew it would be hard telling the others goodbye. They would see the hurt in her eyes and they would pity her. Or it might be one of those you-should-have-known-better-than-to-fall-in-love-with-Derringer looks. In her book, one was just as bad as the other.

Somehow she made it through, but nearly broke

when Zane pulled her into his arms and asked her to stay a while longer. She forced a smile up at him and told him she couldn't, before rushing to her car, getting inside and driving away.

Derringer returned over an hour later. He hadn't meant to be gone that long, but when he'd arrived at the Lattimores' place he had encountered more drama. Ashira had given her father the impression things were serious between them and he had to first break the news to Phillip Lattimore that they weren't. And then he had to let Ashira know that he didn't consider her a candidate as a wife, at least not for him since there was no way in hell he would ever get shackled with someone as spoiled and selfish as she was. Those words hadn't been too well received, and Derringer had found himself stranded on the Lattimore land. He'd had to call Pete to give him a lift back here.

The moment he got out of Pete's patrol car he knew something was wrong. He could understand everyone staring at him, probably wondering why Pete, instead of Ashira, had brought him back. But they weren't just staring at him. They were openly glaring.

"Looks like your family is pissed off at you for some reason," Pete said.

"Yes, looks that way," he responded. "Thanks for bringing me here."

Once the patrol car had driven off, Derringer's gaze roamed over the group that were outside in the yard cleaning up from today's activities. He looked for one person in particular, but he didn't see her. "Where's Lucia?"

It was Canyon who answered in a belligerent tone, "Oh, so now you remember that she does exist?"

Derringer frowned. "What are you talking about?"

Dillon folded his arms over his chest. "You invited Lucia here, yet you took off with another woman without giving her a backward glance. I expected better of you, Derringer."

Derringer's frown deepened. "That's not the way it was."

It was Ramsey who spoke up. "That's the way we saw it."

"And that's the way Lucia saw it," Bailey snapped, losing her cool. "I can't believe you would leave here with one of those 'silly' girls—in fact, the silliest of them all—deserting Lucia and then showing back up an hour later expecting her to still be here waiting on you. You are so full of yourself."

"Like I said, that's not the way it was," he said, glancing around at all his family circling around him.

"You're going to have a hard time convincing Lucia of that," Chloe said, not with the same snappish tone Bailey had used, but there was no doubt in everyone's mind that if given the chance she would clobber this particular brother-in-law right about now.

"Especially when just a couple of weeks ago Ashira paid Lucia a visit at *Simply Irresistible* and warned her that she could get you back anytime she wanted, and that the two of you have an understanding and that she would be the one who would eventually become your wife," Chloe added in disgust.

"Like hell," Derringer snarled.

"Doesn't matter. Ashira came here today to prove a point and in Lucia's eyes, she did."

"But like I said, it wasn't that way," Derringer implored. He then outlined everything that had happened once he'd left with Ashira and the reason that he'd left with her in the first place. "And I won't let that sort of misunderstanding come between me and Lucia," he said, moving toward his truck. "I need to go see her."

She wasn't home when Derringer got there, but according to her neighbor, Mrs. Noel, she had been there, rushing in and then leaving with an overnight bag. Derringer had no idea where she had gone. And she wouldn't answer her cell phone, although he had left several messages for her. He knew her parents were still in Tennessee and wouldn't be returning for another week or so. Thinking she'd possibly driven out to their place to stay for the night, he had gone there too, only to find the Conyers's homestead deserted.

It was after midnight when he returned to his place and rushed over to his phone when it began ringing the moment he opened the door. "Hello?"

"This is Chloe. I just got a call from Lucia. She's fine and asked that you not try seeing her or calling her. She needs time."

"No, she needs me just like I need her. She should have told me about Ashira's visit and I would have straightened things out then. I need to talk with her, Chloe. I can't stand to lose her."

"And why can't you stand to lose her, Derringer? What makes her so different from the others?"

He knew why Chloe was goading him. He was well aware what she was trying to get him to admit, not only to himself, but to her as well, just how he felt about Lucia. "I love her." He drew in a deep breath. "I love her so damn much."

"Then somehow you're going to have to convince her of that, not only in words, but with actions. Good night, Derringer."

Chloe then hung up the phone.

Chapter 12

Lucia sat behind her desk and stared at the beautiful arrangement of flowers that had arrived that morning. She then glanced around her office at the others that had arrived during the week. The cards all said the same thing: *You are the only woman I want.*

She drew in a deep breath wishing she could believe that, but for some reason she couldn't. Maybe it had to do with the haughty I-told-you-so look Ashira had had on her face when she had left that day with Derringer. The two of them had a history. The woman had been after Derringer for years and it seemed as if she had him. And according to Ashira, no matter who he messed around with, *she* would be the woman he married.

So, Lucia couldn't help asking herself, why was she wasting her time and her heart? The latter she knew there was no answer for. She would continue to love him, no matter what. Always had and always would. But she could do something about the former. To spend any more time with him was heartbreak just waiting to happen. Of course, he wouldn't see it that way. Men had a tendency to look at affairs differently. They didn't have a clue when it came to emotions.

At least he was respecting her wishes and hadn't tried contacting her again. She figured he and Ashira were now a hot item, although Chloe insisted otherwise. Of course, she had come up with an excuse for the reason he'd left, which Lucia was certain was the one he'd told everyone. Little did he know that Ashira was spreading another story. She wanted to make sure word got back to Lucia through mutual acquaintances that she and Derringer had left the party to go to his place and have hot, blazing sex. It deeply pained Lucia that he could leave her bed that morning and hop into bed with another woman less than twelve hours later.

Lucia glanced up when she heard the knock at her office door. "Come in."

Chloe stuck her head in and smiled. "Word is around the office that you got more flowers."

She came in and closed the door behind her, admiring the arrangement sitting on Lucia's desk. "They are gorgeous, but then, all the bouquets Derringer has sent have been gorgeous. You have to admit that."

Lucia smiled slowly. "Yes, they've all been gorgeous, but they don't mean a thing."

Chloe took the chair across from her desk. "Because of what Tanya McCoy called and told you yesterday? That she'd heard Ashira and Derringer left my place and had hot, rousing sex over at Derringer's Dungeon? I don't believe that and neither should you. Ashira is just trying to save face. I was there when Derringer returned in Pete's patrol car. Don't let Ashira continue to mess with your mind like that. You need to take Derringer's message on those cards you've been getting with the flowers to heart."

Lucia fought back tears. "I wish I could, but I can't. All these years I've loved him and was fine with loving him from a distance. But then I had to go ruin everything by admitting I loved him and letting him into my space. From now on it's going back to status quo."

"Does that mean you won't ever visit your goddaughter at my place, for fear of running into Derringer?"

"No, but I'm trying to get beyond that."

"Then I think this coming Saturday is the perfect way to start. I suggest you change your mind about coming to the Westmoreland Charity Ball. If you see Derringer, no big deal. Now is your time to show him once and for all that you've gotten over him and you're moving on and won't be hiding out to avoid him."

Lucia nervously nibbled on her bottom lip. "And what if he's there with Ashira?"

"And what if he is? It's his loss. And if he wants her instead of you then more power to him. But if I were you, I would definitely let him see what he gave up. Um, I think you and I should go shopping."

Lucia wasn't convinced making an appearance at the charity ball this weekend would be the right thing to do.

"Just because you think one Westmoreland acted like an ass is no reason to ostracize yourself from the rest of us," Chloe added.

Lucia knew what Chloe just said was true. Gemma had called her this morning and she had yet to call her back. So had Megan and Bailey earlier in the week.

They had been friends long before she'd met Derringer. It wasn't their fault that she had fallen head over heels in love with their brother, a man who would never settle down, fall in love and marry any woman. Except maybe Ashira one day when he got tired of playing the field.

She tossed her pen on the desk and met Chloe's gaze. "Maybe you're right. I can't avoid the other Westmorelands just because my affair with Derringer went sour."

A smile touched Chloe's lips. "No, you can't. So are we going shopping this weekend?"

Lucia chuckled. "Yes, and I know this is more about you than me, Chloe Burton Westmoreland. You'll do anything, come up with any excuse, to shop."

Chloe stood, smiling. "Hey, what can I say? A woman has to do what a woman has to do."

Derringer glanced around. He was surrounded by Westmorelands and he couldn't help but smile. Once a year all the Westmorelands—from the south and west—got together for a family reunion rotating between Atlanta, rural Montana and Denver. At other times they got together to support each other for various events. Earlier this year they had traveled to Austin to be with their cousins: Cole, Clint and Casey Westmoreland had honored their deceased uncle during the Sid Roberts Foundation annual charity ball. And usually every year there seemed to be a Westmoreland wedding. The last one had been Gemma's a few months back.

And now all the Atlanta and Montana Westmorelands were gathered here in Denver with their wives for the Westmoreland Charity Ball. They had begun arriving a few days ago and were all accounted for as of noon today when Thorn and Tara had arrived. Thorn had come straight from Bikers' Week in Myrtle Beach, South Carolina.

"Thanks for putting us up for the next couple of days, Derringer."

He glanced around and smiled at his cousins, the twins—Storm and Chase. But then there were several sets of twins in the Atlanta Westmorelands' group. Storm and Chase's father had been a twin, and his cousins, Ian and Quade, were twins as well.

"Hey, no problem. If there's anything you need, just let me know." At that moment his cell phone went off and when he saw it was Chloe he smiled. "Excuse me while I take this."

He went outside to sit on the porch. "Yes, Chloe?"

"You owe me big-time, Derringer, and I swear, if you screw up, I'm coming after you myself."

He believed her. "Trust me, I've got everything planned. I'm just grateful you got Lucia to agree to come to the charity ball."

"It wasn't easy. Ashira and her girls are out spreading lies, claiming that when you left the cookout, you took her to Derringer's Dungeon and got busy."

Derringer's mouth dropped. They hadn't gone near his home. "That's a lie."

"I know, but she's intent on spreading that rumor. I don't know what you have planned for the ball, but it better be good, and hopefully it will put a stop to Ashira once and for all."

Derringer nodded. "Trust me. It will."

"You sure you're all right, sweetheart?"

Lucia glanced over at her parents, namely, her dad

who had a concerned look on his face. "Yes, Dad, I'm fine."

He smiled. "Well, you look simply beautiful."

And considering everything, she felt beautiful. Chloe had nearly worn her out last weekend. They hadn't just shopped in Denver but had caught one of those commuter planes to Boulder to do some shopping there as well. In the end, she felt like Cinderella entering the ball. And just like good ole Cinderella she feared she would leave the ball without her man.

The moment she and her parents entered the huge ballroom she drew in a deep breath at the number of people in attendance. But then, she really wasn't surprised. The Westmoreland Foundation provided funds to a number of charities and for that very reason the people of Denver were always supportive.

It didn't take long to pick out all the Westmorelands, especially the males. Whether they were from the north, south, east or west, they had similar looks and builds. In their black tuxes, they were all tall, dashing and ultra-handsome and, not surprisingly, even with their wives on their arms most of the other women present had their eyes on them with wishful expressions on their faces.

She had met all of them at Chloe's wedding and again at Gemma's. They were a nice group of people and she thought Chloe was blessed to be a part of the Westmoreland clan.

It seemed Chloe spotted her the moment she arrived and eagerly pulled her from her parents' side, telling her over and over just how ravishing she looked. So did Bailey, Megan, Gemma and a number of the other Westmoreland women. All the men spoke to her and as usual Zane gave her a naughty wink, which made her chuckle.

She released a deep breath, glad no one was acting or behaving any differently toward her, although all that might change once Derringer arrived with Ashira on his arm. She was just speculating and couldn't help doing so when both he and Ashira didn't appear to be present. No sooner had that thought left her mind than she glanced up and Ashira walked in with a couple of her girlfriends. Lucia was surprised she wasn't with Derringer.

A short while later, Lucia was dancing with Jason when Derringer cut in. She glanced up and tried her best not to narrow her gaze at him. The last thing she wanted was to let him know just how badly he had hurt her, although she was sure he had a clue, which was the reason for the flowers. But if he thought he could woo her and sleep with Ashira at the same time then he had another thought coming.

"Lucia."

She wished he didn't say her name quite that way. With that same throatiness she remembered so well. "Derringer."

"You look beautiful."

"Thanks. You look handsome yourself." That was no lie. For some reason, tonight he looked more handsome than ever.

"I'm glad you came."

"Are you?"

"Yes, and I hope you liked the flowers."

"I did, but they mean nothing as far as rekindling our relationship. It's over, Derringer."

He shook his head. "Things will never be over be

tween us. If you read all those cards then you know you're the only woman I want."

She rolled her eyes. "Yeah, right, go tell that to someone else."

He smiled. "I don't have a problem telling anyone else. In fact, I think I will tell everyone."

He turned and gave the orchestra a cue to stop playing and everything got quiet. Also, as if on cue, someone handed him a microphone. "May I have everyone's attention, please?"

Aghast, she tried tugging her hand from his. "What do you think you're doing?" She wanted to run and hide when her words got captured on the mic for all to hear. She was certain before the night was over she would die of shame.

"I'm about to speak from my heart," he said, holding tight to her hand.

"When it comes to the ladies, I didn't know you had a heart, Derringer," Pete called out.

She tried not to glance around since she knew all eyes were on them. They were in the middle of the ballroom's dance floor, and everyone, curious as to what was going on, had moved closer to watch. The Westmorelands, she noted, were standing in a cluster behind Derringer as if to show a united front.

A smile touched Derringer's lips, but when he turned around and met her gaze, his expression got serious. Then he said in a loud and clear voice, "I didn't know I had a heart either until Lucia captured it." He paused and then added, "And that is something no other woman has been able to do."

She glanced away, refusing to believe what she thought she heard him saying. She didn't want to make a mistake about what he was saying. There was no way it could be true.

As if he'd read her thoughts, he tugged on her hand to make her look back at him. "It's true, Lucia. I am so hopelessly in love with you I can't think straight. You are so filled with goodness, warmth and love, I can't imagine not loving you. And it's not anything I discovered upon waking this morning. I knew that I loved you for a while, but didn't want to. I have this fear of loving someone and then losing that person. I think a number of us Denver Westmorelands can't help but feel that way due to the catastrophic losses we've endured in the past. It can do something to you. It can make you not want to take a chance and get attached to anyone.

"But I want to get attached to you. I have to get attached to you. You make me whole. Without you I am nothing."

Lucia couldn't stop the tears that began falling from her eyes. She couldn't believe what he was saying. Derringer was declaring his love and his need for her in front of everyone. His family. Her parents. Their neighbors and friends. Ashira. Ashira's girlfriends. Ashira's parents. Everyone who wanted to hear it.

Evidently, Ashira and her girlfriends didn't. Lucia watched them walk out. It didn't matter to her. The man she had loved for a lifetime was letting her know in front of everyone that he loved her back.

"And when a man has that much love for any woman," Derringer was saying, bringing her attention back to him, "he will choose that woman as his mate for life. The woman he wants for his wife."

She then watched in shock as he eased down on bended knee, gripped her hand tighter and then held her gaze. "Lucia, will you marry me? Will you take my name? Have my babies? And continue to make me happy? In turn, I will be the best husband to you. I will love you. Honor you and cherish you for as long as I live. Will you marry me?"

While she was still swooning from his public proposal, she felt a ring being slid onto her finger. She glanced down. The diamond sparkled so brightly it almost blinded her. She could only stare at it in amazement.

"You have a proposal on the table, Lucia. Please answer the man," someone called out from the crowd.

She couldn't help but smile as she swiped her tears. That had been her father's voice. She met Derringer's gaze. He was still on his knees waiting. "Oh, Derringer," she said through her tears. "Yes! Yes! I will marry you!"

Smiling, he got to his feet and pulled her into his arms in a deep, passionate kiss. She was not sure how long the kiss lasted. The only thing she did know was that the orchestra was playing music again and others were dancing all around them. They didn't care. Tonight was their night and they were going to take full advantage of it.

Hours later, Derringer and Lucia lay together naked in the bed where their adventure all began at Derringer's Dungeon. Upon hearing her wake up during the night, he was ready and leaned up on his elbow and looked down at her, his gaze hot as it roamed over every inch of her naked body.

He leaned down and kissed her and moaned deep in his throat when she returned the kiss with the same hunger he was giving her. Moments later when he pulled back he could only draw in a deep breath in total amazement. Would he always want her to this extreme? He smiled, knowing that yes, he would.

"I love you," he whispered softy. "I regret all the years I didn't make you my one and only girl."

Lucia smiled up at him. "You weren't ready for that type of serious move back then, and in a way I'm glad." She chuckled. "Besides, you needed to impress my dad."

"And you think I did?"

Her smile brightened. "Yes. Going to him and asking for his permission to marry me scored you a lot of brownie points for sure. You're going to be a son-in-law for life."

"Baby, I intend to be a husband for life as well. And you will be my wife for life."

He ran his fingers through her hair as he leaned down and captured her mouth with his. She was definitely a wife for a Westmoreland. She was his, and their love was just the beginning.

Epilogue

A month and a half later

"Okay, Derringer, you may kiss your bride."

A huge smile lit Derringer's features when he pulled Lucia into his arms. She was the woman he wanted, the wife he desired, and as he captured her mouth with his he knew they would share a long and wonderful life together.

He finally released her and turned to their guests as the minister presented them to everyone as Mr. and Mrs. Derringer Westmoreland. He loved the sound of that and wondered why he'd let his fear keep him away from the altar for so long. But as Lucia had said, he hadn't been ready until now.

A short while later, with his wife's hand tucked in his, they made their way around his property, which the women of the family had transformed from Derringer's Dungeon to Derringer and Lucia's Castle. Gemma had returned the week before the wedding and had worked alongside the wedding planner to give Lucia the wedding she deserved.

He glanced down at her and tightened her hand in his. "Happy?"

She smiled up at him. "Immensely so."

He thought she looked beautiful and doubted he would ever forget how he felt the moment he saw her walking down the aisle to him on her father's arm. She was the most beautiful vision in white that he'd ever seen. They had decided to travel to Dubai for their honeymoon, and while they were across the waters they planned to visit Callum and Gemma in Australia before returning home.

"Time for you to throw your bouquet to the single ladies, Lucia," the wedding planner came up to say.

Lucia turned to Derringer and placed a kiss on his lips. "I'll be back in a moment," she whispered.

"And I'll be right here waiting," was his response. He watched her walk to an area where over thirty women— that included his sisters—stood waiting.

"I've never seen you so happy, Derringer," Jason said, smiling as he walked up. "Congratulations."

"Thanks, and I'm going to give you the same advice I gave Zane, Riley, Canyon and Stern this morning at breakfast, although I could tell they didn't want to hear it. Being single is nice, but being married is much sweeter. Trust me, two is better than one."

Derringer figured if he could get any of his single cousins to take his advice it would be Jason. He had been standing with Jason at the charity ball the moment old man Bostwick's granddaughter had made her entrance. It had been obvious that Jason had been spellbound, entranced by the woman's beauty.

He looked over at Jason. "So, have you officially met Bostwick's granddaughter yet?"

Jason smiled. "Yes, I introduced myself at the ball. Her name is Elizabeth but she prefers being called Bella."

Derringer nodded. "Did you let her know you were interested in her land and in Hercules?"

"Yes, we spoke briefly before Kenneth Bostwick interrupted us. I hear she's trying to make up her mind about what she wants to do. I don't think she's interested in hanging around these parts. This is no place for a Southern belle and besides, she knows nothing about ranching."

"But you do. You can always show her the ropes."

Jason looked shocked at the suggestion. "Why would I want to do something like that? She has two things I want—her land and that stallion. The sooner she decides to sell and return to Savannah, the sooner I can get both. I'd do just about anything to get the land and that horse."

Derringer glanced up at Jason and saw his cousin was serious. "Just remember what I said, Jason. Worldly possessions aren't everything. The love of a good woman is."

He then watched as Lucia began walking back over toward him. She was a good woman. She was his life and now she was his wife.

* * * * *

We hope you enjoyed reading
PART OF THE BARGAIN
by #1 *New York Times* bestselling author
LINDA LAEL MILLER
and
A WIFE FOR A WESTMORELAND
by *New York Times* bestselling author
BRENDA JACKSON

Both were originally **Harlequin®** series stories!

Harlequin Desire stories feature sexy, romantic heroes who have it all: wealth, status, incredible good looks… everything but the right woman. Add some secrets, maybe a scandal, and start turning pages!

Powerful heroes…scandalous secrets…burning desires.

Look for six *new* romances every month from **Harlequin Desire!**

Available wherever books are sold.

www.Harlequin.com

SPECIAL EXCERPT FROM

HQN™

Police detective Joy Ingram's commitment to protect and serve has always come first. But her connection to elite security expert Stonewall Courson is instant, undeniable, electric. And just the diversion she needs…

Enjoy a sneak peek of LOCKED IN TEMPTATION by New York Times *bestselling author Brenda Jackson.*

She leaned against the counter. "So, there you have it. I don't want a relationship, steady or otherwise. I'm not ready to let a man back into my space. However, I'm a person with physical needs just like anyone else, and I wouldn't mind getting together with someone to take the edge off every now and then. It doesn't always have to be about sex, mind you. I would also enjoy an occasional movie, dinner, walk in the park, mountain climbing…"

He lifted a brow. "Mountain climbing?"

She chuckled. "Yes. I've never done it before, but it seems like something that could give my body a good workout." She would admit that making love to him had given her body a good workout, as well.

"You've engaged in take-the-edge-off kind of affairs before?" he asked her.

Was she imagining things or was his gaze drifting to her mouth more often than not? She could feel her lips tingling from him looking at them. "No. It will be my first time. Once I moved here and began working, my life was even more hectic than it had been in Baton Rouge. I worked the streets for six months to get used to the city. Then when I became a detective I wanted to do a good job, which meant putting in long hours. No time for a man."

There was no reason to tell him about some of the crap she

took, being one of the few female detectives. She had to earn the other detectives' respect, especially when they found out who her father was. She had to prove she hadn't gotten the job due to any favors.

Deciding to continue to be honest, she said, "I never really thought about men, definitely hadn't shown interest in one until that night I met you." She chuckled. "You definitely caught my eye."

"And you caught mine."

And now here they were, standing in her kitchen after a night of hot, blazing sex. "I'm sure with your hectic schedule you aren't interested in a serious relationship either, right?" she asked him.

He nodded and then said, "Right. I've never dated anyone seriously. In high school I dated but didn't have a steady girl-friend. And then, after I got out of the slammer, I figured I needed to work on improving me and not take on the responsibility of anyone else. I preferred things that way. I guess I still do."

She smiled. "Great! We want and don't want the same thing."

"What I really want is to see you again."

"And I want to see you again, too. Let's keep in touch. Hook up again when we can as a diversion."

"As a diversion?"

"Yes, as a diversion and nothing more. So, what do you think?"

He reached out, wrapped his arms around her waist and brought her body to fit snug against his. "I think if a diversion is all you want, then that's what you'll get, Joy."

And then he lowered his mouth to hers.

What's in store for Joy and Stonewall?

Find out in LOCKED IN TEMPTATION
by New York Times bestselling author Brenda Jackson,
available August 2017.